# Christmas Kisses

### Alison May

**COMBINES:**

*Holly's Christmas Kiss*
*Cora's Christmas Kiss*
*Jessica's Christmas Kiss*

*Where heroes are like chocolate – irresistible!*

Published 2016 by Choc Lit Limited
Penrose House, Crawley Drive, Camberley, Surrey GU15 2AB, UK
www.choc-lit.com

A CIP catalogue record for this book is available
from the British Library

ISBN 978-1-78189-323-4

Printed and bound by Clays Ltd

*For Paul*

# Acknowledgements

Immense thanks first of all to everyone at Choc Lit,
especially to my lovely editor who has held my
hand through all three *Christmas Kiss* novellas.

Thanks also to all those lovely people who make writing
a less solitary experience – all my RNA, ADC and
Pen Club friends, particularly Janet, Lisa and Holly who
are always there with wine/cake/sympathy as required.

And finally, thanks, as always, to EngineerBoy
for so very many different things.

A special thanks to the Tasting Panel readers who were
the first to meet Holly, Cora and Jessica and made this all
possible: Georgie, Michelle T., Leanne, Sarah A., Dorothy,
Betty, Jennie H., Isabelle, Linda Sp., Christie, Jen, Olivia,
Sammi, Nicky, Rosie, Linda G., Hrund, Sally C. and Cindy.

*Holly's Christmas Kiss*

# Chapter One

## Christmas Eve, 1991

### *Holly Michelle Jolly*

I pretend to be asleep while he fills the pillowcase at the end of my bed. I know it's supposed to be a stocking but Daddy says you don't get enough presents in a stocking, so a pillowcase is better.

I peek out of one eye at him. He's wearing his red suit and he's got a big white beard just like in pictures. He sees me looking. He smiles. 'Ho, ho, ho, Holly,' he says.

I smile back. It's not the really real Santa. I know it's Daddy, but in a way that makes it nicer, because I know the secret. I saw him putting his beard in his briefcase and made him tell me, but he swore me to keep it absolutely top secret so I did. At school Jessica Honeybourne went on and on about how she was going to the big department store to see the real Santa, and I didn't say anything.

He finishes stuffing the presents into the pillowcase.

'Time to sleep now, Holly.'

I nod, and pull the covers up over my head until he's gone. I do definitely try to go to sleep. I screw my eyes up as tight as they'll go and I wait and wait for ages but I'm still awake. It's too exciting. The nearly-Christmasness is building up in my tummy, and it's too much to keep in. It's nearly here. My presents are already here. They're right there at the end of the bed.

I pull the top present out of the pillowcase, just to give it a little shake and a squeeze, but I shake it too hard and it falls on the floor. I climb off the bed to pick it up, scrunching the carpet between my toes as they touch the floor. I can see a little tear in the paper at one end of the parcel. I put it on the bed and stare hard at the tear, trying to open it up with my eyes. It does not work.

I must not open my presents.

I must not open my presents.

I have to wait to open my presents in the morning. I have to wait until it's time to climb into Mummy and Daddy's bed. I look at the clock on my dressing table. It has hands that light up so I can see the time even when it is dark. It is not time yet. It is not even nearly time. I stare at the present again; then I hook my little finger under the tear in the paper and give it a tiny pull. It tears a bit more. I stop.

I must not open my presents.

I give it another little tug. Now the hole is big enough to peek through.

'What are you doing, Holly?' I look round and see my dad standing in the doorway behind me. He's in his pyjamas and dressing gown now, but he still looks like Santa in his eyes.

'Sorry.'

He comes into the room, picks the present up and puts it back in the pillowcase.

'Father Christmas came then?'

I nod, playing along with the game.

'Do you think, maybe we should put this out of reach until morning?'

'Ok.'

He grins. 'Or what if we just took a little peek at this one? It is nearly open.'

I can't believe it. 'Mummy will be cross.'

He winks at me. 'Well I won't tell if you don't.'

I pull the paper off, and find a doll inside. It's a sewed together ragdoll. She's beautiful. I decide she will be my favourite, favourite present, whatever else there is in my pillowcase. Daddy holds her up and then pushes her face against my nose like she's giving me a kiss.

'A dolly for Holly,' he says. Dolly, I think, will be her name forever.

## Three days before Christmas, 2013

Holly Michelle Jolly smoothed down her bridesmaid dress and surveyed the room. Fairy lights – check. Christmas tree – check. Thick green garland around the bar – check. She shuddered. A wedding reception the week before Christmas. Michelle couldn't remember precisely which circle of hell that was included in, but it was definitely up there on her list of personal horrors; the tinselled gaudiness of Christmas combined with the ridiculous expense of the wedding, and a London wedding at that. Michelle's inner Yorkshire girl flinched when she remembered the price of the miniaturised fish and chip canapés.

Nonetheless, it was, she knew, Jess's dream wedding. They'd spent many an evening over a glass of wine, in their tiny shared flat, planning this event. Even before Jess had met Patrick, her fantasy Christmas wedding had been clear in her mind. And that was the point, after all. It was Michelle's job to make sure everything went perfectly. She swept her gaze across the room again. People seemed to be enjoying themselves. The mulled wine was proving a hit, and the guests were looking increasingly pink and full of cheer. Michelle shook her head, and looked around for her friend. Jess was ensconced with her new groom, both talking to the best man. Michelle's lips pursed, as her gaze settled for a second.

Sean Munro was a friend of Patrick's from years ago when they'd both lived in Edinburgh. Michelle had met him for the first time the day before the wedding, and was not impressed. He was all floppy hair and stupid grins. She'd tried to get him to sit down and go through the schedule for the day, and he'd tried to get her to put a whole mince pie in her mouth in one go. Michelle had had to explain, quite firmly, that they were here to make sure everything ran smoothly for the happy couple. They were not here to have fun. He hadn't taken her seriously. She had found her carefully typed and bullet pointed list of things he needed to attend to 'On The Day' dropped by his chair after he left.

Michelle glanced at her watch. It was nearly eight. Evening canapés were supposed to be delivered punctually at 7.45 p.m., but there wasn't a white-shirted tray-bearer to be seen. Michelle sighed and set off to find someone to scold before Jess noticed the problem.

'So am I supposed to dance with a bridesmaid or something? That's a best man thing? Right?'

Sean Munro was leaning on the bar, booted and kilted, watching the guests shake, shimmy and sway as the band played *Santa Baby* for about the eighteenth time. He took a sip from his mulled wine and grinned at the bride. She shook her head.

'Michelle's not really the dancing sort.'

He looked around, finding himself hoping that he'd spot Jess's bossy bridesmaid.

'Where is she anyway? I've not had a chance to talk to her.'

'I'm not sure.' Jess turned her head, expensively sculpted bridal hairstyle and all, to scan the room for her friend's distinctive red hair. 'Probably fixing something on my behalf.'

Sean smiled. 'Well, I didn't get these knees out for nothing. If I can't dance with a bridesmaid, I'm dancing with the bride!'

He dragged her onto the dance floor, and spun her round and round. Innocent bydancers were scattered from their path, as Sean twirled his partner with more enthusiasm and gusto than expertise, until the groom decided it was time to rescue his new wife.

'You're gonna do someone a damage mate.' Patrick detached Jess from his friend's exertions. 'Find your own girl to fling about the place.'

Jess took a second to regain her breath before joining in. 'Quite right. I'm sure we can find you a nice girl somewhere amongst my friends.'

Patrick laughed. 'This time next year. Back in your kilt. Doing one of your weird Scottish dances with your new bride?'

Sean felt his face tense but he didn't reply beyond a small shake of his head. He could feel Patrick looking at him with customary concern. They'd been friends since what Sean still thought of as his 'Lost Months', living in Edinburgh straight after 'The Breakup', and Patrick remained on the lookout for a return to those moods, no matter how many times Sean pointed out that the best part of a decade had passed. The silence sat in the middle of the group for slightly longer than was comfortable.

Patrick turned to his bride. 'So, how about a dance with me? A slower dance?'

Jess nodded, and the pair stepped back onto the floor. Sean watched them. He was actually enjoying the wedding. It was several orders of bridal magazine magnitude removed from his own tiny registry office affair. On the dance floor, the happy couple turned and swayed, wrapped in each other's arms. There was something exclusive about their togetherness. You could see, right in that moment, that they only needed one another. Sean turned away.

Across the room something else caught his eye, and lifted his spirits. He walked over to the huge Christmas tree and appraised it. Not dropping much, but you'd expect that with a Nordmann fir. Nice shape. Tall. He wondered how much the hotel had paid for it. The decorations were corporate-classy. Not the right approach, in Sean's opinion. Tree decorations should be personal and have stories attached to them. This was a bit too tidy for his liking. He glanced upwards and realised he was standing beneath a large sprig of mistletoe. His habitual good humour cooled a little. Such a waste.

He turned to walk back towards the dance floor.

And it happened.

A body crashed into his, as he turned without looking. He put out his hands to support the elusive non-dancing bridesmaid who was momentarily pressed against him. His fingers brushed against satin covering soft flesh. His nostrils were filled with the scent of the shampoo from her thick red hair. He blinked. Michelle rested against his body for a second and then staggered backwards, pushing her hand onto his chest for balance.

'I'm sorry.' She stood up straight. 'Sorry.'

'Are you Ok?'

'I'm fine.' She gestured vaguely towards the bar. 'I have things to see to.'

He paused, but only for a second, before he jumped in. 'But you owe me a kiss.'

Sean surprised himself. He looked at the woman in front of him again. Long wavy red hair, pale white skin, bright blue eyes. Something unfamiliar started to stir in the back of his mind. He flicked his eyes upwards towards the beam, which supported the large sprig of mistletoe directly above them.

'Who put that there?' she said.

'What?'

She was frowning. 'There was only supposed to be mistletoe over Jess and Patrick's seats at the top table.'

She glared at the offending decoration, as if the mistletoe had placed itself on the beam with the express purpose of annoying her.

'What does it matter who put it there? It's Christmas.'

'It's not Christmas for another three days.'

'It's near enough. We're under the mistletoe. It's probably bad luck or something not to kiss.' He grinned at her, a soft playful grin that felt strange to him, like something from a different age.

'Bad luck?' He watched Michelle's expression switch from irritation to incredulity. 'What about all the horrid diseases you can catch from kissing?'

Bit harsh, Sean thought. 'I don't have any horrible diseases.'

She shook her head. 'Well I might have. You barely know me.'

Sean grinned again. 'I'll take my chances. I don't have a choice. We're standing under mistletoe. We'd be breaking an important law of Christmas.'

'There's no such thing as a law of Christmas.'

'Of course there is. There's loads of things you have to do at Christmas.' Sean sensed he wasn't winning the argument. 'Well maybe it's not an actual law. Strong convention. We'd be breaking a strong convention of Christmas.'

'Go on! Kiss him!' Jess's voice carried over the music from the edge of the dance floor. Michelle glared at her friend, and sighed.

'Fine.' She lifted her face and puckered her lips.

Sean bent his head to meet her. Without thinking he moved his hand towards her cheek as their lips edged closer. The scent of her skin, the sound of her breath, the warmth of her body, started to play on his senses. He leaned forward, just a fraction more. He was a moment away from her lips. Just one moment.

Crash.

She jumped away from him at the sound. At the far side of the dance floor a waiter slipped and dropped a perfectly balanced tray of canapés to the floor. Michelle pointed in the direction of the unfortunate waiter. 'I'd better go and ...'

Sean watched her stride away. She was all the way across

the room before he noticed that he was holding his breath. Slowly, he exhaled.

## Two days before Christmas, 2013

Michelle's taxi drew up to the drop-off point at Heathrow Airport. Snow was starting to fall as she paid the driver and stepped out onto the pavement. Michelle shivered. She'd always hated winter. Right from the point, usually sometime in the middle of October, when the first person gestured towards the darkening sky and told her it was starting to look Christmassy, she could happily avoid the whole season. Given the option, Michelle thought, she'd probably prefer to hibernate until spring. The thought that this time tomorrow she'd be sipping a cocktail on the beach in the Cayman Islands was the only thing keeping her from jumping straight back into the cab and demanding a ride to the nearest place with central heating.

Her case seemed to have got heavier since she left the hotel. By the time she'd navigated her way to the right check-in area she was sweating despite the cold. Waiting in the queue, she unwrapped her scarf from around her neck and started to undo her heavy duffle coat. At least once she was on the plane she wouldn't have to put those back on for another two weeks.

The doubt she'd been fighting, ever since she'd clicked 'Book' on the online travel site, popped back into her head. It was so much money. Could she really justify it when she spent her working life telling her clients not to overspend? She swallowed. It was what her mother had wanted. A small inheritance, not much once the funeral was paid for, but enough to allow Michelle to take the holiday of a lifetime. That was what her mother, quite uncharacteristically, had instructed her to do, and it was up to Michelle to ensure that it was worth every penny.

With her coat balanced on top of her suitcase she took a moment to look around. The queue for check-in was nearly all adults. The Caribbean at Christmas must be a preference of those without young families. She glanced around again. The queue was also exclusively couples, apart from Michelle. She stood up straight. There was no shame in going on holiday alone. In fact, she'd probably have a better time than all these women with boyfriends or husbands in tow. She wouldn't be worrying about making someone else happy.

Michelle spent the whole year sorting out other people's problems: planning Jess's wedding; helping Jess move; running around after her boss; running around after her clients. She remembered her mother's instructions: 'Put yourself first, Michelle.' That was the plan.

The couple in front of her embarked on a sloppy and prolonged kiss. Michelle looked away, decidedly ignoring the memory rushing into her mind of a moment that got away. She was definitely better off on her own.

The queue inched forward, until Michelle was called in front of a smiling check-in assistant with tinsel pinned to her uniform and reindeer antlers on her head.

'Merry Christmas!'

Michelle didn't reply. It might be nearly Christmas. That didn't mean she had to pander to the fact. She lifted her bag onto the conveyer and held her ticket and passport out to the assistant.

'Thank you, Miss ...' The woman glanced down at the passport. '... Jolly! Oooh, how festive!'

Yeah. Nothing beat being called Jolly at Christmastime. She caught the check-in woman looking at her full name. Holly Michelle Jolly. She could see that another set of jokes she'd heard a thousand times before were already forming in the woman's mind.

'I use Michelle.'

The woman suppressed a smirk. 'Did you pack this bag yourself Miss Jolly?'

'Yes.'

'And has anyone asked you to take any items on the flight with you?' The girl asked the question by rote, in the sing-song voice of someone so used to saying the words that they'd forgotten the meaning a long time ago.

Michelle shook her head.

'Excellent. Window or aisle?'

Michelle paused. She did prefer a window seat. She remembered the one time she'd been on an aeroplane with her dad, and how he'd let her take the window seat. She'd been transfixed by the sight of the clouds drifting below them. Knowing her luck though, she'd get sat next to someone who'd stink to high heaven, regale her with stories of what they'd got up to at their office Christmas party, and then fall fast asleep for the next seven hours, leaving her pinned in her seat. Aisle would mean she could get up and stretch her legs. She didn't want to risk a deep vein thrombosis.

'Aisle, please.'

The assistant tapped a few keys, before another thought struck Michelle. She remembered a documentary she'd watched about plane crashes, and how to survive them.

'And within seven rows of an exit.'

The woman raised an eyebrow, and tapped the keys some more. Eventually the boarding pass printed out.

'You'll be boarding around a quarter to three. We don't have a gate yet, but if you go through security and watch the monitors, it'll come up about thirty minutes before we board.'

'Thank you.' Michelle took the boarding pass and her passport from the assistant and turned away.

'Thank you, madam. Merry Christmas!'

Michelle suppressed a grimace. Hopefully, once she got

to Grand Cayman, people would be more relaxed and not quite so irritatingly perky.

The queue for security was more suited to Michelle's mood. By this stage, people were tired of waiting, and the ritual of removing jewellery, belts and wristwatches was being completed with bored faces and a refreshing lack of festive cheer.

Michelle stuffed her coat and belt into a plastic tray and put the rucksack she was carrying as hand baggage onto the conveyer. She walked through the bodyscan, only to hear the machine bleep. The security guard stepped forward and gestured her back through the scanner. She emptied her pockets fully, and removed the plain gold studs from her ears before walking back through the contraption.

The machine bleeped again and the red light flashed above her head. Michelle followed the guard's instructions to stand with her arms outstretched and legs apart. The woman flicked a handheld device over Michelle's body. Michelle's face flushed red. She knew this was a perfectly everyday occurrence, but she couldn't help but feel that people were staring at her.

The security guard checked with a colleague and then smiled at Michelle. 'Ok. No problem. On you go.'

Michelle dropped her arms. She didn't want to have to go through all this on the way home. 'What set it off?'

The guard shrugged. 'Sometimes it just goes off. You're fine.'

Michelle didn't consider that a satisfactory answer, but the guard had moved on to wave her detector at some other poor innocent. Michelle started to collect her belongings from the tray.

'You managed to talk your way out of that one then?'

The distinctive Scottish accent made her stop dead. She turned round slowly to see Sean Munro smirking at her. Her eyes were drawn straight to his mouth, to those inviting lips that … She shook her head and forced her gaze away from his face.

'You're not wearing your kilt.' She blurted the words as her glance dropped to his legs.

'No.'

What was she saying? Of course he wasn't wearing a kilt. Just because he wore a kilt in her imagination, didn't mean he always wore a kilt. Not that she'd been imagining Sean. She was tired, she decided, and flustered from the security check. Yes. Flustered. It would pass.

'What are you doing here?' He obviously had no right to be here. This was her holiday. She was supposed to be getting away from any distractions.

The smirk extended into a grin, 'Don't pretend you're not pleased to see me.'

Michelle took a breath. She'd simply run into an acquaintance. They would exchange the time of day and go their separate ways. There was no reason to be getting worked up. His deep green eyes weren't a reason. The slight crumple to the T-shirt he was wearing wasn't a reason. The flash of tight muscled torso she glimpsed as Sean rubbed his hand over the back of his neck wasn't a reason. The warm intoxicating smell as he leant towards her definitely wasn't a reason to lose her composure. Wait a minute. He was leaning towards her.

Michelle stepped sideways, away from the heat of Sean's body. He lifted her rucksack off the table and swung it over his shoulder, raising his eyebrow slightly at her jump to the side.

'But, what are you doing here?' Michelle spluttered out the question again.

'I'm catching a plane.'

'Yes.' Well, obviously. 'A plane to?'

'Home for Christmas.'

'Home?' Of course home. That's where people went for Christmas, wasn't it? They spent it with family. They had traditions, and customs that they shared with their parents and passed on to their children. Was that what Sean's Christmas would be like? Michelle swallowed the thought.

Sean was still talking. '... near Edinburgh.'

Michelle nodded, hoping she hadn't missed anything important.

'Are you heading home too?'

Michelle shook her head. There wasn't really a home to head to any more. Her mother had passed away. And her father was ... well, her father was not somebody she would choose to spend her holidays with.

'To the Caribbean. On holiday.'

'Who with?'

'Just me.'

'At Christmas?'

The hint of concern in Sean's voice made the muscles in Michelle's neck twitch. 'What's wrong with that?'

'Nothing.' He regrouped quickly. 'When's your flight?'

She paused and took a breath. 'Three.'

Sean nodded and started striding away from the security area and into the main departure lounge. Michelle scurried to keep up with his longer legs.

'So, what do you fancy?'

What do you fancy? Michelle opened and closed her mouth with no sound. What did she fancy? She gave up. The less she said the less likely it was that she'd see the teasing grin reappear at Sean's lips.

He gestured towards the large, fluorescent-lit store in front of them. 'We could see how many perfumes they'll let us test before they realise we're not buying.'

Michelle shook her head. It was a ridiculous thing for a grown man to suggest.

Sean glanced around, and pointed at a coffee shop. 'Hot chocolate? We could get cream and marshmallows and see if we can drink it without getting cream on our noses?'

Hot chocolate had always been what her dad would bring Michelle if she caught a cold. She had a picture in her head of him sitting on the edge of her bed with a big steaming mug for each of them. If Mum was out he'd buy the synthetic cream in an aerosol can and spray that on top. If Mum was around she would shout at him for daring to bring aerosol cream into her kitchen. Apart from at Christmas. At Christmas, she used to let him have his way. That was a very long time ago, but Michelle could taste the memory of the cheap sugary cream dissolving on her tongue. She smiled.

Sean returned the smile. 'So hot chocolate?'

'No, thank you.' This holiday was about time alone, not about playing like children with a man who was old enough to know better. 'Can I have my bag please?'

Sean placed the rucksack strap into her outstretched hand.

'Thank you. Now, if you don't mind, I'd rather be on my own. I'll be quite happy reading my book.'

His eyebrows rose slightly, but the smile didn't leave his lips. 'If that's what you'd prefer.'

Michelle adopted a light tone. There was no reason not to be cordial. 'Have a nice Christmas.'

Sean didn't move as she walked away. He'd met this woman twice now. This time he'd even made her smile, but both times he'd ended up watching her leave. It wasn't a situation he was used to. If Sean was honest, in recent years he'd tended to be the one doing the walking away. It was safer that way.

It seemed a shame, though, Michelle holidaying alone at Christmas. He let the thought settle in his brain. Even during his lowest moments, Sean couldn't imagine spending Christmas away from his family and friends. That was it. He felt sorry for her being alone. Obviously if she'd told him she was flying out to meet a boyfriend he would have been fine with that. Completely fine.

Sean wandered without much intent around the departure lounge duty free stores. He remembered the first time he'd flown from Edinburgh to London, back before travelling for work had been part and parcel of his life. He'd been a twenty-year-old farm boy who'd never boarded a plane before. He remembered the shops at Edinburgh's airport. Aisles and aisles of perfume, scotch whisky, books, scarves, jewellery, and bags, all potential gifts for his hostess. In the end he'd plumped for perfume. A bottle of he didn't remember what, a tiny bottle, but much bigger than he could afford at the time. The assistant had smirked, and told him it was the perfect scent to get a young girl to fall in love with him. Maybe that had been his mistake all those years ago. He didn't ask what would be the perfect scent to persuade a girl who'd fallen out of love with him to change her mind.

His phone pinged in his pocket. He took it out and glanced at the screen. A new text. He rolled his eyes at the name. Speak of the devil and he will appear. That was the saying, wasn't it? Cora went one better. You only had to think of her and she popped up.

The text was breezy and flirtatious in tone. What part of no didn't she understand? Sean paused as he read the end of the message. 'Hope to see you over Christmas.' She must think he was staying in London. No chance. He'd be safely in Scotland, and he couldn't imagine Cora gracing the ancestral home with her presence for the holidays. She would, no doubt, have a much more glamorous option lined up.

# Chapter Two

## Christmas Day, 1996

*Sean*

Mum's wielding her pudding ladle.

'Who's for seconds?'

Bel shakes her head. She never has seconds, because she's watching her figure. I don't know what she thinks is going to happen to it. I shake my head too. It's twenty to three already. There isn't time for seconds. Nobody else seems to care. The rest of the family dig in. I push my chair back from the table.

'Where do you think you're going?'

'Out for a bit.'

Dad shakes his head. 'Not until everyone's finished.'

It's not fair. Now I have to sit here and I don't get any more pudding. And old people eat so slowly. Granddad's the worst. His teeth don't fit properly, so he can't really chew. I have to sit and listen to every gummy mouthful. Eventually he puts down his spoon.

'I'm going out for a bit.' I dash up to my room and grab the present from my drawer, and then I'm out of the house, across the yard, and through the first field at a run. I scale the gate into the second field and start to slow down. I want to get my breath back before I see her. After Christmas, we're definitely going to tell people. Then I'll be able to walk up to her front door like normal. I climb over the far fence, into the next field, and onto the Strachan estate.

She's waiting at the edge of the field, arms wrapped across her body, and scarf pulled up to her ears. I stuff my hands in my pockets and drop my head.

'All right.'

'Hi.' She's got her eyes down to the floor, but she looks up at me through her lashes. 'I thought you weren't coming.'

'Dad made me stay 'til everyone had finished dinner. I'm probably gonna get bollocked anyway for not helping wash up.'

She wrinkles her nose, probably at the idea of having to do chores. 'Did you tell them where you were going?'

I shake my head.

'Cool.'

'They wouldn't mind. Bel's boyfriend stays over all the time.'

'She's older than you.'

'Not much.'

She shakes her head. 'Mine'd go mental.'

'Why?'

'Cause they're stupid.'

I'm pissed off now. 'They think I'm too rough for you.'

'It's stupid.' She doesn't deny it though.

I look across the fields to Cora's house. It's big and it's modern. My dad calls it a bloody eyesore, but that's just because he's not used to buildings that aren't held together with duct tape.

Cora takes a step towards me. 'Don't be grumpy.'

She reaches her arms up around my neck. 'It's more fun this way anyhow. Sneaking about.'

She presses her body against mine. 'It's sexy.'

She's got round me. She always does. I slide my arms around her waist and squeeze her bum through the layers.

She smiles. 'So where's my pressie?'

# Chapter Three

## Two days before Christmas, 2013

Michelle found a seat, wedged between a Chinese family and a man fast asleep across two chairs and a table, at one end of the departure lounge and tried to calm her breathing. Resting her hands on her lap, she realised that she was shaking slightly. What was happening to her? She hoped that she wasn't coming down with some sort of virus that would mean a holiday wasted tucked up in her hotel room.

A battered pair of Converse at the bottom of a pair of denim-clad legs was heading towards her. She looked up and offered a half smile. The stranger nodded a little uncertainly and carried on. She dropped her head. It wasn't Sean. Of course, it wasn't Sean. There were probably thousands of people in the terminal. Not all the men wearing jeans would be Sean. And she wasn't interested if it was. Sean Munro, so far as Michelle could tell, was an immature little kid trapped in a grown-up body. She'd seen him twirling Jess around the dance floor like a maniac, and he was no better today, talking about getting cream on his nose and suggesting playing pranks in shops.

She tried to focus on her book, struggling through a couple of unengrossing chapters. She wriggled in the hard angular seat. Time crawled by. She glanced at her watch; it was half past two. Her flight would be boarding soon, and she'd be on her way. She looked up at the departure board. The screen was full of the dreaded word: DELAYED. She scanned down the list for her flight: 'Wait In Lounge.' She sighed with relief. The idea of a long delay didn't appeal one little bit.

Twenty minutes later, the display was still flashing, 'Wait In Lounge.' Michelle closed the book she was hardly reading anyway. Surely, they would be boarding soon. Either way, she needed to stretch her legs. She stuffed the book into the top of her rucksack and picked up her bag. As she stood up, she was taken aback by how stiff she'd got, sitting on the hard seat for so long. She walked slowly across the lounge and turned a corner. In front of her was a full floor to ceiling window with an uninterrupted view of the runway. On a normal day this would be the ideal spot to watch the planes taking off from one of the busiest airports on the planet. Today there was no such view.

Michelle walked up to the window and placed her hand against the glass. The runway was silent. Nothing was moving apart from the snowflakes which danced and fell in front of her, creating a cover of white across the ground. She turned back towards the departure lounge, looking out for a display board.

15:10 BA345 Grand Cayman DELAYED.

It really was just her luck. Her first proper holiday in more than twelve years, and her flight was delayed. She blinked hard. No point getting downhearted about it. The only sensible thing to do was go back to her seat and wait.

She made her way, more briskly now, back across the main lounge, and saw that her earlier seat had been taken. Searching the departures hall she couldn't see an available place to sit. She walked in between the rows of chairs, clambering over bags, pushchairs and people's legs. There wasn't a single seat free. Eventually she dragged her rucksack back to the window overlooking the runway, dumped it down on the floor and tried to get comfortable sitting on her bag. It was not a dream start to her dream holiday.

The time passed slowly, too slowly. Michelle shifted around, trying to find a comfortable position on the cold floor. She read for a bit, looked out of the window for a bit, closed her eyes for a bit trying to rest. As the ache in her back grew, she silently cursed her mother for forcing her into this holiday. The money would have been put to far better use invested in her ISA, or topping up her pension pot.

Outside the snow continued to fall. Michelle shifted and stretched to get a view of an information board. Her flight was still listed as DELAYED. She scanned for details of the Edinburgh flight. It wasn't on the board. She glanced at her watch. Nearly five o'clock. Sean must be on his way already. An unfamiliar feeling crept into her tummy. Disappointment? Michelle told herself not to be so silly. She settled, as best she could, back onto the floor, trying to use her rucksack as a pillow. She gazed out of the window. A thickening white layer was covering the runway, crying out for a child in wellingtons to jump full-footed into the unspoilt snow. It was a silly thought, and it made Michelle shake her head. Jumping in snow was just the sort of frivolity that she could do without; every bit as foolish in its own way as spending your last few pounds on a present that would hardly get played with, or a turkey that would barely fit in the oven. She remembered her father bringing home a turkey on Christmas Eve and her mother complaining that it was too big, and she remembered eating turkey soup and turkey fritters long into January. At least her mother understood how to plan ahead.

'I bought you a hot chocolate, just in case.'

The voice interrupted her thoughts, and Michelle tried, unsuccessfully, to scramble to her feet. She ended up half kneeling, half squatting, eyes level with Sean's crotch, her hair halfway out of its ponytail and sticking to her face.

'I thought you'd gone.' She tilted her head towards his face and decided to carry on as if this was a quite normal position for chit-chat. 'Your flight's not on the board.'

Sean smiled. 'You noticed.'

'Well, I was, I didn't particularly ...' Michelle let her voice trail off. She'd noticed, and now he knew she'd noticed. She wished she hadn't said anything.

Sean held out his hand and Michelle let him help her to her feet. The touch sent tingles through her body. She dropped his hand and tried to regain her composure. Sean wasn't her type. She liked men who were put together, not ones who looked like they'd fallen into their clothes by happy accident.

He held the hot chocolate towards her. 'It's got cream and marshmallows, but I suppose you can keep the lid on if you don't want cream on your nose.'

She took the drink from him, realising that she'd arrived at the airport nearly five hours ago and not had anything to eat or drink since. She kept her gaze firmly towards the floor, or at best Sean's shoes. Calm and under control was her new mantra. 'Thank you.'

'You're welcome.'

Michelle felt herself smiling. That was probably the first bit of normal conversation they'd managed. She swallowed, raised her head and met Sean's gaze.

He nodded towards the snowy scene outside the window. 'My flight was cancelled.'

'Oh no! I'm sorry.' She put her hand out to touch his arm in sympathy, but pulled it back before her fingers made contact. There was really no need for any more touching. 'What are you going to do?'

He shrugged. 'Stand here. Drink my hot chocolate. Watch the snow. What about you?'

'Well, my flight's only delayed. I'm still going ...' Her voice trailed off as she saw Sean's eyebrows flick up.

'I'm sorry. I don't think anyone's flying out of here today.'

'It still says delayed.' She looked forlornly at the departures board and then back out through the window.

The snow was still falling, covering the scene outside in an ever-deepening blanket of white.

He paused as if deciding what to say next. Eventually he smiled softly. 'All right. I guess we'd better make ourselves comfortable for the wait then.'

'We?' Michelle could hear the horror in her own voice. Sean, however, seemed to be immune, or, at the very least, choosing to ignore it. He had put his own drink down, taken off his jacket and laid it out across the floor.

'Madam,' he took Michelle's drink out of her hand and gestured toward the coat. 'Hardly the full Walter Raleigh, but the best I can do.'

He nodded back towards the main departure lounge. 'There's not a seat to be had through there.'

'But you don't have to wait. Your flight's cancelled. You can go home.'

'And leave you all alone? Never.'

'Why are you still here?'

'There is nowhere I would rather be.'

Well that made no sense. What was the point in hanging around at an airport after your flight had been cancelled? Michelle opened her mouth to argue, but stopped herself. Bringing her a drink had been kind. She should probably try to be gracious. Very slowly, she lowered herself onto the coat and wriggled to one side, leaving space for Sean to sit beside her.

He sat himself down and picked up his hot chocolate. He pulled the plastic lid off, and took a generous gulp, allowing the cream to settle on his top lip and the tip of his nose. Turning his face towards Michelle he grinned and raised his eyebrows in challenge.

'Don't be silly.'

'Why not?' He looked disappointed, but wiped the cream from his nose and lip with the back of his hand.

'Because you're a grown-up, not an eight-year-old.'

'No. It's Christmas. Everyone gets to act like a kid at Christmas.'

'Don't be stupid.'

'Why not? Nothing wrong with embracing your inner eight-year-old.'

Michelle rolled her eyes. 'Apart from that it's completely unrealistic. I have a grown-up life, a grown-up flat, a grown-up job.'

'What do you do?'

'I'm a money adviser.'

Sean rolled his eyes. 'Like in a bank?'

Michelle shook her head vigorously. In her line of work, banks were usually on the opposite side of the argument. 'I'm a debt adviser. I help people who can't cope with their debts.'

Sean laughed. 'Figures.'

'What?' There was something about his tone that Michelle didn't care for.

'Jess said you were always trying to fix things for everyone, you know, make everything better.'

'What's wrong with that?'

'Nothing.' Sean shook his head. 'Seriously, nothing. But wouldn't it be nice to take a break from being sensible?'

What a preposterous idea. It was just the sort of thing Michelle fancied her father would think. She closed the door on the thought before it had chance to take hold.

'You can't take time off from being grown-up.'

Sean considered her answer in silence. 'What about running away to the Caribbean for Christmas? That's taking a break.'

'Not from being responsible.' Michelle's voice raised. She twisted uncomfortably to face Sean. 'This holiday is all about taking responsibility for myself, not needing someone else to look after me.'

Sean raised his hands in submission. 'Sorry.'

They fell into silence. After talking about the importance of being grown-up she realised that refusing to let it go would look childish. Beaten by her own argument. She swallowed the warm creamy chocolate and let out a breath. 'It's Ok.'

They sat for a moment looking out at the white landscape beyond the window.

'Excuse me madam.' Michelle turned around and saw a young woman in airline uniform approaching them from behind, clutching a clipboard.

The woman gestured towards the airline insignia on her jacket. 'Can I ask if you're booked on a flight with us today?'

Michelle nodded.

'Can I ask your name?'

'Michelle Jolly.'

'Oh! Very festive.' The woman smiled the smile of a person who knows that they get to go home at the end of the day. Michelle glowered. 'And, can I ask which flight you're booked on?'

'Grand Cayman.'

'I'm terribly sorry. That flight has been cancelled today.' The woman flicked through the pages on her clipboard to avoid eye contact.

Michelle sighed in disbelief. Obviously she could see the snowbound runway, but she'd been telling herself that somehow her flight would be different.

Next to her, Sean scrambled to his feet. 'And is it being rescheduled?'

The woman glanced back at her clipboard. 'And you are?'

'Sean Munro.'

'And are you booked on the same flight?' Her eyes were scanning the clipboard as she spoke.

Sean shook his head. 'I'm just a friend.'

'All right,' she replied, in a tone that implied that friends weren't really all right, but would be tolerated in these unusual circumstances. 'The flight will be rescheduled.'

Michelle's mood brightened and she dragged herself to her feet. So she could stay in an airport hotel tonight, and fly tomorrow. Yes, her holiday would be a day shorter but it wasn't the end of the world. The woman was still talking.

'... so you see, with the forecast as it is, and Christmas, and our aircrews are all over the place, that's really the best we can do.'

'What is?'

'The twenty-seventh. We should be all back to normal by then.' The woman smiled brightly but without sincerity. 'Maybe the twenty-eighth.'

Michelle was dismayed. The twenty-eighth of December. That would be five days off her holiday, and, even worse, she was stuck in the UK for Christmas.

'But, I've booked a hotel and all the money ...'

Her half-formed thought was met with another disengaged smile and a sheet of paper pulled from the woman's clipboard. 'For financial compensation, refunds and any other complaints, you'll need to fill in this form, and return it to the address at the top. Merry Christmas!'

The woman hurried away, as if too much talk of refunds and complaints might dent her brittle cheerful shell.

Michelle turned to Sean and for a second her bottom lip trembled, before she snapped her usual brisk exterior back in place. 'Oh well, no point hanging around here.'

Sean looked momentarily confused. 'No. I suppose not. So are you going to head home?'

Michelle nodded. 'Not much else to do.'

She held her hand out in front of her. 'Thank you for the hot chocolate.'

He shook her hand uncertainly. 'No problem. You don't want to share a cab or anything?'

'No thank you. I'll be fine from here.' Because nothing had changed. This Christmas was about independence. Chance meetings and almost-kisses didn't mean anything. She picked up her rucksack and walked briskly into the crowded departure hall.

Sean watched her leave, before collecting his own jacket and bag, and tossing the empty hot chocolate cups into the bin. Why had he waited with her anyway? He could have been well on the way to Edinburgh by now. He was behaving like the old Sean. He'd sworn off acting on impulse a long time ago.

He glanced at his watch. If he managed to find a cab, he probably had enough time to get back into London and catch the sleeper train north, if there was space, and if everyone else who was on his flight hadn't left with the same idea hours earlier. He rubbed his eyes. At the moment it wasn't just the best plan; it was the only plan.

He jogged across the departure hall, jumping and jostling to get past the crowds of people berating the airline staff. He resisted a smile at the sight of the woman who'd spoken to him and Michelle looking significantly less bright and festive. Partway across the room he realised that he had no idea where he was going. The whole layout of the airport was designed to stop people leaving from the departures area. Once you were through security, you were supposed to leave on a plane.

He stopped and looked around. The bright festive woman was peeling herself away from another group of disgruntled looking passengers.

'Excuse me.'

'Yes?' The smile snapped back onto her face, but it wasn't quite as glossy as it had been earlier.

Sean beamed at her. 'Tough day?'

She fluttered her eyelids slightly in the full wattage of his smile. 'Well, you know ...'

'Sure. Look ...' he glanced for a name badge but found none. 'I was wondering if you could help me get out of here?'

'Oh. Yes.' The woman pointed towards an escalator at the far end of the hall. 'If you go up there and follow the corridor round, they've opened up the doors through to Arrivals.'

Sean grinned again. 'Thank you. Happy Christmas.'

'Yes.' The brightness was returning with vigour, and she shouted a festive greeting at Sean's departing back. 'Merry Christmas!'

Sean resumed his half-run, half-leap across the bustling hall and jogged up the escalator two steps at a time. The corridor upstairs was quieter. It didn't seem like many people had worked out how to get out of the departure lounge yet.

Sean followed the signs to Arrivals, and came out at a junction with signposts to 'Baggage Reclaim' and 'Buses and Taxis.' He followed the Baggage Reclaim sign and saw his case circling on the nearest carousel. So that was one benefit of hanging around at the airport for an hour after your flight was cancelled – no wait for your baggage. He grabbed his case and bounded towards the sliding doors to the outside world. The cold outside air hit him in a blast. He pulled his jacket tight around him and fastened the zip, but it wasn't the cold that made him stop. It was the quiet.

He'd been visiting London most of his adult life and was a regular through Heathrow. He couldn't remember seeing the arrivals area so quiet. It made sense. If there were no planes taking off, presumably there weren't any landing either. And if there were no planes coming in, then Arrivals would be deserted. Hardly any cars coming and going. A few people milling around, waiting for buses. Only two taxis waiting at the rank. And what noise there was, was being deadened by the soft floating fall of the snow. In the middle of an international airport, in one of the busiest cities in the world, he had managed to stumble into a truly silent night.

Sean smiled. Despite the flight being cancelled, and his day being a huge mess, he could feel the stirrings of Christmas excitement in his gut, exactly the same as when he was a kid seeing the first decorations going up or spying the tins of biscuits and treats stowed away on top of the kitchen cupboard waiting for Christmas to officially begin. He grinned and walked towards the first of the taxis.

Michelle waited at baggage reclaim. Seriously, how long could it take for one bag to come through? It wasn't as if they had to unload it from the aeroplane hold. So far as she could work out, the luggage had never got that far, but still she was stuck here waiting for her suitcase to re-emerge from the bowels of the airport. Slowly the baggage hall started to fill up with miserable faces. Parents alternately bickering and placating fractious children. Couples standing in strained, disappointed silence. Airline staff with clipboards looking harassed and tired. People on their phones trying to beg rooms for the night and lifts home from the airport.

That made Michelle think. At least she knew she had somewhere to stay over Christmas. Of course, Jess would be looking forward to her first Christmas with her shiny new husband, but Michelle was sure she'd be more than welcome once she explained her predicament. She started to brighten. It might even be fun. She could help with the cooking. Having another pair of hands would be useful anyway.

She walked a few feet away from the crowd and pulled her phone out of her pocket. She hit Jess's number on her speed-dial. It rang for a few moments before she answered.

'Hiya. Are you there already?'

Michelle had to think for a moment before she remembered where she was supposed to be.

'Er no. Not exactly. They've cancelled my flight. I'm not going after all.'

'Oh no.' Her voice was full of concern. 'What are you going to do?'

'Well, I was wondering if I could stay with you, just over Christmas ...' She stopped, waiting to hear Jess's assent.

Her friend paused. It wasn't a long pause, but it was enough. 'I'm sure you can. That'll be fine.'

Jess drifted into silence. Michelle could hear Patrick talking away from the phone. His voice was light, happy, intimate. Michelle's image of herself cooking a perfect Christmas dinner fractured in her mind. This was their time to do things like that together. Michelle would be an intruder in their blissful little bubble.

'Actually, I might head back to Leeds.'

'Oh. Are you sure?' Jess sounded surprised, but not disappointed.

'Yeah. Some people had invited me over on Boxing Day, and Christmas Day on my own might be nice.'

'Oh. Ok.' She didn't try to talk her out of it, which only served to confirm that it was the right decision.

'Yeah. Have a good Christmas.' Michelle fought to keep the crack out of her voice.

'You too.'

'Ok then. Good ...' Click. Jess hung up.

Michelle turned back towards the baggage carousel. The carousel at the far end of the hall seemed to be slowly creaking into life. This was fine. She would collect her bag, get a bus or the tube to King's Cross station and head back to Leeds. Christmas was just one day after all, so spending it on her own would be fine. It was what she'd planned. All her books could still be read. It would be big jumpers and pots of tea, rather than bikinis and cocktails.

She made her way through the bodies lined up around the baggage carousel. Her suitcase was one of the first to come through, and she hauled it off the belt and started to fight her way back through the throng. Her eyes were stinging slightly, but she refused to allow herself to cry. Michelle Jolly did not cry.

No flight. No one to spend Christmas with. She looked at her watch. Would it be too late for the train by the time she'd made it to King's Cross? She added the fact that she had nowhere to stay tonight to her list of things she absolutely wasn't going to get upset about, and tugged at her bag. Her muscles strained from the exertion after lying on the hard floor.

She paused before the double doors that led out to the bus stops to put her scarf back on and button her coat. So much for two weeks of guaranteed sunny weather. The cold air stung her cheeks and she could feel the tears starting to well up. They weren't proper tears, she decided, just her eyes watering from the cold.

Michelle gave herself a stern talking to in her head. She hadn't cried when Jess moved out of their shared Leeds flat to come to London, even though Jess had been in a flood. She hadn't cried when Mum had forbidden her from attending her half-brother's Christmastime christening service. She hadn't even cried at her mum's funeral. She wasn't going to cry because she was stuck on her own in the cold.

Bundled up in her duffle coat, and with her scarf pulled around her head, Michelle dragged her suitcase towards the bus stops. At the first shelter she stopped and read the sign. Of course, it didn't help. She didn't know where she was going, so she had no idea which bus to get. Had she missed the last train? Should she head to the railway station and try to sleep there and catch an early train in the morning, or should she look for a hotel? Would all the airport hotels be full with so many flights cancelled? Should she really be paying out for a night in a hotel, when she was at risk of losing so much money on her holiday already? Maybe she should have stayed put in the departures hall. At least it was warm in there.

All at once, the decisions overwhelmed her, and she felt the proper tears start to fall. Fat, salty, gulpy tears poured down her face and she cried, for the first time she could remember, in a public place. It was humiliating, and the realisation that it was humiliating made her cry more. Michelle pulled the end of her scarf over her face, and sobbed into the wool, paying no heed to anything but the sound of her own distress.

She didn't notice the car stopping and the door opening right in front of her until, wiping the scarf across her face, she looked up. Sean's taxi had pulled up in the bus lane directly in front of her, and Sean was already lifting her suitcase into the boot.

'What are you doing?'

'Thought you could use a lift.'

Michelle opened her mouth to tell him she could manage perfectly well on her own, but stopped herself. Given that he'd found her at a bus stop, weeping like a Best Actress winner, he was probably justified in thinking she might need some assistance.

'I don't know where I'm going.'

As soon as she spoke the tears started up with renewed gusto.

'Woah!' She felt Sean's hand on her arm. 'Where do you live?'

'Leeds.'

'Right. Is there anyone you can stay with?'

Michelle shrugged, and swallowed, struggling to compose herself. 'I'm going to head home, I think.'

She saw Sean glance at his watch. 'Do you know what time your train's at?'

Another wave of tears started to well up behind her eyes.

Michelle shook her head and took a deep breath. Enough crying already. Of course she didn't know what time the train was. She hadn't been planning on going home.

Sobs finally subsiding, Michelle realised that Sean's hand was still on her arm. Saying a silent prayer of thanks for the layers of jumper and duffle coat between his skin and hers, she pulled her arm away, and tried to adopt a more businesslike attitude. 'A lift towards King's Cross would be great. Thank you. I'm sure I can find a hotel if I've missed the last train.'

Sean stood next to the cab, holding the door. 'After you.'

He watched her climb into the car. She sank back into the seat and closed her eyes, shutting herself off, he couldn't help but feel, from any conversation with him.

He opened his mouth to say something and then stopped. The moment of indecision confused him. Usually people seemed to have no trouble opening up to him. And usually he had no trouble at all being charming. Sean had what his fifteen year-old nephew would call game. Maybe it was only situations requiring something more than an easy line that gave him a problem.

He turned to look out of the window, and watched the snow falling, hoping to summon the flutter of Christmas excitement back into his mind. Watching the fat flakes landing on the verges brought a smile to his lips.

'What are you smiling at?' Michelle interrupted his thoughts.

'The snow.'

'It's wet, cold and miserable.'

'It's fantastic. It changes everything.'

Michelle seemed to think for a moment before answering. 'Jess said your family has a farm. I thought farmers hated bad weather.'

Sean shrugged. 'I'm not working today. Snow's great when you don't need to get anywhere.'

Michelle tsked at him. 'But we do need to get somewhere. You need to get to Edinburgh.'

'And you?'

'Back to Leeds, like I said.' There was a spark of irritation in her tone.

Sean paused. That feeling was there again in his gut. The same feeling that had made him stay at the airport with her. The same feeling that had made him stop his cab to pick her up. He told himself it was simply Christmas spirit. 'You're sure there isn't anywhere closer you could stay?'

'I could go to Jess's, but they only just got married. I don't want to intrude.'

Michelle turned away, apparently watching the snow falling outside the window, before turning back with a smile fixed in place. 'Besides I was always planning on spending Christmas on my own. It'll just be in Leeds rather than in the Caribbean.'

Sean grinned and matched her light tone. 'I'm sure you'll barely notice the difference.'

'Quite.' Michelle turned back to the window.

Sean let a silence fall between them. She'd asked to be taken to King's Cross to look for a train or hotel, so why hadn't he passed that request on to the driver? They were heading towards the apartment on the South Bank. As soon as he'd seen Michelle crying in the snow he'd abandoned the idea of catching the sleeper train to Scotland and decided to stay in London another night. But why? Because it was Christmas, and he felt bad about her being alone? That's what he was telling himself, but she patently didn't want his assistance. He thought about how she might react to arriving at the apartment. No matter how he played the scene out in his mind he couldn't see her taking it well. In the worst case scenario, he realised, it could be seen as a wee bit kidnappy.

'Michelle?'

'Yeah?'

'It's getting late.'

She nodded.

He took a deep breath. 'Look, I've been staying at a …' He paused. '… at a friend's flat. She's away. We could both crash there without paying for a hotel and then get a train in the morning?'

She shook her head. 'I'm fine, really. It's very kind, but …'

'But nothing. Why pay for a hotel when I'm offering you a spare room?'

'A spare room?' The hint of suspicion in her voice brought the grin back to Sean's lips.

He nodded. 'What did you think I was suggesting?'

She reddened. 'Nothing. I don't want to impose. A hotel will be fine.'

'What if I insist?' He could see the indecision in her eyes, the wish to be independent, to not be reliant on anyone, competing with her tiredness and need to curl up and feel safe.

She sighed. 'You're sure it's no trouble?'

'None at all. In fact, it'll save me money, if the cab goes straight there.'

She shook her head. 'I'll pay for the cab, as a thank you.'

Sean wasn't really an insisting on paying sort of guy. He'd never felt emasculated by splitting a bill, and he could see that by paying for the cab, Michelle was able to tell herself that she wasn't relying on him. It made it a fair businesslike exchange rather than an act of charity.

'Ok.'

'Ok.'

She looked away from him again. Sean wasn't taking her acquiescence to imply that the drawbridge had been lowered for him to ride through. Why was he so interested in this woman? The almost kiss? That was certainly part of it, but that wasn't the beginning. He kept thinking of their first meeting before the wedding. She'd had spreadsheets and lists galore detailing every possible bridal need on the wedding day. It was obsessive. It was insane. It was a level of care for other people that touched something in Sean, something he'd started to believe might have been beyond repair.

' … the driver?'

He realised she was talking. 'Sorry?'

'What about the driver? You didn't tell him we've changed where we're going.'

Sean grinned in what he hoped was an innocent absent-minded sort of a way, and leaned forward. 'Straight to Ostler's Wharf, mate. On the South Bank.'

The driver shot a glance at Sean in the mirror but didn't comment. Sean rested back in his seat and raised an eyebrow at Michelle.

The journey continued, off the motorway and into the city. Michelle focused her attention out of the window. The city was still bustling with shoppers, tourists and commuters rushing through the snow, hurrying to pick up last minute presents, or to get to the bar for Christmas drinks with friends. Everyone was moving like they had somewhere to be. Michelle realised that she had nowhere. She had a charitable offer of a place to stay from a virtual stranger, but nobody would be checking the clock and wondering when she'd be joining them.

The cab made it onto Westminster Bridge. The view down the river was stunning. The lights of the London Eye shone against the cloud-covered darkness, and the snow continued to fall around the wheel. You only needed the outline of a sleigh against the moon to make the perfect Christmas card. Michelle turned away.

A few minutes later she stood in the doorway of the flat and gasped. Firstly this wasn't a flat. Michelle lived in a flat. It had a bare patch in the carpet in front of the gas fire, and the spare room doubled as an airing cupboard. This place wasn't a flat; it wasn't even an apartment. This was a penthouse. The open plan kitchen-lounge-diner was bigger than her entire place in Leeds, but that wasn't what made her gasp. Sat right at the top of the building, the room was surrounded on three sides by glass, with views across the river to St Paul's Cathedral and the whole of the city beyond. Without thinking, she walked towards the window and stood for a moment, still and transfixed by the lights of the city spread out before her.

She heard Sean behind her carrying her bag into another room and then strolling back into the lounge.

'You like?'

'It's amazing.'

'I know. Shame it's not mine.'

'It must have cost the earth!' As soon as the words were out of her mouth, Michelle apologised. 'Sorry. I just meant … your friend must be doing Ok.'

'Yeah.' Sean paused. 'Yeah. I guess she is.'

Michelle registered the 'she' without comment. Obviously, he could have female friends. That didn't mean that he was regularly and athletically bending them over the polished glass table. The thought caught Michelle by surprise. She must be tired, she decided. She clearly wasn't herself. She turned around to avoid Sean's eye and took a proper look at the rest of the apartment. It was elegantly furnished, but something seemed missing. 'Does she live here all the time?'

Sean nodded.

Michelle looked around again. There was a glass dining table surrounded by eight leather backed black chairs, a large L-shaped settee, a flat screen television and sound system mounted against one wall, and a gleaming gloss-black kitchen. 'Where's all her stuff?'

'What do you mean?'

'Well books, ornaments, DVDs, magazines. There's nothing here.'

Sean shrugged as if he'd never thought about it before. 'I don't know.'

She was being rude, commenting on his friend's home furnishing, which was not nice behaviour when he was letting her stay with him.

'There's a Christmas tree.' She gestured towards the modest tree in the corner of the room. It was the only personal touch she could see.

'I got that.'

Michelle was surprised. 'You're not even going to be here for Christmas!'

'You've got to have a Christmas tree.'

Michelle shook her head at the extravagance. She ought to be making herself useful. She glanced at the clock. It was nearly ten.

'Are you hungry?'

Sean nodded. 'I didn't get any dinner.'

'Well, that's not on. You've got to take care of yourself.'

The grin she was getting accustomed to spread across his face. 'I appreciate the concern for my well being.'

She met his eye. No obvious sarcasm. He was apparently sincere. Michelle looked away. 'It's silly not to eat.'

'Have you eaten?'

'That's not the point.'

Sean's grin widened. 'So let's eat.'

Michelle walked around the counter into the kitchen area and opened the massive American style fridge. 'There is nothing in here.'

'That's not true.' Sean walked up behind her and surveyed the fridge. 'There's eggs.'

He picked them up and peered at the box. 'And they're in date.'

Michelle turned and considered the options in the back of the fridge door. A small, slightly hard piece of cheese, an unopened bottle of wine and half a pint of milk.

'Right. Is there any bread?'

Sean shook his head.

'Well what else have you got?'

Sean looked around at the cupboards before flinging one open. It was full of plates. He furrowed his brow and tried the next cupboard along.

'How long have you been staying here?'

'Couple of weeks.' He shrugged. 'I eat out a lot.'

'Clearly.'

The picture in Michelle's mind was of Sean all suited up pouring wine in an elegant restaurant for an even more elegant woman. It wasn't great but it was an improvement on imagining what he might have got up to with the owner of this apartment. At least she could look him in the eye while she thought about him going out on dinner dates.

Sean's intrepid exploration of the cupboards revealed a sugar bowl, and half a bag of dried spaghetti. 'Pasta?'

'Is that all there is? Seriously?'

'Like I said, I eat out a lot.'

'Ok.' She took the bag of pasta and popped it down on the counter along with the cheese, milk and eggs. 'Cheesy pasta then.'

'Sounds good.'

'Sounds like the only option.'

Michelle busied herself in the kitchen, finding that she seemed better able to work out where his mysterious lady friend stored the cooking essentials than he was.

Twenty minutes later she was spooning pasta into bowls and Sean was pouring wine into glasses. They sat opposite each other at one end of the dining table. Sean swirled a big mouthful of spaghetti onto his fork and tucked in. 'It's good. Cheesy.'

Michelle took a gulp of wine and allowed herself a smile. 'Considering the raw ingredients, it's practically miraculous.'

'You've worked wonders. Do you cook a lot?'

She nodded. 'It's a useful skill.'

'To make cheesy pasta?'

'To make something out of not very much. Clever cooking is a great way to save cash.'

She took another sip of wine and Sean topped up her glass. She glanced at the goblet. She was drinking more quickly than she was used to.

'My mum taught me to cook.'

Why was she telling him that? The wine. It must be the wine.

'You're close to your mum?'

'I was. It was actually her idea that I take this trip of a lifetime holiday.'

Sean raised an eyebrow in question.

Michelle swallowed. 'It's what she wanted me to spend my inheritance on. She died. At the end of last year. Cancer.'

'I'm sorry.'

'It was very quick. She wasn't even ill really.' That still rocked Michelle. She'd had people close to her pass away before. Mum's sister, Auntie Barb, for one, but there'd been a progression: treatment; improvement; then more treatment; and a long interminable decline. There had been tasks Michelle could do; things that needed organising.

With her mum it had been different. A routine visit to her GP on Monday. Admitted to hospital on Tuesday. Officially dying by Wednesday. There had been conversations about hospices and specialist nurses, but there hadn't been enough time for any of those things. Tanya Jolly had been told by an official looking man in an official looking white coat that she didn't have much longer and her body had taken him at his word.

They fell silent. Normally Michelle would do anything to avoid talking about her mother, but tonight something felt different.

'People say I look like her.' She blurted the words out, pointing at her long red hair. 'I get this from her.'

'Lucky you.'

'Hardly. I sort of hate being ginger.'

'It's beautiful.'

Michelle wasn't sure how to respond. It was flattering, but she'd already let him get her back to this apartment and then drunk too much of his wine. Compliments were easy.

'What about your dad?'

Michelle shook her head. 'I don't really see him any more.'

Sean leaned towards her across the table and rested his hand on top of hers. 'I'm sorry ...'

'I'm fine. They split up years ago.' She pulled her hand quickly away. 'I should clear these things away.'

'I can do it.'

'Right.' Michelle stopped half standing, half leaning over the table. 'I might go and er ... could I take a shower?'

'Sure. Through the bedroom at the end of the hall.' He pointed to an archway beyond the lounge area.

Michelle strode down the hallway and found her case already sitting on the bed in the spare room. What was she doing, telling a virtual stranger about her personal life? This Christmas, she reminded herself, was about her independence.

The shower was excellent, not like the spluttery electric thing in her own flat. The water rushed over her body and numbed her sight and hearing, forcing her further into her own thoughts. She found herself back at her Auntie Barb's house, ensconced in the kitchen, as she and her mother generally were in the weeks after Dad's affair had been revealed. She remembered sitting on a high stool, with Dolly gripped tightly in her hand, watching her mother and her aunt making fairy cakes and biscuits, stews and pies, quiche – which Barbara insisted on calling flan – and sauces. She had seen how nothing was wasted. Tonight's leftovers were tomorrow's lunchtime soup.

Michelle stood under the shower, and relived all those moments. Time and time again she'd seen her mother proved right. Relying on other people left you in a mess. She'd seen clients who'd happily doled out cash to other halves who'd sworn blind they were going to use it to pay the council tax or the electric, and then been left alone, in debt and with threats of disconnection hanging over their heads. She'd seen countless friends through countless break-ups who all told the same story. They trusted him. They loved him. They thought he loved them. Michelle shook her head to clear her thoughts. Let other people make those mistakes. She'd been taught, by her mum, how to get along on her own.

And then she remembered watching Auntie Barb feeding the Christmas cake, pushing a skewer deep into the mixture and pouring a little brandy into each hole. Michelle paused on that memory for a second – revisiting the rich smell, and the sound of Auntie Barb's laughter when Michelle had poured far too much brandy. That must have been when she still thought they'd be going home to Daddy for Christmas. She remembered something else. Her mother standing in the corner of the kitchen, dabbing her eyes, refusing to join in with even the tiniest preparation for the festive season.

One final, more recent, memory snuck in uninvited. A single moment under a sprig of mistletoe. She stepped out of the shower, busying herself wrapping her hair and body in towels to distract from the unwelcome thought. She padded into the bedroom, to hear her phone buzzing in the pocket of her jeans. She fished it out. Jess's name was flashing on the screen. Maybe she'd changed her mind about having a best friend to stay for Christmas. With relief, Michelle swiped the screen to answer the call.

'Hi.'

'What am I going to do?' Jess's voice screeched down the phone.

Michelle pulled her towel tight around her and sat down on the bed. 'About what?'

'Patrick's present! It hasn't come yet.'

'Right.' Michelle didn't respond for a second before she forced herself to swallow her irritation. Jess needed her help, and helping each other out was what friends did. 'What were you getting him?'

She listened as Jess explained about the website, the perfect gift, and the unfortunately missed delivery man. Michelle made suggestions about contacting the warehouse, and failing that about making Patrick a 'voucher' for his perfect gift to open on Christmas Day. With her friend calmed, she relaxed a little; it was nice to have a few minutes to catch up with Jess after the excitement of the wedding. 'So are you excited about Christmas apart from that?'

'Yeah. Course we are.' Jess talked quickly. 'Thanks, Michelle. I'd better go.'

And she hung up. Michelle flicked her phone off and got dressed. Jess was bound to be preoccupied at the moment. They would have plenty of time to catch up in the New Year, she was sure.

Sean finished the washing up in silence. So Michelle had lost her mum. Was that what gave her the hint of vulnerability he kept seeing under the tough shell? Sean tried to picture his own life without the ever-growing gaggle of his family. Not possible. Family. Home. They were what made him who he was. They were what made Christmas what it was. They were what had kept him going when he thought he'd lost everything.

He dried his hands and turned the television on. There wasn't much to choose from with the time rapidly running towards midnight. He was still flicking between the channels when Michelle padded back into the room wearing a T-shirt and sarong tied around her waist.

She gestured towards the outfit. 'I packed for the Caribbean.'

'You look great.' He gestured towards the TV. 'This won't keep you awake, will it?'

She shook her head. 'Actually, I'm not that tired. Eating late, you know, I think I've confused my body clock.'

'We could watch a movie?'

'Ok.' The idea of a film appealed to Michelle. She could imagine losing herself for a couple of hours, not having to think about her missed holiday, or about Sean, and definitely not having to think about Christmas. She squashed down into the corner of the L-shaped sofa, apparently trying to take up as little space as possible.

'Relax. Put your feet up. It's what it's designed for.'

Michelle stretched her legs out in front of her, causing her sarong to split apart revealing a long pale-skinned leg. Sean's eyes travelled up the leg and settled for a second on her thigh. He swallowed hard and turned back towards the television. 'Ok. Film. Wait there.'

Michelle watched Sean jog from the room and reappear with an armful of DVDs. 'Ok. I thought something festive would be in order. So *It's A Wonderful Life*? *White Christmas*? *Mary Poppins*? That one's not technically Christmassy but near enough. *The Santa Clause*? *Elf*?'

'Christmas films?' Her face was incredulous. 'I'm assuming those came with the apartment?'

'No! My mum buys me a new Christmas movie every year. I own them all. What do you fancy?'

'I'm not sure.' Michelle's heart sank. She couldn't think of a worse way to pass her time than being forced to sit through a saccharine fantasy of Christmas. She was Sean's guest though, and she had agreed to watch a film with him. She sighed. 'Which is best?'

'You mean you haven't seen them?'

Michelle shook her head.

'None of them?'

'Mary Poppins, maybe, when I was a kid.' Michelle swallowed the memory of Christmas Eve, with her Dad, before things changed. 'None of the others I don't think.'

Sean was insistent. 'Then it has to be a classic. *It's A Wonderful Life.*'

Sean put the DVD in the machine and leant back into the sofa clutching the remote. 'It's a bit cheesy but, you know, it's Christmas.'

Michelle watched the opening to the film in silence, uncomfortably aware that Sean was glancing at her to check her reactions. As time passed she lost herself in the story and forgot his attention. Sean had been right. The movie was pure cheese. As she watched George Bailey decide to end his life, Michelle rolled her eyes. She'd never had any time for self-pity. Life was tough and there was nothing to do but get on with things.

The film went on. The eye-rolling stopped. Michelle felt a lump rising in her throat, as George realised how many people in his life loved him. She swallowed it, and bit the inside of her cheek to distract herself.

As the credits rolled Michelle turned to see that Sean's eyes were streaming. He grinned at her. 'I love that film.'

Michelle looked away, giving him a chance to wipe his eyes. It was embarrassing, getting emotional in front of someone you hardly knew. Sean didn't seem to mind.

'I always cry like a baby though.' He grinned again. 'Very cathartic.'

'I don't really cry.'

'Erm, what about this afternoon?'

Yeah. He'd found her blubbing like a baby just a few hours earlier. She couldn't really argue with that. 'That was an aberration.'

'But didn't you feel better for it?'

Michelle thought for a second. Did she feel better? Well, possibly, but that was down to the meal, and the shower and the bed for the night. She felt better because her practical issues had been resolved. Sobbing on the pavement hadn't been any help at all. 'Don't be silly. Crying doesn't change anything, does it? It's far better to get on and deal with things.'

Sean shook his head at her. 'That's silly.'

The muscles in Michelle's jaw started to tense. How dare he call her silly? Silly was exactly what she wasn't. Silly was wasteful and irresponsible. Silly was childish. The Christmas tree twinkled in her peripheral vision. Christmas was silly. Michelle was not. She stood up from the sofa. 'I'm not silly.'

'You are if you think you can ignore your emotions. Feelings don't go away because it's inconvenient. Everybody has feelings they can't control.'

'Maybe not everyone.' Michelle paused. Maybe he was right. Maybe everyone else was a seething mass of love and hate and jealousy and compassion. Maybe there was something wrong with her.

'You've never had an emotion that overwhelmed you?' He stood up and moved towards her as he asked the question.

Caught off-guard her mind jumped back to the day when Auntie Barbara had unexpectedly collected her from school, and explained that Michelle and Mummy would be staying at Barbara's house for a little while. Daddy, she had been told, would not be coming with them. 'Never.'

Another step towards her. 'What about your family? There must have been highs and lows.'

'Of course. Just not ...' She paused again. 'Just nothing worth dwelling on.'

'Fair enough.' Another step towards her. She could feel the warmth of his body radiating. 'What about passion? A boyfriend?'

'No one serious.'

He'd almost closed the gap between them now. Michelle wondered why she wasn't moving away, but she couldn't seem to make her feet shift. He reached one hand forward and touched her fingertips. The softest, most fleeting of touches, almost like a dream or a memory of a touch, and then he wrapped the arm, suddenly, decisively around her waist and clamped her body against his.

'You've never been completely caught up in a moment of joy or passion? A moment where you couldn't think about anything else, where you have to do what you feel?'

Michelle shook her head mutely. Sean bent his head towards her. Involuntarily, she lifted her face to meet his. She could feel his breath on her cheek, his heart beating against her chest.

'You've never given in to a moment of desire?' He whispered the question against her skin.

'No.' Her answer was barely audible, muffled against his jaw.

His mouth hovered over her cheek.

'Fair enough.' He stepped away, releasing her from his arms. 'I guess we're all different.'

Michelle couldn't speak for a second. Her body was tingling from his closeness, and aching from the sudden distance between them. How dare he take advantage of her like that! A small voice in her head pointed out that firstly, no advantage taking had actually occurred, and, secondly, Michelle wouldn't have minded one bit if it had. Michelle ignored the voice.

'So you go with whatever you're feeling, do you?'

'Of course.' He glanced at his watch. 'Time for bed, do you think?'

His normal playful tone was back, which in this case, made the question sound even more like an invitation.

Michelle marched past him towards the spare bedroom. 'I'll see you in the morning.'

She undressed quickly and pulled the bedcovers around her like a cocoon. One more sleep, she told herself. One more sleep before you're back into your own flat, safe from all Sean's silliness. The only thing sillier than silliness, Michelle decided, would be falling for silliness.

In the lounge, Sean switched on his laptop. While he waited for it to boot, he pulled his phone from his pocket, and flicked back to the message from Cora. Cora Strachan – he'd noticed a few weeks ago that she'd dropped the double-barrelled Strachan-Munro from her e-mail signature. He skimmed through the message again and sighed.

She'd stopped using his name, but she still kept texting. He'd sworn that they were over for good, but here he was staying in her apartment. He shook his head. Cora should be ancient history. He didn't keep slipping back into old habits because she was the love of his life. It was because it was easy. It was because it was safe.

He remembered finally quitting smoking two years ago. He'd spent five years trying. Patches, gum, hypnosis, cutting down gradually; he'd tried them all and nothing had worked. Then he'd stopped. No one-off sneaky smokes. No substitutes. He'd just stopped. Cold turkey. Maybe it really was the only way.

His laptop pinged into life and he clicked his way to a train booking site, scrolled through the options for trains up the east coast the next morning and settled on the 11.41 from Kings Cross. As he clicked, an idea was forming that shoved any worries he had about Cora unceremoniously out of his mind. Maybe he could invite Michelle to spend Christmas with him? It would be in the spirit of Christmas, wouldn't it? An act of Christmas charity.

He glanced down the corridor, but the light in her room was already out. Best not to wake her. He clicked to select two tickets to Edinburgh, and paused for a second before clicking 'Confirm.' It would be fine, he told himself. Totally fine.

## Christmas Eve, 2013

Michelle was surprised to be woken by the sound of pots and pans crashing around in the kitchen. She pulled on the jeans and jumper she'd worn to the airport and headed into the lounge-diner in time to see Sean plating up the biggest cooked breakfast she'd ever seen. Bacon, sausage, fried eggs, fried bread, tomato, mushrooms and beans were being heaped vertically onto plates only designed for normal human-sized portions.

'There's enough here for about eight people!'

Sean nodded. 'Convenience stores don't really do single rashers of bacon. I had to buy a pack.'

'You've been shopping? What time is it?'

He glanced at his watch. 'Nearly ten.'

'Sorry. Oh God! Have I made you late for your train?'

'Not at all. I've booked us both on the 11.40. There's a cab coming at 11. Loads of time.'

'Right.' Michelle bristled at Sean's presumptuous attitude. 'I could have arranged my own train ticket, you know.'

'I don't doubt it, but I was booking mine.'

Michelle looked at the food and then at Sean. She remembered the state of the kitchen cupboards the night before. He'd clearly gone to a lot of effort to get breakfast ready. She must be sounding horribly ungrateful. 'Well, thank you. I'll pay you back for the ticket.'

He spread his palms in a 'no worries' gesture, and carried the heaped plates to the table.

Michelle sat down opposite him. 'Well this looks ...' She surveyed the mountain of food, unsure how to finish the sentence. 'This looks massive.'

Sean laughed. 'It's a long way to Edinburgh. Who knows when you'll get to eat again?'

'I'm going to Leeds.'

'Leeds. Edinburgh.' He chewed a forkful of beans and fried bread. 'Actually ...'

Before Sean could explain, Michelle's phone buzzed in her pocket. 'Hold on.'

She got up from the table and hovered in the kitchen to answer the phone. 'Hello.'

It was Jess again. 'They didn't have any pigs in blankets.'

'What?'

'The supermarket didn't have any pigs in blankets.'

Michelle laughed.

'It's not funny!' The pitch of Jess's voice escalated. 'I want it to be perfect.'

'It will be.' She felt for her friend. 'It's your first Christmas together. It won't be ruined because you don't have pigs in blankets.'

She heard Jess harrumph. 'That's what Patrick said.'

'Well then.'

They chatted for a few more minutes about how long roast potatoes took to cook, and whether you could still be viewed as a domestic goddess if you bought ready-made stuffing, before Jess hung up.

Sean had nearly finished his food mountain by the time she sat back down at the table.

'Sorry about that.' She waved her phone. 'Jess.'

Sean rolled his eyes. 'What's up with Princess Perfect?'

'What?'

'Jess.' He grinned. 'You've gotta admit, she's a bit spoilt.'

'Don't be rude.'

He laid down his fork and shrugged. 'Sorry. I know she's your mate.'

'Yes.' The comment had struck a nerve. She felt disloyal thinking it, but she wondered if Sean was right. 'She's a bit stressed about their first Christmas together. Wants it to be perfect.'

'Nah. Christmas isn't supposed to be perfect. It's supposed to be sort of disorganised. If you don't eat at least an hour later than you intended, you're probably not doing it right.'

Michelle didn't respond. She'd only eaten one proper Christmas dinner in the last twenty years, and that one she'd prepared herself. It had been served precisely on schedule.

An hour later, they were on the concourse at Kings Cross station. Michelle let the noise and bustle wash over her, while Sean collected their tickets from the machine. All she had to do now was pay him for the ticket, make a polite excuse about being tired and preferring to sit on her own, and she'd be able to get back to her plan of spending Christmas alone as far away from tinsel or, indeed, mistletoe as possible.

She peered at the overhead display board. The 11.41a.m. to Edinburgh, calling at Leeds, was on time. Her mood darkened, remembering that, by rights, she should be sunning herself in the Caribbean by now.

'Er ... there's a little bit of a problem.'

She turned round to see Sean standing behind her, his rucksack slung over one shoulder and his hair flopping in front of his face. 'It's probably my fault, but ...'

'What?'

'I think I must have clicked Edinburgh twice.' He held the ticket out to her.

'What?' She looked at the ticket. First class to Edinburgh. 'You did this on purpose.'

The words were out of her mouth before she had time to think about them, but as soon as she'd spoken she realised it was true. Sean was staring at the floor.

'Why?'

He took a breath. 'I'm sorry.'

She repeated the question. 'Why?'

'I was trying to be nice.' He paused. 'I should have asked you.'

Michelle didn't respond.

'Look, it's Christmas. It's horrible to be on your own. Why not come with me?'

'Because I barely know you.'

He stepped towards her. 'You could get to know me. I'm delightful.'

'You're a presumptuous little rich boy, who's too used to getting his own way.' Michelle took a breath. 'Write your address down and I'll send you the money for the ticket.'

Sean was disappointed and it showed on his face. 'It's reserved seating. I'm afraid we're next to each other.'

Michelle shook her head. 'I'll find somewhere else to sit.'

She picked up the handle of her suitcase, and set off wheeling her way through the throng towards the platform. There was no way she would be sitting next to that man. What on earth had he been thinking?

On the platform, she ignored the first class carriages and dragged her case down to the standard class part of the train. It was busy with people heading home for Christmas. Bodies, luggage and bags filled with presents were jammed into every available space. Michelle fought her way through, reading the reservations displayed above each seat, and discounting everything that started 'London to'. Eventually she found a single window seat which was only reserved from Newcastle onwards. She stripped off her coat and left it on the seat to stake her claim while she manoeuvred her suitcase onto the luggage rack.

Michelle sank into the seat and closed her eyes, but she couldn't relax. The carriage was filling up around her. Across the aisle was a mother with two young children and a bored looking teenage boy, who slumped into his seat and immediately started fiddling with his phone. In the aisle a group of older teenagers, students she guessed, were talking loudly and trying to make space to sit on the luggage rack.

'Finally!' The voice was female, the tone haughty, but with an undercurrent of thick West Yorkshire, which, Michelle guessed, the speaker had spent years trying to eradicate. The stranger gestured at the empty aisle seat next to Michelle. 'This is me.'

Michelle squashed tightly against the window to let the woman sit down and got a proper look at her companion as she did so. She was wearing a navy blue suit over a crisp white blouse, with dark court shoes. Her hair was cropped short and was unapologetically white. The outfit suggested conformity, but the hair said she didn't really care.

The woman eased herself into her seat and glanced at Michelle. 'Do you mind?'

She gestured towards her feet, which she was already easing out of the court shoes.

It seemed a little unusual, but Michelle smiled. 'Make yourself comfortable.'

As the train pulled away, and Michelle tried to concentrate on her novel, she realised the woman was staring at her.

'I know you.'

'I don't think so.' Michelle smiled and turned back to her book.

'I do. I don't forget a face.' The woman pursed her lips, as if her inability to remember was Michelle's fault. 'Turn your head that way.'

The instruction was delivered with such certainty that Michelle obediently turned her face so the woman could observe her profile.

'I'll work it out. Where are you from?'

'Leeds.'

'Ah-ha! How old are you?'

'Twenty-nine.'

'Too old.'

'I'm sorry.' Michelle responded without thinking. The woman tutted. Again, Michelle felt as thought she was somehow at fault.

'Brothers or sisters?'

'Not really.'

'You're not sure?'

'Half-brothers. A lot younger than me.' Michelle petered off. Was the stranger expecting a full family tree?

Apparently not. She held up a hand. 'Don't tell me. It's coming!'

She screwed her face up in concentration. 'Joseph Jolly! And Noel Jolly. You're Noel Jolly's big sister.'

Michelle opened her mouth in surprise, but the woman stopped her again. 'I said don't tell me. Polly? Molly? Holly! Holly Jolly! Two hundred new children to learn every year, and twice as many parents, but I never forget a face.'

'People call me Michelle.' Michelle peered at her companion. 'Mrs Bickersleigh?'

'Miss!' The tone was imperious.

'Sorry, Miss Bickersleigh.' Michelle heard herself chorusing the words like a schoolgirl, which was ridiculous. The woman had never been her teacher. So far as she could remember she'd only actually met her once, at Noel's nativity play. That must have been twelve years ago. Apparently, she truly never did forget a face.

'You can call me Jean. And, now I know this, you're Barbara Eccle's niece, aren't you?'

Michelle nodded.

'Barbara and I go way back. My brother took her to see

The Beatles in Scarborough. 1963 it must have been. Waste of the price of a ticket that was. She wouldn't let him past her cardigan.' The woman sighed. 'So what brought you down to London? Do you live here now?'

Michelle explained about the wedding, the cancelled flight, and the train ticket debacle. She skimmed over the mistletoe and the cheesy, weepy movie.

'You poor thing! You'll need a little something to perk you up after all that.' Jean produced a hip flask from her handbag, followed by two plastic cups. Michelle raised an eyebrow at the contents of the lady's handbag. Catching the look, Jean smiled.

'You never know when you might need a little pick-me-up. Chin! Chin!'

Michelle didn't even try to refuse. Drinking during the day wasn't her usual style, but she sensed that no argument would be brooded. She took a sip and felt the whisky burning her throat.

'That's the stuff. Now tell me about this boy.'

'Which boy?'

'The one whose house you slept at last night. Why aren't you living it up in first class with him?'

Michelle took another sip of her whisky.

'Don't play with it girl. Drink up!' Jean topped up her cup. 'And tell me about the boy.'

'He's just a boy.'

'No. He's not. The ones people say are "just a boy" are always something more.'

Michelle didn't answer immediately. She knew she was lying. Sean wasn't just a boy. He was all man. For all the floppy hair and mischievous attitude, there was nothing boyish about the way he'd pulled her into his arms. Outwardly, she shrugged.

'Nothing much to say.'

'Bollocks.'

Michelle gulped at the unexpected expletive, and looked again at her travelling companion. Jean rolled her eyes.

'Tell me about Noel then. Was it his mother I heard about a few months ago? Tanya Jolly? The one who died.'

Michelle shook her head. She really must stop drinking before talking to people. Her normal reserve had been shattered to pieces over the last twenty-four hours.

'Good.' Jean pulled a face. 'Horrid to lose one's mother too soon.'

'Actually that was my mother.'

'Oh. I see. I knew they were related somehow. Were you close to her?'

Michelle nodded. 'It was mainly just me and her when I was growing up.'

Michelle's plastic cup was topped up. She took another sip.

'So your parents split up? Your father married again?' Miss Bickersleigh was not, it appeared, a great respecter of personal boundaries.

'Yes. I didn't see him that often really.'

'That's a shame. Girls need fathers.'

The conversation was getting far too personal for Michelle's liking. She picked up her book and tried to look engrossed. Jean didn't seem to mind, but Michelle couldn't concentrate on the words. What was happening to her? Different faces swum across her imagination. Her dad. Sean. Auntie Barbara. Miss Bickersleigh. Sean. Her mum. Sean. Sean.

And then her dad again. A card every birthday. A letter every Christmas, always with an invitation to join him and Noel and Joe and The Elf. She'd never gone. She'd always said it was because of her mother, but why not this year? The letter had arrived a month before Christmas like it always did. She'd recognised the writing on the envelope and thrown it away.

And then Sean's face again. Those stupid green eyes glinting at her, challenging her to loosen up, relax, have fun. Those green eyes that clearly didn't understand anything about losing people that you loved, or about taking responsibility for yourself or anyone else. What Michelle needed wasn't Sean. It was simplicity, time on her own with no commitments. If she did happen to decide she wanted a relationship in the future, she would use one of those internet dating sites, where she could set criteria, and control who contacted her. It sounded much more orderly.

Finally, her mum. She would always think of her at this time of year, even though she'd hated Christmas with a passion. She remembered Christmas dinners after they'd moved out of Barbara's cramped terrace and into the flat – enchiladas, or homemade pizza, whatever Mum could think up that clashed with the season. She'd even written a cookbook based on the same idea – 'The Anti-Christmas Cook.' She wasn't exactly the new Delia but it had sold reasonably well, and given Tanya a career for the first time in her life.

Michelle's own book dropped onto her lap and her eyes settled closed, lulled by the rhythm of the moving train.

'Excuse me.' The voice seemed to be coming from outside. 'Excuse me!'

It was louder now, and closer.

'Excuse me!' Michelle opened her eyes, and looked around. She was still on the train, but Jean had gone. There was an empty seat beside her and a couple standing in the aisle. The man was glaring at her. 'These are our seats.'

Michelle rubbed her eyes and shook her head. 'No. This is only reserved from Newcastle.'

'Yes.' The man's tone was increasingly impatient.

'But we've only just left …' Michelle petered out as she looked around her. The family across the aisle had gone. The teenagers resting on the luggage rack had also vanished. She looked out of the window and saw unfamiliar buildings. She turned back to the couple. 'Where are we?'

'Leaving Newcastle, and these are our seats.'

'Right. Sorry.' Michelle swung her legs around and slipped past the man into the gangway. She hurried along the aisle, grabbed her case off the luggage rack and dragged it out of the packed carriage. She paused by the door and read the list of stations. Next stop: Edinburgh. Michelle groaned. Why hadn't someone woken her up?

Never mind. She'd have to get off at Edinburgh and then catch another train back to Leeds. Her immediate problem was finding somewhere to sit. Her hand went to the ticket, stuffed in her pocket. She had a reserved seat in first class. Of course, that would mean Sean. It was at least another hour to Edinburgh. She turned and peered back down the train, hoping desperately for a free seat.

Sean stared out of the window as the train moved away from the built-up outskirts of Newcastle and on to cling to the coast towards Berwick. This part of the journey was always when he started to feel as though he was nearing home. Home for Christmas. He smiled to himself.

'Is this seat still free?'

He was jolted out of his reverie by the voice, but he didn't turn away from the window. After her reaction to him that morning, he wasn't minded to throw down the red carpet. 'I thought you were only going as far as Leeds.'

There was a pause. He glanced up at her.

'I fell asleep.'

Despite his resolution to be cool with Michelle, Sean's face cracked into a laugh. 'I guess you're stuck with me then.'

Michelle slumped into the seat beside Sean. 'Only until Edinburgh. I'm getting the first train back to Leeds.'

Sean paused. An idea, only half formed was jumping up

and down in his head, demanding his full attention. 'What if ...'

'What?'

'Look. I know we've only just met, but it's Christmas. It's silly to be on your own. Why don't you come with me?' The question surprised Sean almost as much as Michelle. He'd seen her reaction to the ticket to Edinburgh. At this point a sensible man would have known that it was time to give up, but he couldn't let go. He felt like his accelerator pedal had got stuck hard to the floor, and the only option was to hold on and enjoy the ride.

Michelle's lips pursed. 'We've been through this.'

'For goodness' sake. You're already halfway there. You'd really rather go back to an empty flat?'

Michelle's expression shifted slightly. He'd done enough sales pitches to see that she was interested, but she wasn't on the hook yet. Think Sean. What do you know about her? She's practical. Sensible. Somehow, he needed to make running away for Christmas with a virtual stranger sound sensible.

'Do you even have any food in your cupboards?'

Michelle shook her head.

'Right. Well, it's Christmas Eve now. What are you planning on eating tomorrow?'

Michelle shrugged. 'Anything but turkey.'

Sean shifted in his seat to face her.

'We're not discussing this any more,' he tried.

No response. He was going to need to grovel at least a bit before he laid down the law. 'I'm sorry I bought the ticket to Edinburgh. It was out of order. I should have asked you first.'

'You should.'

There was a note of acceptance in her voice that hadn't been there before. Sean's stomach jumped. She might actually agree.

'Ok. What about a deal? It's Christmas Eve. What if you give me forty-eight hours? Two days. After that I'll drive you home myself. Forty-eight hours in the warm, with plentiful food and lots of Christmas spirit.'

'I'm not really a fan of Christmas.'

'Then I've got two days to change your mind. Deal?'

'Don't be silly.'

'It's not silly.' Two days. She might go for that, and it was only two days. Nobody could get their heart broken in two days. Sean grinned. This was it. This was his pitch. 'It's practical. It saves you wasting time and money travelling home. It saves you wasting more money at home on food and heat, and we both get some company.'

He held a hand out for her to shake, and waited. This was the sort of thing he used to do so naturally, follow his instincts because something felt right. Well, he'd done it now. No option but to stick with the idea and hope she didn't notice him trembling.

Eventually she took his hand. 'But only because it saves me a long trip home.'

Sean exhaled. 'Ok. Now for the terms and conditions.'

'What?'

'I'm a businessman. It's important that contracts are clear upfront. It saves all sorts of problems later.'

'But you can't add things now.'

'I'm clarifying our agreement. You have to enter into the spirit of things. No refusing to "do Christmas". No standoffishness. Basically you have to go along with whatever I say.'

'Whatever you say?'

'Absolutely. Forty-eight hours. I'm in charge.'

Michelle scowled. 'You're not in charge of me.'

'And you're pulling a face, which isn't very festive.'

'It won't make any difference. Christmas is for kids. We are not kids.'

Sean shook his head. 'What's wrong with being a kid at heart?'

Michelle didn't reply.

'So you agree to my terms?'

She nodded.

'Good.' Sean turned his face back to the window to give himself a moment to regroup. This was fine. It was only two days. Time limited. Just a bit of fun. He glanced back at Michelle settling back into the seat beside him, and felt his stomach lurch again.

# Chapter Four

## Christmas Eve, the previous year, 2012

*Michelle*

'This is going to be great.' Jess is pouring champagne into two glasses.

'Isn't it a bit early for that?'

'Lighten up.' She shrugs. 'It's Christmas.'

'It's Christmas Eve, and it's half past nine in the morning.'

'It's exciting.' She carries her champagne into the living room and I follow her, leaving the second glass on the kitchen counter. 'Christmas with no family. It's going to be amazing.'

I ought to reply. I open my mouth but I can't make any words come out.

She claps her hand over her mouth. 'Oh my God! I'm sorry. I didn't mean "no family" like ... Sorry.'

'It's Ok.' She didn't mean anything by it, and it's been two months. Mum wouldn't be impressed if she thought I was moping. I force myself to smile.

Jess giggles. 'Is it wrong that I'm happy my parents have gone on a cruise over Christmas?'

I shake my head.

'So what about a cruise?'

'What?'

'With your money.'

'I don't think so.' I can't really see myself playing quoits with a party of retired librarians from Barnsley.

'Well you have to book something.'

I know I do. Mum was very clear about me spending the inheritance on a holiday. 'I don't even know how much it is.'

Jess's brow furrows again. 'I thought you saw to the solicitor yesterday.'

'Er ... no.' I tried to go to the solicitors. I had an appointment. I got as far as the door. They had a Christmas tree in the reception. I could see it through the glass. It was a real one, like Dad used to bring home. I could remember the smell of the tree. I could remember Christmas with Mum and Dad still together. It wasn't the right thing to be thinking about. I'm supposed to be thinking about Mum. I didn't go in. I put a smile on for Jess. 'I'll phone them after Christmas.'

She takes another sip of champagne. 'So have you got everything we need?'

'What for?'

'For Christmas!'

I gesture towards her glass. 'Well we did have champagne.'

'You know what I mean. Turkey, little tiny sausages wrapped in bacon, Christmas pudding.'

'I don't like Christmas pudding.'

'Neither do I, but that's not the point. It's Christmassy.'

I close my eyes for a second. I was hoping for a quiet Christmas. 'Me and Mum never really bothered with Christmas food and stuff.'

Jess doesn't answer, but I can see her nose start to wrinkle and a furrow appears between her eyebrows. 'I thought it would be nice, after everything.'

I'm being ungrateful. She's right of course. It will be nice to make an effort, and at least doing the traditional Christmas dinner will be different from all the years with Mum. 'Ok. What do we need?'

'Can we get a Christmas tree?'

I shake my head. 'No.'

I find a pen and paper and start to make a list. Jess, it turns out, has very firm ideas about what constitutes a proper Christmas. I put my foot down over the tree and insist that for two of us we only need a chicken rather than turkey, but apart from that it's Jess's perfect Christmas all the way.

The thought of braving the supermarket to get all this stuff on Christmas Eve doesn't appeal, but we can go together, and we've got all day. 'Do you want to drive to the shops?'

She wrinkles her nose again. 'Actually, I'm meeting Patrick for lunch.'

'Oh.'

'I mean, he's going down to London this evening, and I'm not going to see him until Boxing Day.'

Two whole days.

'You don't mind going to the shop, do you?'

'Course not.' Well someone has to go, and I'm not doing anything else, so I might as well make myself useful.

Jess skips off to make herself beautiful for the sainted Patrick. I collect my bag from the kitchen and get in the car. As soon as I sit down in the driver's seat I have one of the moments. I've never had anything like this before, but since Mum went they come every couple of days. It's not an upset feeling or anger or even anything you could recognise as grief. It's just the absolute certainty that everything in the world is just too vast and too empty and too pointless to contemplate. I sit in the car, staring straight ahead, and wait for it to pass.

### Christmas Eve, 2013

At Edinburgh station, Sean swung Michelle's case from the luggage rack and hopped from the train onto the platform. He set off towards Left Luggage and had checked in his rucksack and Michelle's suitcase before she had time to object. He strode out of the station towards the city.

'Aren't we going straight to your house?'

'Not yet. It's Christmas Eve. We're in the middle of the best city on the planet.'

Michelle opened her mouth.

'Don't argue. The best city on the planet, with a beautiful woman who says she doesn't like Christmas. This is part one of persuading you otherwise.'

Michelle made a face. 'It'll be really busy.'

Sean grinned. 'Full of potential new friends.'

'And cold ...'

'Cold is Christmassy.' Sean leant towards her, the now familiar scent of his skin filling Michelle's senses. 'We had an agreement. You said you'd go along with me for forty-eight hours. You're barely out of hour one.'

Pulling her duffle coat tight around her, Michelle followed Sean out into the city. There was snow on the ground, turning to slush as last-minute shoppers charged through it, rushing to get everything done in time for Christmas.

Michelle stopped as the cold air hit her. Sean paused alongside her, reached down, and took her gloved hand in his.

'What are you doing?' She pulled her hand away.

'Come on!' Sean leant towards her and retook her hand. 'You've got to hold hands on a first date.'

'This is not a —'

'Go along with it.'

'No.' Michelle stood still in the station entrance. 'I said I'd go along with Christmas. Holding hands is romantic not Christmassy.'

Sean sighed and let go of her hand. 'Ok. Come on then.'

Michelle was caught off guard as he strode away from the station and made his way over the bridge, away from the bustle of the Princes Street shops. She ran after him. 'Where are we going?'

'This way!'

She followed him along the road which twisted to climb steeply up the side of a long hill. Partway up, Sean turned and continued to climb up a narrow staircase between the buildings. Eventually they came out at the top of the hill and Sean settled leaning against a railing, looking out across the park and city in front of him.

'What have we come up here for?' Michelle came to a stop next to Sean, panting for breath after the steep, quick climb.

'Just look.' Sean placed his hands on her shoulders and gently turned her around to face the view.

The park below them was full of light and movement. She could make out the gleaming white of a skating rink, and a Ferris wheel towering above the ant-like people on the ground. Next to the wheel there was a maze of tiny market stalls, all framed with sparkling lights. Beyond the market and the fairground, she could see trees across the park lit up with thousands of white lights, and beyond that Princes Street, still bustling in the last few hours of shopping time. It was only four o'clock but darkness had already descended, making the lights below sparkle even more brightly. Michelle gasped.

'You like?'

'It's very pretty.' The scene below her was like a piece of moving artwork.

'Excellent. Let's get down there then!'

Michelle sighed. 'It'll be really busy, and everything's always very overpriced at these sorts of things.'

Sean stopped dead in front of her. 'Forty-eight hours. You promised. Come on.'

And they were off again, racing back down the hill. Michelle had to skip and jog to keep up with Sean's irrepressible bounds, and was out of breath all over again by the time they got down into the market. She watched Sean weaving his way between the stalls, bumping into other shoppers, and shouting random apologies and excuse me's in every direction. Michelle followed more cautiously, squeezing herself between bodies, trying to blend in with the crowd.

And then she was alone. She looked around, and saw only strangers, unknown bodies jostling her, shopping bags bashing against her legs. She stood on tiptoes and craned her neck to see where he'd gone, but Sean had rushed too far ahead of her and was out of sight. She told herself to breathe. She forced her way through the crowd, and stopped at the end of a row of stalls. Behind her, a group of buskers were singing *God Rest You Merry Gentleman* but Michelle was deaf to their instructions to 'Let nothing you dismay.'

Sean had vanished. She was cold. She'd been shoved and buffeted through the crowd from every direction. She hadn't had a chance to catch her breath from the run up and back down the hill. She was stuck in an unfamiliar city hundreds of miles away from home, and thousands of miles from the beach she was supposed to be lying on. And everywhere she looked there was bloody Christmas.

She walked a few metres in each direction, scanning the crowd. No Sean. She was absolutely, resolutely alone. She would have to go back to the station. Her case was there. Her only chance of getting back to Leeds was there. Of course she didn't have the ticket for the left luggage, and she had no idea whether she was too late to catch a train, but at the moment it was her only option. She stuffed her hands deep into her pockets and started to walk.

'Michelle!' At first the voice didn't seep into her brain.

'Michelle!'

'Hey! You in the red hat. Get that woman for me! Her! There! With the ginger hair!'

A hand touched Michelle's arm. 'Er, I think that man wants your attention.'

She turned to look where the stranger was pointing.

Sean. Of course Sean. He appeared to be levitating above the crowd a few feet in front of her. He waved. 'I thought I'd lost you. Wait there!'

She watched as he clambered back down into the crowd, seeing that he had actually been standing on a high table in front of one of the glühwein stalls. He climbed down leaning on strangers, who seemed perfectly happy to assist, and lolloped through the throng to her side. 'Where did you go?'

'You were in front.' Michelle didn't smile. 'You went away from me.'

'I thought you were just behind me.' He beamed as a new thought entered his head. 'I told you it would be better if we held hands.'

Seeing that he was not, in any sense, forgiven, Sean changed track. 'Look. This was supposed to be about going with the flow. Trying to experience the joy of Christmas. You have to trust me.'

'I don't see how I can trust someone who runs off like a child the moment my back's turned.'

'I didn't run off. I went to see what was going on. You don't dive in.'

'Well, I'm sorry to be such a disappointment. If you give me the luggage ticket, I'll get my things and be on my way home.'

He could let her go. She'd probably still be able to get a train home. His brain was telling him to let her walk away. That would be safer. There was still a chance he wasn't in so deep that he couldn't swim back to shore.

He ran after her. 'Wait!'

He caught up within a few paces, and fell into step beside her. 'Now of course, you could go back to Leeds. You could. But, I can't help but wonder if that's really what you want.'

She shot him a look that left little doubt.

'Ok, so you do really want to do that, but I can't help but

wonder if it's truly for the best. You're pissed off with me. I get that, although to be fair to me, if we'd held hands like I suggested we'd never have got separated.'

Another look.

'Anyway, you're here now. We're almost home, well my home anyway. There's a warm bed there.'

A further look.

'More than one warm bed. You'll be quite safe. Come on. If you go home now, you'll arrive back too late to go to the shops. You'll have no food in, and you won't be able to get anything until Boxing Day. It makes more sense to stay.'

'You think staying with you is sensible?'

Of course he didn't. Staying with him was clearly insane. 'Yeah. Dead sensible.'

Sean had played more than a few hands of pub poker in his time, but those guys had nothing on Michelle. He had no idea which way she was going to jump.

'All right.'

'Really?'

She nodded.

'Come on then.' This time he grabbed hold of her hand and she made no attempt to wriggle free. He pulled her through the crowd to the foot of the Ferris wheel and into the queue.

Michelle pulled a face.

'What?'

'We've already seen the view for nothing from the top of the hill.'

'Well I'm going on it. You can stay down here if you want.'

Michelle looked up at the wheel turning slowly above their heads.

'No. I'll come on. I assume you're paying.'

Sean laughed. 'If it gets you to do something festive I'm more than happy to pay.'

They moved to the front of the queue and climbed into a gondola, sitting opposite each other, knees touching in the middle of the car.

Sean's eyes never moved from Michelle. As the gondola climbed into the sky and paused at the top of the wheel, her whole face changed. The closed, guarded expression gave way to something else. Something joyful. She was smiling as she watched the people on the ground below. Finally, he seemed to have found something she liked.

The wheel turned them back to the ground and then they started to rise again. Michelle turned to face him.

'You're enjoying this?' He couldn't keep the hint of accusation out of his voice.

'Maybe. I haven't been on one of these things for years.'

'When was the last time?'

She shrugged. 'I don't know.'

'Liar.' The dig was friendly. 'Look, it's forty-eight hours and then you never have to see me again. What's to lose by telling me all your dark secrets?'

She laughed, quietly, tentatively. 'I don't know if I have any dark secrets.'

His responding laugh was generous and uncontrolled. 'Shame. Just tell me about the Ferris wheel then.'

'It was with my dad. We used to go to the fair near where we lived on Bonfire Night. We went every year, until they split up.'

'He didn't take you after that?'

'A couple of times. It wasn't the same. Mum would ask all these questions when I got home. And he used to bring The Elf with him.'

'The Elf?'

Michelle shook her head. 'Too long a story.'

'I wish I could say, "Well it's a long ride," but sadly it's not.'

They were coming towards the bottom of their third spin

and the ride was slowing. Sean stepped off, and turned to help Michelle down, holding out his hand like a footman helping a grand lady from her carriage.

'What now?' Michelle was still smiling from the Ferris wheel.

'Food?' Sean suggested. 'And then I suppose we should probably head for home.'

'Ok. Where can we eat?'

Sean gestured towards a row of stalls. 'Hot pork rolls?'

Michelle nodded.

'And because it is Christmas, and the Ferris wheel was fun, but it's not technically Christmassy, you have to have glühwein.'

Michelle didn't argue, and they ate their rolls, crunching on crackling and giggling as the fat and apple sauce dripped onto their chins. The ride on the Ferris wheel and the comforting salty taste in her mouth were combining into a fun evening.

'Tell me something about you then.'

'Like what?' Sean glanced at her.

'I don't know.' She looked down at the floor, hoping he wouldn't see how awkward talking about herself still made her. 'I told you about my mum and the Bonfire Night thing. It's only fair.'

'Ok. What do you want to know?'

Michelle thought for a moment. 'Why do you love Christmas so much?'

She looked at his face while he thought about the question. His expression was almost wistful. 'It's because nothing can break Christmas. You can have the worst things happen one year, but then next year it's Christmas again and it's still exciting and brilliant. It's like Christmas is too special for real life to spoil it.'

'That's easy to say if you've never had a really bad Christmas.'

Sean shook his head. 'Oh, I've had lousy Christmases.'

'What happened?' Michelle didn't believe him for a second. If you had a really bad experience, you learnt from it. You learnt not to get your hopes up the next time.

'I once got dumped at Christmas.'

'Really? When?'

He waved his hand as if to dismiss the memory. 'A long time ago.'

Michelle sensed that she'd reached the end of Sean's willingness to talk. She'd almost drained her glühwein, and opened her mouth to ask if Sean wanted another. She realised Sean wasn't drinking. 'You're not having any.'

'I have to drive.'

The information didn't make it through the glühwein fuzz in her brain until they were back at the railway station, collecting their bags. 'What do you mean drive? You said you lived in Edinburgh.'

'My flat's in Edinburgh. Christmas is at home.'

'Whose home?'

'Mine. Well technically, it's mine. Mum and Dad still live there.'

'Who's going to be there?'

'Just family.'

A full-on family Christmas? 'I can't come to Christmas with your whole family. I don't know them.'

'You know me.'

'Barely!'

Sean shrugged. 'Well you promised you'd do Christmas. Christmas means family I'm afraid.'

Michelle scowled, but knew that without anywhere else to go, she was well and truly beaten. 'Where is it then?'

He paused for a second. 'Near Edinburgh.'

He strode across the station to the car hire window and started talking and filling in papers for the assistant. Michelle watched in silence.

Once he'd collected the keys she followed him to the car park. 'How near Edinburgh?'

'Not too far.'

Something about his tone made her suspicious. 'How far exactly?'

'Couple of hours.' He looked at the snow starting to fall gently from the sky. 'Maybe three.'

He clicked the car key and opened the boot of the hire car. 'Would have preferred a four wheel drive in this weather to be honest.'

'What?'

'It'll be fine.' He glanced back at the snow. 'Probably.'

Without much other option, Michelle climbed into the car. It was clean and fresh, and had the recently valeted new car smell. She leant back into the passenger seat and settled to watch the scenery go by as Sean set off to drive out of the city. The radio was on, and a mix of cheesy Christmas music washed over them both. The snow falling had a hypnotic quality and the combination of the snowy cold outside and warm glühwein inside was cheering. She listened to the music, watched the snow, and resolved to try to follow through on her promise to embrace the Christmas mood. Life seemed to be giving her lemons. She would follow her mum's example, and do her best to make lemonade.

Her last conversation with her mother came into her head. 'Put yourself first, Michelle,' and then the instruction to use her inheritance for a holiday, a trip of a lifetime all for herself. She'd taken that as her mum's last lesson in independence, but what if she'd meant something else entirely? Put yourself first. Good advice, if you knew what yourself wanted.

Sean's voice interrupted her thoughts, as he swore quietly under his breath. They were well out of the city now, on winding narrow lanes. Sean switched off the engine. Why had they stopped?

'What's wrong?'

'Bit of snow.' He grinned over at her. 'Don't worry. Wait here a minute.'

He jumped out of the driver's seat and walked around the car. Straining in her seat, Michelle saw him stop and pull his phone from his pocket. After a minute he stuffed the phone back in his pocket and jogged back to the car. 'At least you're awake now.'

'I wasn't asleep.'

'You were drifting off before we left the station.'

'Oh.' That explained how quickly they seemed to have got out of the city. 'What's the problem?'

Sean smiled sheepishly. 'Should have got a four wheel drive.'

He turned the key in the ignition and flicked the headlights on so she could see the narrow country road ahead more clearly. It was covered in a deepening layer of white.

'I told you snow was a pain. What are we going to do?'

'We'll be fine. We're nearly there. I've ordered us a taxi.'

'A taxi won't get through this!'

He laughed. 'This one will.'

'What do you mean?'

'Trust me.'

A few minutes later, Michelle heard a sound in the lane behind them. She spun her head. It was a tractor. 'That's never going to get past us.'

Sean had already jumped out of the car and was waving his arms in the middle of the road. He disappeared into the gloom. After a second, Michelle got out of the car to see Sean embracing an old man in a wax jacket that had probably seen its better days sometime before she'd been born. The man, apparently, went with the tractor, and, as soon as he released Sean from the hug, he was lifting bags out of the boot of the hire car and stowing them in the cab.

'Come on then.' Sean bounded back to her side of the car. 'Our lift's here.'

'What?'

'Oh. Sorry. Michelle, meet my dad. Dad, this is Michelle.' The old man stepped forward. 'Alun.'

Alun turned to his son. 'Another one for dinner tomorrow then?'

Sean nodded, and Alun returned his gaze to Michelle. 'The more the merrier.'

Sean found a perch alongside his dad in the tractor, and leant down to take Michelle's hand, pulling her into the cramped cab.

'Not much space, I'm afraid.' He grinned and pulled Michelle onto his lap. 'Hold on.'

Michelle balanced herself on Sean's knee, her torso pressed against his body, his arm wrapped tightly around her waist to keep her in the cab. The journey couldn't have lasted more than twenty minutes but Michelle felt every second. Sean's breathing against her neck, his arm around her waist, his fingers inside her duffle coat gripping the fabric of her top to hold her steady on his lap. Heat raced through her body. Was he feeling it too? If he was there was no sign of it. He was chatting to his dad. Something to do with work and a farm she gleaned, but she struggled to concentrate on the conversation. She still didn't know what Sean did for a living. He seemed to be doing all right, if his willingness to buy first class train tickets for virtual strangers was any guide, but beyond that she had no idea, which made the heat in her body and the lightness in her head even more confusing. Relationships, in Michelle's world, were based on shared values and common interests, not on physical attraction, fairground rides and glühwein.

The tractor jolted over a bump, and Sean's arm braced to keep her secure on his lap. It was a long time since Michelle had spent this long this close to another human being. Her mum had never been one for big displays of affection, and Michelle had thought she was the same.

Another bump marked the entry to a farmyard. Through the dark and snow, Michelle could make out various outbuildings to one side of the yard, and a house to the other. The tractor pulled to a halt. Alun jumped down, and offered his hand to help Michelle out of the cab.

'You coming, son?'

'Sure.'

Alun dragged Michelle's case down from the cab and gestured towards the house.

'Right in there. Sean'll show you what's what.'

And he headed off.

Michelle glanced at her watch. After midnight. She turned back towards the tractor. 'Are you Ok?'

Sean grinned and stretched to uncurve his cramped spine. 'Fine. Let's go in.'

He jumped from the cab and grabbed hold of her case. 'Don't mind my dad. Man of few words. You'll understand when you meet Mum.'

Michelle followed Sean towards the house and into the darkened hallway. The ceiling was low and the stairway was narrow. She got the impression of an old cottage, which had probably been extended and remodelled by generations of occupants. Sean leant past her to shut the door, moving his body in close to hers. A hush fell over them. She could hear his breath, and feel the warmth from his body. She raised her face to meet his lips. The kiss was softer than she expected, and more lingering. Without thinking about it, she parted her lips and reached her hand to his waist. Sean raised his fingers to her cheek, and traced her jawline, sending a flush of warmth through her body. The world beyond the tiny dark hallway faded away.

Sean pulled back.

'Sorry.' He turned his head away from her face. 'That was out of order.'

'It's Ok.' She mumbled the words into her chest.

'Yeah.' He tried to arrange a smile on his face. 'Just got a bit carried away. Christmas spirit and all that.'

He took a big step back from her. 'Right. Wait here. I'll go find you some towels and work out who's sleeping where.'

He disappeared up the staircase at the end of the hallway. Michelle leant back against the wall. Her heart was beating hard and fast. Stupid, stupid, Michelle. Clearly Sean had instantly regretted what had just happened. He had just been being friendly. Nothing more.

Sean jogged back down the stairs, arms now full of towels and bedding, and stopped a clear two metres out of touching range. 'It's a bit of a full house.'

'Who's here?' Michelle remembered that she wasn't just spending Christmas with a man she barely knew; she was spending it with his whole family.

Sean waved a vague hand towards the upstairs. 'Oh, people.'

He pushed one of the doors off the hallway open. 'Brilliant. No one down here.'

He turned back to Michelle. 'I'm sorry. Are you all right on the sofa?'

She nodded.

'Good.' Sean busied himself spreading sheets, blankets and pillows over the sofa.

'There's a shower room down here too, through the kitchen.' He pointed towards another doorway, and flung a towel over the arm of the settee. 'So are you sure you're Ok there?'

Michelle nodded again. 'Where will you be?'

Sean shrugged. 'On a floor somewhere by the looks of things.'

'You could ...' Michelle stopped herself. She'd already made a fool of herself with the kiss. She wasn't going to get rejected again.

'What?'

'Nothing. I'll see you in the morning.' Michelle nodded brightly.

'Right. Goodnight then.'

Michelle sat on her makeshift bed and listened to Sean's footsteps disappear upstairs. She found the rumoured shower room and brushed her teeth. Back in the lounge, she snuggled down into the surprisingly comfortable cocoon he'd built for her, and tried to think about anything other than that kiss.

Upstairs, Sean tried to settle on the floor of his sister's childhood bedroom, which was already occupied by his brother, Luke, in the bed, and fifteen-year-old nephew on the foldout bed. A quick survey had told him that it was the least occupied room in the house, as his sister-in-law and the baby were packed into the old nursery, and his sister, her husband and the twins were all but stacked vertically in his and Luke's old room. A full house for Christmas – just how his mum liked it.

The floor was hard and he'd been left with the oldest, least presentable of the available bedding, but it wasn't discomfort that was keeping him awake. Normally he could sleep anywhere without a problem. What had he done? He'd brought a girl he hardly knew all this way on an impulse. His thoughts turned back to the last time he'd acted on impulse in a relationship. Cora. Perfect, particular Cora. The promise to build a life together. For better or worse and all that. Promises made on impulse, Sean knew, were easily broken, and the hearts that made promises were collateral damage at best.

Broken promises. Broken hearts. Both those things were

hard to mend. Sean's thoughts raced between two extremes. He was dismayed with himself for bringing Michelle here, for kissing her, for stopping kissing her, but, at the same time, the Christmas Eve feeling was growing in his gut. The feeling of anticipation, the childlike wondering about what tomorrow might bring. It wasn't a feeling he was used to any more, but somewhere in the back of his mind he knew exactly what the feeling was. One more sleep, he thought.

# Chapter Five

## Boxing Day, 2002

### *Sean*

It's six o'clock in the morning. I'm wide awake. Nobody should be awake at six o'clock in the morning on Boxing Day. Boxing Day is the ultimate lie-in day. There's nothing to get out of bed for on Boxing Day.

That's bollocks, of course. We live on a farm. My dad got up hours ago. I should get out of bed and do some work, but I don't. I lie and stare into the darkness and wait for Cora to be awake too.

It's too dark to see, but I know the pile of paper is still sitting on the chair at her side of the bed. The prospectus. The acceptance letter for the course starting in January. The application form, two-thirds completed in my wife's best writing, for single person's accommodation.

Really, this is my fault. I was pissing about last night, asking where she'd hidden my Christmas present. I said it didn't matter if she told me now, because Christmas was over, and then I started pretending to look in places that it might have been. She told me to behave like a grown-up. She tells me that a lot lately. I pulled this shoebox down from the top of the wardrobe and she went mental.

I opened the box. I shouldn't have opened the box. If I hadn't opened the box I wouldn't have found all that stuff, and I wouldn't know. If I didn't know it would still be like this wasn't happening. I wouldn't be lying awake on Boxing Day morning waiting for my wife to wake up so we can chat, like the grown-ups she wants us to be, about precisely how and when she's planning to leave me.

# Christmas Morning, 2013

*Michelle*

'What is she?'

What was happening?

'She's a lady.'

Two voices wrenched Michelle from sleep.

'I know that. What is she doing here?'

She opened one eye. A girl, in pink pyjamas, clutching a teddy bear.

'Maybe Santa brought her.'

Michelle opened the other eye. A matching boy, blond curls sticking every which way, tiny glasses perched on his button nose, clinging to his sister's arm.

'I think she's awake.'

The girl extended a hand towards Michelle. 'Good morning, lady. My name is Chloe Patterson. Did Santa bring you?'

Michelle freed one arm from the blanket and shook hands with Chloe Patterson. 'No. I'm Michelle. I'm Sean's ...' She searched for a word. '... friend.'

The girl nodded. 'Like Amy McAvoy. She is my friend.'

Michelle smiled. 'Yeah. Like Amy McAvoy.'

She turned to the boy and extended her hand. 'And you are?'

The boy peered at Michelle uncertainly, and let his sister carry on the talking. 'He's Joseph. You can call him Joe or Joseph, but not Joey because it makes Mummy cross. He is shy.'

'Very good.' She thought for a second of her own half-brother, Joseph. What was his family Christmas like? Michelle focused her smile on the Joe in front of her. 'Nothing wrong with being shy.'

'Mummy said we could pick one present from under the

tree to open with breakfast.' Chloe pointed towards the Christmas tree in the corner of the lounge.

In the beginnings of the morning light, Michelle considered the tree properly for the first time. It was beautiful. Thick, dark, green needles. Tall and full at the base. She swallowed. 'It's a lovely tree.'

Chloe nodded. 'It's one of Uncle Sean's. He always gets Nana and Granddad the best tree.'

One of Uncle Sean's? Who has more than one Christmas tree? Michelle put the thought aside as a misunderstanding of a little girl. The children had lost interest in her and were happily pulling presents from under the tree. Sitting up on the sofa, Michelle listened. She could hear people moving around in other parts of the house. So this was it. Christmas morning in a family home. She took a deep breath.

'What are you two doing?' An older woman bustled into the lounge, wearing a pinny over her dressing gown.

'Mummy said it was all right.'

The woman sighed. 'Oh, did she now?'

Her attention finally alighted on Michelle. 'Oh, hello my dear. You must be Sean's friend. Alun told me he'd brought someone back. I can't tell you how pleased I am. It's been so long since he brought anyone home. I was starting to think that it would never happen, or that he'd started batting for the other team. Not that I'd have minded that of course. Alun might have had a cow, but I'd have said to him, "Alun it's the twenty-first century. These things are all the rage these days." So I wondered if that was it. I thought maybe he was shy about telling his Ma. Cameron MacGregor was like that, you know. He didn't say a thing. Of course his mother had known for years. She heard it from someone in her knitting circle, as it goes. But anyway, here you are. All woman.'

Michelle wasn't sure how to respond. She hoiked the blanket up a bit higher over her boobs.

'You'll be wanting some breakfast. I'm sorry I didn't have anything for you last night. If I'd known he was bringing someone I'd have left something out. There's a bit of ham needs using. You could have had a sandwich. Or egg. We've always got eggs. Do you like egg?'

Michelle nodded.

'Well, everyone does. You rarely meet a person who doesn't like egg. Mind you, I was at school with a girl who wouldn't eat the whites. Yolks, not a problem, but never the white. Made scrambled egg a right performance.'

'Chloe!' A new voice shouted from the hallway before coming into the room. Another woman, maybe a couple of years younger than Michelle. 'Oh! Hello.'

The older woman continued. 'This is Sean's friend. Isn't it wonderful? Can you remember the last time he brought someone home? I was telling her how we were starting to wonder...'

The younger woman cut in. 'Hi. I'm Bel. Isobel. People call me Bel.'

'Michelle.'

'I'm Sean's sister. Do you want some breakfast?'

Michelle nodded, noticing that the older woman was still chatting away quite happily, oblivious to the fact that her audience was moving on. She followed Bel into a kitchen-dining room, where the other woman poured herself a generous cup of coffee and an equally generous Buck's Fizz. Michelle gladly accepted the offer of the former, declined the latter, and sat down at the massive wooden table.

'Don't mind Mum going on about Sean.'

Michelle smiled. 'I won't. We really are just friends.'

The other woman smirked. 'Course you are.'

'We are.' Michelle could feel her cheeks colouring. 'I actually only met him two days ago.'

'Woah!' Bel pulled out the seat opposite Michelle and sat down. Her face opened up into a big wide toothy smile with echoes of Sean's own familiar grin. 'Talk about acting on impulse. He must have got it bad.'

'No!' Michelle shook her head. 'It's not like that. I got stranded in the snow. I think he took pity on me.'

Because that was all it was, Michelle told herself. The kiss last night had clearly meant nothing to him. It was an aberration, best forgotten.

'If you say so. Really don't mind Mum. I don't know why she got it into her head that he might play for the other team. I mean, he got married for goodness' sake!'

Married? Michelle swallowed hard, pushing down the bile that was rising in her throat. Married. Well, that was that then. Any interest he might have had in her was nothing more than a mouse playing while its cat was away.

'Oh my God!' Bel clamped her hand over her mouth. 'You knew that didn't you? I haven't massively ballsed things up, have I?'

Michelle shook her head and tried to make her lips into a smile. They didn't seem to remember where to go. 'We really are just friends.'

'Thank God! Seriously, I'm getting worse than Mum with my mouth. Don't know when to stop talking. That's my trouble.'

Michelle made another attempt at a reassuring smile, but she wasn't sure how convincing her unconcerned act was. She wasn't that convinced by it herself.

The tension eased as the room filled up and Michelle was introduced by Bel to her husband, her other brother, Luke, and his wife and children. She had a cuddle with the baby, and busied herself with introductions and chit-chat and anything that wasn't thinking about Sean. She was almost managing it, when the man himself surfaced and poured himself an even bigger mug of coffee than his sister.

She watched him lean against the kitchen worktop sipping his coffee. Married. He got married. That's what

Bel had said, not that he was married now. Michelle felt her stomach flip. It might only have lasted a few weeks. It might have been a quickie wedding of convenience to get some poor Ukrainian farm worker a visa. His wife could have left him years ago, or he left her, or she died. Michelle's hopes rose with the thought, and then she felt guilty for wishing this stranger dead. Her stomach flipped again. Bel hadn't said that he wasn't married now either though. Michelle forced herself to take a deep breath. It was irrelevant. She didn't care for him either way.

After breakfast, Sean watched his family bustle Michelle away into the lounge. He hung back, unexpectedly uncertain how to approach her. Should he pretend the kiss hadn't happened? Go back to their nice safe agreement, that this was forty-eight hours of Christmas cheer and then back to their normal lives?

Sean's father was sitting alone at the table. 'What are you doing?'

Alun raised a finger to his lips and then pointed at the open door behind Sean. He closed the door and sat down at the table.

'Getting some quiet. It's a mad house through there.'

Sean laughed. 'Always is in this place.'

Sean's phone beeped in his pocket. He scrolled quickly through the text, hit delete and switched the phone to silent.

His father raised an eyebrow in question.

'Cora.'

'Ah, and what does the former Mrs Munro want this fine morning?'

'This and that.'

'And I trust she'll not be getting either of them from you any more?'

Sean shook his head.

'Probably best.'

'What am I going to do?'

'About what?'

Sean didn't answer.

'Let me guess. About the fine young red-headed lassie you managed to bring home?'

Sean nodded.

'You like her?'

Sean paused. He nodded again.

'I should imagine the best thing would be to just go for it. You don't get anywhere in life sitting on the sidelines.'

Sean shook his head. 'Not this time.'

'Ah, you're not still on Cora.'

Cora. The last time Sean had dived right into a relationship, and it hadn't worked. He had to rebuild his whole idea of who he was and what love was, and it didn't involve diving straight in any more. 'Well look where I ended up.'

'You ended up here.' Alun sighed. 'Look. I don't do so well with talking. I leave that for your mother.'

'She doesn't give you much choice.'

'Watch what you're saying about your mother.'

Sean's head dipped. 'Sorry.'

'I should think so. Anyway, you jump in if that's what you want to do. Since Cora you've been cautious when it comes to the girls. It's not you. You're a jumping in with both feet man.'

'I don't know.'

'I do. Look at this place. I retired five years ago. You increased the business more in your first year than I did in the last twenty-five, by just going for it. I was terrified the whole time. Thought you were going to lose me my house, but no. You went for it and it paid off.'

'I'm scared.'

Alun grunted. 'Well that's no good reason not to do anything now, is it?'

Could it be that easy? Could he really step up to the edge of the cliff and jump with no idea at all whether she'd catch him? No safety net of telling himself he'd never see her again. No pretence that this was forty-eight hours of madness and then he could walk away. Could he?

'I don't know.'

His father shook his head. 'Well you'd best make your mind up. I just don't reckon you can change who you are. Not doing something because you're scared. It's not you.'

Sean pushed his chair back from the table and stood up. 'Right then.'

Michelle spent the morning discovering that one of the joys of a big boisterous family, desperate to include her in all their activities, was that it made it surprisingly easy to avoid one specific member of that family. She went upstairs with Bel to find some clothes to borrow. She admired the twins' new toys, and allowed them to pull her into an elaborate game of dolls versus dinosaurs, a pastime that appeared to be well-established as their joint favourite. She won grudging kudos from Sean's teenage nephew by working out how to get music to download onto his brand new Christmas present smartphone. She won grudging respect from Alun with her ability to chat about savings rates and pensions options. She offered to help Sean's mum prepare dinner, and was decisively bustled out of the kitchen. And that was her mistake, because that left her in the hallway alone and unchaperoned.

'Get your coat.' Sean was leaning on the wall next to the front door.

'Why?'

'I want to show you something.'

Sean watched Michelle as she looked down at the skirting board, rather than at him. So he hadn't been imagining it earlier. She was avoiding him. He'd blown it with that kiss.

'Look if it's last night, I'm really sorry. I was out of order. It won't happen again.'

His eyes flicked to the floor as he spoke, evading her gaze. He shouldn't be promising that. It was pretty much the opposite of what he should be saying.

She blinked hard. 'Fine.'

'So you'll let me show you?'

She nodded, a small curt nod. He grabbed both their coats from the hook in the hall before she could change her mind. Then he stopped in the doorway. 'Wait. What shoe size are you?'

'Six or seven. Why?'

He scrabbled on the floor in the porch and came up with two wellingtons. 'Don't want your shoes getting messed up.'

'Where are we going?'

'Just outside, but you are on a farm. Remember?'

Michelle kicked off her shoes and pulled the boots on. 'These aren't a pair.'

'Do they both fit?'

'Sort of.' She glanced at his face. 'Probably good enough.'

Sean grinned. 'All right then. Come on.'

He bounded out into the farmyard, noticing that the hire car they'd abandoned last night was parked next to the small barn. His dad must have gone out at first light to collect it. He carried on across the yard. He really did want to show her this. It had been in his mind since he very first suggested the whole 'forty-eight hours of Christmas' plan. He glanced at the sky. It was clear and blue, and last night's snow was crisp and untrodden on the ground. Perfect. He led the way across the farmyard and between the two biggest outbuildings to a padlocked gate which he climbed over.

'Are we allowed through here?' Michelle had stopped at the gate.

'Course. It's my land.' Sean walked back to the gate and held out his hand to help Michelle climb over. She didn't take it, managing to get over on her own.

'Well your parents' land.'

'No. Mine.' He carried on along the track beyond the gate before turning to climb a second gate on the right into a field. Again, Michelle refused his help.

He stopped at the edge of the field. 'Look.'

'Wow!'

She couldn't stop the exclamation escaping her lips. Even for a Christmas non-believer, the sight in front of her was breathtaking. Stretched out across the field was row upon row of miniature Christmas trees, waist high, all covered in a dusting of white snow.

'These are for next year.'

'You farm Christmas trees?'

Sean nodded, smiling broadly. 'Dad started it as a sort of sideline to the farm. Locals could come and pick their own tree. When I took over I turned the whole thing over to trees.'

'Seriously? You make Christmas trees?'

'Grow Christmas trees.'

Michelle pulled a face. 'You know what I mean.'

Sean nodded. 'We've got a bigger growing site over by Loch Lomond. Most of these we still sell locally. The main site's for trade, garden centres, local councils, hotels, that kind of thing.'

'So you actually make your living out of Christmas?'

'I own another nursery, and a tenanted farm the other side of Edinburgh. Not good business to have all your eggs in one basket, but yeah. Christmas trees are my main thing.'

'But you still love it?'

Sean looked confused. 'Wouldn't do it if I didn't love it.'

'Don't you get sick of all the Christmas?'

Sean shook his head. 'Never. Why do you hate Christmas so much?'

She shrugged. It wasn't a question she wanted to answer. It was a joke amongst her friends and colleagues – the idea that she was a bit of a Scrooge. She went along with the jokes to avoid anyone asking her the question too seriously.

'What was Christmas like when you were a kid?'

She kept her eyes fixed forwards, looking out towards the field. 'Depends when you mean exactly.'

'What do you mean?'

'My dad was insane about Christmas. Always made a massive deal of it. He was Santa for this big department store every year. Properly obsessed with Christmas.'

'Cool.'

'Maybe.' Michelle paused. She didn't usually talk about her dad, but this felt different. She was far away from home, and Sean was easy somehow. Even with all the question marks in her head, when she was alone with him things felt safe. And anyway, she'd promised him forty-eight hours. What did it matter what you said to somebody you were never going to see again?

'I remember sitting on my dad's knee when he was all dressed up as Santa. I knew it was him, but it didn't matter. It felt like magic.'

Sean nodded. 'That's the point of Christmas. You can know it's all tinsel and costumes and a dead tree, and still love the magic.'

'Maybe.'

'So what about the other times?'

'What?'

'You said Christmas depended on when it was.'

Michelle nodded. 'I told you about their break up, Mum and Dad. Mum kind of avoided Christmas after that.' Thinking of her mum, Michelle suddenly felt disloyal.

Her mum had been there for her right through the year. Christmas was just one day.

'And she was right. Do you know how much the average adult spends on Christmas every year?'

Sean shook his head.

'I do. £592. That's nearly £29billion across the country. It's insane.'

'But it's not about the money. It's about family and getting together and that feeling of ...' Sean dried up for a second. 'That feeling of anticipation, of hope. Don't pretend you don't understand that.'

'It's a commercialised excuse to overspend. Anyway, it's for kids really, isn't it?'

Sean wasn't having that. 'I saw your face.'

'When?'

'When you saw all this, the trees and the snow, and when you were talking about your dad and the magic.'

'This is quite pretty.'

'It's not just pretty. It's Christmas. We're standing in a field, in the freezing cold, and you gasped because it's Christmas.'

'Maybe.'

'Do you still talk to your dad?'

Michelle shook her head. 'He's got my number. He texted to say Merry Christmas.'

'You should ring him.'

Another shake of the head.

'Why not?'

'Too much water under the bridge.' Christmas or not, she didn't want to play at happy families.

'When did you last talk to him?'

She shrugged. 'I e-mailed him when Mum died. I thought he ought to know.'

'Did he come to the funeral?'

'I didn't invite him.'

'Ok. Look, it's Christmas. It's about family. A two minute call couldn't hurt.'

'I don't have signal.'

'No excuses. Does he Skype?'

'I don't know.' She paused, realising that Sean wasn't going to let this drop, and that she didn't want him to let it drop. It was an odd feeling. Someone else was taking care of her. That was what Sean was doing. Picking her up at the airport, taking her to the Christmas fair, getting her to talk about her family – they were all the acts of a man who was thinking about what might be best for her. She pulled her phone from her pocket.

'I thought you didn't have signal.'

She scrolled back through her phone and found the message she was looking for. 'He sent me his Skype name though.'

'Come on then.'

Ten minutes later she was sitting in front of the computer in Sean's office, downstairs in a newer extension to the family home.

'I'm not sure about this.'

Sean shrugged. 'It's two minutes out of your life.'

'He's probably not even online.'

He was online.

Michelle waited as the image came up on the screen, and Sean adjusted the speakers so she could hear properly.

'Holly!' Her father was, as always, in his Santa costume. If he was surprised to hear from her after such a long time, it was hard to tell under the thick white beard and the Father Christmas hat, but she saw him turn and gesture to someone out of sight of the camera. 'It's Holly!'

He turned back to face the screen. 'Ho! Ho! Ho!'

'Hi, Dad.'

In the background she could see other figures moving around, her half-brothers, tall gangling teenagers now, not the snotty kids she remembered.

Behind her she heard Sean stifling a chuckle.

The image on the screen was of Santa's grotto packed into a terraced house in Bradford. There were lights, dancing Santas, illuminated reindeer, inflatable snowmen, tinsel, so much tinsel, all jammed into the tiny living room. Another figure came into the shot.

'Holly!' The woman was clearly in her late forties, but dressed, apparently without embarrassment, as an elf. The Elf. 'Happy Christmas!'

'Happy Christmas, Sandra.' Michelle forced the words out through clenched lips.

Her father took over the conversation, eagerly telling her about their family Christmas. Michelle listened.

Her father paused. 'You know you're always very welcome here, don't you?'

Michelle nodded. He'd always been clear about that. He'd never tried to make her pick sides, but that is what she'd done. She'd chosen to be Tanya's daughter.

'And your mother, I didn't know if you'd want me to come ...' He looked away. 'I am sorry.'

'Yeah.' It was all Michelle dared say.

'Good.' He looked smaller somehow.

Michelle pushed a smile onto her face. 'Well I'd better get on. I just wanted to say Merry Christmas.'

'Thank you, pet. I appreciate it. I do.' He paused. 'Maybe in the New Year you could come for a visit?'

She gave a tiny nod. It wasn't much, but it was something, and that was more than they'd had before. Michelle could feel herself starting to tear up. She took a breath.

'Ok. Better get going.' She clicked the disconnect button quickly before Sean saw her get any mushier.

'Woah.' She was still staring at the screen when the voice behind her cut in.

'What?'

'They really go for it with the Christmas decorations.'

'You don't know the half of it.'

Sean swung himself onto the desk in front of her. 'Tell me.'

Michelle turned to face him. There didn't seem much point lying about it now.

'The decorations aren't because it's Christmas.'

'What?'

'He has it like that all the time.'

Sean's face convulsed as he tried not to snigger, turning redder and redder until his eyes watered, and he gave up under the pressure. A gale of laughter shook his whole body. 'You're kidding?'

She shook her head. 'He wasn't as bad when I was little, but after they split up it got more and more and more.'

'Wow! That must have been brilliant when you were a kid. Christmas all the time!'

'It was mortifying. I could never take a friend there. And my mum hated it.'

'Fair enough, but you're not your mum.' Sean stepped towards her. 'I mean, it's bonkers, but it is kind of fun.'

'I guess.'

'Do you know why they split up?'

Michelle nodded. 'He had an affair with the elf.'

Another torrent of laughter. 'I'm sorry.'

'Well, men have affairs with their secretaries all the time. His job was being Santa, so he had an affair with his elf.'

'Right.'

Michelle sighed. 'I guess they probably are better suited really.'

'Wow.' Sean shook his head. 'Your dad is a bit mad.'

'Yeah.' Michelle looked up at Sean. Her dad was mad. That was her shame, but Sean didn't seem horrified at all. She stood up and stepped towards him. Maybe Christmas was getting to her. 'Thank you.'

'What for?' His voice was quieter than normal, less certain.

'For persuading me to call him. And for letting me stay.'

'It's Ok.' Sean grinned. 'One more thing though?'

'What?' She could see the beginnings of more laughter in his eyes.

'Holly? They called you Holly.'

Now she could feel her cheeks reddening. 'It's my real first name.'

'And I'm guessing your dad picked it.'

She nodded. 'I hate it.'

'Why?'

'Jolly Holly! Prickly Holly! You must have been born at Christmas! Every boy wants a bit of Holly at Christmas!' She recited the familiar jibes from her youth. 'I could go on.'

'I like it.'

She shrugged.

'It's part of you.' Sean smiled. 'You can't change who you are.'

Maybe not, but for the first time in many years, Michelle thought maybe you could. Maybe you could be braver. Maybe you could take more chances. Maybe you could put what you wanted first. She took another step towards him. Sean stayed stock still, leaning on the wall behind the desk, watching her, breathing deep and slow. Michelle balled up her courage and took the final step, letting her fingertips move across his stomach. She felt his body tense. She tilted her face towards him and let her lips brush against his.

Relief flooded through her as he responded. Strong, safe arms encircled her and pulled her tight against his body.

Sean's tongue pushed against her mouth and she parted her lips, responding hungrily, instinctively to the feel and taste of him. His hand moved downwards and tugged at her jumper. Michelle raised her arms from around his neck and moved her body away from him a fraction, just enough for him to start to undress her. Sean flung the jumper to the corner of the room and wrapped her back into his arms. Michelle needed more. Lip against lip was intoxicating. She needed skin against skin. She pulled at his shirt, fumbling with buttons until he dragged it roughly over his head. She ran her fingers over his skin, feeling every hair, every bump through her fingertips. Her lips brushed his chest and she heard him sigh in response. She moved to his belt. Sean's hand clasped her wrist, slowing and stopping her.

She glanced up.

'Are you sure?'

She nodded.

Sean breathed deeply. 'We should probably talk ...'

Michelle shook her head.

Sean closed his eyes for a second. 'I wanted to tell you about ...'

She didn't want to talk. She didn't want to think about what the problems might be. Something was opening up inside her that she couldn't bear to see shut down. She needed to be close to him. 'Later.'

He nodded, and then all at once he was in control. He moved hungrily, desperately, in perfect time with her. They wrenched and tugged the rest of the clothes off each other's bodies, constantly touching and kissing, celebrating each new inch of undiscovered skin.

He lay her down on the rug at one side of the room. The fur caressed her back, and she watched Sean lower himself to her side. She pulled him towards her, rolling him above her, wrapping herself around his hips.

'Wait.' Sean's voice was a low whisper.

Michelle's stomach clenched. He'd changed his mind. The cold familiar feeling of steel edged back into her gut. She sat up. 'What's wrong?'

Sean was rooting through the pocket of his jeans. 'What? Nothing. I ...'

His voice tailed off as his fingers pulled a condom from the recesses of his wallet.

'Oh.' Relief bubbled from Michelle in a little nervous laugh. 'I thought you'd changed your mind.'

'No.' Sean's answer was instant and emphatic. 'Definitely no.'

Michelle lay back and watched him move across the room. Lean and strong, skin still tanned in the depths of winter from days and weeks working outside. He dragged a chair over to the study door and wedged it firmly closed. He grinned. 'Just in case.'

Michelle hadn't even thought of his family in the next room. 'Won't they wonder where we are?'

Sean shrugged. 'Probably won't even notice we're gone.'

Eventually, he came back to her. They moved more slowly now, taking their time, daring to start to believe in what was happening. He finally sank into her with one long easy stroke. She gasped. Her body tensed, holding him deep inside her.

'Ssshhhh,' he murmured.

She buried her face in his shoulder, lips pressed against his skin, breathing him in and out, muffling her moans from the house beyond. He made love to her. Slowly. Deeply. Sincerely. And then faster. Deeper. More urgent. More insistent.

Wave after wave of warmth streamed through Michelle's body as they came together, moaning and gasping against the other's sweat salted skin. He relaxed onto her for a second and she felt the weight, the utter solidity of him, before he rolled to the side.

'Wow.'

Michelle giggled. 'Yeah.'

Sean propped himself up on one elbow. 'Michelle?'

'Yeah.' She was still lying on her back, looking up at him now. Hopeful but uncertain. His body hadn't lied, she thought. He'd felt something and so had she. The word for that feeling hovered on the edge of her consciousness. She wasn't quite ready to let it in, but it was there insistently growing, ready to overwhelm her.

Sean opened his mouth. 'I do need to tell you about ...'

A knock rattled the chair he'd wedged against the door. They both sat up. Another knock. Sean scrambled to his feet. There was a low clearing of the throat outside the door.

'Lunchtime,' called Sean's dad. 'Your mother asked me to come and find you.'

Michelle jumped up, grabbing her knickers from the desk where they'd been thrown earlier.

Sean stifled a laugh. 'We'll be there in a minute.'

They jostled round the room, picking up clothes, pulling them on hurriedly, without speaking. Michelle could feel her cheeks burning. What must Sean's family think of her? Turning up for Christmas with a man she'd only met a few days ago, and then disappearing to ... to ... erm ... to have ... her brain wouldn't allow her to think it aloud. She leant against the desk to pull her socks on, and then stood in the middle of the room smoothing down her jumper, unable to look at her ... at her new ... at Sean.

'Right then.' She started towards the door. Sean stepped behind her, grabbed her hand and spun her to face him.

'They can wait a minute longer.' He bent to kiss her, soft and strong and loaded with good intentions. Michelle responded, feeling her nerves settling.

Another knock.

Sean pulled away, resting his forehead onto hers. 'Once more unto the breach then Macduff.'

Christmas dinner in the Munro household was perfect in its imperfection. Gravy was spilt; siblings talked over one another; wine was spilt; children bickered over the last lonely pig-in-a-blanket; Sean's mum fretted about whether the turkey was cooked right through; her children reminded her, loudly, that she had the same panic every year and it was always, predictably, fine. Michelle was able to eat her meal quietly, squashed on one corner of the table, with Sean to one side, and the sharp tablecloth-covered drop to the children's table on the other.

She watched the family without her usual feeling of claustrophobia and discomfort. She'd hated family events with her dad and The Elf. She'd been shoehorned in, like they were trying to force her stiff, hard edges into a smooth, round hole. Here no one seemed to care where or how she fit; it was assumed that she would, and the family morphed and shifted around her to make space.

Listening to the chatter and eating her meal were small distractions from the thing taking up the rest of her attention. Sean. Sean, who was sitting right next to her. Sean, whose leg was brushing against her own. Sean, who was bending down to pick his dropped napkin from the floor and running his hand up her calf and thigh as he sat up again. Sean, whose mere proximity was making her senses tingle. Sean, who had finished his meal, and placed his hand, quietly, unobtrusively, hidden by the tablecloth, on her thigh where he was stroking small insistent circles, moving higher and higher.

Michelle gasped, and saw heads turn towards her. She covered quickly with a loud theatrical cough. Across the table, she could see the laughter in Bel's eye.

'You all right there?'

Michelle nodded. 'I'm good.'

# Chapter Six

## Christmas Afternoon, 2013

### *Michelle*

'Look who's here!'

Michelle looked up from an involved game of post-lunch Monopoly to see Bel ushering a stranger into the lounge. The newcomer was about Michelle's age, but that was their only point of similarity. This woman was radiantly beautiful, and exquisitely dressed. She pulled off her long wool coat to reveal leather boots below a fitted pencil skirt and soft silk blouse. The woman scanned the room before her gaze settled on Michelle.

'You're new.'

'Michelle is a ...' Bel paused. '... a friend of Sean's.'

'Friend' sounded like a euphemism for something sordid. The newcomer smiled. 'How wonderful. I'm Cora.'

She stepped forward and leant to clasp Michelle's hand before Michelle could get up, leaving Michelle awkwardly half sitting and half standing.

'Sean and I go way back,' the newcomer continued. 'So many stories I could tell you about him.'

I bet there are, thought Michelle. She pulled her hand away and dragged herself to her feet. There was no mistaking the hint of fight in the stranger's tone, although it must have been clear that Michelle was not much opposition, stylish, as she was, in leggings and a borrowed Munro family Christmas jumper. She plastered on her most dazzling smile. 'Really? I'm not sure he's mentioned you.'

The woman paused, and pressed home her advantage. 'I wonder why not. You wouldn't think getting married would slip someone's mind, would you?'

Trying to pretend the thrust hadn't hit a nerve, Michelle parried. 'Oh I knew that. I guess he must have forgotten to mention your name.'

Neither woman's smile faltered.

'Cora?' They both turned towards the doorway where Sean was standing. 'What are you doing here?'

Sean's mum bustled past her son, bustling any answer Cora might have offered away at the same time. 'Cora! Lovely to see you. Will you have a drink?'

Cora was hidden from view for a moment as Sean's mother, then father and niece and nephew, enveloped her in hugs and welcomes. Michelle was isolated. Sean was still hovering in the doorway, but everyone else was treating Cora like visiting royalty. However friendly they might be, Michelle reminded herself, she wasn't part of this family. She was an outsider. They'd made her feel welcome, but it was nothing more than a feeling. Michelle knew better than to rely on those.

Cora disentangled herself from the hugs. 'Chloe, why don't you take a look in the hallway? There's a bag you might be interested in.'

The twins dashed into the hallway and re-appeared dragging a bulging sack of presents. Cora waved a manicured hand. 'Well, you can't come visiting at Christmas empty-handed, now can you?'

Presents were pulled out of the sack and handed round. Cora sat herself down in the centre of the sofa.

The group redrew itself around her. Extravagant gifts were opened. Drinks were offered and accepted. It was the picture of the perfect Christmas scene, except in Michelle's heart. It was true. Sean had a wife, and she wasn't imaginary or far away or hideously disfigured and only able to eat through a straw. She was real and here and hideously beautiful and put together. Michelle wanted to run, but she was trapped in this house until at least the following morning. Even if she tried to leave now, she had no way of getting back to civilisation, unless …

'Anyway, darling, I do need a quick word with you.' Cora was talking to Sean who was still hanging back near the door.

He nodded and the couple walked out into the hall.

Sean led the way into the study and closed the door.

'What are you doing here?'

'I came to see you. It's Christmas.' She slinked across the room towards him, smiling her perfect lipsticked smile. 'I texted.'

'Well, you've seen me.'

She pouted. 'Why so hostile? I thought after I let you use the flat, we might be back on better terms.'

Sean took a breath. 'We're on fine terms. I appreciate the use of the flat, but you asked me. You said it would help you out to have someone housesitting. I could just as easily have got a hotel.'

Another pout. 'So businesslike. You didn't used to be so businesslike.'

That stuck in his throat. 'And isn't that why you left me? You wanted someone with a bit more ambition.'

She perched on the edge of the desk. 'But then you turned out all ambitious. There was a piece about you in Scottish Life you know.'

'I know.'

'Apparently, you're an eligible bachelor.'

Sean didn't respond.

'So why don't we?'

'What?'

'You know.' She was being coy now, but Sean knew what was coming. 'We were always great together. We could rekindle?'

She stood up and moved right in front of him. 'I always

turned you on, didn't I? We never had any problems in that department. And you loved me, didn't you?'

'Yeah.' Sean couldn't stop the tiny nod of his head.

'So you and me? It always worked.'

Sean was distracted for a second by a sound in the hallway. He moved past Cora to the door and looked out. There was no one there. He closed the door again and leant against the frame.

'It didn't always work, Cora. We got divorced.'

She stuck out her bottom lip.

Sean closed his eyes. 'You've got to stop doing this. We can't keep going back.'

'It's not just me.'

It was true. There were plenty of times in the past decade when he'd met up with Cora for a drink, to clear the air, just as friends, and ended up falling back into the pattern, back into her bed, but it wasn't real. 'I know, but it's got to stop. Neither of us is happy. Neither of us is moving on.'

'Is this because of that ginger girl?'

'Not just her.'

'I miss you.' She was wheedling now, not accepting that she was beaten, trying to get around him.

'Then you shouldn't have left.' As he said the words Sean realised that it really could be that simple. 'But you did, a long time ago.'

Cora took a step away from him and shook out her hair. She arranged her face into a smile. 'No need to be grumpy. I'm only messing around.' Sean didn't answer, allowing her to save face.

'Best get back to the olds then.'

Sean nodded. 'Give them my love.'

He walked her to the door and they stopped, unsure how to say goodbye. A kiss on the cheek? A hug? A shake of the hand? In the end she just left.

\* \* \*

A few minutes earlier, Michelle had darted away from the study door as she heard Sean's footsteps come towards her. She pressed herself against the wall, out of sight, as he glanced to see who was in the hallway, before closing the door and going back to the tête-à-tête with his wife.

Michelle breathed through the wave of nausea that hit her. They were going to get back together. She wasn't just betrayed; she was humiliated, and it was her own fault. She'd had years to learn not to trust a man who treated life like a game. She put her hand against the wall to steady herself. Sean's perfect wife wanted her perfect life back. There was no way Michelle could stand in the way of that. She wasn't even the wronged party here. She wasn't her mother. She was The Elf.

She swallowed as hard as she could, trying to force her lunch to stay where it was. There was a table at the end of the hallway. She saw a set of keys lying amongst the discarded gloves and junk mail. She grabbed them.

'Are you off somewhere?'

Sean's dad was standing behind her.

'I ... I've got a friend who lives quite near. I thought I'd pop and visit. You know, as it's Christmas.'

'Aye.'

'Right.' Michelle picked up the car keys and fled the house. She had no idea where she was going, but she had to get away. She couldn't watch the happy couple being reunited. She jumped into the hire car and drove out of the yard. She followed roads at random, driving too fast, brain flitting in every direction and landing on one single thought. What if she was wrong?

She moved her foot to the brake to slow down. She felt the car slide beneath her. She slammed her foot hard on the brake, cursing herself at the same time. 'Never brake into a skid,' she heard the voice of her geriatric driving instructor in her head. Too late.

# Christmas Day, 1992

We're having something called fajitas. I made Auntie Barbara write it down for me. It is written f-a-j-i-t-a, but you say it fa-heeeee-ta. Auntie Barbara says it is from Mexico, which is a special type of Spain. Auntie Barbara isn't staying for lunch. She said there was plenty of turkey for us at her house, but Mummy said that she wasn't in the mood for all that business.

Then they went in the kitchen and talked in quiet voices but I could still hear them because Dolly wanted to play in the hallway so I had to go with her. Dolly sometimes does things like that. She is much braver than I am.

'It's not right for a child at Christmas.'

Mummy doesn't answer that.

'I mean, I understand why you're not feeling like it this year, but come on.'

Mummy laughs. 'I'm sure they'll have the full spread tomorrow at her father's.'

I'm having a different Christmas just with Daddy tomorrow. When we came back here from Auntie Barbara's house I thought it might be so we could all see Daddy for Christmas, but Mummy says that Daddy doesn't live here any more, and this house is just mine and hers now. Mine and hers and Dolly's.

They've forgotten that they're talking quietly now, and Mummy starts to shout at Auntie Barbara. I tell Dolly that I think we should play in the lounge. There's a spot in between the sofa and Mummy's sewing box where I can squeeze right in, with Dolly, and make myself small. I squash into my spot and sing *Away in a Manger*. Last year Mummy and me sang Christmas carols together before bed on Christmas Eve. She didn't want to do that this year.

I'm going to make sure Mummy has a lovely Christmas. When my fajitas come, I'm going to eat them all up and make 'Mmmm' noises even though they've got yellow bits in them, and I don't know what they are. Dolly doesn't like yellow bits. She might leave hers on the side of the plate.

'Are you having a nice day dear?' Mummy asks.

'Yeah.'

'Good.' She seems pleased. 'Christmas is a bit of silliness really. It's much nicer this way, isn't it?'

I nod. I think that's what she wants me to do.

# Chapter Seven

## Christmas Afternoon, 2013

### Sean

Sean watched Cora stalk back to her car, and headed back into the lounge. 'Where's Michelle?'

Bel looked up from the Monopoly board. 'She's gone. She said she had friends to visit.'

What? That made no sense. Michelle didn't know anyone around here. It didn't matter. All that mattered was that she had gone.

'When?'

Bel shrugged. 'Ten minutes ago maybe.'

'Did she say anything?'

A shake of the head. 'No.'

Sean ran into the yard. The hire car, as he expected, was gone. He quickly counted back through the day. Coffee at breakfast time, even though his mum and Bel seemed to have been quaffing Buck's Fizz from first light. One glass of wine with lunch. That was Ok. He ran back into the house.

'Car keys!'

'What?' His parents, brother and sister all stared at him. 'I need to borrow someone's car. Any car!'

He caught the first set of keys that came flying towards him and ran outside pressing the unlock button. Luke's Land Rover sprang into life. Thank the Lord. He'd said any car, but he was relieved not to be chasing the woman of his dreams in his mother's bright yellow smart car. He started the engine, pulled away and immediately stopped. Which way had she gone? He silently thanked the Lord again, this time for the snow, and for the fact that Christmas Day meant there weren't many tracks coming in and out of the yard. He could see footsteps, presumably Cora's, going off across the field. He could see where his dad had brought the hire car back, but those tracks were already part covered in fresh snow. He turned out of the yard, following the newest tyre marks.

This was crazy. He could wait until after Christmas, get her contact details from Patrick and Jess, give her a call sometime calm and quiet. He could be sensible. He could take things slow. He didn't have to dive straight in. Sean grinned to himself, pressed his foot to the clutch and moved up a gear.

He followed the lane from the farm for about a mile, to the crossroads. The lack of Christmas Day traffic meant that even out on the road there were only a few tyre tracks. The freshest seemed to go straight on. He followed them.

The lane rose and fell with the landscape, and then started to rise more sharply as the road climbed into the higher hills. Sean glanced at the sky. The fresh snow was falling more heavily, and the snow on the ground was getting thicker as he climbed higher. Would the hire car make it through this? He shuddered to think of Michelle alone and probably lost.

He rounded a bend, and brought the Land Rover to a rapid stop. The hire car was half off the road in front of him, nose into the ditch. He threw his door open and ran. The front of the car was crumpled, but the car was empty. The driver's side door was open. He spun around scanning the road and fields. No Michelle.

His heart pounded. Where was she? Was she hurt? Cold? Out there somewhere alone? He imagined the landscape he loved through Michelle's eyes. Freezing. Forbidding. Dangerous. He ran back to the four by four and opened the boot. Good old Luke. You could always spot a boy who'd been brought up on a farm. There was a waterproof jacket, along with a shovel and first aid kit. Sean pulled on the coat, and headed back to the hire car. He dragged his phone out of his pocket. No signal. He hadn't thought there would be. No sign of Michelle in or near the car. No key in the ignition. He tried to tell himself that was a good thing. It looked like she'd got out and walked away. Steeling himself, he ran his hands over the steering wheel and driver's seat. No obvious signs of blood.

'Sean!'

He spun round to see Michelle standing in the lane. There was blood on her hand, but she was standing and breathing and talking. His heart rate started to slow. He ran towards her.

'You're Ok?'

She nodded. 'What are you doing out here?'

'Looking for you.'

He saw her open expression snap closed. 'That's not necessary. I'm …'

'If you're going to say "fine" then I'm going to point out the car in the ditch and the blood on your arm. You're not fine. You need help.'

She nodded but made no attempt to move towards him.

'I'm sorry if you don't want my help, but I'm all that's here, so sit down.'

He flicked the tailgate open, and gestured towards it. Michelle sat down while Sean leant into the car and dragged a first aid kit from the glove box.

'Roll up your sleeve.'

The cut was on the back of her wrist and wasn't as bad as Sean had first feared. He found an antiseptic wipe and started to clean.

'I can do that.' Michelle took the wipe off him with her good hand and started to deal with her own wound.

'Why did you run off?'

Michelle shrugged. 'It seemed perfectly clear that I wasn't wanted.'

'What?'

Michelle swallowed, still holding the wipe against her arm. 'Look. I'm sure you were trying to be nice, and this probably isn't your fault but I don't do things like this. I don't ride Ferris wheels. I don't play in the snow. I don't run away with strange men. I don't ...'

She tailed off, as if the other things she didn't do were too numerous to list.

Sean laughed, trying to keep the tone lighter than he felt. 'You do now.'

'No. I don't.' Michelle lifted the wipe from her wrist. 'I need to put something on this.'

Sean accepted the distraction. 'I don't think there's a plaster big enough.' He fished around in the first aid kit.

'Hold this.' He pressed a pad against the cut, and started wrapping a piece of bandage to hold it in place. 'I thought there was something good happening here.'

Her face was pinched and closed, like it had been when he'd first met her, like it had been before he'd persuaded her to ride the Ferris wheel, and shown her the Christmas tree field. She wouldn't look him in the eye. 'Apparently not.'

Sean swallowed. 'What happened?'

She glared at him. 'Seriously? I thought ... it doesn't matter.'

'You thought what?'

'I thought you might, sort of, want to ...'

Sean smiled. 'I did. I do. I very much sort of, want to ...'

'Well that's not going to happen.' She took a breath. 'Well not again.'

Sean paused in his bandage wrapping. What had happened? Things had been going well. Things had been going really well. 'Help me here. I'm confused.'

Michelle pulled her hand away. 'What's confusing? You had a bit of fun. It didn't work out.'

'What?'

She set off walking back along the lane. He ran after her. 'Seriously. I'm getting really tired of watching you walk away.'

'Then why don't you let me go?'

'Because I don't want to.' He yelled his answer back at her, and the shouting was exhilarating. 'Because I'm sick of being cautious and sensible. Because I want to jump in with both feet, and I don't care if I get hurt.'

'You don't care about getting hurt?'

'Not even a little bit. I think you might be worth it.'

Michelle let out a small bitter laugh. 'And what do you reckon your wife would think?'

'What?'

'Your wife?'

Oh. Sean was stupid. Cora. Of course she'd have told a possible rival she was his wife. That was exactly what she'd do. He took a deep breath. 'Look. I can explain.'

'I'm not interested.'

'I tried to tell you before we … before we did anything. You didn't want to wait.'

'How long would it have taken to mention your wife?'

'She's not my wife.'

Michelle was still striding away from him.

He tried another tack. 'You can't walk anywhere from here. It's freezing. I know, for a fact, that that's not your jumper, so you have to take it back. Come on. You don't even know where you are.'

She stuck out her chin. 'I do.'

'Where?'

Her chin lowered. 'Scotland.'

'Excellent. Well I'm sure that's all you'll need to tell the AA for them to pop out here on Christmas Day and pick you up.' He saw her shoulders drop. 'Come back to the Land Rover. Let me explain.'

She walked past him without speaking, and sat back down on the tailgate. 'Two minutes.'

Two minutes. What could you explain in two minutes? The big stuff, he guessed. If you were going to jump right in, you couldn't be half-hearted about it. 'I'm not married.'

She raised her eyes.

'I was married. I'm divorced. I should have told you that. I tried to tell you that.'

She folded her arms across her chest. 'So tell me about it now.'

'Ok.' What to say? 'It was a long time ago. We were seventeen. We were in love. I leapt right in, didn't think, didn't hesitate. I wanted to be with her.'

'What went wrong?'

He looked at her. 'Apart from being seventeen?'

She laughed, a small quiet laugh. It was beautiful.

'We stayed together quite a while actually, living with my mum and dad. Then, when she was twenty-one, she started thinking about all the stuff she'd missed out on. University. Wild nights out. Growing up, I guess.'

'And that's why you broke up?'

'She didn't tell me until she already had the place at college. One day I thought we were fine. The next she was moving to London to do Business and Economics, and I wasn't invited.'

He closed his eyes.

'I'm sorry.'

'I haven't really jumped into a relationship since then.'

'Once bitten?'

Sean nodded.

'Are you still in love with her?'

'What?'

'I heard you talking at the house.'

'I knew there was someone in the hall!' He paused and shook his head.

'How do you know?'

'I know.' He turned to face her. 'Honestly. I'm not in love

with Cora. She's cool in her own slightly self-involved way. We have history, but I think I've been kidding myself that we can be mates. She's part of my past. That's all.'

Michelle didn't answer.

'So what about the future?'

'What?'

Sean leant towards her. 'Well, officially you still owe me another twenty-four hours.'

Michelle shook her head. 'That was always a silly idea.'

'I know.' Sean swallowed. He was all in now. No pretending this was just him taking pity on a girl who was alone at Christmas. No pretending that when the two days were over he'd be able to stand by and let her walk away. 'I was kidding myself about the forty-eight hour thing as well. I don't want a couple of days with you. It's not enough. I don't want to be safe. I don't want a time limit. I want to take care of you. I want to spend time with you. I want … I just want you.'

Michelle kept her head bent away from him as she spoke. 'I don't think I can do that.'

'Do what?'

'Jump right in. What if it doesn't work? What if I've seen this whole relationship play out before?'

'What do you mean?'

'My mum and dad. He was so impulsive, so much fun, and she was like me. Careful. Cautious. It didn't work for them.' She lifted her head towards Sean. 'Why would it work for us?'

That was it. That was her biggest fear. She'd loved her dad so much, but he'd let her mum down. He'd let them both down. 'Well, for starters, I'm not like your dad. Yes. I'm a bit impulsive, but I don't quit. I'm not going to run off with an elf …'

Michelle opened her mouth, but Sean kept going.

'… or a secretary or my ex-wife or a foxy Christmas tree

saleswoman or whoever it is you're worrying about. When you're around, I don't see anyone else. I only see you. I see you taking care of everybody, and I want to take care of you.'

Michelle shook her head again. 'You'll get bored of me. Sensible Michelle.'

'There's nothing boring about sensible Michelle.' Sean grinned. 'And if I get bored of sensible Michelle, I've always got Holly.'

'Shut up!' The hint of a smile was returning to Michelle's voice.

'And so what if you are your mother's daughter? Your mother's dying wish was that you went on holiday to the Caribbean. That's hardly sensible.'

Michelle sighed. 'I suppose not. I think maybe she thought she'd stopped me having fun when I was younger.'

'So maybe you're both your parents? Sensible Michelle and impulsive Holly?'

'Maybe. Actually, when I was little I had a dolly, called Dolly ...'

Sean grinned. 'What else?'

'I used to make her do the things I was too scared to do.' She smiled at the memory. 'Like I had to be Michelle but she could be Holly in my place.'

She shook her head. It was a silly idea. 'You could still break my heart. My dad broke Mum's heart.'

Sean shrugged. 'And you could break mine.'

'I wouldn't do that.'

'Good.' He took a deep breath. 'One question then, when we're together, do you see anyone else?'

Did she? She paused for a second. Normally her head was full of plans and things to do and problems to solve, but the last twenty-four hours had been different. She'd managed, mostly, to just be in the here and now, because the here and now with Sean in the middle of it had been all she could see. Michelle shook her head. 'It's just you.'

Sean leant towards her and she found his lips. Soft, chilled from the cold air, intoxicating but safe. Maybe she could trust a feeling. Maybe she could jump into the unknown and let him catch her. She kissed him back.

She pulled back a fraction. 'I crashed your hire car.'

'Yep.'

'What are we going to do?'

'Dunno.' He glanced at the car in the ditch. 'I can probably tow it back somehow. Don't worry about it today. It's Christmas.'

'Oh.' She sounded sad.

'What's up?'

'It's getting dark. Christmas is nearly over.'

'I thought you hated Christmas.'

'Maybe I'm a convert.'

Sean laughed. 'Well, in that case, can I interest you in New Year?'

'What?'

'Well, this is Scotland. Really Hogmanay is what it's all about. We'll go to Edinburgh.'

She squirmed. 'I don't know. Isn't New Year a big waste of money?'

Sean shook his head. 'I'll do you a deal. Give me another week. I'll get you to love New Year. I promise.'

'Just one week?'

'Well, a week until New Year.' He pulled her closer. 'After that, we can start planning next Christmas.'

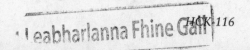

*Cora's Christmas Kiss*

# Chapter One

*What is perfection? Cora Strachan knows. Perfection is a beautiful apartment and a successful career. Perfection is being in control of your own life and never relying on anyone else. Perfection is the state of being perfectly independent.*

*And Cora Strachan had the perfect life. She had the apartment. She had the job. She had the wardrobe and the social life and the bank balance. She had it all. Had. Past tense.*

*There are people who say that sometimes you have to lose everything to appreciate what you had. There are people who say that 'setback' is just another word for 'opportunity'. Those people are stupid. That's another thing Cora Strachan knows.*

## December

Cora stared at herself in the mirror on the wall of the staff toilet. She was a vision in brown felt and nylon. Behind her Mrs Atkins was smiling broadly. 'And now your antlers.'

Cora picked up the offending items and arranged the set of antlers attached to a head band on top of her head. Her face was coated in brown face paint, with the end of her nose picked out in scarlet. Apparently plastic noses were rather too common for Golding's department store. She kept her gaze fixed on the mirror. 'I thought I was going to be an elf.'

Mrs Atkins shook her head. 'You've got to have a Rudolph. The children love Rudolph.'

Cora frowned. 'But it makes no sense. Rudolph doesn't talk or stand on two legs.'

The older woman heaved her sizeable bosom. 'The children like Rudolph. It's part of the magic of Christmas.' Her tone implied that no argument with the magic of Christmas would be brooked from her employees. Cora's best approach seemed to be to shut up and put up. She'd already had to knock the idea of travelling home to Scotland for Christmas on the head because she couldn't afford the cheap bus, let alone the train or a flight, and she wasn't particularly welcome in her parents' home at the moment, not after the last time she'd seen them.

She stared at the downcast reindeer in the mirror. If she didn't keep hold of this job the lack of money for the train would be the least of her worries. She smeared a final dab of pink onto each cheek and forced what she hoped was a festive smile onto her lips. This wasn't the time to be thinking about the horror of a thirty-year-old woman dressing up as a make-believe magical reindeer. This wasn't the time to be thinking about the Christmas bonus she'd been busy spending in the expensive stores on Fifth Avenue this time last year. This wasn't the time to be thinking about anything other than being the best damned reindeer Golding's department store had ever seen, in the vague hope that there might be a job for her after Christmas.

She turned to face Mrs Atkins, who gave her a once-over that would have passed muster with most regimental sergeant majors, before deciding that Cora was ready to be allowed near the grotto. 'It's a lot of responsibility being Rudolph, you know?'

Cora nodded. 'Yes, Mrs Atkins.'

'And we've got a new Father Christmas this year, so you're going to have to be on your toes.' She paused. 'Maybe I should give Rudolph to one of the more experienced girls. Some of our elves have been with us for years, you know.'

Cora didn't know, but she nodded anyway. 'I can do

it Mrs Atkins. I promise.' She could hear the feigned enthusiasm in her voice. It disgusted her.

She followed Mrs Atkins onto the shop floor. It was twenty minutes until the doors opened to customers. They wound their way through sports equipment and luggage and into toys. One end of the floor was dominated by the grotto. It wasn't like any grotto Cora had ever been taken to. They'd been plastic-y affairs crammed into an unloved corner of a shopping centre. This was something else. This was the North Pole transplanted to Knightsbridge. At the front there was what looked like real grass with model robins and woodland creatures nestled amongst foliage. Cora resisted the urge to reach down and touch the green blades. Beyond the grass, the scene gradually shifted from green to white as you followed the path the children would walk along to see Santa himself. The actual grotto was at the end of a winding lane of glistening ice and snow. Despite herself, Cora smiled.

A gaggle of elves were already waiting for instructions. Cora stood alongside them, while Mrs Atkins inspected the rest of her team. She stopped. 'Where's Father Christmas?'

One of the elves gestured in the direction of the staff staircase. Cora followed the pointing finger. A big-bellied figure in the familiar red suit was making his way across the shop floor, partly obscured by displays of ski equipment and a six-foot teddy bear. Mrs Atkins tutted pointedly. 'Hat and beard on at all times please, Mr Carr.'

Cora caught a flash of dirty blond hair brushing against a stubbled jawline. Something about the line of his jaw was familiar, but she couldn't think what. Before she had time to dwell on the mystery, the man pulled a thick white wig over his hair, and secured the white beard across his face. He ambled over to the group of elves, catching Cora's glance as he passed. Sparkling sky blue eyes met hers. Cora felt a smile bubble spontaneously to her face. She swallowed it down. She wasn't here to make friends. She was here because she had no choice. She dropped her gaze from the stranger in the Santa suit and looked away.

'Very good.' Mrs Atkins folded her arms. 'For those of you who are new to us, a few ground rules. You are to remain in costume and in character at all times. You will be at your posts before the store opens and you will not leave until the final child has left at the end of the day. You are employed for six days each week. On late night shopping evenings the grotto will close for twenty minutes to allow the changeover to the evening Father Christmas, who will also cover the role on Sundays. Mr Carr you will leave the floor before the evening Father Christmas enters. We do not want the children to catch a glimpse of the two of you together now, do we?'

Next to Cora, the man in the Santa suit stifled a laugh. 'What about breaks?'

Mrs Atkins sucked the air through her teeth as if she suspected breaks were an unnecessary modern innovation. 'There is a break area at the rear of the grotto specifically for the use of yourself and your reindeer. You will exit the store through the break room behind the grotto, and not across the shop floor. And there is to be absolutely no smoking in costume. Father Christmas and his faithful elves should not be seen puffing on a roll-up in front of the store. Is that clear?'

The assembled magical characters nodded. Mrs Atkins continued, explaining that the role of the elves was to manage the queue of children waiting to see Father Christmas, and to ensure that gold ticket holders were shepherded to the front of the queue without causing a riot amongst the less favoured little ones. Access to see Father Christmas was already sold out for the final few days before Christmas and for every Saturday during December. Inside the grotto, it was Cora's job to act as Father Christmas's faithful attendant, ensuring that there was an appropriate gift to hand for each child, and keeping an eye on the time. The whole operation was overseen by the Chief Elf, a rather softly spoken woman who apparently worked in childrenswear most of the year but had grafted her way through the elven ranks to the top job. She reported, in turn, directly to Mrs Atkins. Cora hadn't quite worked out yet what Mrs Atkins' actual job was, but it seemed to involve being officious and particular, and Cora was clear that she didn't want to get on her bad side. Depressing though it was, Cora needed this job. A year ago, less than a year ago, that would have been unimaginable. How on earth had she ended up here?

Inside the Father Christmas costume, Liam Carr grimaced. He'd bloody kill Raj for persuading him to take this job. No amount of 'getting out of the house' was worth committing to spending the whole of December shaking his belly like a bowl full of jelly and 'Ho ho hoing' at everyone who passed. At least Raj had been right about one thing. With his costume, wig and beard on, nobody was likely to recognise him, which made a refreshing change. The dictator lady finished her rundown of the immutable rules of the festive period at Golding's department store and approached him, beckoning one of the other poor costumed saps over. 'So Father Christmas, this is your Rudolph. She'll be the one handing out the gifts to the children. You'll need to work together. We need to run a tight Christmas ship.'

Liam thought he heard the faintest hint of a sigh next to him, but he kept his eyes fixed straight ahead as he nodded.

Mrs Atkins drew her bosom up to its full height. 'Well off you go then.'

Liam followed the glittering path into his grotto. Inside there was a chair, a throne really, covered in plush dark green velvet. Alongside that there was a sack overflowing with perfectly wrapped presents. Mrs Atkins marched into the grotto behind them, directing the reindeer's attention to the presents. 'Blue and green wrapping is for boys. Pink and purple is for girls. Yellow and orange are ...' She paused and a flicker of distaste danced across her face. '... unisex. The darker the shade of paper, the older the child. So pastel paper for babies and little toddlers. The brightest ones for three to sixes, and darker paper for older children. You understand?'

The reindeer nodded, shaking her antlers as she did so.

'One more thing. At Golding's we host Father Christmas's grotto. Not Santa Claus. Santa Claus comes from Holland by way of America. Here we celebrate a traditional British Christmas. So ...' She turned to the reindeer. 'You will refer to your colleague as Father Christmas throughout the period of the grotto. Am I clear?'

Another antler-shaking nod. Apparently satisfied, Mrs Atkins made her way out of the grotto, pausing in the entrance. 'First child in twenty minutes. Look jolly.'

Liam waited for her to leave before turning to his reindeer companion. Looking closely now he could see that somewhere under the make-up and the antler hairband, there was probably an attractive young woman. The costume wasn't helping her. He held out a gloved hand. 'I'm ...'

He saw the smile in her eyes as she held up her own hand to stop him. 'You're Father Christmas.'

He laughed, and then he thought about it. Her not knowing his name might not be such a bad thing. She hadn't recognised his face under the costume – if she didn't know his name either he might even get through the whole month without her figuring out who he was. 'You can't call me Father Christmas all month. Not when we're on our own.' He shuddered. 'It makes me feel like a creepy old man asking you to come, sit on my knee and rummage through my big sack.'

'Well I can't call you Santa.' The reindeer laughed again. 'It's forbidden.'

'Okay.' Liam paused. 'Then I'm Chris, short for Christmas.' He held out his hand again. 'Hi. I'm Chris.'

She shook the offered hand. 'And I'm Rudy?' She said it with a hint of a question.

'Okay.' So maybe he wasn't the only one who was hiding out. Rudy was fine, better than Rudolph anyway.

They muddled their way through the first morning. It was still a few weeks before Christmas and schools hadn't broken up yet, so the pace was slightly less frenetic than they expected, and the children were still at the age where they were either terrified or absolutely believing in their attitude to the big man in the red suit. At twelve-thirty the Chief Elf stuck her head into the grotto. 'Lunchtime! I've put some sandwiches in your break room fridge. You'll have to get your own from tomorrow though. And don't tell Mrs Atkins. I don't think she's a fan of acts of kindness.'

The break room was tiny with one high window, a worktop big enough for a kettle, a sink and a mini fridge. Two plastic chairs were wedged around a small table. Next to the worktop was another door to the bathroom and a corridor, which Liam presumed led somehow into the bowels of the store. He raised an eyebrow to Rudy. 'Palatial.'

She nodded and opened the fridge. 'Tuna mayonnaise or chicken salad?'

Liam accepted the chicken sandwich and squeezed himself, belly and all, into one of the plastic chairs. He was going to have to take his beard off to eat. He pulled the scratchy white beard away from his jaw and glanced at Rudy. He saw her eyes scan across his face, as she lowered herself into the other chair, but there was no hint of recognition. That was something.

A month. A month hadn't seemed that long when Raj

had talked him into it, but a month of lunch breaks with this stranger trapped in their tiny break room box suddenly felt like a really, really long time. He glanced at his trusty reindeer. It was impossible to make out much of her face under the make-up, but she had long dark hair and the tights and leotard combo didn't leave much to the imagination in terms of her body. He forced himself to look away. There was no point thinking about her like that. The idea of trying to start a relationship at the moment was absurd and far, far too risky.

Next to him, she clicked her tongue against the roof of her mouth. 'So ...'

He nodded encouragingly, hoping she might have something they could talk about. 'Yeah?'

She nodded back at him. Clearly she had nothing. An idea struck. He was sick to death of Raj telling him he should talk about what was on his mind, but why not? He was never going to see this woman again. She had no idea who he was, and he didn't even know her real name. 'So ... I had the weirdest year.' He stopped. 'That is ... I've got this friend ...'

He saw her eyebrow shoot heavenwards. 'A friend?'

'Yeah. I've got this friend who had the weirdest year.'

She shook her head. 'It can't have been worse than mine.'

'Yours?' There was a hint of a challenge in his voice.

She glanced up and held his eye for a second. Her eyes were gentle brown pools, but they weren't giving anything away. She smiled slightly. 'Well not me. This friend of mine.'

Liam nodded. 'You go first then.'

'What?'

'Tell me about your terrible year.'

'*My friend's* terrible year?'

'Of course.'

She took a deep breath. 'Okay. Well my friend – we'll call her Cora ...'

'Pretty name.'

She smiled. 'Well it sort of started last Christmas ...'

## Christmas Day, one year previously

Married at seventeen. Separated at twenty-one. Divorced by twenty-two. Yet Cora Strachan still considered Sean Munro to be by far her most successful relationship. He was, and perhaps would always be, the one that got away – although in fairness he hadn't got away. She'd run from him, away from his family home in the depths of the Scottish countryside, and she'd kept running. She hadn't stopped until she'd finished university and got her foot on the career ladder, and then more than a foot, and she'd hauled her way up to the corner office and the penthouse – technically sub-penthouse – apartment on London's South Bank. She might have run away from her marriage but, to her credit, she had really committed to her escape. Until now.

'I miss you.' Cora could hear the wheedling tone in her voice. She despised herself for doing this, for being here. She knew he wasn't interested. She couldn't argue he'd been equivocal about that. Sure, there had been times when they'd both fallen back on the comfort of hooking up with their ex, rather than enduring the perpetual pain of putting themselves out there, but recently she'd sensed him moving on.

Opposite her, Sean shrugged. 'Then you shouldn't have left, but you did. A long time ago.'

Cora fought to ignore the punched-in-the-stomach feeling. He was right. Of course he was right. It wasn't even that she desperately loved and missed him. She knew that. Sean was her emotional comfort blanket. Sean, she'd thought, was easy – a safe harbour in the midst of the storm. She wasn't in love with him. Cora stepped back and arranged her face into a smile.

'No need to be grumpy. I'm only messing around.' She glanced around the room. Sean's study. When she'd lived here, the schoolgirl bride moving in with her husband's parents, this room had been his father's office. Everything changed, thought Cora. 'Best get back to the olds then.'

He nodded and moved towards her. For a second she thought he was going to kiss her, one of those soft wistful goodbye kisses that happen in films and stories but are ripe for misinterpretation in real-life. She dipped her head, and walked away. She didn't stop to say goodbye to his family, who would offer drinks and mince pies and subsume her in a fug of festive cheer. She didn't stop to find out the identity of the red-headed woman who'd been playing with Sean's niece and nephew when Cora arrived. He'd moved on. She didn't need to pore over the details.

She slammed the front door closed, and pulled her thick wool coat tight around her in the chill December air. Snow was falling, covering her footprints as she went. How many times had she walked this way before? Over the fields between her parents' house and Sean's, clambering over gates and fences to meet for a teenage snog at the edge of his family's land. She crunched through the snow along the edge of the field of baby Christmas trees being cultivated for next year. Twelve months to grow strong and healthy, and then they'd be chopped down and brought into overwarm living rooms to die. Cora fancied she knew how they felt. She'd had eight years in London, growing strong and independent and now she was back here, falling into old habits, feeling the new Cora ebbing away.

She shook her head. It was Christmas. Christmas was an odd time. That must be what was making her feel adrift. Her mind turned back to her real life for a second. The corner office. The penthouse apartment. The work-hard, play-hard schedule that filled her time. Or that had filled her time. She pushed her hand into her coat pocket and pulled out the crumpled letter that she'd stuffed there two days before. She knew the contents backwards, but she found herself reading it over and over, trying to glean some further meaning from between the lines.

She skimmed through the first four paragraphs, which detailed the exciting new developments for her company and the forward-looking opportunities to shift their working paradigm into a new era, and settled her gaze on the much shorter final paragraph.

*Therefore, we are notifying you that your post is at risk of redundancy. You are invited to a consultation meeting on 3rd January at 9 a.m. to discuss this further.*

And that was it. At risk of redundancy. At risk wasn't the same as redundant. Cora took a deep breath. She could deal with this. She would go back to London. She would go into work. She would go to their meeting and she would convince them to keep her on. She would adapt. She would reinvent. She would do whatever it took to hold on to the life she'd built.

# Chapter Two

## December

Cora glanced across the break room as Chris stuffed the last of his sandwich into his mouth. He shrugged. 'So you got knocked back by an ex? That is nowhere near winning you the prize for the weirdest year.'

'You mean nowhere near *my friend* winning the prize. Obviously none of this happened to me.'

'Of course.'

Cora wrinkled her red nose, and let her mind drift over the last twelve months. 'I'm only just getting started. We're not even into January yet.'

She glanced up into the face of her companion. 'So what was so weird about your year?' She paused, and corrected herself. 'Your friend's year.'

He flicked his eyes up to the clock on the wall and shrugged. 'No time Rudy. I'll have to tell you tomorrow.'

Liam picked his beard up from the table and hooked it back around his ears. He followed Rudy into the grotto and took his seat. The Chief Elf stuck her head around the door. 'I was about to come and get you. Ready?'

They nodded, and the first child of the afternoon toddled in, followed by a woman who looked as though she'd been plopped down onto the earth fully formed and pristine. Perfect hair, perfect nails, sparkling white jeans under a Chanel jacket. The mother rather than the au pair, Liam guessed. He forced his face into an avuncular smile. He hadn't exactly taken this job through choice, but a performance was still a performance.

As soon as the little girl clapped eyes on Father Christmas the need for parental support was forgotten. She dived onto his lap and started regaling him with the Christmas wish list to end all wish lists. 'I wanna pony, and I wanna wendy house, and a tree house, and an iPad, and I wanna toboggan. Oliver's already got a toboggan and Daddy says it's 'cos he's bigger, but that's not fair, so I should get one too.'

Liam bounced the little madam on his lap, and glanced at the child's mother. Mother was nodding along with all her daughter's requests, with the smug smirk on her face of a parent who knows that all her little angel's wishes are destined to be granted. Something flipped inside his head. 'So you want Father Christmas to bring you a pony?'

The little girl nodded.

'Not a hippogriff?'

The child's brow furrowed.

He shrugged. 'I suppose those are for the older kids really. Not everybody gets one.'

The little girl's eyebrows were practically knitted together now. 'I want a hippogriff.'

'Then Father Christmas will see what he can do.'

The mother's face had paled somewhat. Rudy scooped the little girl off Liam's lap, and thrust a present into her grasping hands. 'Well Merry Christmas!' She bustled the pair out of the grotto before she the laughter bubbled onto her face. 'That was mean.'

'She was spoilt.'

'But still ...'

'Sorry.' He pulled the beard from his face and rubbed his chin. It wasn't the little girl's fault she was growing up in the lap of luxury; and it wasn't her fault he was struggling with the idea of undeserved riches either. 'She's getting a pony and an iPad. I think she'll be fine.'

The afternoon went by, and then the next day, only interrupted by Liam's auntie phoning him at lunchtime and wittering about plans for Christmas for the full forty-five minutes. On the third day, he poured water over the teabags in their mugs, shuffled to manoeuvre his belly padding around the tiny kitchenette, and smiled. 'So come on Rudy. January?'

She shook her head. 'You're supposed to be telling yours as well.'

That was true. A promise was a promise. He hesitated and then grinned. 'Ladies first.'

## January, earlier in the year

Cora shifted in her seat and waited. Her head of department, Angus, was talking. He'd been talking for nearly an hour and, so far as Cora could discern, he hadn't said anything meaningful. He mentioned 'dynamic systemic challenges' four times and 'increasingly divergent realities' twice. Cora was lost. Normally she would have claimed to speak fluent corporate hogwash. She could inform a client that 'economic actualities suggested an optimum moment to refocus his investment medley,' rather than simply telling him he was at risk of ending up dead broke with the best of them, but today her bullshit interpreter seemed to be on the blink. There was a lot of talk going on but none of it was answering the basic question of whether Cora had a job any more.

She forced herself to swallow down her anxiety. Of course she would keep her job. Cora was invincible. She was the woman who'd got herself hired at the height of the credit crunch. She'd not only ridden out the storm; she'd prospered through it. When other teams were laying off staff and talking in dark tones about natural wastage and 'last-in-first-out,' Cora's team had exceeded every target they'd been given. Cora was good at her job, but as well as good she was something even more important for an investment banker. Cora was lucky. At least that's what she'd believed.

Across the table, Angus steepled his fingers and glanced sideways at the woman from HR who'd been dragged into the meeting. Then he tilted his head and smiled at Cora. 'So I think that wraps up the situation, as we see it, within current parameters.'

Cora felt herself nodding. 'Wait. Sorry. Am I being made redundant?'

Her manager sucked the air through his teeth in a way that suggested a possible second career as a car mechanic if the business really did go belly up. 'Well, as I was saying we are facing some exceptional external stresses in relation to the monetary flow ...'

Cora clenched her fist under the table. 'Yes or no?'

Angus glanced at Mrs Human Resources. In the end he shrugged. 'We don't know.'

'You don't know?'

He shook his head.

'And when will you know?'

'Well ...'

The woman from HR interrupted. 'I expect final decisions when they review the full end of year figures.'

Cora stood up. 'Thank you.'

She walked out of the room and kept walking past the lifts. As she expected the stairwell was deserted. Despite the money expended by her colleagues on personal trainers and stepper machines, very few of them would ever dream of actually using the stairs. She stopped, leant back against the wall and forced herself to breathe. Three months. It was still three months until the end of the financial year. Cora could turn this around. She could make herself indispensable. A doubt crept into her head. She'd thought she was already indispensable. She quashed the sneaky little misgiving. She would simply make herself even more indispensable.

She descended the two flights to the fifth floor where her office sat in a circular glass hub at the centre of a large open plan room. Her team hot-desked at work stations arranged outwards like spokes from the centre of a wheel. Everything was light and bright and unremittingly modern and Cora loved it. As soon as she stepped out of the lift Denise and Colin pounced. Denise was the only woman working in Cora's team; Welsh, hard as nails, shorter – by a clear foot – than any of the men, and about three times as fierce. Colin was tall, freckly and ginger, the polar opposite of the traditional slick salesman, but Cora had nabbed him for her team within twenty minutes of him walking into the company recruitment day a year earlier. It was his very unsalesmanlike demeanour that made him so good. Clients didn't even realise they were being sold to until they were halfway home with three quarters of their wealth tied up in whatever failure-proof scheme Colin was pushing on that occasion.

'So what's happening?' Denise stopped Cora in the doorway to the floor.

'Something and nothing.' Cora smiled, keeping her tone of voice light. 'Just the usual end of year jitters.'

'So we're not all screwed then?'

Cora shook her head. 'We're gonna be fine. Although we'd be fine a hell of a lot quicker if you got back to your desks and did some work.'

Colin muttered something into Denise's ear.

'Sam Allery in acquisitions told Colin the whole sales team was done for.'

Cora felt her stomach clench. *Indispensable* she reminded herself. 'Not likely.' She strutted past Denise and inspected the whiteboard at the side of the room. *High Value Client Support Centre* – that was what they did according to the lettering across the top. Support was a euphemism for selling, of course. And High Value meant filthy rich. It was their job to present investment products to rich individuals. They earned good commissions and hedonistic bonuses.

She glanced down the list of names on the board and then around the office. 'Where's Dave Three?'

In addition to Denise and Colin, there were four shiny-faced, slick-haired salesmen on Cora's team, collectively known as The Daves. Cora was vaguely aware that at least one of the Daves was actually called Toby, but that wasn't the point. They all had a general sense of Daveishness about them.

Dave Two, or possibly One, looked up. 'Lunch with Vasilyev and his spoilt daughter.'

Cora nodded. 'I've got a lunch too.'

Dave Two frowned. 'It's not on the board.'

Cora shrugged. 'Well neither is Dave's and you knew about that.'

She picked up her plush wool coat from the stand in her office and jumped in the lift. Out in the street she pulled the soft layers tight around her body against the January chill. She wasn't sure why she'd lied. She ought to be in her office calling contacts, cracking the whip over her team, but she wasn't. Instead she was outside walking the ten minutes away from her office, across the river to Bankside. She went into the Swan bar, ordered a large glass of expensive wine and sat facing the window. Even in January, with the theatre closed, a steady trickle of sightseers and tourists strolled along the riverside in front of her. Cora watched them amble past, no sense of urgency, nothing they needed to get done. There was a twinge of something. Envy, maybe, only it couldn't be envy. Cora took a sip of wine. She'd worked and worked to get herself to this point. The point where she was always busy. Always in demand. People thought she was a success because she had an expensive apartment and nice clothes, but that wasn't what was important in Cora's mind. What was important was that she'd got it all for herself. Nothing was paid for with Daddy's money. Nothing was bought for her by a husband or a lover. Everything she had she'd earned. Cora downed her drink and stood up. Time to get back to work.

Across the river, Liam bounded away from the Embankment and along the Strand. He grinned as he glanced at his watch. With a bit of luck he'd be finished with whatever it was that was dragging him to a solicitor's office at the crack of dawn, and make it to work by lunchtime. It was just rehearsals this morning, and he was only in a couple of scenes, but his producer hated lateness.

He crossed the street and turned onto Chancery Lane. He was ninety per cent certain this whole trip was a waste of his time anyway. Almost certainly a hoax. Probably a hoax. Unless …

He'd received the letter between Christmas and New Year. Franked first class and typed on thick headed paper, inviting him to meet with Mr Daley at Daley, Callendar & Associates at his earliest convenience. He'd phoned the number more out of curiosity than expectation, but the woman who'd answered the phone had refused to offer any more information. The only way to find out what on earth the letter was about had been to arrange to come down to Mr Daley's London office to discuss what the woman on the phone persisted in referring to as 'the matter' face-to-face.

Liam hadn't been near a solicitor's office since he moved out of Mama Lou's house. There was usually at least one of her extended brood in court for something, and Liam remembered sitting in corridors playing on his second hand Gameboy waiting for whichever of the older kids was in trouble that week. He walked further up Chancery Lane, away from the bookmakers and shops and towards what he suspected was some seriously expensive office space. He passed the grand building of the Maughan Library before he spotted the plaque next to the door on his left. *Daley,*

*Callendar & Associates.* This was the place. The offices were located in what, Liam presumed, had originally been a generous townhouse, with stone pillars at either side of the door.

Inside, everything was plush carpeting and elegant understatement. Immediately Liam wished he'd pulled something smarter than ripped jeans out of his wardrobe, and taken a minute to clear the two-day stubble from his chin and run a brush through his messy blond hair. Given that he had the luxury of an acting job where none of his audience ever got to see him, vanity about his appearance wasn't a vice Liam afforded much time to. He approached the desk at one end of what would have been called the waiting room, but for the lack of anyone doing anything as vulgar as waiting. The receptionist looked up from her screen.

'I've got an appointment with Mr Daley.'

The woman glanced at his face and for a second Liam thought he registered a flicker of surprise. 'You're Mr Carr?'

Liam nodded.

The woman clicked on her screen. 'You can go right through.' She gestured to an archway to the right of the desk. 'First door on the left.'

Liam followed the directions. At the door to the first office he paused. Before he'd raised his hand to knock the door swung open. The man on the other side was short, greying and bespectacled. He wore a sharply tailored three piece suit and a neatly knotted bowtie. He was the very personification of dapper. He held out a hand. 'Mr Carr?'

'Liam.'

'Good. Good. Come in.' He stepped aside to let Liam into the office. 'Take a seat.'

Liam sat opposite the big old-fashioned desk that dominated the room. 'So what's this about?'

The older man muttered to himself as he sat. 'Yes. Yes.

It has been a bit cloak and dagger. It's just that with the sum involved, we thought it better not to make anything public. We've had situations before where every Tom, Dick and Harry is queuing outside trying to get their hands on a share. I'm sure you understand.'

Liam shook his head. 'Not really.'

The man paused. 'No. Of course not. Let me get down to brass tacks.'

'Please.'

'So we have identified that you are one Liam Carr. Liam David Alexander Carr?'

Liam nodded.

'Born on the nineteenth December nineteen eighty-four?'

Liam nodded again.

'At the Broomfield hospital in Chelmsford?'

'That's what I'm told.'

'And your mother was one Catherine Carr.'

Liam tensed. Giving birth to a child did not make you a mother. Cath had died nearly eleven years ago, and up until then her involvement in her eldest son's life had been sporadic and disruptive. Liam remembered their last meeting. It was the week before his recall audition at RADA. She'd laughed in his face. So far as Cath was concerned Liam's life with his foster carer, Mama Lou, had given him ideas well above his station. His last memory of Catherine Carr was leaving her at the bus stop, ignoring the shouted requests for cash that she threw at his back as he walked away. He swallowed. 'Biological mother. Yes.'

The man nodded.

'And you've brought the documents we asked for?'

Liam nodded and pulled his passport and folded birth certificate from his back pocket.

The man inspected them, opened a file on the desk, checked the birth certificate again, and closed the file. 'Very good.' He handed the documents back across the table. 'That all seems in order. One can't be too careful in situations like this.'

'Like what?' Liam could hear the pitch of his voice rising. He took a breath. 'Sorry. Look. I do need to get to work, so if we could ...'

'Yes. Yes. Of course. Well it is now a simple matter of transferring over the money.'

Liam was confused. 'Hold on. I don't owe anyone ...'

The man waved a hand. 'No. No. Of course not. I doubt you'll ever owe anyone again. We need to transfer the money to you.'

Liam shook his head. 'What money?'

'The inheritance. The twenty million dollars.' The man continued to smile benignly behind his desk.

Liam could feel his mouth opening and closing. He had no idea whether there were words coming out. He closed his eyes. He opened them again. The office, the chair, the well turned out solicitor – they were all still there. On balance it seemed unlikely to be a dream, apart from, apart from. 'Twenty million?'

'Twenty million US dollars. I believe it's only around twelve million in pounds sterling. The draft is drawn up and ready in the safe if you'd like me to check.'

'This is a wind-up.'

Mr Daley shook his head. The look on his face suggested that he'd never knowingly engaged in any sort of wind-up in his life. Liam heard himself laugh. Only twelve million pounds. Well that was perfectly fine then. Hardly worth dragging himself down here for. Another thought broke through the disbelief. 'You said inheritance.'

Liam knew he didn't have any rich relatives. He didn't have any relatives at all actually, so it was a fairly easy conclusion to reach. 'Inheritance from who?'

The dapper little man squirmed slightly. 'That information is, I'm afraid, not in the public domain.'

'What?'

'That is to say, I am not at liberty to disclose the benefactor behind the sum in question.'

Liam closed his eyes. 'But it's an inheritance. So it's someone who's died.'

The man's lips pursed slightly. 'That would be a logical inference.'

Liam shook his head. Nothing about this made sense. He didn't know anyone who had that sort of money. His family were, well the people he thought of as family were a disparate bunch of waifs and strays who'd come together under the roof and good graces of Mama Lou, and not one of them had anywhere near this sort of money. His friends were mostly from his acting course, and largely subsisted as waiters and barmen in some of the less salubrious parts of the capital. Liam managed to make rent, and enough money for food and beer beside and was generally considered quite the big spender amongst his social circle. 'Are you sure you've got the right person?'

'Quite sure.'

'But nobody would leave me twelve million quid.'

Mr Daley steepled his fingers. 'And yet somebody did. The details of the inheritance and the identity of the recipient are very specific. You are the correct Mr Carr.'

Liam stepped out of the office a few minutes later with a banker's draft for just over twelve million pounds. A banker's draft, Mr Daley had been keen to explain, was as good as cash. Essentially he had twelve million quid in his pocket.

Liam walked along the street, arms folded across his chest, eyes darting over the scene around him. He'd always loved London, ever since he moved here when he was eighteen. He'd breezed through life in the city, developing the traditional London attitude to crime and security. Sure – bad things happened, but they generally happened to other people, and were a small price to pay for living in the most incredible city in the world.

Today was different. Today, for the first time in his life, Liam had more money in his pocket than he could afford to lose. He had more money in his pocket than he could even start to imagine, and somehow, he was sure, everybody knew. Every passer-by was suddenly a threat. The old lady with the shopping trolley inspecting the cut flowers outside the newsagent was a potential criminal mastermind, plotting to relieve him of his unearned fortune. Liam headed over the bridge to the South Bank of the Thames. It wasn't on his way to work. It wasn't on his way to anywhere. He just kept walking. He headed into the bar next to the theatre and ordered a beer. The barman waited for him to count out the change to pay. He was ten pence short. Liam heard himself laugh. Twelve million pounds and not enough money to pay for a pint. He pulled a credit card out of his wallet.

The barman shrugged apologetically. 'We only take cards if you order food.'

Liam closed his eyes for a second. 'What's the cheapest thing on the menu?'

'Probably the soup. Or you could just have a side?'

Liam opened his mouth to order the soup, before closing it again. Hold on a minute. 'And what's the most expensive thing?'

One hour, and one astonishingly expensive tasting platter later, Liam had discovered that he very much liked lobster, but couldn't really see the point of truffle oil, and he'd barely scraped the surface of his twelve million. Two questions were crystalizing in his mind. One – who on earth had left him all this cash? And two – what on earth was he going to spend it on?

Obvious things sprung to mind. He could buy a car or a house. Even in London he couldn't picture himself spending more than a few hundred thousand on somewhere to live. He could very easily picture Mama Lou spitting at the extravagance if he spent more. He knew there were plenty of penthouse oases for the super-rich but Liam was a single bloke. He had no use for a split level master bedroom suite, or basement utility room with underfloor heating. The idea of even beginning to spend this amount of cash was overwhelming. Extravagance for him was ordering extra onion rings with his Sunday evening takeaway.

Maybe he'd be better off focusing on the first question. He swallowed the last of his beer. Decision made. He'd do nothing with the money until he'd found out where it came from. In Liam's mind there was still a good chance this was an administrative cock-up anyway. Self-control was the right choice. No going out and buying a yacht just because he could. He didn't want a yacht. He didn't really know where a person would go to try and buy one, and if he found out, then he'd still be Liam, but Liam with a yacht he never used. He'd get to the bottom of where the money came from, he decided, and then he'd think about what to do next.

The barman stopped his train of thought, clearing plates from the table in front of him. 'Can I get you anything else?'

Liam glanced at his empty glass. Well one more beer wouldn't break the bank.

# Chapter Three

## December

Rudy opened and closed her mouth. 'You're kidding?'

Liam shook his head.

'But that's brilliant.'

Liam didn't answer for a second. That is what any normal person would think. Twelve million quid. By most measures it was hardly the worst start to the year, but Liam didn't judge it by most measures. He judged it, like he judged everything, by the voice in his head – the voice that belonged to Mama Lou. Responsibility. Self-reliance. Work hard. Earn what you need.

He turned his attention back to Rudy. She was staring at him. Thinking. He pushed the beard higher up his face. 'What did you say your friend's name was?' she asked.

Liam paused. He could come clean. She was going to work it out at some point. He'd be best off just coming clean, but ... he glanced up, catching Rudy's dark brown eyes. There was something about telling the story that seemed to be helping. Pretending it all happened to somebody else made that easier. He shrugged. 'I'm not sure I did.'

She shook her head but didn't push him. 'Well, whatever. Inheriting twelve million pounds is hardly a terrible year.'

Liam rolled his eyes. 'Well your friend's isn't so bad either. She didn't lose her job. That sounds okay to me.'

Rudy stared at him.

'What?'

She gestured at her brown nylon costume. 'Trust me. It's not gonna end well.'

He clasped his hand to his chest in faux agony. 'But that's you Rudy, not your friend.'

She laughed. 'Of course.'

He waved his arm around the break room, taking in the chipped formica worktop and the wobbly mismatched chairs. 'Anyway, what's wrong with this? We're living the dream.'

He watched her eyes follow his gesture before she crumpled forward in laughter. 'Yeah. Perfect.'

'Knock, knock?' The voice came from the small door at the side of the worktop – the one that led away from the grotto. Liam understood that that exit took you into the bowels of the store, and that somehow a person with sufficient stamina and a good supply of breadcrumbs to trail behind them might find their way out to the street. So far he'd stuck with the safer plan of arriving early and leaving late and walking across the sales floor. A dreadlocked head popped itself around the door. 'Can I come in?'

The woman made a beeline for Rudy, enveloping her in a generous one-armed hug, while clutching a tupperware in her free hand. 'You've already eaten?'

''Fraid so.'

The woman frowned. 'I brought you some couscous.'

Liam saw Rudy smile. 'Did Charlie make that for your lunch?'

The woman nodded.

'And what did you have?'

The dreadlocks slumped slightly. 'Bacon sandwich.'

Rudy shook her head and turned to Liam. 'This is Trish. She does the shop's website, and she's one of my housemates.'

Liam nodded at the stranger, and tried to keep his surprise out of his face. She wasn't the sort of housemate he'd have pictured for Rudy at all, and certainly not for someone living in the high-powered corporate world of her story.

Rudy continued. 'And this is ...' her voice tailed off.

Liam hesitated. The anonymity thing was stupid, but he'd come this far. He grinned at Rudy and turned back to her housemate. 'I guess you can call me Chris.'

The dreadlocked woman gathered up her tupperware, muttering about the innate health dangers of a lack of fat and sugar in the diet.

As Trish ambled out, Rudy took the last sip of her tea. 'So what happens next?'

Liam straightened his beard. 'No spoilers.'

She laughed, and started to make her way back to the grotto. Liam watched her brown nylon bottom wiggle in front of him as she walked. Anonymous. Impersonal. No complications. That's what he'd wanted when he agreed to take this job. No complications at all.

He followed Rudy into the grotto. 'So no hints on what happens to the lovely Cora next?'

She raised her eyebrows. 'You think she's lovely?'

'So far. Why? What does she do next?'

Rudy shook her head. 'Nothing she's particularly proud of, I'm afraid.'

## February, earlier in the year

Cora shook Mr Anderssen's hand as the lift door opened. She waited until he stepped inside and the doors slid closed behind him, before she punched the air. Another day. Another dollar. She mentally added the deal she'd just closed to the rest of the deals listed on the office whiteboard. It was good. It wasn't quite good enough, but she still had six weeks to go before the end of the quarter. Six weeks was plenty of time. She strode back to her team and added the deal to the running total on the board. She'd let one of the Daves draw the chart this quarter, which was a mistake, because what she'd ended up with was a picture of a massive grey willy that was gradually turning pink as team members coloured in sections relating to the size of the deals they'd done. Cora shook her head. One day, she thought, she'd get a job in an office with girls. Not even girls. Old women. Just her and a group of quiet grandmothers who would spend their break times knitting and wouldn't be even remotely amused by a picture of a willy and balls.

She retreated into her own office and logged into the client account system. As she scrolled through the recent sales, something caught her eye. A gap where the staff initials registering who was managing an account ought to be. She scanned across to the client name. Nemo Kanenas. She didn't recognise the name, and it shouldn't be possible to create an account on the system without linking it to an account manager. Cora frowned.

She stuck her head out into the open plan office. 'Do any of you have a client called …?' She glanced back at the screen. 'Kanenas? Nemo Kanenas?'

The Daves shook their heads. Denise looked up. 'You're trying to find Nemo?'

Cora scowled. Colin leant back from his computer. 'Nemo means nobody in Latin, you know?'

Denise stared at him. 'No Colin. We didn't know that. Didn't particularly want to either.'

Cora left them bickering and headed back into the office. Something rankled. Nobody? She went to her web browser and searched *Kanenas meaning*.

She scrolled through the results. Nobody again. Kanenas was an English spelling of the Greek for nobody. So Mr Nobody Nobody? Cora pushed her door closed and flicked back to the account system. The account had been opened earlier that day. Nearly four million pounds had gone in and then straight out again – recipient account not listed, which implied overseas, somewhere not averse to a little banking secrecy. She caught herself tapping her fingers against the desk, and balled her hand into a fist. It looked as though someone had created a fake account and used it to move three point eight million pounds off shore. And it was on her team's system. She took a deep breath, and clicked on the full details of the account. No staff name. No login details. Nothing to suggest who was really behind it. It was possible to take the staff name off an account, in case somebody left and their clients were reallocated, but that had to be done by the team manager. By Cora.

She logged off, and grabbed her bag and coat. 'I'm heading out for a minute.'

She needed to clear her head. That was all. She'd go for a walk. She'd get some perspective, and when she got back she'd sort out what was almost certainly a simple administrative error.

Cora waited for the lift and pressed the button for the ground floor. By the time she reached the bottom she was all but ready to go straight back upstairs. She was obviously overreacting. The lift doors slid open. Cora froze. Through the plate glass at the front of the building she could see at least four separate police cars. As she stared, bodies flooded through the main doors. At the front of the oncoming swarm was a tall, bespectacled woman, probably ten or fifteen years older than Cora. The receptionist made a grab for her phone. 'Put it down,' the woman yelled.

She handed a piece of paper to the receptionist. Cora couldn't hear what was being said, but she could guess. She pressed the button for her floor and watched the doors slide closed in front of her before anyone else could get in. Maybe she hadn't been overreacting after all.

Upstairs the rest of the team were working away quite happily, still oblivious to the situation unfolding storeys beneath them. Cora rushed past them and along the corridor. She rounded the corner and stopped in the entrance to her boss's office. The room was in disarray. Documents were piled on the desk and floor, and Angus was frantically feeding papers into the shredder. He glanced up. 'Cora!'

Cora didn't reply.

He pointed towards the laptop on his desk. 'Be a pet Cora, and see if that's finished reformatting the disk.'

Without thinking Cora took a step towards the computer before she stopped herself. The police were probably only seconds away. There was no way she was going to get caught red-handed for something she hadn't even been involved in. 'What have you done?'

Angus shrugged. 'Nothing that everybody else wasn't doing too.'

'Step away from the shredder.'

The voice behind Cora came from the same policewoman who'd led the charge into reception. Cora turned to the officer. 'What's going on?'

'We have a warrant to search these premises. We're simply asking everyone to stay at their desks, but please don't use your computer.'

Cora nodded. 'My office is through there.'

The policewoman stepped aside to let her pass. 'And your name?'

Cora told her.

Back in her own office the team were huddled in one corner while uniformed officers took over their desks, packing laptops and mobile phones into clear bags and boxing them up. One of the Daves looked up as she came into the room. 'What's going on?'

Cora shrugged. 'I don't know.' Although that wasn't quite true, was it? She knew one thing that was going on. She stepped towards the nearest police officer. 'Can I show you something?'

He shrugged but followed Cora into her office, where her computer hadn't yet been bagged up and packed away. She quickly logged into the account system and showed the officer the rogue account. She wasn't at all sure it was the best thing to do, but somebody had done this in a way that made it look like it was her fault. She didn't think corporate loyalty extended to taking the fall for that.

Twenty minutes later she was sitting at the wrong side of her desk with the policewoman in charge peering over her spectacles at the screen.

'So who else could have created this account?'

Cora shrugged. 'I don't know. Anyone senior to me I guess.'

'Mr Smith?'

'Angus? I suppose so.'

The policewoman nodded and smiled. At least somebody was having a productive work day. 'Well that's something I suppose.'

Cora frowned. 'So all this was for Angus? You'll arrest him and the rest of us can get back to work?'

The policewoman laughed. 'Sorry. No. All this is for something incredibly complex to do with rate fixing and insider trading and something called "short selling". So far as I can make out this whole industry invents money, and then some clever buggers come up with ways of pocketing the invented money. I don't understand half of it, but I have forensic accountants who promise they do.' She nodded at Cora's computer screen. 'Mr Smith is just a tiny little fish who got caught in the net.' She smiled. 'Good old-fashioned thieving though. I understand that.'

'So I'm in the clear?'

The officer nodded. 'For this at least.'

Relief flooded through Cora. It was going to be okay. So they'd lost a morning's work, but she could still hit her targets. 'So when can we get back to work?'

The policewoman shrugged. 'Well we should be out of here in a couple of days, but I don't know.'

Cora was confused. 'But you said we were in the clear?'

The woman at least had the grace to look sympathetic. 'Did you watch the news the day Lehman Brothers went bust?'

Of course Cora had watched the news. She remembered seeing the hordes of workers, personal possessions in boxes, standing purposeless on the pavement outside their office. She nodded.

The policewoman stood up. 'Well this is going to be worse.'

Cora jumped into her seat and typed and clicked her way to the company's current share price. It was in freefall. She closed her eyes for second. This wasn't part of the plan. The plan was simple. She'd come to London and make her fortune. She had the good job. She had the nice apartment. She opened her eyes again. She'd taken her last four bonus payments in shares. As she stared at the screen their value dwindled down to next to nothing.

'Cora!'

Denise yelled at her from the outer office. Cora followed her down the corridor and into the break room, where staff from across the floor were staring up at the TV screen bolted to the wall showing one of the twenty-four hour news channels. The reporter was standing in the street right outside, on a patch of pavement that Cora walked across at least twice a day, every single day. Normally the break room was a bustle of gossip and conversation. Today it was full of people, silent, apart from the reporter on the screen.

'... the collapse of London Fairweather will send new shockwaves through the financial industry and the wider economy, which many commentators believed had weathered the worst of the storm. The immediate shock, of course, will be to the staff here at London Fairweather's headquarters. It is our understanding that many of them came into work this morning with no idea of the problems facing the company.' The reporter paused. 'And we're now being told that London Fairweather has formally ceased trading. No great surprise for those of you who've been watching this story unfold throughout the morning. Back to the studio for more on that announcement.'

Cora watched in silence as the coverage shifted to the studio and the station's business editor confirmed that the company had declared bankruptcy leading to the loss of nearly two thousand jobs. So that was that. She was one amongst the two thousand. Another tiny fish caught up in a big old net. She wasn't the great all-conquering Cora who'd come to London and made her own way in the world. She was an afterthought, one two thousandth of a much bigger picture.

Across town, in a much less palatial corner of the banking world, Liam Carr leant back in his seat and skimmed through the headlines on his phone. Some investment bank in the city had gone bust, which apparently was a bad thing. Liam scrolled down to the sports news.

'Mr Carr?' The woman standing in front of him was wearing a dark blue polyester uniform with one of those scarves tied at the neck that you only ever saw on bank clerks and flight attendants. 'Would you like to come through?'

Liam followed her through some doors at the back of the branch, and into a partitioned office.

'I understand you want some investment advice.'

Liam shook his head. 'Not really.'

The woman frowned. 'My colleague was under the impression that you had a ...' She paused. 'A significant amount to invest.'

'I just want to pay it in.' He uncrumpled the cheque and pushed it across the table. He'd meant to pay it into the bank the day he got it, and then the next day, and then definitely at the weekend, and then absolutely, positively next week. But next week had turned into the week after and then the week after that, and somehow he'd never quite got beyond taking the banker's draft out of his wallet and staring at it.

'Er ... into your current account?'

Liam nodded. Of course into his current account. It was the only account he had, the only account he'd ever had, opened for him by Mama Lou. Opened on his sixteenth birthday with fifteen pounds and a promise of twenty pounds more at Christmas, if he managed to keep hold of the original amount for the week between the two dates. He hadn't, of course, but he'd kept the account and overall, he thought, he'd just about been in the black more than the red over the years.

'People don't normally hold this amount of money in a current account.'

Of course they didn't. In Liam's experience people didn't normally have that sort of money.

'Some sort of investment package really would be more efficient.'

Liam raised an eyebrow. 'More efficient?'

'Make you a better return.'

Liam was aware that he was looking blank.

The woman sighed. 'Make you more money.'

The laugh bubbled up from his gut and shook his whole body. He swallowed hard. 'I think I've got enough money.'

Two hours later after a lengthy discussion with supervisors and branch managers, and one slightly weary threat to take his business elsewhere, it was agreed that Liam could pay his twelve million pounds into an instant access savings account. He stuffed the paperwork into his rucksack as he stood up to leave. The bank woman pushed her business card across the table towards him. 'I've popped my mobile number on there too.' He glanced at her face. She was peering at him under her eyelashes. 'Use it anytime.'

He stuffed the card into his bag as well. Normally he'd be chuffed with that. She was attractive. A bit high-maintenance looking for Liam's usual tastes. Most of his girlfriends had been drama students, or dancers, or actors. There tended to be a lot of leggings and loose fitting tops, of the sort that would allow the wearer to pretend to be a bird or a giant or a tree at short notice. The bank woman was rather more primped and preened, but normally he wasn't the sort to look a gift horse in the mouth. If a woman offered her number, he would usually call. He didn't think he would this time. He couldn't escape the feeling that the glint in her eyes was more to do with pound signs than Liam himself. She was, he suspected, hoping to get a call from 'the guy who paid twelve million pounds into his account.' Real Liam would only be a disappointment.

He strolled across the street to a coffee shop, bought himself an Americano and slumped into a corner sofa. Five weeks. Five weeks since the cheque had first started burning its hole in his life, and he hadn't done a thing about it. He hadn't told his housemates. He hadn't told his colleagues. He hadn't told his agent. He'd gone into work every day that he was needed, done script read-throughs and recordings. He'd taped interviews for three different local stations about his upcoming storylines on *Lamplugh and Sons*, Radio 2's long-running soap on which he'd played the youngest Lamplugh son pretty much since drama school. In short, he'd carried on as normal.

Liam sipped his coffee, grimacing as it burnt his tongue. Why wasn't he behaving like he should? He knew exactly what a thirty-year-old guy with no responsibilities and twelve million pounds in the bank should be doing. He should be out spending it. Casinos. Holidays. Beautiful women and fast cars. Fast women and beautiful cars. The world was Liam's oyster, but he was still travelling on his Oyster travelcard. He closed his eyes. He remembered that

Christmas when he was sixteen, and Mama Lou had refused to give him the extra money for his new bank account because he hadn't stuck to their agreement. 'Promises have to be kept,' she'd told him. 'Rewards have to be earned.'

And this one wasn't earned. The more he thought about it the more he concluded that there were only two options. Either the money had been left to him by mistake, or it had been left to him by somebody who thought he was the right person to inherit their fortune, and fortunes passed, in the usual order of things, from father to son.

Liam felt his hand clench around his cup. He'd never had a father. So far as he was aware, Catherine hadn't even known for sure who he was, but what if that wasn't true? What if he had a dad out there somewhere, a dad who'd thought enough of him to leave him enough money to make the rest of his life a bed of roses, but not enough to pick up a phone? How would he find out something like that? The solicitor had been clear that the bequest was confidential. In *Lamplugh and Sons* his character would probably hire a private detective. Characters were forever hiring private detectives in soapland. He shook his head. He'd never been able to afford anything like that. Not until now.

# Chapter Four

## December

Cora paused at the entrance to the tiny break room. Chris was already stashing his lunch in the fridge. It had only been a week, but already coming here was starting to feel like coming home. She caught herself smiling at the idea. 'How was your Sunday?'

Chris looked up and shook his head. 'I have no idea. I slept til about half four. It's knackering being Santa.'

A sharp cough from the doorway startled them both to attention. Mrs Atkins stomped over the threshold. 'At Golding's we do not use the S-word, Mr Carr.'

Cora could hear Chris fighting to suppress a laugh. She kept her eyes fixed on the floor as he managed to splutter an apology.

'Very good.' Mrs Atkins surveyed her Rudolph and Father Christmas. 'Now I do like to do a little review with all our new festive characters at the start of week two, just to nip any problems in the bud. Mr Carr if you wouldn't mind waiting in the grotto.'

Chris lumbered out and Cora found herself alone with Mrs Atkins. 'Miss Strachan, I have had reports.'

Her tone brooked no possible misunderstanding that the reports were good. Cora frowned. She was stuck being Rudolph but she'd been the best Rudolph she could possibly be. She needed this job too much to be half-hearted. 'Reports?'

'I understand that at least one five year old was given a pre-school age gift on Saturday?'

Cora kept her gaze fixed to the floor. 'Sorry Mrs Atkins.'

'Sorry is easy Miss Strachan. Action is what counts. Consider this your first and last warning. I shall move you to a junior elf role if I have to.'

Cora doubted that. Both the junior elves were pushing five foot ten. There was no way either of them would fit into the tiny Rudolph leotard. 'Yes Mrs Atkins. It won't happen again.' Cora heard herself parroting the words like a school girl caught out by a teacher. *Yes Mrs Atkins. Sorry Mrs Atkins. Three bags full Mrs Atkins.* She bit her lip.

'Very good. Apart from that you're punctual and well turned out. You're not caked in make-up like some of these girls.'

Cora frowned. Her face was covered in brown pan stick and the tip of her nose and the buds of her cheeks were marked out in scarlet. Apparently Mrs Atkins was sufficiently in thrall to the Christmas magic that she thought that this was Cora's actual face. 'Thank you, Mrs Atkins.'

'Good. Now if you could wait here. I'll talk to Mr Carr in the grotto.'

Cora nodded. She leant on the radiator in the tiny room and folded her arms across her body. *Mr Carr.* Inside her head a penny started to drop but didn't quite hit the ground. She kicked one brown bootie against the other in frustration. She knew she recognised his face from somewhere. And the story about the money rang a bell too. And something about the shape of his nose and the colour of his eyes, but it was all but impossible to get an idea what he looked like with his hair always hidden under hat and wig, and wobbly belly strapped to his front. She was going to have to wait for the end of the story to find out. And she had made an agreement. In here, she was Rudy and he was Chris. It was stupid, but it was giving her the confidence to talk about her horrible year, and it was a lot cheaper than therapy.

Chris ambled into the break room from the grotto. 'Well apparently my Ho, ho, ho lacks gusto.'

Cora furrowed her brow. 'I think you have a delightful Ho, ho, ho.'

He grinned. 'Thanks. It's good someone appreciates my efforts.'

Cora watched him fiddling with his beard. 'Do I know you from somewhere? Y'know somewhere before here?'

'No.' The answer was instant but his eyes dropped straight to the floor. 'Don't think so.'

She regretted the question as soon as it was asked. He obviously had his reasons for wanting to be someone else. And who was she to judge? 'Okay. So what happens next in the story?'

Liam shook his head. 'You have to wait til lunchtime.'

'Give me a clue.'

'Okay. It involves a private detective.'

'I'm intrigued.'

'Good.' He was smiling. Cora could barely see his lips under the mass of white beard, but his eyes glinted. 'Roll on lunchtime.'

## March, earlier in the year

Another day. Another faceless office. This one lacked the elegance of Daley, Callendar & Associates, but made up for the absence of grandeur with a cheerful embracing of all things MDF. Across the desk from Liam a slightly pink-faced middle-aged woman scrolled down her computer screen. Liam had to admit that he was disappointed. From his email contact with Sam Bartolotti, he'd been picturing a short, wiry Italian-American guy, complete with Private Investigator uniform of trench coat and trilby. The real-life Sam Bartolotti was a slightly dumpy woman in her mid-fifties, who spoke with the noticeable remnants of a Welsh accent.

'So now Mr Carr, you've got yourself rather a nice little problem, haven't you?'

Liam shrugged. 'I just want to know where it came from.'

The investigator nodded. 'And I think I can help you there.' She paused. 'Cup of tea?'

Liam shook his head.

'Right.' Sam looked around the desk for a second. 'Kit Kat? Pink wafer biscuit?'

'No.' Liam heard the tension in his own voice and forced himself to breathe. 'Thank you. I'd just like to know what you've found out.'

'Okay.' The woman stared at her screen. 'Well I've identified who left the bequest. That was relatively straightforward.'

Liam desperately wanted to hear what she knew, but for a second more general curiosity won out. 'How? Sorry. It's just …' He glanced across the desk at the plain woman in her tunic top over leggings and sensible boots. 'How do you find that sort of thing out?'

Sam laughed. 'Oh my dear. Middle-aged women are invisible. We can pass the time of day with anyone anywhere and nobody bats an eyelid. Twenty minutes after you leave this office you won't even be able to describe me.' She smiled. 'Which is fine. It's a good career to be forgettable in.'

Liam nodded. It made sense. 'So what did you find out?'

'Well, a name essentially. Robert Alexander Grey. He was an American businessman. Bit of a Howard Hughes type from what I can make out. Eccentric, reclusive, incredibly private, but rich, filthy, filthy rich. What he left you was only a fraction of his estate.'

Robert Grey. Liam ran the name through his head. No bells rang. 'But why leave any of it to me?'

'You're sure you never knew him? Grey isn't a family name?'

Liam shrugged. 'I never knew my father. It could be, I guess.'

Sam nodded. 'Well I'm afraid the name's all I've got for

you. I couldn't get a full copy of the will. The girl at the solicitors was putting her neck on the line letting me peek at the name.'

Liam swallowed. He was disappointed not to have a complete answer, but a name was something, and it was a lot more than he'd had before. 'That's fine.'

'I do have a few more details for you. His date of birth. Known addresses. Some college stuff from years back. I'll print them out.'

Ten minutes later, Liam leant on the wall outside the office and skimmed through the details Sam had provided. Apart from not being able to come up with a reason for Mr Grey's generosity, she'd been impressively thorough. Robert Alexander Grey, he learnt, had been born on the 4th August 1931, and died in 2013, three days short of his eighty-second birthday. His initial wealth had been inherited from his grandfather but Robert had invested wisely, if somewhat eclectically, and by the time of his death was rumoured to be a billionaire. It really did look as though Liam's twelve million was small change.

So far he'd still barely touched the money. Sam's services had cost him a few hundred quid, but that hadn't made much of a dent on his new bank balance. He'd half suggested that he might buy a new PlayStation for the living room, but his housemate had asked how he could afford it and he'd abandoned the idea. The bottom line remained the same. It didn't feel like his money. The fact that it had been left by a total stranger didn't change that. In fact it made things worse.

Liam glanced at his watch. 11 a.m. He was only in a couple of scenes scheduled for today so he didn't have to be at work until two. Technically he should still be doing work. He had scripts he'd promised his agent he'd look at, and he definitely would, but he needed to get this sorted out first. He pulled his phone out of his pocket and scrolled through the numbers until he found what he was looking for and hit dial. He negotiated with the switchboard to be put through and waited.

'Philip Daley speaking.'

Liam took a breath. 'Mr Daley, it's Liam Carr. I saw you a couple of months ago about an inheritance.'

There was a pause at the end of the line. When the conversation resumed Mr Daley's tone was suddenly warmer. Twelve million pounds could do that. 'Mr Carr, what can I do for you?'

Liam swallowed. Even in his head the decision sounded insane, but it was the only right thing to do. 'It's about the money.'

'Yes?'

'I want to give it back.'

# Chapter Five

## December

'You're insane.'

Liam shrugged and sipped his cup of tea. Rudy and he had got into a nice rhythm at lunchtimes. She would show the last child of the morning out. He'd have the kettle on by the time she got back. They were working their way through the selection of poor orphan mugs in the cupboard, all slightly chipped, and presumably abandoned by past employees long since moved on. The second day Rudy had got the same two mugs down as the day before, but Liam had switched them. Somehow the idea of leaving mugs unused and unloved on the shelf made him melancholy.

'You tried to give it back.'

Liam nodded. 'My friend did.'

'To a dead person.'

Liam nodded again. 'Apparently you can't do that.'

Rudy shook her head. 'No.'

Liam was aware that he was telling her details of his story that nobody else knew, even though the whole world thought they knew it all. He glanced around the small, cold room. The bleakness of the room, the anonymity of the costume and the fact that he was talking to a total stranger – a total stranger who hadn't officially told him her real name – gave the whole thing the air of a confessional. Only this was better than confession. This worked both ways. He grinned. 'So what about you?'

'What?'

'We're up to March. What were you doing?'

'Well *I* wasn't doing anything.'

Liam shook his head. 'Okay. What was *your friend* Cora doing?'

Rudy glanced at the clock. 'No time.'

'Tomorrow?'

She nodded. 'Tomorrow.'

## March, earlier in the year

In a very nice apartment on the top floor of a very nice building on the South Bank, Cora fastened her very nice blouse and looked in the mirror. Today would be the day. Three weeks after she'd found herself unceremoniously unemployed. Fourteen application forms. Three interviews. Five recruitment agencies. Today recruitment agency number six would come through for her. It was what she had to believe.

Her landline rang. Cora paused. It would be someone trying to sell her something. Unless ... there was still one interview from the week before she hadn't officially heard back from. She picked up the phone. 'Cora Strachan speaking.'

'Cora, love ...' Her mother's voice purred down the line. Cora closed her eyes. '... you never pick up your mobile any more.'

It was partly true. Cora had stopped picking up her mobile to her parents. Since she moved to London, phone calls and visits home had been for one purpose only: to make sure her parents knew how well she was doing without their help. Cora knew she'd been very lucky. She was told it often enough. She'd grown up never wanting for anything, but also never having to earn anything. At seventeen she'd committed what had felt like the ultimate act of rebellion when she'd married the farm boy from the next plot over. Four years living with Sean and his family had made her realise that she hadn't rebelled at all. She'd simply run away. Sean's parents worked every moment of the day, and as soon as they were old enough, their children were expected to follow suit. Everything the family had was the product of their own hard work. Cora was the much-adored cuckoo in the nest, living in their home but never being treated as less than an honoured guest. She'd tried to chip in but her efforts were met with the gratitude afforded to an unexpected kindness, not the indifference offered to real members of the tribe.

'Cora, are you there?'

Cora dragged her attention back to the phone call. 'Yeah. Sorry. I'm just in a bit of a rush.'

'Where to?'

Cora paused. Last time she'd spoken to her parents she'd had to admit that she'd lost her job. It had been all over the six o'clock news so she could hardly pretend everything was going swimmingly at the bank. She'd been resolutely upbeat though. Confident she'd have a new job within days. And that was still true. She'd just been unlucky so far. 'A meeting,' she hedged.

'For work?'

'Mmmmm.' *Mmmmm* couldn't be lying could it? And the meeting was for work – trying to find work at least.

'Oh that's wonderful. I told your father you'd be back on your feet in no time.' Her mother's voice broke into a chuckle. 'And he said you'd be back here with your tail between your legs!'

Cora's stomach clenched. That would be what everyone was expecting. Spoilt Cora went to London and ended up back home licking her wounds. That was not going to happen. She laughed, slightly too much, down the phone. 'No! No! Everything's fine here.'

'So ...'

'Anyway I'd better go. Don't want to be late.'

'But ...'

'Talk soon. Bye!' Cora slammed the phone back onto the cradle, as if sheer force would make it less likely to ring again. *Mmmmmm* and *Everything's fine* – she definitely hadn't lied. It wasn't her fault if people made assumptions.

She really was risking being late though. She dashed out of the flat and towards the tube, where she swiped her hated Oyster travelcard. The days of black cabs weren't over, she told herself, simply on hold until she got over this minor hiccup. She'd found work before in the depths of the recession; it would be easier this time around. It was just a question of finding the right job.

Today's agency was on the Shepherds Bush Road, a long way from the sleek offices of the square mile or the stately Georgian buildings she'd been visiting up until now. Cora pushed the thought out of her mind and forced herself to think positive. Today could very easily be the day. The building itself did little to inspire, a side door next to a newsagent with a Perspex sign wonkily stuck above it. *Careers Now* it confidently proclaimed which was definitely what Cora needed. She pushed the door open and climbed the stairs.

The actual office was nicer than the signage had suggested. There were three low seats for waiting clients at the entrance to an open plan office housing seven desks. Cora approached the nearest desk, staffed by a pasty teenager, and held out her hand confidently. 'Hi. I've got an appointment.'

The boy nodded. 'Name?'

'Cora Strachan.'

He glanced around the room until his gaze alighted on a colleague who didn't look too busy. He shrugged. 'You can like see Patrick then.' The youth pointed to a desk two down on the window side of the room. 'Over there innit.'

Cora followed the direction of the pointing finger and found herself standing in front of a man whose name badge proclaimed him to be Patrick, and also *here to help*. He didn't look up. Cora cleared her throat. No response. She peered at Patrick. Nice shirt, beautifully pressed. A flash of a silver watch at his wrist. Clean shaven. Well-groomed hair. He glanced up. Dark, chocolate-brown eyes, and a flash of brilliant white teeth when he smiled. Wow. Cora felt her knees quiver, and her heartbeat hasten. She put a hand on the back of the chair in front of her to steady herself. This was a business meeting. She was supposed to be coming across as professional and in control.

'Have a seat.'

Oh no. He was Scottish. Cora had always had a weakness for the accent of her homeland. She sat down and swallowed hard to moisten her suddenly dry mouth. 'Thank you.'

The smile flashed back onto his face. 'A Scot? Whereabouts are you from?'

Cora caught herself cocking her head and twirling a strand of hair. She dropped her hand and sat up straight. *This was a business meeting.* 'Tiny village. You wouldn't know it. Finbarr.'

She thought she caught the merest hint of a pause before he shook his head. 'Edinburgh boy I'm afraid. So, erm ... let's get started. Did you bring a CV?'

Cora pulled the repeatedly tweaked and toiled over document from her bag and handed it over.

'So you're Cora? Cora Strachan?'

She nodded.

Was that another tiny hint of a pause? 'Great.' He scanned through her CV and she saw an eyebrow shoot up. 'London Fairweather?'

She nodded. The bank where she'd made her career was still front page news. She was starting to wonder if employers thought she was toxic by association.

'Sorry. That must have been rough.'

Cora was surprised. She'd just got on with things. Old job fell apart, so she'd set out to look for a new one. She hadn't allowed herself to dwell on how unfair the whole thing was. 'I hadn't really thought about it.'

He glanced at her CV. 'But it says here that you're thoughtful and detail-oriented?'

Cora ruffled. 'Well I am thoughtful. I meant ...' She glanced into his face. He was grinning. She stopped and smiled back. Neither of them looked away.

Eventually he blinked. 'Well you look great.' He stopped and held up the CV. 'I mean on paper. You look great on paper. Not that you don't look great in real ...' He stopped again and closed his eyes. Cora watched as he opened them again, taking a deep breath. 'I'm going to stop talking now.'

Cora dropped her chin and giggled slightly. 'It's okay.' Were they flirting? Cora didn't generally do much accidental flirting. She did meeting appropriate, professional men who had been carefully screened either online or by mutual acquaintances, and it had been said that her dating conversation technique was indistinguishable from her recruitment interviewing technique, but Cora was a firm believer in knowing where she stood. She hadn't acted on romantic impulse since Sean, and if she was honest with herself, getting married at seventeen had had more to do with the romance of running away from her parents than the romance of falling in love. She returned her gaze to the man across the desk. Normally her dating choices were carefully considered, but here she was inadvertently affecting a girlish giggle for a total stranger. He was gorgeous, but there was also something about his clean-cut good looks and frequent smile that Cora read as trustworthy. Someone trustworthy might be a refreshing change, given her recent employment history. She watched his lips, and forced herself to focus on what he was saying.

'So, I'm sure we can find something to keep you busy.'

Cora felt her cheeks reddening. She could imagine a good number of ways in which Patrick could keep her busy. Of course that wasn't what he meant. He was a recruitment consultant. She was just another client. A flash of something metallic caught her eye as he shuffled the papers on his desk. A wedding ring. Obviously. She took a deep breath, and tried again to focus on what he was saying.

'I mean you're really well qualified. I'll need to make some calls though. I don't think I have anything on the books today.'

Cora's heart dropped. So that was that. He would make positive noises, like everyone she'd sat across a desk from in the last few weeks had, and then she'd never hear from him again. 'You don't have anything?'

He shrugged. 'I've lots of jobs, but nothing that really matches your skills.'

'I could branch out.'

He laughed. 'Well, if you were prepared to consider getting your fork lift licence?'

Cora sighed.

'Look, what if we schedule a meeting in a couple of weeks? I'll make some calls, put some feelers out, and I'm sure I'll have some options for you by then. It's a really fast moving market at the moment. We work with some absolutely blue chip companies. I promise – I bet something fantastic is just around the corner.'

Cora nodded. Another couple of weeks felt like an age, but it was the best she was going to get. They set up a date and time, and Cora stood up. Patrick leant across the desk to shake her hand. 'Thank you Cora. It was intriguing to meet you.'

Intriguing? Maybe she hadn't lost her romance radar after all. Maybe this was what flirting felt like. She pulled the appointment card out of her pocket. Patrick Howard. The delectable Patrick Howard. Stop that. The married Patrick Howard, who would end his day by sauntering off home to the, presumably, equally delectable Mrs Howard and possibly a whole brood of tiny Howards. Cora stuffed the card in her bag and set off for home. Alone.

# Chapter Six

## December

Chris sipped his mug of tea. 'Why did she lie to her parents?'

Cora folded her arms across her costumed chest. 'Who?'

'Your friend in the story. Why didn't she tell them she was still unemployed?'

Cora paused. Why hadn't she? It wasn't that they weren't supportive exactly, it was more that she could live without their sort of support. 'I think she wanted to prove that she wasn't their little princess, you know. Prove she could do something for herself.'

Chris nodded. 'That makes sense, I guess.'

'I mean she could have run away back home, and they would have housed and fed and clothed her, but it would have been like confirming that all she was really good for was being a good little daughter or a nice little wife.'

'And my friend could have just spent the money.'

'Exactly, but he didn't earn it.'

He paused. 'Unlike the pittance we're getting paid to do this. We're earning every last penny of this.'

Cora grinned and checked the clock. 'Still got time for another cup of tea though.'

She stood up and flicked the switch on the kettle.

'You're smiling.'

'What?'

He was watching her with the hint of a smirk peeking through his beard. 'You were smiling.'

Cora pulled a face. 'Oh God. All the Christmas stuff must be getting to me.'

He laughed. 'Do you think we're institutionalised?'

'What do you mean?'

'You. Me. The kids. The presents. The poxy little kitchen.

That's all there is in my world. I'm going to need therapy in January just to go out of the house.'

Cora laughed but she felt a shiver down her spine. January. It was only two weeks until Christmas, and then this would be over. No more Rudy. No more Chris. No more telling each other stories. She was in a bubble, but it was a bubble that was about to pop.

She turned her attention back to her task, dropping fresh tea bags into mugs and lifting the kettle off its stand. As she poured Chris's tea, her grip slipped on the handle. Cora squealed as boiling water splashed across her free hand. The skin flushed red. There was a moment of quiet and still inside Cora's head, and then the pain rushed in in a hot searing wave. She heard herself gasp.

Chris reached from behind her, prised the kettle from her fingers, and put it safely back on its stand. 'Come on.'

His voice pulled her back into reality. He pressed gently on the small of her back and guided her to the sink. She let him lean around her and turn on the cold tap. 'Hand under the water.'

She did as she was told, letting the cold stream run over the reddening skin. Stupid Cora. She wasn't normally clumsy. Normally she liked to have everything under control. She caught Chris's eye. 'Sorry about this.'

He shook his head. 'It was just an accident.' He reached towards her. 'Can I?'

She nodded.

He took her fingers in his and peered at the burn. 'It doesn't look too bad.'

Cora followed his gaze. She wasn't sure when anyone had last held her hand. Her most recent ex hadn't really been one for great public displays of affection. She was mesmerised for a second by the way the light caught the tiny blond hairs on the back of Chris's hand. She reminded herself to breathe.

He'd said something hadn't he? That must mean it was her turn to talk. She stared at their interlocked fingers. She wasn't quite sure she could remember how to make words.

'Are you two coming?' The Chief Elf's voice rang around the door to the kitchen.

Chris dropped her fingers and stepped back. 'Sorry.' He gestured towards the sink. 'Just doing a little bit of first aid.'

The Chief Elf bustled efficiently towards Cora and peered at the burn. 'There'll be cream in the first aid kit. Excuse me.' Cora stepped to one side to allow her to flip open the cupboard under the sink and pull out a first aid box. She let the helpful elf dry her damp skin and rub ointment onto it. 'There you go.'

'Thanks.' Cora glanced at Chris. He'd put his beard on, but she could feel his watchful blue eyes on her. There had been more than just friendly concern in those eyes when he'd held her hand so gently under the cold water. A fizz of anticipation bubbled up inside Cora. She had to ignore it. Chris was a nice guy. When he heard the rest of her story there was no way he'd want anything to do with her. And he'd be right. However hard she tried to do her best, Cora always seemed to hurt good people. Chris would be better off without her.

### April, earlier in the year

This was not how things were supposed to be going. Six weeks. Forty-three days to be exact. That's how long Cora had been unemployed. Her healthy savings were dwindling at an alarming rate. Her mortgage payments were huge. She realised that she'd never really thought about how huge. She'd bought her flat seven years ago for an obscene sum that was still only a fraction of what it would have cost her just six months earlier. She remembered her glee at the bargain, accompanied by only the vaguest awareness that the bottom falling out of the housing market wasn't only a boon for her, but a catastrophe for others. She also remembered her absolute cast iron confidence that it was a catastrophe that would never befall somebody like her.

She looked in the mirror. Today was her follow-up appointment with the dishy recruitment consultant on the Shepherd's Bush Road. She smoothed down her suit, and waited for the positive, determined thoughts she was so used to living by to pop into her head. It didn't happen. She set out for her meeting resigned to another disappointment, secretly looking forward to getting home again and back into her pyjamas, rather than feeling fired up for the inevitable success in front of her. Back in February every meeting had been an opportunity, every interview full of possibility. Two months on they were trials to be endured before the inevitable monotony of life at home under the duvet could resume.

Her appointment was at nine, and Cora arrived early. She made her way along the street to the entrance next to the newsagent, and stopped. Patrick was standing on the pavement, staring at the door. She stepped towards him. 'Am I too early?'

His head turned slowly, as if processing her presence and the question, before turning back towards the door. 'No. You're too late.'

She followed his gaze. A scruffy piece of A4 had been stuck to the door. She read the words scrawled across it in marker pen. *Business in administration.* 'What?'

Patrick turned and started to walk away from her. Cora wasn't having that. She set off after him. 'Wait! We've got an appointment.'

Patrick turned abruptly and ran past Cora towards the door. He crashed into it, shoulder first, before staggering back wincing in pain. 'Well that looks easier in films.'

'What are you doing?'

'My mug's in there. And there's a Snickers in my desk drawer. They're not having my sodding Snickers.'

Patrick marched away from the door and took another run. This time the door seemed to give a little, but remained defiantly closed.

Cora watched open-mouthed. She remembered the last day at London Fairweather. Collecting what she could from her desk, and having to let some jumped up little constable check through it before she could leave. Sneaking down the back stairs and out of the fire escape with Denise and Colin, who had, she remembered, promised faithfully to keep in touch. She'd not heard a word from either of them. She remembered the indignity of skulking away from the job she'd worked so hard to get, and she started to feel something new. Not her usual determination to make the best of things. Not her growing resignation to her hopeless situation. This feeling was darker, stronger, different from what she'd been dealing with so far. Without thinking, Cora kicked off her shoes and, gripping one tightly in each hand, she lined herself up with the offending door. 'Get out of my way.'

'What are you doing?'

Cora ran across the pavement, her scream of rage ripping the air, and crashed into the door. She felt it shift, and she forced her whole body weight against it. The door didn't want to open, but the door wasn't channelling Cora's fury with the world. She felt it shift again, almost imperceptibly under her weight, and then everything happened at once. A creaking noise turned into a crack and then a crash, as the door lost the fight and collapsed inwards. Cora fell into the building with it, hitting the floor with her knee, then hip, and finally hand.

She lay on the floor at the foot of the stairwell, breath rushing in and out of her lungs. She looked up and found herself staring into dark chocolate eyes. 'What are you doing?'

She had no idea, but whatever it was it was exhilarating. She shrugged. 'I fancied a bit of Snickers.'

She let Patrick lean forward and pull her to her feet. 'Well come on then.'

The upstairs office was deserted. Patrick flicked the light switch, but nothing came on. He shook his head. 'Disconnected?'

Cora followed him over to his desk. 'So what happened?'

He shrugged. 'I've been off. This was my first day back.'

'So nobody let you know?'

He stopped rummaging through his drawer and turned towards her. So far he'd seemed angry, but now Cora saw something new. He closed his eyes for a second and rubbed his hand across his face. 'What do you think?'

She remembered the shock she'd felt the last day at London Fairweather, but at least she'd had people around her who were in the same rapidly sinking boat. 'I'm sorry.'

He turned his attention back to the desk. 'Bad news.'

'More bad news?'

'It looks like someone nicked my Snickers while I was away.'

Cora giggled. It was ridiculous. There was nothing to laugh at. She took a deep breath. This was his life, she reminded herself. A better person than her would be offering comfort. She glanced around the deserted office. There wasn't much comfort to be had. 'Look at it this way. If you'd come in on a normal day and found that, it would have seemed like a much, much bigger deal.'

'Fair point.' He picked up a Snoopy mug from the desk. 'Well then ...'

They drifted into silence. Neither of them had any reason to hang around but, Cora realised, neither of them had anywhere else to go either. 'What are you going to do now?'

He looked around the abandoned office. 'I have no idea.'

'Guess you're probably heading home?'

She saw his face tighten for a second, before he broke into a smile. 'Nah. Let's do something.'

'What?'

'Let's do something. Go somewhere.'

Cora laughed. 'Go where?'

He shrugged. 'Let's go to the beach.'

Cora wasn't sure how to respond. He grinned at her. Something inside Cora remembered what it felt like to be seventeen and sneaking out of her parents' house to meet her boyfriend. It was a silly thought. She wasn't that girl any more.

'Clacton. We'll go to Clacton. Come on. It'll be a laugh. I went there last year with ...' his voice tailed off.

'Who with?'

He shook his head. 'It doesn't matter.'

Cora stared at Patrick, and shifted her gaze to his left hand. No ring. He'd definitely been wearing one last time they'd met. 'You're not wearing your wedding ring.'

He peered at his hand, as if he was surprised at its nakedness. 'No. I'm not.'

Okay. So he wasn't wearing his wedding ring any more, and she knew he'd had some time off work – it didn't take Einstein to put two and two together. 'You broke up?'

He didn't reply.

'It's okay. I'm divorced. I know what it's like.' Did she know what it was like? In her head she'd left her marriage behind when she moved to London. She'd left Sean to deal with the fall out. His family. Her family. She'd moved away and moved on.

'Yeah.' He nodded. 'It's been really tough.'

A broken marriage. A career meltdown. Nowhere else to go. She watched Patrick as he surveyed his crumbled professional life. Was it possible? In the midst of a truly horrible few months, could she really have stumbled upon a kindred spirit? She glanced around the empty office. 'And now all this?'

He laughed, just slightly. 'I don't want to think about it. Let's have one day of living in the moment.'

'In Clacton?'

'Absolutely. Living in the moment in Clacton.' He held his hand out towards her. 'Are you in?'

Cora paused. She needed to get on with things. She needed to call a whole new set of recruitment agents, redo her CV, trawl the internet for more jobs to apply for. She looked up. Patrick's eyes danced and glinted in front of her. She stepped forward and took his hand. A shiver ran up her arm and down her back as they touched, and then they were moving. She found herself skipping and clattering in her heels, trying to keep up with him as he darted down the stairs and out into the street. They dodged between shoppers and commuters and into the tube station. On the platform they finally stopped. Patrick kept her hand clasped tight in his. Suddenly his free arm wrapped around her waist.

'What are you doing?'

He didn't reply, but bent his head towards hers. Instinctively, she raised her lips towards him. Everything faded away, like no kiss Cora remembered before. Just for a second the kiss was all there was, and then he pulled away.

'Seriously, what are you doing?'

'Living in the moment.'

A tube ride later, they boarded the train to Clacton, fingers entwined around each other, giggling like teenagers.

'Is this seat taken?'

Liam leant over the seat opposite them, across the table, and gestured to the empty space.

# Chapter Seven

## December

'That's not what happened.' Rudy wrinkled her painted red nose.

'What?'

'They weren't on the same train.'

Liam grinned. 'They might have been.'

'I'd have remembered ...' she tailed off, apparently recognising that she was beaten.

'But you weren't there! Did "your friend" definitely tell you that there wasn't a devastatingly handsome man opposite her on the train?'

Rudy giggled. 'Devastatingly handsome?'

He held her gaze. 'Sure. Anyway, my friend went to Clacton in April too, and he definitely told me there was a really nauseating couple opposite him.'

'Don't push your luck.'

Liam laughed. 'I promise you, when they make a movie of all this they'll be on the same train, and the camera will linger for a second over the near-miss.' Liam could picture it in his head. It would be one of those cute moments where the hero and heroine don't quite meet, but the audience know that everything is going to be all right in the end.

Rudy shook her head. 'Why would they make a movie of it?'

Liam froze. Of course this wasn't the plot of a film. At some point she was going to recognise him, and then she'd run a mile. Even if she didn't, what did it matter? From what he was hearing it sounded like there was another guy well and truly in the picture. He dropped his chin to his chest, so she wouldn't see the disappointment on his face.

Across the table, Rudy rolled her eyes. 'Just get on with the story.'

## April, earlier in the year

Liam slung his rucksack onto the overhead shelf and settled into the seat, trying not to bash his knees against the woman opposite. The couple were engrossed in one another. He turned his gaze out of the window, stuck his headphones in his ears, and tried to let his thoughts drift away.

They wound their way out of the capital, towards the coast. Normally Liam liked train journeys. They were time to simply let his mind wander as the scenery scrolled by. Today he was on edge. The thought he'd been rolling around and around in his head was now lodged firmly front and centre. Robert Grey. Who on earth was Robert Grey?

He jumped off the train at Clacton, behind the nauseating, canoodling couple he'd been stuck opposite for the whole journey. He grabbed a cab, and sat back for the last few minutes of the journey to Auntie Val's bungalow on the edge of town.

Walking up the driveway was an eleven step journey back in time. Auntie Val was Mama Lou's younger sister, a carbon copy of her sibling. Big, brassy and overflowing with affection for the waifs and strays that made up Lou's constantly evolving household. The door was open before he'd had chance to ring the bell, and Liam found himself enveloped in hugs, kisses and Val's expansive bosom. He followed her cheerful stream of chat about how grown-up he was, and how proud of him she was, and how very much prouder Mama Lou would have been, into the kitchen, and took a seat at the well-worn table in the middle of the room. Tea was offered, refused and brought anyway, along with biscuits and homemade fruit cake. The kitchen was exactly how he remembered it, and for a second he felt bad. Since

Mama Lou had died he hadn't been home to see Val half as often as he ought. He'd do better in future, he promised himself.

Eventually Val was satisfied that her guest was sufficiently fed and watered and filled in on the local gossip, and she took a seat opposite him. 'So what brings you all this way, Liam?'

'I inherited some money.'

Val raised one eyebrow. 'I see. And who might that be from?'

Liam sighed. 'I was hoping you might be able to help me with that.'

He pulled the printout the private investigator had given him from his rucksack and pushed it across the table. 'This guy. Robert Grey.'

Val's brow furrowed.

'Did you know him?'

His aunt didn't reply. She pulled her reading glasses from the top of her head on to her nose, and worked through the papers in front of her. Liam waited. 'Do you know who he was?'

His aunt sighed. 'Sorry love. The name means nothing to me.'

Liam closed his eyes. 'I thought maybe he was something to do with my father?'

Val glanced at the papers again. She shrugged. 'I don't see how. How would a recluse from Tennessee run into your mam?'

Liam had to admit that this part made no sense to him either, but neither did anything else. People didn't leave big chunks of their fortunes to total strangers.

'Tennessee!'

'What?'

Val jumped up from the table. 'Wait there.' She marched out of the room, and Liam heard her rummaging around in the lounge. After a few minutes she came back, clutching a battered green box file. 'These are papers and that from Lou's. Tennessee. There was definitely something.'

She tipped the contents onto the table and started to sort through. She gave Liam one of her looks. 'Well don't just sit there.'

'What am I looking for?'

'Airmail letter. From America. I've definitely seen it.' Under the layers of yellowing children's drawings, and faded bank statements, her hand alighted on the envelope. 'Here.'

She pulled the letter out and scanned the contents before handing it to Liam.

*Dear Mrs Jones,*

*I am writing on behalf of a client here in Nashville, Tennessee, who is seeking his son. Our client visited the UK briefly in the spring of 1985 and became involved in a liaison with a Miss Kate or Katy Braun. Our client is led to believe that as a result of this liaison Miss Braun gave birth to a son on or around 10th December the same year.*

*It is our understanding that you currently have a young person in your care who might be the child in question. We appreciate that this is a sensitive matter, and wish to reassure you that our client has only good intentions towards your family and his son, should it be proven that this is the child in question.*

*Our client has considerable means at his disposal and simply wishes to ensure that his son is in good health and well looked after. It would assist us greatly if you could contact myself on the number provided to discuss this matter further.*

*Yours,*

*Nathan Glover.*

Liam glanced at the contact details at the top of the letter. Nathan Glover was, apparently, the representative of a large firm of private detectives based in Nashville, Tennessee. The letter was dated 1989. 'This came when I was five?'

'It wasn't that long after you came to Lou's. I think she copied it and passed it on to social services to deal with. To be honest I'd not thought another thing of it until today. I mean we didn't even know if it was genuine, and he was barking up the wrong tree anyway.'

Liam nodded. The estimated date of birth of the child the detective was looking for was a year after his own. Almost exactly a year. And his mother was Catherine Burn, not Braun, and, so far as he knew, she never went by Kate. Easy enough mistakes to make – to simply misread a date or a name, but there was no way he was the child they'd been looking for all those years ago. If anything, it looked like the investigator was grasping at straws. He screwed his eyes tightly closed and tried to think. None of this made any sense. He wasn't the child in question, so if the client had been Robert Grey, why had Grey still left him an inheritance? 'Can I take this?' He gestured towards the letter on the table.

Val nodded. 'Don't see why not.' She paused. 'He wasn't your dad love.'

'I know.'

'I mean, not knowing who was must be hard, but this fella wasn't.'

Liam nodded. In fact not knowing the identity of his father had never been that much of an issue for Liam. So far as he could make out he'd done a hell of a lot better than some of the kids who came to live at Mama Lou's who knew both their parents. He'd never thought of his childhood as a sad story. He'd had amazing foster carers, and so far as he was concerned Lou was enough parent for any child. 'It's not that ...'

Val tipped her head to one side and narrowed her eyes. 'What then?'

'It's not that I'm wondering about my dad. It's the inheritance.'

'What about it?'

Liam took a gulp of air. He still hadn't told anyone, apart from the investigator he'd hired, about the bequest. 'It was kind of a lot.'

'Money?'

He nodded.

'How much?'

'Twelve million.'

Watching Val's face was fascinating. He wondered if he'd run through the same range of expressions that day in the solicitor's office. Incredulity. Confusion. Joy. And then back to incredulity. 'You're kidding?'

Liam shook his head.

'Are you sure it's not some sort of scam?' Val was constantly wary of being scammed. She hadn't switched on her computer for a week after Liam had set up her broadband 'just in case.' Liam put it down to watching too many daytime consumer programmes.

'Nope. The money's already in my bank account.'

Finally her expression settled on something more serious. 'So what's the problem?'

Liam shrugged. 'Well it's not mine, is it? I never met the guy. It's some sort of mistake. For all I know he left it because he thought I was his son.'

'So?'

'So I don't deserve it.' Liam laughed nervously. 'I tried to give it back.'

'To a dead man?'

'Yeah. Apparently that's a problem.'

Val smirked, and then patted his hand. 'Of course you deserve it love.'

Liam shook his head.

'Well you deserve it as much as anyone else. You deserve it a lot more than you deserved to be abandoned by your mother ...' Val crossed herself absent-mindedly. 'God rest her soul. You're a good boy.' She shuffled around the table and put her arm around his shoulders. 'What would Lou say if she was here?'

'Lou would say that you have to work for what you want.'

Val laughed. 'Rubbish. Lou would tell you to go out and get raging drunk and enjoy yourself. You're young. You're rich. You're good-looking, and you're wasting your life feeling maudlin about it in my kitchen.'

Maybe she was right. Maybe he should simply be enjoying this unexpected good fortune. Liam tried to push the idea to the front of his brain, but something niggled. However he thought about it, he hadn't earned the money and that meant it couldn't really be his.

# Chapter Eight

## December

'I've changed my mind.' Rudy was sitting hugging her knees with her toes pulled up onto the seat in front of her.

'What about?'

'It's not the same as my friend not telling her parents she's still unemployed. I'm with the Auntie Val woman. Not spending twelve million quid is bonkers.'

Liam stared into his mug of tea. 'But what about the old man?'

Rudy shrugged. 'With the best will in the world, I don't think he cares any more.'

'But what if he died all alone desperate to reach out to his long lost son, and believing that he'd left his fortune to his only child. Spending it wouldn't be right.'

Rudy shook her head. 'You're insane.'

'I'm insane?'

She rolled her eyes. 'I mean your friend's insane.'

Liam grinned. Pretending they were telling stories about somebody else was stupid. They both knew that wasn't what was happening, but it was safe. However much he wanted to take her hand, tell her his real name and beg her to stay away from charming recruitment agents, he wouldn't. He needed somewhere he could talk all this through without judgement, and somehow he figured he wasn't the only one. 'Your turn.'

## May, earlier in the year

'Why can't you stay over?' Cora pouted at Patrick, who was sitting on the edge of her bed pulling his shoes on.

'I told you. It's my ...'

'I know. Your father. He gets confused.'

Patrick's father suffered from dementia, and was increasingly the bane of Cora's life. Patrick's father needed routine. Patrick's father needed taking to the hospital. Patrick's father relied on him. She took a breath. She was behaving like a spoilt teenager. Patrick was a devoted son, and a caring man, and the one and only good thing that had happened so far in this unremitting hell hole of a year. She glanced at the clock. 'Do you have to go straight away?'

Her lover checked his watch. 'Well a few more minutes would probably be okay.' He kicked his untied shoe back onto the floor and threw himself across the bed wrapping Cora's naked body in his embrace.

## December

Liam winced at the image. He'd signed up to listen to the story. That didn't mean he had to be happy about the appearance on the scene of this Patrick guy. 'I get the picture. It was going okay with this Patrick guy. Can we fast forward to a fully clothed bit?'

Rudy giggled, her antlers wiggling on the top of her head. 'Prude.'

Hardly, but Liam didn't want to dwell on what his real problem was. He'd known Rudy two weeks. He'd never even seen her face without a layer of pan stick across it. He didn't officially know her real name. There was no way he could be jealous of some guy she'd had a fling with seven months earlier. Unless Patrick wasn't just a fling. Maybe it wasn't over. Liam pushed the thought out of his mind. He closed his eyes for a second. 'Let's just stick with the PG version. Okay?'

## May, earlier in the year

The following morning Cora was woken by her phone

buzzing on her bedside table. She glanced at the screen. *Patrick*. Accept call.

'Come downstairs.'

'What?'

'Come downstairs.'

'I'm not dressed. You come up here.'

'Tempting.' He laughed on the other end of the phone. 'No. You come down.'

'Okay. Give me five minutes.' Cora pulled on jeans and a top. She'd promised herself that the last two weeks of April were an aberration. Once May started, she'd decided, she'd get back to the job hunting. She'd properly rein in her spending. She'd stop counting wine and nachos in front of Pointless as a proper meal. In short, she would get her life in order. It was nearly the end of May. Cora stuffed her purse into her bag, grabbed a jacket and ran downstairs. June, she thought. In June she would do all that stuff.

Outside, the late spring sun was high in the sky, and the South Bank of the Thames was crowded. She spotted Patrick leaning on the railing next to the river and stopped for a second. He was gorgeous. She'd been in love before, or at least she thought she had. She'd been married, for goodness' sake, but somehow Patrick sent her right back to that teenage girl, climbing over the fence on her daddy's estate to run away and meet Sean. He made her feel like he was the only thing in the world that mattered. She smiled, and ran across the busy pavement to her lover, ready to be wrapped up in his arms and his kisses. She looked around. 'It's busy.'

'It's the bank holiday.'

Cora wrinkled her brow. Over the past few weeks she'd lost track somewhat of days of the week. One merged very much into the next, and her pre-Patrick routine of getting up at 6.45 a.m., like she had when she was at London Fairweather, and going to the gym in the basement of her building, and then getting dressed in proper work clothes to signify how she was treating her job hunt as her new full time job, had disintegrated into mornings in bed and days and weeks that bled into the next. Patrick was still dressed in shirt and suit trousers. 'So what are we doing today?'

He grinned. 'Today is a day of culture.'

She raised an eyebrow. 'Really?'

He nodded. 'Really. Look.' He pulled two tickets from his pocket for her inspection. They were for the Globe that evening.

'Don't you have to get back to your dad?'

He shook his head. 'Not tonight. He's got a carer coming. New scheme thing. From the council.'

Cora's brow furrowed. 'I thought they'd cut all that sort of stuff.'

Patrick bristled. 'What? You think I'm making it up?'

Cora shook her head. 'That wasn't what I meant. I just … you hadn't mentioned it before.'

His face set into a frown. 'So do you wanna go to the theatre or not?'

Cora felt a knot of tension in her stomach. Now Patrick was cross with her. Sweet, kind Patrick who'd done nothing but light up what could have been a dismal start to summer. She couldn't blame him. If she allowed herself to dwell on her situation for too long, Cora increasingly found she was cross with herself. 'Of course I want to go. Thank you.'

He lifted his gaze. 'Good.'

'So what else?'

'What?'

'You said a whole day of culture.' Cora had an idea. 'We could go to Tate Modern!' It had been on her to do list ever since she'd moved to London, but somehow with college and work she'd never quite managed it.

'Really? When we could go back upstairs and make our own fun?'

Now Cora pouted. 'You made me come all the way down here.'

He laughed and wrapped a possessive arm around her middle. 'And then I saw you, and remembered how much more fun we could be having in your bed.'

Across town, Liam looked at his watch for the first time in hours. Ten o' clock. He blinked. That must be ten o'clock in the morning, because he was pretty sure he remembered ten o' clock last night. He looked around the room. No clocks. No natural light. Fully air-conditioned to ensure a perfect constant temperature. No clues whatsoever as to how much time had passed, apart from the sallow faces of his few remaining companions. That meant that he'd been sitting at this roulette table for at least six hours. He stared at the stack of chips in front of him, took a swig of the very fine single malt he'd been putting on his tab all night, and tried to piece together exactly how he'd ended up here.

The decision to come to the casino had been sound. Having listened to Auntie Val's advice that he should enjoy his sudden wealth, he had made more than one serious attempt to spend the money. He'd been to car showrooms, clothes shops, department stores, but somehow when the moment came to key in his pin number he couldn't quite persuade himself to commit.

The bottom line hadn't changed. It wasn't his money. He hadn't earned it. He didn't deserve it. Through no fault of his own he'd come by it through false pretences, and spending it felt like stealing.

Gambling, he'd reasoned to himself, would be different. He'd get to enjoy it, like Auntie Val had said, but he wouldn't gain anything from the experience beyond a few hours of fun, because the thing you had to understand about gambling was that the house absolutely, definitely, without exception, always won. If he really committed, Liam reasoned, a casino would be the perfect place to unburden himself. Liam looked again at the stack of chips in front of him. As plans went, it wasn't entirely working out.

He'd started on the poker table, and he'd lost the first few hands, and was soon down by £5000. That was good. It wasn't enough to make a significant dent in his bank balance, but it was proof of concept. The gambling plan was sound. Only then, he won a hand, and then another, and then another. After two hours at the poker table he'd more than doubled his original stake. No matter, Liam had thought. Poker was a silly choice. It had an element of skill and he'd played enough late night hands at drama school, for matchsticks and beer money, to consider himself a half-decent player. He'd moved to the blackjack table, and again he'd lost a bit, but then he'd won a bit more, and overall ended up breaking even. Time for roulette. Nobody won at roulette. It was pure chance and the house kept the odds just the wrong side of 50:50 to make sure that, over the long run, they would always come out on top. Liam didn't know how long he'd been playing roulette, but however long it was, it wasn't enough for the laws of probability to even out. He was winning. He was winning big. He'd started with £10,000, assuming that he'd be able to run through that pretty quickly. If he really rode his bad luck, Liam had figured, he could easily be down half a million by the end of the night. He wasn't. He was up. He was up nearly £200,000. Sod this, he thought. He waved a hand at the croupier and changed his huge stack of chips for higher denominations, and then pushed the whole pile onto thirteen. He heard mutters from the few remaining gamblers around the tables. When he lost it all he'd still only be down his original £10,000 so as an attempt to burn through his unearned gains the evening hadn't been a great success, but at least he'd be down something.

The wheel spun. Round and round and round she went.

Liam watched intently. There was no need. It landed exactly where he'd suspected it would. Thirteen. Of course. A smattering of applause broke out around the table, as the croupier piled chips onto Liam's stack and slid them across the table. He leant forward to shove the whole lot back into play, and felt a hand on his arm. An old guy smiled at him from the next stool, blue eyes twinkling above a thick white beard. 'I'd quit while you're ahead son.'

Liam shook his head. 'You don't understand.'

The man still smiled. 'Probably not, but I think it's time to call it a night.'

Liam hesitated. Maybe white-beard was right. The way he was going, he'd only end up winning more anyway. He nodded, scooped up his chips, cashed up and walked blinking into the morning sun.

Thinking it through, his plan had failed on two counts. Not only had he failed to get rid of any money, he'd failed to enjoy himself too. He'd picked the casino because of a recommendation from Ted, the old stager who played his father on *Lamplugh and Sons*. He'd decided it was the right place when Ted had laughed out loud at the notion that Liam could afford to go there. That was what he needed – somewhere where losing tens of thousands of pounds in an evening wouldn't make him stand out as a high roller, but it wasn't his sort of place. Those late night poker games in college, fuelled by cheap beer and youthful exuberance, had been fun. They'd rarely gambled for money, because none of them had any, but there'd been laughter and the company of friends. The casino was a joyless, sanitised, efficient machine for extracting money from people who were either too rich or too far gone to care.

Attempt to enjoy his undeserved wealth number one: Total fail.

# Chapter Nine

## December

Cora watched Chris bouncing the current visitor on his knee and caught herself smiling. There was an awful lot she still detested about this job, but apart from the costume, the tiny wage, the occasionally annoying parents and the odd bit of baby vomit in her hair, the festive spirit was starting to get under her skin. Spending all day every day dispensing Christmas cheer must be it. She tore her eyes away from Father Christmas. Yep. It was seasonal high spirits that were putting the unexpected smile on her face.

Cora pulled a toddler-appropriate present from her sack and handed it to Chris, who sent the child scurrying back to his mother clutching his brightly-wrapped prize. He glanced at Cora. 'What do you reckon? One or two more before lunch?'

'One I think.'

She stretched her arms upwards and rolled her head from side to side to ease the tension. She was ready for her lunch break. The grotto entrance swung open and the Chief Elf ushered the next family in. Two kids, one small enough to have reins dangling from his back and a slightly older girl. The little boy charged happily into Chris's leg before he was scooped onto the safety of Father Christmas's lap. The little girl hung back slightly, clutching her father's leg. Cora took in the whole family for the first time. No mum. Just dad and the kids. Her gaze settled on dad. It was Dave Two.

Cora spun around and busied herself with the present sack. Dave Two was here. Dave who used to be her underling was here. She glanced up. The expensive looking suit, recently cut hair, and preoccupation with checking his phone, even in the middle of a picture perfect family moment, suggested that he'd landed on his eminently employable feet since the collapse of London Fairweather.

She couldn't let him recognise her. Being here was one thing. Not actively hating it was another, but the thought of her former colleagues seeing how far she'd fallen made her feel sick. The imperious Cora Strachan reduced to dressing up in brown nylon for minimum wage. She swallowed hard. Father Christmas was engrossed with the children, and Dave was keeping a close eye on his phone. Nobody was watching her. She edged slowly away until she felt the door handle to the break room digging into her back. As quietly as she could she opened the door and slipped through. It wasn't fair on Chris, but it was all she could do.

She leant back on the wall in the kitchenette and lowered herself to the floor. In any other year this moment would have been her lowest ebb. This year, hiding from a former colleague in a drab kitchenette barely made the top five. She looked around the kitchen. The peeling Formica and cheap linoleum weren't just symbols of her failure any more. Instead they represented laughter and friendship and the fact that, despite everything, she was still here. She'd lost her job. She'd struggled to find a new one, but she was making the best of her situation. There was nothing to be ashamed of. So what if every last one of her former employees was now heading their own hedge fund or claiming the crown of a small eastern European nation? Cora was earning a living, sort of, and paying her own way, just about. She could hold her head up high.

She pulled herself to her feet and slipped back into the grotto. She took two presents from the sack and passed them across for the children, and then she drew herself to her full height, looked her former employee squarely in the eye and smiled. 'Merry Christmas to you.'

Dave Two stuffed his smartphone into his pocket and nodded. 'You too. Come on kids.'

He lifted the younger child into his arms and ushered them both out of the grotto. Cora stood stock still. He hadn't recognised her. Okay, so she was under a heavy layer of make-up, but they'd worked in the same office for three years. He hadn't simply failed to recognise her. He hadn't even seen her. So far as he was concerned Cora wasn't even a person any more; she was the help.

She followed Chris into the break room and waited for the kettle to boil.

'Where did you sneak off to?'

She didn't meet his eye. 'That guy. The dad. I used to know him.'

'An ex?' There was an edge to his voice that she'd never heard before.

Cora shook her head.

'Knock! Knock!'

Two heads popped around the back door to the break room. Cora's housemate, Trish, was the first. 'I found this one wandering the corridors looking for you two.'

A young Asian guy was loitering behind Trish, giving the impression for all the world of having been dragged along in her wake. He held up a large white box. 'I brought this for Santa.'

Cora and Chris shook their heads in unison. 'Don't say Santa.'

Chris laughed. 'We only say Father Christmas at Golding's, don't you know?'

'Okay.' The man laid the box down on the tiny table, completely filling the space. 'But presumably you're off duty now, so I can just call you Li—'

'Chris!' Chris interrupted the man. 'It's short for Father Christmas.'

The man stared at Chris for a second and then turned to Cora. 'I'm Raj. I'm his flatmate. I work in the food court.'

Cora smiled. 'Nice to meet you.'

He turned back to his box. 'And this was supposed to be picked up yesterday and it wasn't, so it was going cheap.' He grinned. 'Happy Birthday!'

Cora winced. It was his birthday. 'I'm so sorry. I didn't know.'

Chris shrugged. 'That's okay.'

He flipped the box open to reveal the cake inside. 'It says "For Your Bar Mitzvah."'

Raj shrugged. 'I can't really control what people don't collect, can I?'

Cora managed to find four clean-ish forks. Plates were a rather more scarce resource. The four of them stood over the cake clutching a fork each. 'I guess it's every man, woman or reindeer for themselves then.'

'Cool.' Trish didn't need to be asked twice, leading the charge and plunging her fork straight through the B of Bar Mitzvah. Cora hung back watching the others digging in. Three years she'd worked side by side with Dave Two every single day, and she didn't even remember his real name. She'd never known that he had children, and he hadn't even recognised her face. Less than three weeks with Chris and she'd met his flatmate and told him more about herself then she'd told anybody since Sean. No. Anybody including Sean. She'd told Sean about parts of herself. Chris was getting the no holds-barred version but, in a few months' time, he'd probably walk past her in the street without a second glance too. Cora's stomach clenched. Suddenly she didn't fancy the idea of cake.

## June, earlier in the year

The security intercom buzzed next to Cora's front door. She glanced at the clock. It was only half past nine. Patrick had said he'd come round at lunchtime. He must not have been able to stay away. She pressed the button. 'Hi!'

'Hello dear.' Cora froze. That was not Patrick. She fiddled with the button that activated the video screen and waited for the tiny image to flicker into life. Definitely not Patrick. Why hadn't she checked the screen first? She could very easily have pretended to be out. 'Mum! What are you doing here?'

'Well if you ask us up, we'll tell you.'

'Okay.' Cora pressed the door release, and raced back into her bedroom. A minute at the most. That was how long she had to clean her entire apartment, get dressed, and come up with a reason that a gainfully employed successful career woman might be at home at nine-thirty in the morning. She settled for throwing on some clothes and scooping the worst of the dirty dishes into the dishwasher, before the knock at the door called time on her panicked preparations.

Her parents were, as always, impeccably turned out. Her father's beard was always trimmed; her mother's shoes always matched her bag. She let them in, and then retreated to the kitchen to make tea, hurriedly hiding the empty wine bottles under the sink. 'So why are you in London?'

Cora's mother sipped her tea and gazed out across the balcony towards St Paul's. It wasn't a view Cora could really afford any longer, but she'd always loved having an apartment where people's jaws dropped as they walked through the door. Her mother sniffed. 'You should have some greenery here to frame the view.'

Cora nodded. There was always room for improvement. She tried her question again on her father. 'Why are you in London?'

He was sitting bolt upright on one end of the L-shaped couch. 'We went to the National Theatre last night, dear. We've got tickets for the Vikings exhibition at the British Museum later.'

'I see.' That made sense. Her parents liked an occasional

trip south to take in some culture. It helped them maintain their sense of superiority over their friends back home.

'Have you been to the Vikings exhibition?'

Cora shook her head. Of course she hadn't. She lived here for goodness' sake. She intended to go to things. She didn't actually do it.

Her father narrowed his eyes. 'And you're not at work today?'

'Not today. No.'

He didn't reply.

Cora forced a smile onto her face. 'You should have told me you were coming.'

Her mother tapped the toe of her court shoe on the polished floor. 'I would have dear, but you don't answer your phone.'

'I've been busy.'

'Of course.'

They fell into silence. Cora remembered the culture shock when she moved in with Sean's family. All the talking. All the time. Everyone talking over everyone else, telling stories, sharing jokes and moans. Her house had never been like that. She'd once overheard her mother on the phone to one of her friends from the Townswomen's Guild, gossiping away as if small talk was quite normal to her. To Cora it had sounded like a stranger's voice. She swallowed. 'So it's getting warmer.'

Her father nodded. Her mother continued to sip tea. Her father looked at his watch. 'Well, we'd better get on.'

'Right.' Cora leapt off the sofa. She was probably supposed to exhort them to stay longer, but their presence was exhausting. She could try opening up to them, admitting that she was still out of work, explaining that she was struggling, but where would that get her?

Her father put his cup down on the coffee table and paused. 'What's that?'

Cora followed his gaze. There was a pile of envelopes on the floor under the coffee table, the top one labelled clearly with the logo of the Department of Work and Pensions. Her application for Jobseekers' Allowance. She swallowed. 'It's taking a bit longer to find a new job than I thought.'

A bit longer than she thought? The recruitment agencies she'd signed up with had all stopped calling. Her daily scouring of the internet had dropped down to a weekly browse. Her father nodded. 'I see.'

Was that it? No comment? Cora nodded. 'Right.'

Her father stood and clapped his hands together, turning his head to his wife. 'Well you've had a good run down here I suppose.'

Cora's mother stepped towards them. 'But you're not getting any younger.' She reached out and patted her daughter on the shoulder. 'Maybe time to move home.'

Cora's stomach clenched. 'This is my home.'

Her mother laughed. She actually laughed. 'Well, for your twenties maybe, but ...' She surveyed Cora's carefully chosen minimalist décor. 'It's not a place for settling down, is it?'

And there it was. Cora's big bold move to London reduced to a youthful phase, which had now passed. She gritted her teeth. 'I'm going to find a new job.'

Her father frowned. 'There's plenty of jobs at home for a bright young woman.'

Her mother nodded. 'The big veterinary surgery are advertising for a new receptionist. Your father could put a word in.'

'I don't want to be a vet's receptionist.'

She saw her mother bristle. 'Well that would only be part-time. There'd be other things. The Young Farmers. The Townswomen's Guild are very welcoming to young folk these days.'

Cora shook her head. She wouldn't argue. She wouldn't make a scene. That wasn't what they did. She kept her voice calm. 'I'm not moving. I'm going to stay here and find a new job.'

Her father shook his head at the folly of youth. 'Of course you are.'

Her mother smirked. 'But I'll get a decorator to look over your old room, just in case.'

Cora opened the front door and forced a mask of a smile to her lips. 'Enjoy your Vikings.'

'So we need to raise our profiles a bit.'

The cast of *Lamplugh and Sons* had just finished the read-through for the next two week block of episodes. Their producer was now addressing his troops from the head of the table.

Next to Liam, Avril Barker, a forty year old woman who'd been playing the octogenarian Nana Lamplugh for nearly twenty years winced. 'What do you mean "raise our profiles"?'

The producer shifted from foot to foot. 'You know the sort of stuff. Get yourselves in the papers. Maybe some of these reality TV things.'

Liam shared Avril's discomfort. He'd been an actor his entire adult life, and had managed to be moderately successful without ever being famous. The idea of becoming a celebrity horrified him. He'd had an acquaintance at drama school who'd dropped out in the final year because he got a movie part. Six months later Liam had read in the paper that the guy was sleeping with his married co-star. For three months after that you hadn't been able to open a paper without seeing Liam's former classmate. During the fourth month, it was reported, he checked into rehab, and in the sixth month he had a very public relapse. He hadn't actually worked as an actor since. Celebrity, so far as Liam could tell, was an utterly poisoned chalice. 'But we're a radio soap. None of us are actually famous.'

'Quite. And that's the problem.' The producer leant forward, hands spread on the desk. 'We're not attracting younger listeners. They're all about Justin Bieber, and the Kardashians.'

Avril leant towards Liam and whispered. 'Off Star Trek?'

Liam shook his head. The producer was still talking. 'We need a bit of razzle dazzle to attract younger viewers. So talk to your agents. Any offers that would raise your profile, I'll be happy to accommodate time off.'

He turned away from the table. The actors remained in their seats, chuntering to one another. The general consensus seemed to be that this was nothing more than pandering to the lowest common denominator. Liam wasn't sure. Celebrity did mean interest, and interest meant ratings. Ratings meant keeping your job. Somebody was going to have to take one for the team. He really hoped it would be someone else.

# Chapter Ten

## December

Across the tiny table, Rudy narrowed her eyes.

'What?' Liam dropped his head. He hated it when she looked at him like that, like she knew, like she recognised him. Obviously she was going to recognise him. He was getting closer and closer to the part of the tale where that became inevitable, but not yet. He wanted to stay in this fantasy world where he was Chris and she was Rudy and nothing else intruded a little bit longer.

'I have to go.'

'What?' It was only lunchtime. So far neither he nor Rudy had ventured out of the store until the end of their shifts.

'I've got an afternoon off.'

Liam pulled a face. 'Who's going to be my faithful assistant?'

She shrugged. 'I think you've got an elf standing in.'

He shook his head. 'It won't be the same. Where are you going anyway?'

She dropped her eyes to the floor. 'Just this thing I've got to do.'

He didn't push her. She'd probably end up telling him once she got up to December in her story anyway. Another thought struck him. She didn't have to be here for the afternoon shift, so she could have gone at the start of the lunch break. She didn't have to sit around listening to him, did she? Liam smiled at the thought.

Cora traced her way along the back corridors to the staff locker room, cleaned her make-up off as best she could at the sink in the ladies' loo, and changed into her one surviving work suit. Why hadn't she said where she was going? It was just an interview. She'd had interviews before. She knew why. If she told him she had an interview, he'd come in tomorrow and ask her how it went. If she ballsed it up horribly she didn't want people to know she was a failure. She didn't want Chris to know she was a failure.

Her interview was in another part of the store. She wasn't even completely sure what the job was. Trish had heard somebody talking about a job that had, in her housemate's words, 'something to do with numbers and that,' and she'd told them they absolutely had to interview her friend. So they were. It was a pity interview, or possibly a terrified-of-Trish interview, but still, it was more than she'd had in months so she was going to make the best of it.

She navigated her way through the back corridors, clutching a folder with her CV and references to her chest, and knocked on the door marked *Accounts*.

'Come in.'

The office was decorated in a range of shades of beige and brown, and housed three desks; one occupied by a grey-haired lady who was frowning at her computer screen, the second home to a slightly younger, bespectacled woman who was knitting furiously, and the third currently empty. The grey-haired woman looked up. 'Can we help you?'

'I'm Cora. I'm here about the job.' She held out the folder. 'I brought my CV.'

The woman waved her hand. 'I'm sure you're very competent.'

'Okay.' It seemed like quite a big assumption, given that the stranger knew nothing about Cora, but she went along with it.

'Sit down. Sit down. Let's get down to brass tacks.'

Cora sat on a brown plastic chair opposite the woman and tried to look keen.

The woman leant forward. 'I'm Mags.' She pointed at her

colleague. 'That's Sadie.' She turned her head. 'Sadie who is only supposed to knit during her breaks.' Back to Cora. 'We do accounts, payroll, petty cash and expenses. It is not desperately exciting work, but, if you're the sort that can find pleasure in a spreadsheet that balances, it has its little satisfactions. You don't have to put up with talking to the general public, but you do have to be nice to departmental heads who couldn't check an employee's expenses claim to save the life of their own dear sweet mother.' She pointed at the empty desk. 'You would sit there. It's got the biggest monitor, but it's also next to the window so you get glare on your screen and spend half your time in summer opening and closing the damn thing when one of us moans that we're too hot or too old. It's Monday to Friday nine until five. You get half an hour for lunch, and I cannot recommend the staff canteen. It's twenty-one thousand a year, so I hope you don't have expensive tastes.'

Well not any more she didn't. In her experience interviews normally involved being asked questions. This one was much more informative. She'd worked at Golding's for more than two weeks and this was the first whisper of the existence of a staff canteen.

'Do you have any questions for us?'

Cora shook her head.

'Good.' The woman turned to her colleague. 'Do you want to say anything Sadie?'

Sadie peered over her knitting. 'What about the tea?'

Mags nodded. 'Good point. We have a kitty for tea. How many cups a day do you have?'

Cora paused. An actual question. 'I'm not sure. Three or four.'

The women exchanged a glance. Mags seemed satisfied. 'The last girl only had two and then tried to claim she should pay less. It was a right mess.'

Sadie cleared her throat. 'And do you knit?'

Cora shook her head. As she looked up she caught a warning look in Mags' eye. 'But I'd love to learn,' she added.

'Okay. So we'll see you first day back in January then?'

Cora nodded. In the corridor she stopped. She had a job. A job with a salary she would have laughed at a few months ago, but a job nonetheless. She'd probably have to keep living with Trish and company, at least for the time being, but she would be able to pay the rent she'd already committed to.

The new sense of purpose carried her all the way home on a cloud. Her other two housemates, Charlie and Fake Alan, were ensconced on the sofa watching a made-for-TV Christmas movie. She squeezed in next to them, and tried to make sense of the story. From what she could tell there was a family from the big city who had somehow become stranded in a small town that didn't celebrate Christmas at all. 'Why don't they celebrate Christmas?'

Fake Alan shrugged. 'It's not clear.'

Charlie shook her head. 'I don't think the *why* is important in this sort of film. What's important is that they're all going to rediscover their Christmas spirit and everyone will get along in the end.' She leaned in front of Fake Alan. 'What are you doing for Christmas?'

Cora shrugged. She didn't exactly have many options. Places where she would be welcome, and which fell within her travelling budget, were limited.

'You should stay here. I'm making a nut roast.'

Fake Alan groaned. 'But it'll be all right. I'm doing a proper turkey.'

'Are you sure?' Cora had only been in her shared home a few weeks.

'Course.' Charlie nodded vigorously. 'Everyone's welcome at Christmas.' She pointed at the screen. 'That's probably the sort of thing that this lot'll figure out before the end.'

Fake Alan nodded. 'That and something about how people are the most important thing.'

'Absolutely.' Charlie was on a roll now. 'And love. Love and people are the most important things.'

'And the spirit of Christmas. The three most important things are love, people, the spirit of Christmas and helping your neighbours.'

'You've gone all Monty Python now.'

Fake Alan shook his head. 'Hold on. I'm going to get this. The four most important things are love, people, the spirit of Christmas, helping your neighbours, and a fanatical devotion to the Pope!'

Cora closed her eyes. He was right though. Not about the Pope thing, but the other stuff. Christmas was about helping people. She jumped off the sofa, and flipped her laptop open on the dining table. She couldn't afford to get Chris a proper Christmas present to say thank you for listening, but maybe there was something she could do.

She clicked on to the search engine, and started typing: *Tennessee private detectives*. Two hundred and sixty two thousand results. Cora sighed. This was going to take a while.

## July, earlier in the year

The first letter came in the second week of July, which was unsurprising because it was in the first week of July that Cora missed her first mortgage payment. The tone of the letter was pleasant, friendly. Cora was still a valued customer. She'd never missed a payment before. Some sort of administrative error, the letter assumed, but one that needed resolving at her earliest convenience.

Cora screwed up the letter, and crawled back into her warm bed and Patrick's warm arms. Obviously, she'd been lax in her job-hunting, but she would definitely get that back on track very soon, and everything would be fine again. She'd catch up with the mortgage, and she'd deal with her credit card, and her other credit card. She just needed a tiny bit more time.

'Let's go out and do something.' Cora found that she wanted to be out of the apartment. She could feel her limbs sinking into the mattress, but suddenly it was cloying rather than comfortable.

Patrick shook his head. 'S'more fun here.' He pulled her on top of him and grinned.

Cora straddled his hips, and felt the familiar jolt of electricity as he reached up to touch her body. Today she was not to be persuaded. If they went out she'd be doing something, not any of the things she was supposed to be doing, but something. 'We can do that anytime. Come on. I want to go out in the sunshine.'

Patrick pulled a face. 'All right. Where do you want to go?'

She shrugged. 'Just out.' She glanced at the clock. It was nearly eleven, and she hadn't had breakfast. 'We could get coffee. Croissant.'

'Come on then.'

They threw on clothes, Patrick still in his habitual shirt and trousers. Cora narrowed her eyes.

'Why do you still wear that?'

He paused. 'What do you mean?'

'You look like you're dressing for work, not to come and see your girlfriend.'

He turned away, tying his shoe laces. 'Habit, I guess.'

Cora tied her hair back, chucked her purse into a bag and led the way to the elevator and into the street. They wandered to a coffee shop, and took seats in the sunshine at the front of the shop. She leaned across the table and grabbed Patrick's hand. 'We've got to stop doing this.'

'What?'

'Bunking off.'

He shrugged. 'We're not bunking off. We're ...' He stopped, cup halfway to his lips, sentence incomplete. His gaze shifted to the pavement in front of them. 'I'll be back in a minute.'

He pushed his chair back from the table, dropped his head low, and sidestepped into the café. Cora followed the direction of his gaze. Two people had stopped on the pavement in front of the café, perusing the menu displayed in a plastic case at the front of the seating area. They were older than Cora, about her parents' age. They had the look of a nice, suburban retired couple having a day out in the big city. Cora imagined they were the types who came here twice a year, stayed one or two nights, took in whatever the big new show was, and then scurried back to their nice house and nice garden feeling terribly cosmopolitan for having coped with the tube for two whole days. They didn't look like assassins, or undercover police officers, or benefit fraud investigators – she was fairly sure both their jobseekers' allowance claims were supposed to involve some level of jobseeking – or anything else that might cause her boyfriend to run and hide in the gents' at the very sight of their faces.

She sipped her hot chocolate and forced herself to think about her situation. She wasn't a stupid woman. She prided herself on the fact, but somehow she'd ended up in a relationship with Patrick. Wonderful, sexy, intoxicating Patrick. Cora shut down that train of thought, and tried another. Patrick who, she knew, had lost his job two months ago but still wore work clothes every day. Patrick who spent all day every day with her but could never stay overnight. Patrick who, however much she tried to forget, Cora absolutely knew had been wearing a wedding ring the first time they met.

The man in question pushed open the door to the café, glanced side to side down the pavement. The couple had moved on, and were now strolling away along the riverside. Patrick sat back down. 'Sorry. Call of nature.'

Cora didn't reply. She didn't know what to say. Nothing was an option. Nothing felt like a really good option. If she said nothing then things could carry on as they were. Her perfect summer could meander on with lazy mornings in bed, and even lazier afternoons in front of the TV. She could carry on drinking him in like a medicine that inoculated her against real-life. She knew what the old successful Cora would have done, the Cora that had never needed anyone enough to be scared of the answer to a simple question. She took a breath. 'Patrick?'

'Yeah?'

'Are you married?'

She watched his face. Was there a flicker of something there before he settled into the confident shake of the head? 'No. What? What would make you think that?'

The knot in her stomach loosened but didn't untie. There was too much that didn't add up. 'Who were those people?'

'Which people?'

'The couple that walked past. The ones you were hiding from.'

He opened his mouth.

'Don't lie.'

He closed his mouth again and shut his eyes.

'It's complicated.'

'So tell me.'

Cora waited, watching Patrick's chest rise and fall with his breath.

'You were wearing a ring the first time we met.'

Patrick didn't meet her eye. He nodded.

'But you told me you'd split up?' *Had he though?* She tried to remember.

'That's right.'

Cora grasped the confirmation. Her instincts were wrong;

her instincts often were these days. There didn't have to be a big, dark secret hiding behind every odd coincidence. She didn't quite believe it enough to stop asking. 'But you were hiding from those people?'

Patrick nodded. 'I've been stupid.' He sighed, staring into the distance for a moment. 'I didn't want to tell people that I'd lost my job.'

'What people?'

He shrugged. 'At home.'

Suspicion returned. 'Who at home?'

Patrick shook his head and broke into a grin. He reached towards her and cupped her face in his hands. 'I'm not married Cora! I'm with you.' He was suddenly serious, voice low and insistent. 'I love you.'

Cora gasped. He loved her. Did she love him? She'd abandoned all her good intentions for finding a new job and getting herself back on her feet to spend her whole summer with him. She must love him, mustn't she? This must be what love felt like.

'So this is about your dad?'

Patrick nodded. 'That's it. He needs routine and familiarity. He gets scared if things change, so to start with I just didn't want to upset him, but once I'd put my shirt and tie on one day and headed out of the house like normal, it got harder and harder to say anything.'

'Have you told your mum?'

A flicker of confusion danced across Patrick's perfect brown eyes. 'Erm … no. I should have. I've made a mess of things, haven't I? You must think I'm a total idiot.'

He turned his head towards her, and Cora's heart melted. She was too suspicious. Patrick was a bit messed up, but he'd started out from a good place – not wanting to upset an old man with dementia. That was nice. Something still niggled. 'So who were those people?' The penny dropped. 'They know your parents?'

Patrick nodded. 'Yeah. So I didn't want them to see me out drinking coffee when I'm supposed to be at work.'

Cora could understand that. If her own parents hadn't dropped in unexpectedly they'd probably still be none the wiser about her situation too. 'You'll have to tell them at some point though.'

'My parents' friends?'

'No. Your parents.'

'I know.' Patrick shook his head.

Cora laughed. 'I mean, how are you going to explain me to them?'

'What?'

Cora wanted her seat to tip up and deposit her into a convenient hole in the ground. She'd all but suggested that he take her home to meet the folks. That wasn't Cora's style. Was she the girlfriend sort? She'd tried being the wife sort once, and she'd ended up moving four hundred miles to extract herself. 'Sorry. I didn't mean I wanted to meet them. Not that I don't want to meet them. Just ...'

Cora forced herself to stop talking. Patrick was all she had at the moment. However confused she felt, she couldn't scare him away. She risked a look at his face. He was smiling.

'It's okay. It's just my Dad. He's really confused. He doesn't cope that well with meeting new people.'

Cora nodded. Maybe that was for the best for them, at least for the time being. Meeting parents was real, and real-life could sting.

In Liam's flat delivery men were hauling a brand new 48" plasma screen into the living room, while rival delivery men moved the old sofa out to make space for a five-seater leather L-shaped monster of a settee.

Liam's housemate, Damon – a horrendously unsuccessful actor, but surprisingly decent bar manager – stared at the new arrivals. 'What did this lot cost?'

Liam shrugged. 'Not that much.'

'Bollocks.' Damon pointed at the telly. 'We were gonna get one of them for the bar for the World Cup. They cost a tonne.'

Liam tried to look non-committal. 'It was on offer.'

The third member of the household, another jobbing actor mate from drama school, Raj, wandered into the living room, just out of bed in boxers and a crumpled T-shirt. 'What on earth?'

Damon turned to his mate. 'Liam bought all this shite.'

Liam bristled. 'It's not shite. It's good stuff.'

'It's expensive stuff.'

Raj surveyed the new purchases. 'So do we all have to, like, chip in?'

Liam shook his head. 'It's my gift to the household.'

Damon narrowed his eyes. 'Why?'

'Why not?'

'Did you get some big part or something? Are you gonna be like Thor's bum double in the next Avengers film?'

Liam shook his head. 'I bet he does his own bum work.'

Damon pulled a face. 'So how can you afford all this?'

Should he tell the truth? These were his best mates, friends since eighteen, housemates since graduation. If he couldn't tell them, he couldn't tell anyone. And that was the problem. He couldn't tell anyone. Money changed things. He'd never really had any before, and, if he'd thought about it at all, he'd probably have imagined that having more would be good. It wasn't. A guy with twelve million pounds in the bank would never just be a guy. Friends would interpret generosity as showiness. New acquaintances would always be viewed with a tinge of suspicion. Liam shrugged. 'They were on offer.'

Damon nodded. 'Well you should have asked us first.'

'I'm not expecting you to contribute.'

Raj sat down on the newly installed settee and put his

feet up. 'Nah. We split bills.' He ran a hand over the back of the seat. 'This is nice.' He turned to Damon. 'Come on. The old one was bollocksed. It's not like either of us would have got round to doing anything about it.'

Damon sat down next to his housemate. 'Fair point.' He grinned at Liam. 'You gotta let us know what we owe you then.'

'It really doesn't matter.'

His housemates laughed. 'Don't be stupid.'

Liam shrugged. He wasn't going to win the argument without telling them the truth, and that still didn't feel like an option. He wandered into the kitchen, and flipped his laptop open on the table. His email pinged with new messages. He scanned the subjects and senders. One caught his eye. It purported to be from the son of a West African diplomat who had been tragically killed whilst attempting to smuggle a significant amount of family money away from the clutches of the corrupt regime. This money was now, the email stated, in the hands of the son who was keen to come to the UK and would happily share his wealth with someone who could provide the pounds sterling to grease the wheels and solve a few small administrative matters. Liam sighed. He couldn't gamble his money away. He couldn't buy things for people with it. Maybe he could let himself be conned out of it. He ran his finger over the mouse pad and clicked 'Reply.'

# Chapter Eleven

## December

Cora convulsed in giggles, spitting her tea across the kitchenette.

'What?'

'You replied to one of those emails?'

He raised an eyebrow at her.

She sighed. 'I mean, *your friend* replied to one of those emails? What happened?'

Her companion looked at the floor. 'He never replied.'

Another wave of laughter took over Cora's body. Her eyes started to water. Nobody had made her laugh that hard since ... she paused. Old professional Cora hadn't really been one to let herself go like that, and she hadn't laughed that much with Patrick. She'd been too busy holding on. Laughing uncontrollably without a second thought to how she looked felt new.

Chris stood up and pointed at the clock. 'Come on. Pull yourself together.'

The afternoon was something unusual for the inhabitants of the festive grotto. Today was the day that Golding's took temporary leave from the world of all things expensive and consumable and gave something back to the wider community of the city. Cora was prepared to admit to a certain cynicism about the store's motives in inviting children from hostels in the poorest parts of the capital to meet Father Christmas, but that didn't mean that the kids didn't deserve a good show.

Mrs Atkins was patrolling the grotto, a sack of gifts at her side.

'What's this?'

Mrs Atkins lifted the new sack into the place normally

occupied by Cora's bag of presents. 'Different presents for these children.'

Cora understood. The poor kids weren't going to get their hands on the good stuff. 'Why not the normal presents?'

Mrs Atkins didn't meet her eye. 'No particular reason.'

Cora rifled through the sack, expecting cheap wrapping around token gifts. She was wrong. Each present was individually labelled with a child's name. Somebody must have contacted each child's carer or parent and found out what they wanted. 'Who organised all this?'

Mrs Atkins folded her arms. 'It might be all these little ones get. I like them to have something a bit special.'

So Mrs A had a soft side. Whoever would have thought?

'You'll make sure they get the right presents?'

Cora nodded.

'There are two Calums, but I've put their ages on the cards.'

Cora nodded again. Such care for the children of strangers. She swallowed down the lump from her throat, and set about the afternoon's work. The kids were really no different from the children who came through the grotto every other day. Some were brats. Some were shy. Some were talkative. One wet himself. But the parents were from another world. Photos were taken. A few quiet tears were shed. Nobody was simply ticking off another thing from their Christmas to do list. This was a real treat. For the first time she could remember, Cora felt proud of her work.

She led the last little girl, happily clutching a wrapped purple parcel, back to her mum, and turned back to Chris. His eyes were fixed on the floor, but Cora was sure she could see the beginnings of a tear glistening. A huge part of her wanted to go to him. It would be the simplest thing in the world to put an arm around his shoulder or a hand on his. She hesitated. 'Are you okay?'

He swallowed and rubbed the back of his arm across his eyes. 'I'm fine.'

She paused. They'd bared their souls over the sins and follies of the past. Here and now was different. 'Do you think we made a difference to those kids?'

Chris sighed. 'Not enough.'

She knew what he meant. 'It's weird. Nobody thinks about money until they haven't got any.'

'Or til they've got loads.'

'I know we said no spoilers, but did your friend ever find out why that guy left him all that money?'

Chris shook his head.

She thought of the list of private detectives sitting on her bedside table. She'd half-decided that trying to contact them was too big a task but seeing Chris choked up over the little bit of love they'd been able to share today pulled at something inside her that she'd never known was there before. Cora remembered the time and effort that Mrs Atkins had taken to find the perfect gift for every child they'd seen that afternoon. Maybe no task was too big if you had the right motivation to finish it.

## August, earlier in the year

'I'm really sorry.'

Liam listened to the woman's voice on the other end of the line. 'It's not your fault.'

'I feel awful.' He heard her gulp back what sounded like a sob. 'You trusted me. I'll refund what you paid me.'

Liam shook his head. 'Don't be silly. You did your job. This is bad luck.'

He heard another gulp. 'Thank you. You've been so understanding.'

'Well, like I said, not your fault.'

He hung up the phone and tried to process the conversation. Sam Bartolotti, the investigator he'd hired earlier in the year, had called to tell him that her office had been burgled. That in itself wasn't a big deal. What had upset her was the call she'd had a few days after the break-in from a tabloid journalist who was taking particular interest in two of her cases. One involved the wife of a minor government minister who had hired her to investigate the minister's proclivities beyond the marital bed. The other was Liam.

Sam's guess was that her burglar had been an enterprising sort who spotted the actor and the politician and wondered if they could make a quick buck selling the stories to the press. Liam sat on his bed and thought about the situation. He was lucky, as an actor. He had a regular income and regular work without being famous. He very much liked being able to go to the supermarket without feeling that passers-by were assessing the contents of his basket. He liked being able to play pub league football without a crowd of paparazzi and teenage soap fans on the touchline. Very occasionally, if he went out to a quiet restaurant, somebody at the next table would recognise his voice, but radio soap fans tended more towards the polite awkwardness than hormonal mobbing, so he was rarely interrupted for more than a moment's polite chit-chat between main course and dessert. Despite his boss's encouragement to court the celebrity lifestyle Liam was not the sort of soap star that tabloids photographed falling out of nightclubs.

He held the phone in his hand for a moment before accepting the inevitable. Even if the chances of the story going anywhere were negligible, he ought to try to keep on top of it. He hit seven on the speed dial and waited to be put through to his agent, Tony. 'Liam, what can I do for you?'

Liam ran through the bare bones of the situation, the burglary, the loss of some personal information, the potential upcoming newspaper story. He skimmed over the key detail.

'What sort of personal information?'

He took a deep breath. 'I inherited some money.'

He could almost hear the indifference on the other end of the line. 'Well unless you were flashing sideboob while you did it, that's hardly news.'

Liam took another breath. 'It was twelve million pounds from somebody I've never met.'

'Shit.'

'Yeah.'

'Twelve million.'

'Yeah.'

'Twelve actual million. In actual pounds. Not like Cambodian lira or something?'

'Cambodia use the riel.'

'Really?' There was a pause. 'How would you feel about doing Celebrity Mastermind?'

Liam closed his eyes. Tony was great, but he had something of a butterfly mind. 'The money.'

'Right. Yes. Why the hell are you still pissing about on *Lamplugh and Sons*? You could be doing anything. You could be in movies. You could set up a production company. Get backers. Do whatever you like. You could change your whole life.'

Liam sighed. 'I don't want to change my life. I just want you to kill this newspaper story, if there even is one.'

Tony laughed down the phone. 'Oh there'll be one.'

'You reckon?'

''Course. They'll print anything.'

Liam winced. 'Just kill it.'

'Kill it?'

'Yeah. That's something you can do, isn't it?'

Tony laughed. 'Not really. I can make some calls. Find out what they're planning though.'

'I'd appreciate it.'

He hung up the phone again. Tony had to make the story

go away. If he couldn't, then Liam wouldn't be Liam any more. He'd be Liam the millionaire. He'd be Liam who'd lied. Liam who'd hidden his money from his friends, from the people he was supposed to be closest too, for months and months. The money would make them suspicious of him, but the lies would make them right.

## December

Liam Carr. Liam Carr. Of course he was Liam Carr. She could see it now, even through the beard and the costume. He was Liam sodding Carr. How on earth could she have failed to recognise him? He'd been all over the tabloids for months. It was like Lois Lane not noticing that if Clark Kent popped his specs off he was a dead ringer for that mysterious superhero she was so keen on.

Cora stared at his face. His gaze darted from the floor to her face. She stared back into those familiar bright blue eyes. The usual hint of a smile had been replaced by a new guardedness.

'What?'

She could tell him that she knew who he was. She could come clean. But then what? She wasn't in any position to judge. Half of the stories in the papers would have been made up anyway, and there were still some unpalatable truths she hadn't told him about herself. She shook her head. 'Nothing. So do you want to hear about the rest of Cora's summer?'

He stared at her a second longer, before his face creased into a grin. 'Of course.'

## August, earlier in the year

Across the city, Cora checked her post. The day had a lacklustre sort of feel to it. Patrick was tied up taking his father to the hospital, which meant that Cora was at a loose end. She'd already skimmed through her Facebook, wondering if there was somebody she could call up and arrange to meet for coffee or lunch; something to give structure to the time that swam in front of her before she could reasonably crawl back under the duvet and sleep away the remaining hours until tomorrow. She'd realised that, without work and without Patrick, she was entirely alone. Her news feed was made up of women she'd been at school with posting photos of overweight toddlers demonstrating earth-shattering skills like clapping and standing upright. In between those there were occasional updates from former work colleagues, bemoaning the nine to five, or smugly bigging up their new self-employed status. None of them were actually friends.

She carried her handful of envelopes up to her apartment and sorted through them. Two notices telling her direct debits for bills had not cleared. Another letter from her mortgage company. This was the third. They were getting less polite. The last two had mentioned court action. Cora placed them all in the growing pile at the end of the sofa, where post she didn't want to think about went to gather dust and be ignored.

The final envelope was different. Cream-coloured, soft paper, her name hand written in fountain pen on the front in writing she didn't recognise. She opened it carefully, and pulled the card out from inside.

*Mr Sean Munro & Miss Holly-Michelle Jolly*
*cordially invite you to their wedding*

Cora stopped, blinked and read again.

*Mr Sean Munro & Miss Holly-Michelle Jolly*
*cordially invite you to their wedding*

Cora put the invite down on the sofa and went into the kitchen. She put the kettle on, made a cup of tea and came back to the elegant cream card. The wedding was six weeks away, in the middle of September, in Scotland near Sean's family home. Surely it was a courtesy invite. Nobody wanted their ex-wife at their wedding, did they? The easiest thing would simply be to decline the invitation. She could invent some prior engagement, or minor health problem, send them a gravy boat and that would be that but, Cora realised, she wanted to go. It would be closure on a chapter of her life. Sean had obviously moved on. It would be good to show that she'd done the same.

She picked up her phone, scrolled through the contacts and hit dial.

'Cora?'

She got straight to the point. 'I got your wedding invite.'

'Yeah.' The voice on the other end of the line sounded uneasy. 'I wasn't sure whether I should tell you first, or whether you'd want to come.'

'Do you want me to come?'

'I do.'

Cora was not convinced. 'Honestly?'

'Well, it was mum's idea.' That made sense. Sean's mum had an endearing willingness to view anyone who crossed her threshold as a permanent member of the family.

'But,' Sean continued. 'You were a big part of my life. Maybe it would be good to show that there are no hard feelings. And Holly thought it would be nice to ask you.'

'Your fiancée?'

He laughed. 'Yeah.'

Cora did some mental calculations. The last time she'd fallen into bed with her ex was less than a year ago. 'And when did this all happen?'

'Christmas.'

Eight months. Eight months from single status to getting married. 'You don't hang around.'

He paused. 'Well, when it's right, it's right.'

It was a nice thought. Had Cora ever been that sure?

'So will you come? I'd like you to come.'

She waited for the pang of regret or envy. It didn't happen. She was genuinely happy for Sean. 'Then yes. I'd love to.'

'Great.'

They chatted idly for a few minutes more. Sean explained that his fiancée didn't have very much family, so it was going to be a relatively small wedding and reception, or as small as it could be to accommodate the growing Munro brood. 'Hence the lack of plus one,' he explained. 'Sorry. Did you want to bring someone?'

Cora glanced at the invitation. She hadn't even noticed that there was no plus one on the invite. She thought of Patrick. 'No. He probably wouldn't be able to get away.'

'So you're seeing someone?'

'I am.' She told him a bit about her new relationship, but found herself skimming over the lack of job or income that was blighting the rest of her life. Sean might be friendly, but anything she told him would get back to his mother, and anything his mother knew would be around the village in seconds. Cora's parents knew she was down on her luck, but she was betting they hadn't shared that with the neighbours.

She finished the call and went online. Current account – overdrawn. Savings account – empty. Credit cards – numerous and all nearing their limits. She used one of them to buy a £5 return bus ticket to travel to Edinburgh, and another to pay a few pounds off her electricity and phone bills. Enough to keep the bailiffs from her door for a few more weeks, but not enough to make a difference. And then, for the first time in weeks, she clicked on a recruitment website and started to search.

# December

'Can I ask you something?'

Cora nodded.

'Why did she stop looking for a job?'

Cora swallowed, but didn't reply.

'I mean I get that she was all loved up, but ...' He met her eye. 'It sounds like your friend kind of gave up.'

Cora bristled. Who was he to comment on her life? Twelve million pounds in the bank and here he was, hiding behind a stick-on beard. 'Look who's talking.'

'What do you mean?' Neither of them was shouting, yet, but there was an edge in their voices that hadn't been there before.

Cora picked up her mug and dumped it in the sink. 'I'll be in the grotto.' She stalked out and sat on the floor in the grotto, half-heartedly sorting through the present sack. Chris was a virtual stranger. She'd only known him for a few weeks, and the few cross words they'd just exchanged barely constituted a proper argument. They'd only just reached the level of slightly grumpy, but even that made her ache. She felt herself calm down, almost as fast as she'd got wound up to start with. Did she even have a reason to be cross with him? He was right. She had given up.

'Rudy.'

She looked towards the voice. He was leaning on the door frame. 'Sorry.'

She shrugged. 'It's okay.'

He manoeuvred his Father Christmas belly to squat on the floor next to her. 'No. I was out of order. It's none of my business.'

Over the last few weeks she'd told him the gory details of her year. She hadn't sugar-coated anything. She'd simply told him the truth. Now it was time to decide whether that should be the whole truth. 'I think I ...' she paused. 'I think my friend did give up. When she moved to London it was like she had this plan to get the perfect job, and the perfect home and it all worked out. I think ...' Cora stopped again. She'd barely admitted this next part to herself. 'I think when it fell apart she felt like she'd failed. And then when she couldn't get it all back together again straight away, all the fight went out of her.'

Chris leaned towards her and squeezed her fingers. His thumb brushed over the back of her hand, sending tingles up her arm. He swallowed. 'You know, I think your friend's too hard on herself.'

'Hardly.'

'Definitely. Plans don't always work out. Sometimes you just have to enjoy what life throws at you.'

Cora opened her mouth.

'I know. I know. Twelve million pounds.'

She smiled. They fell into silence, still holding on to each other's hands. 'Well I guess we ought to ...' She looked around the grotto.

'Yeah. Work. Right.' He pulled his hand away and stood up.

Cora watched him get settled on the green velvet chair. Enjoy what life throws at you? Maybe he was right.

# Chapter Twelve

## September, earlier in the year

'I've got to go. I'll call you back.' Damon hung up a call on his mobile as Liam walked into the living room. Despite his housemates' initial reluctance, the new couch and TV had turned out to be enormous hits. Damon was lounging on the settee watching *Homes under the Hammer*.

Liam glanced at the screen. 'Any stupids today?'

Damon shook his head. 'Nah. They all got surveys done before they bought.' He shrugged. 'Maybe the ones that don't aren't stupid. Maybe they've got money to burn.' He swung his legs off the sofa. 'I've gotta go out.'

It was over a month since he'd called his agent in a panic about the newspapers getting hold of a story about him, and nothing had happened. For the first week, Liam had Googled himself from his phone before he even got out of bed, convinced that today was the day everything was going to come out. By the third week, he'd got it down to a scan of the front pages as he passed the newsagent on the way to the tube. By now he'd concluded that he'd been right all along, and he simply wasn't famous enough to make running the story worthwhile.

His sense of relief was enormous. It was also entirely misplaced. Four hours later, as he was getting a coffee from the machine at work, his phone rang.

'Liam Carr?'

'Yeah.'

'This is Maddie Jones.'

Liam wracked his brains. He wasn't exactly a player but there were girls in the world who had his number. Maddie Jones didn't ring a bell. On the other end of the line the woman was still talking.

'It's awful isn't it?'

'What?'

'The stuff in the papers.'

Liam's gut clenched. 'What stuff?'

'Oh, you know, just tittle tattle. How are you feeling?'

'I don't know what you're talking about.'

'Oh come on. Twelve million quid from some old guy in America? What did you do for him Liam?'

'I've never met him!'

The woman on the end of the line laughed. 'Outright denial? Well I guess it's a line. I don't see our readers swallowing it.'

Readers? Liam's brain whirred into gear. 'Who are you?'

'Maddie Jones. I said that. From the Echo.'

Liam pulled his phone away from his mouth and hit 'End Call'.

It rang straight away. This time he recognised the number. His agent.

'Liam, the story's out. Don't answer your phone. Don't talk to anyone.'

Great. Now he told him. Liam sat down on the floor, and swiped to the web browser on his phone. He searched for his own name. The Daily News website had the story linked from its front page, but from the headline Liam would never have guessed it was his story. Nothing about an inheritance. Nothing about the mystery of the benefactor. Simply this: *Soap star doubles as rent boy?*

Question mark. That all important question mark. The paper wasn't saying he was a rent boy. They were simply posing that as a possible explanation for why an eccentric old man would leave him a fortune. *One can only imagine what sort of services the Thor-lookalike rendered to end up £12 million richer. We hope it was worth it Liam.*

A wave of nausea rocked Liam's body. He forced himself to read the rest of the article. At least it couldn't get worse. It got worse.

Carr's oldest friend, the actor Damon Samuels, commented: 'We're all concerned for Liam. Getting involved in something like this, and then hiding it from all his mates. You've got to assume there's something else going on. Drugs or some sort of breakdown. We're all so worried for him.'

Carr had a troubled childhood. His mother was a notorious drug addict, and Carr grew up in a foster home that locals describe as being more akin to a hippie commune than a loving family home. Maybe with that background it was inevitable that Liam himself would go off the rails. And with £12 million in the bank how much further could he go?

It was Liam's life, but not as Liam knew it. Disbelief, dismay, betrayal, confusion, anger. Emotions punched him again and again in the gut, as Liam's brain failed to keep up with the number of different ways in which he was outraged.

His phone rang again. *Raj.*

Could he trust Raj? It didn't seem like he could trust Damon. He answered the call. 'Where are you man? There's photographers outside. What's going on?'

'You don't know?'

'No.'

Liam closed his eyes. 'Have you got your computer on?'

'Yeah.'

'Go to the Daily News website.'

Liam stayed sitting on the floor in the corridor next to the vending machine while his mate searched the web. He could hear muttered responses on the other end of the line. 'What—Twelve mill—Oh my ...' After a second Raj raised his voice. 'Bastard.'

'Me or Damon?'

'Damon. He sold you out.'

Liam smiled for the first time since he'd answered the call from the Echo. 'You're not pissed off with me?'

'Nah. 'S'none of my business if you're shagging some dead American.'

'I wasn't shagging him! I've never met him.'

He could picture Raj shrugging to himself. 'Whatever. I'm chucking Damon out of the flat.'

'We can't do that.'

'Course we can. He's an idiot.'

Liam heard himself laugh. Raj had many good qualities, but his ability to see the world in simple terms was probably the best of them all. Liam was all right. Damon was an idiot. To him it was that simple. 'So we're all right?'

'Course. You're buying the beers for the next few months though.'

'Seems fair. Do you want me to come home and deal with the paparazzi?'

'Nah. You're better off staying there. I'll tell them you're out offering blow jobs to members of the House of Lords or something.'

'Please don't do that.'

Raj sighed. 'You spoil all my fun.'

## December

'That's awful.' Cora shuddered. She'd known that this was coming. She'd seen some of the stories, but hearing it from him was different. It made her hot with anger. Anger with the journalists. Anger with the housemate she'd never met. Having your private life as the main topic for village gossip was one thing, but the whole country thinking they knew your business didn't bear thinking about.

He shrugged. 'I guess you have to find some way of separating yourself from it. Some way of being someone different from the guy in the papers.'

That made sense. 'And have you ...' She corrected herself automatically. 'Has your friend found a way to do that?'

He looked down at his red velvet suit and laughed. 'In a way.'

They fell into silence. This could be the moment to tell him what she'd found out from all her internet research. She took a breath.

He put down his sandwich. 'So what about the story of Cora? What happens to her next?'

Cora glanced at the clock. They had a couple minutes of lunch break left. Not long enough to explain the outcome from sending hundreds of emails to America, and not long enough for the next instalment either. She shuddered slightly at the thought. She wasn't looking forward to telling him what Cora did next. 'That might have to wait until tomorrow.'

She dumped her mug in the sink and headed back into the grotto. The Chief Elf was already poking her head around the door. 'Are you ready?'

Father Christmas took his seat and Cora nodded. The first child of the afternoon bowled in, a perfect little ball of toddler energy, shouting at the adult she was trailing in her wake. 'Come on Uncle Patrick.'

Cora's eyes shot up. Of course it was him. Who else would it be? She forced herself to breathe. Dave Two hadn't recognised her. Maybe Patrick wouldn't either. The mature, sensible thing to do was to keep her head down, be professional and do her job. She ran back into the break room, and she kept going, through the kitchenette and all the way into the corridor beyond. Her hands were wet with a thin layer of sweat, and her heart raced faster and faster. She forced air into her lungs. Four months since she'd last seen him. Four months since everything had gone wrong. She closed her eyes. She was lying to herself. Everything had been going wrong anyway. Patrick had been a sticking plaster on her broken life.

'Are you okay?'

Chris was standing in the door of the break room.

'Have they gone?'

He nodded.

'That was Patrick.'

'Oh.' He paused for a second. 'So what went wrong?'

Cora shook her head. There'd be a queue of children waiting. 'I'll tell you tomorrow.'

# Chapter Thirteen

## September, earlier in the year

Cora stretched out her shoulders as best she could in the confines of the coach seat. The overnight bus to Edinburgh was cheap and had saved her from having to choose between a night in a hotel or staying with her parents, but her back was screaming at having been squashed into her chair for eight hours straight. The tabloid paper she'd nicked from the guy across the aisle lay on the seat beside her. Soap actors doubling as rent boys for huge sums of money; it was bizarre what passed for news. For a second Cora wondered how much she'd get for her body – it could be an option to solve her personal credit crunch. Thinking about it, she probably wouldn't get as much as she might have six months ago. Early morning visits to her building's gym had fallen by the wayside, along with earning a living and wearing fitted clothes. Even her perfect relationship was starting to pale. The feeling that he was hiding something wouldn't go away. The old Cora would never have pushed that feeling down and pretended everything was fine. She shut down the thought. Patrick was great. Being happily in love was the only thing she had going for her at the moment. There was no way she was going to fail at that as well.

The wedding was at the local church in the village she'd grown up in. Cora changed her clothes, and washed as best she could in the bus station toilets before checking the boards for the local bus she needed. It was cancelled. Cora cursed under her breath. A harassed-looking man in a bus company uniform strode past her.

'Excuse me!' The man didn't slow down. Cora tottered after him on her heels. 'Excuse me?'

'What?'

'The Finbarr bus?'

'It's cancelled.'

'I know. When's the next one?'

'It'll be on the screen.' The man strode away.

Cora sighed and checked her watch and then the information board. She still had time. It meant she was cutting it fine, rather than destined to be stupidly early. She found a corner of a cold metal bench and settled down to wait.

Two hours later, the local bus ambled its way out of the city and into the countryside. It seemed to Cora that the passengers were unusually slow to get on and off, and soul-destroyingly ponderous as they delved in pockets and purses for their last few coppers for the driver. She checked her watch again. She was going to be late.

She ran from the bus stop, along the main street and up the path to the doors of the church. The bridal car was parked outside, empty. She paused outside and listened. The service must have already started. She pushed the door as quietly as possible and crept inside. She found a seat at the end of the back aisle. At the front of the church Sean was standing next to his brother, Luke, with the bride at his other side. A cascade of deep auburn hair fell down her back. She turned to face her groom. Both were smiling, eyes following the other throughout their vows and the exchange of rings. A few metres away her ex-husband was repeating the promises he'd once offered her, to his new bride. Cora slipped quietly out of the back of the church, pulling her phone from her bag. She scrolled through the contacts to Patrick's name and hit 'Call.'

Suddenly she knew what she wanted. She wanted what Sean had. All those niggling fears could be misplaced. She and Patrick had been living in a bubble, but he loved her. Why couldn't they make their bubble into something real? They could get a place together, near to Patrick's parents, so they could still help out with his father's care. They could find new jobs, and go shopping for furniture and have rows about what colour to decorate the downstairs toilet. They could do something. She listened to the phone ringing, waiting for him to pick up. The click came. 'Patrick, I wanted to—'

She stopped, listening to his voice on the end of the line. '... not here right now, but leave me a message and I'll call you back.' And then the beep. Cora smiled. She'd been about to declare her deepest feelings to his voicemail. Probably not the most romantic move in the world. When a relationship was right, it was right. And Cora was determined. Even if it wasn't spot on, she could make it right.

Voices behind her pulled Cora out of her reverie. The wedding guests were pouring out of the church, led by Sean and his new wife, followed by the best man and bridesmaid, and then the groom's parents. Cora smiled. She'd wondered how it would feel to see Sean remarry, but all she was feeling today was joy, enough of it to spread around. She stepped towards the happy couple.

'Congratulations.'

Sean leant forward to kiss her cheek. 'Thank you. I don't think you've met Holly properly.'

Cora smiled at the redhead in the beautifully simple white gown. 'Congratulations.'

The bride nodded in response. 'Thank you. And thank you for coming.'

Cora shook her head. 'Thanks for inviting me. I'm glad Sean's found someone who makes him really happy.'

The group fell into silence for a second. How friendly were you supposed to be to your ex's new wife? Cora wanted desperately to tell her that there were genuinely no hard feelings, but wondered if that would sound like she protested too much. The bridesmaid interrupted, 'Are you ready for the photos?'

The bride nodded. 'Where's your husband? We need one of the four of us.'

The bridesmaid smiled, peering around the congregation thronging around the small church garden. 'He's over there. Hold on.'

Cora's gaze followed the bright pale blue dress, as the bridesmaid scurried through the crowd towards a man standing with his back to them by the church door. There was something about the line of his hair above his collar, and the slope of his shoulder. The man turned, revealing the outline of his nose and the curve of his lips. He kissed the bridesmaid. Cora stopped. She couldn't talk or think or move or breathe. She stared. The deep chocolate-brown eyes. The cleanly shaved jaw, every inch of which she knew by heart. Everything around her swum out of view apart from him, and the woman leaning towards him. The woman who'd gone to fetch her husband.

Her husband.

Cora's lover.

Patrick.

Cora's own heartbeat was the only thing she could hear. The voices all around her were suddenly far away. All she could see was the bridesmaid leading her man through the throng of wedding guests. Step by step, second by second, closer and closer; she was waiting for the executioner's axe to fall, unable to step out of the way.

'Here he is.' The bridesmaid was all smiles and ringlets. Cora stared at her. She was petite with honey-blonde hair and big blue eyes. Cora forced herself to look at Patrick. His face was frozen. That was almost funny. You could see every situation from another point of view, if you chose. To him, Cora supposed, she was the one holding the axe.

'Hi.' Eventually Patrick spoke.

Cora nodded. 'Hello.'

His wife furrowed her brow and peered at Cora, and

then at the bride and groom. 'Oh you must be Cora.' She turned back towards her husband. 'You two must know each other from years ago?'

'Yeah.' Patrick nodded.

'When?' A flicker of confusion danced across Sean's face. 'I don't remember ...'

Patrick nodded vigorously. 'Course you do. It was at the thing.'

So that's what was going to happen, was it? Polite pretences and well-oiled lies. She watched the man who'd planted kisses down every inch of her spine slip into the character of an old acquaintance. What was one more deception to him anyway? Cora felt Sean's gaze shift across her face. She couldn't force a smile, but she managed to find the words. 'Yeah. You remember that thing, don't you?'

He looked at Patrick, and then he nodded. 'Yeah. 'Course. That thing.' Sean wrapped an arm around his bride. 'Shall we get on with these photos?'

The bridal party wandered further into the garden, under the instruction of a short, balding man with a camera around his neck and a self-important head on his shoulders. Cora watched Patrick being pulled across the grass by the bridesmaid. She corrected the thought immediately – by his wife.

She couldn't stay here. She had to get away. Her return ticket was for the overnight bus back from Edinburgh. She'd planned to be back home in time to meet Patrick for a croissant and coffee before they tumbled back into bed for the rest of the day. She walked along the side of the church building to get away from the crowd. She caught a glimpse of her parents, making chit-chat with the vicar, and quickened her pace. The wedding was replete with a full complement of people she could do without talking to. Her ex. His bride. His parents. Her parents. Her lover. His wife. She appeared to have achieved a full house of social discomfort.

'Are you all right?'

The voice belonged to a stout white-haired, white-bearded man sporting a natty red waistcoat under his suit.

'Actually I was just going.'

The stranger seemed to consider her for a second, before he smiled sending a twinkle to his eyes. 'Don't run away.'

'What?'

The old man smiled again. 'It's none of my business, but if you run away now that might set you on completely the wrong path for where you need to be.'

'What?' She stopped. It wasn't good manners to argue with befuddled elderly people. She peered around the corner of the church. The photographer seemed to be gathering everyone for a whole group photo. Maybe the old man was right. Why shouldn't she be in the picture? She'd been invited. She had every right to be here. She turned back to ask the white-bearded stranger if he was coming too. He was gone.

She positioned herself at the furthest edge of the group, as far from Patrick as it was possible to stand. Unfortunately that left her open to attack from her flank. 'You never told us you were going to be here?' Her mother's light friendly tone did little to disguise the hint of accusation in the question.

Cora shrugged. 'Last minute decision.'

In front of them the photographer moved tall people out of the front row, and tried to bring the most attractive children to the fore. Cora realised the children must be Sean's nieces and nephews. When she'd lived here, she and Sean had been the children of the household. Now Sean ran his family business and there was a whole new generation creating headaches for the grown-ups. Everything changed.

Her mother tutted. 'Well I hope they're expecting you. They'll have catered for a number.'

Cora nodded. 'I'm sure it'll be fine.'

Her mother pursed her lips, as the flash bulb popped for the first time. 'And you'll be wanting to stay I imagine?'

Cora held her face in an unmoving smile as the photographer fired off another round of shots. She answered through gritted teeth. 'I'm going straight back.'

'Oh. No time for family then.'

'I'm very busy.'

This time her mother paused to plaster a smile on her face while the camera clicked away. 'Busy with work?' There was no masking the hope in her voice.

Cora paused for second and then nodded. What was one more lie on a day like today?

'I knew you'd get back on your feet.' Her mother turned towards her. 'You don't need to tell people you've been unemployed though, do you?'

Cora nodded. Of course not. She'd keep up appearances like a good little princess. She accepted the inevitable and allowed herself to be carried along with the throng to the one hotel in the village where she gratefully accepted the glass of champagne she was offered at the door. Ten minutes later she managed to snag a second glass. Ten minutes after that she established that two more glasses of wine would cost her the same as buying a whole bottle, and her plan for the evening was set. She might have to be here. She might be trapped into making small talk with her mother, while the man who'd professed to love her sat engrossed in conversation with his wife a few tables away, but she didn't have to stay sober while she was there.

Food was brought, and plates were cleared. More food was brought, and then coffee and then more champagne. Cora chewed and swallowed and nodded and smiled, without noticing a single thing that went on around her. Her one and only thought was sitting across the room. Each time Cora forgot to stop herself staring, she found her eyes locked on Patrick. Patrick taking a sip of wine.

Patrick wiping a smudge of food from his wife's lip. Patrick sharing a joke with the best man. Patrick, her Patrick, being a person she barely recognised, as if some alien had taken that perfect body and walked it into an entirely different life. He deserved the chance to explain at least. Maybe this was a charade for the sake of his parents. A single molecule of hope rose in Cora's head. That made sense. Maybe Patrick's father would be distressed at his son's separation so his wife had agreed to put on a show at big occasions. That was possible. Maybe. Or maybe he'd married stupidly young – Cora could hardly judge someone for that – and didn't have the courage to end it. That would be bad, cowardly certainly, but maybe something she could come to understand.

At the top table, toasts were being offered and speeches made. Cora watched as the bride stood up. 'I know it's not very traditional, but I wanted to say a few words. Most of you will know that I met Sean at another wedding, a wedding last Christmas where my very best friend Jess ...' The bridesmaid offered a little tilt of her head in acknowledgement. '... got married to the lovely Patrick.'

Last Christmas. That was nine months ago. Cora had met Patrick in March. They'd run away to Clacton together in April. April, when Patrick had been married for four tiny months. The bubble of hope popped. There was no sad story. He wasn't trapped in a long loveless marriage. He was a stupid little kid who'd picked the most expensive toy in the shop and got bored the moment he'd got it home. Cora's heart sank. She was simply his most recent fad.

The bride was still talking. Cora tried to listen. 'Now I didn't used to be the biggest fan of Christmas, but last year was so perfect, and obviously Sean is obsessed with the festive season, so I know a few of you were wondering why we didn't go for a Christmas wedding ourselves. Well, apart from the fact that it's completely impractical to organise a wedding in the depths of the Scottish countryside in the middle of winter, we simply didn't want to wait a second longer than we had to.'

Around the room tipsy aunts and single cousins sighed at the romance of it all.

The bride held up her hand. 'Which it turns out was a good thing, given that we now know that I might be struggling to fit in this dress by December.' Cora raised an eyebrow. That was one bit of news Sean had kept from her, but apparently not from the rest of the guests as there didn't appear to be any great surprise. The bride rested one hand on her belly, and reached the other towards Sean. 'I know that Sean is going to be an incredible husband and a wonderful father. So I'd like you all to join me in raising a glass to the man I'm overjoyed to be able to call my husband. To Sean!'

Cora slipped out, and took refuge in the ladies' toilet. She stared at her reflection. Her sharp cheekbones had been softened by the little bit of weight she'd gained over the summer. Relationship weight, they called it, didn't they? But still, she didn't look stupid. She didn't look like she imagined the sort of bimbos who dated married men would look. She wasn't even a scarlet woman, a proper mistress who didn't care about her man having a little woman back home. She was just a stupid girl who'd believed him when he'd said he wasn't married. She closed her eyes.

'Are you okay?' The pale blue bridesmaid was standing in the doorway to the toilets.

Cora nodded. Could she tell? Did Cora look guilty? Was there a neon arrow above her head emblazoned with the words 'She's sleeping with your husband'? 'I'm fine.'

'Okay.' The bridesmaid bobbed into a cubicle and bobbed straight out again. 'The lock's bust.' She pulled a face at Cora. 'Do you mind standing guard for me?'

'Okay.'

Cora leant on the basin and waited. Every fibre of her being wanted to run away, but she couldn't. Ladies' toilet etiquette did not permit it. All right, so she'd been conducting a six month affair with this woman's husband, but that didn't exempt her from the implied solidarity of the ladies' loo.

The blue bridesmaid reappeared. 'So today must be a bit awkward for you?'

Cora froze. 'No. It's fine. Everything's fine. What do you mean?'

The bridesmaid giggled. 'Just being at your ex's wedding. It must be weird.'

Cora forced herself to exhale. 'It's fine. He seems happy. We've been divorced a long time.'

The bridesmaid shrugged. 'I didn't have any exes at my wedding. I think Patrick's mother tried to slip one of his onto the guest list, but I crossed her off.'

So this woman didn't like exes. Cora wondered how she'd feel about 'currents'.

'Our wedding was massive though. To be honest anybody could have been there. So long as they brought a gift, I wouldn't have noticed.'

Curiosity overcame discretion. 'You got married at Christmas?'

'Last December. Yeah. In London. Patrick's parents are minted so they helped.' The bridesmaid paused to inspect her lipstick in the mirror. 'There's no way we could have paid for it all. I'm a teacher and Patrick works for a recruitment agency. We're hardly millionaires.'

Red flags popped up all over the place. Patrick's parents? Patrick works for? Not used to work for? Works for, as in present tense? Cora picked one question out of the many. 'And is Patrick's dad okay?'

The bridesmaid's brow furrowed. 'Course.'

'Oh.' Cora rallied. 'I thought I remembered him being ill. It was a long time ago.'

'When you met Patrick before?'

'Right.'

'No. His parents were supposed to be here, but they've gone off on some cruise somewhere. Like I said, minted.' The bridesmaid shot a final look at her reflection and was evidently satisfied with what she saw. 'Better get back to it.'

Cora nodded. 'I'll be out in a minute.'

So the wife wasn't an ogre, or in a coma, or any other thing that might explain why a man who'd barely made it home from his honeymoon would be spending half his time in somebody else's bed. She looked at her watch. About one more hour, she thought, and then she could reasonably claim that she needed to get back to Edinburgh for her journey home.

Patrick was waiting in the corridor outside the toilets.

'What did you say to Jess?'

Cora didn't reply. She didn't have the words. She hadn't had time to mentally pore over the fantasies of what she'd say to him when they finally spoke. If she'd thought about it at all she would have assumed that his opening salvo would have involved at least an element of apology. She shook her head. 'I didn't say anything.' A detail popped into her head. 'I'm glad your dad's feeling better.'

'What?'

'Your wife told me your dad was fine. On holiday, apparently, so that's nice. Quite impressive for a man who was housebound with dementia this time yesterday.'

Now she'd started talking, it was surprisingly easy. 'And I hear you're working again? That's great Patrick. Really great, because your wife obviously would know what you were doing for work.'

Slowly pieces began to slot into place. Alcohol and shock were making Cora's brain fuzzy, but her tongue was remarkably perceptive. She kept talking. 'She doesn't know you lost your job, does she?' As soon as she'd spoken, Cora knew she was right. The shirt and tie. The daytimes out of the house. 'And she doesn't know you've been sleeping with someone else since April, obviously. And your dad's never been ill, has he? That's just what you told me so that I wouldn't demand an explanation for how you could never stay over at night. Which of course you couldn't because you're married!'

Cora shoved Patrick hard in the chest and stormed past him. The corridor was short, just a couple of metres. She rounded the corner still fuelled by indignation. She stopped. The pale blue bridesmaid was standing with one hand on the wall, looking as though that was the only thing anchoring her to the ground. The pink tinge in her cheeks had drained to deathly white.

She stared at Cora, took a step forward, and then crumpled, sliding down the wall to the floor. Cora froze. She was in the middle of a nightmare, but it was only partly her own. What should she do? She wasn't the right person offer comfort, but technically she was also a wronged party. It was possible that her boyfriend's wife wouldn't see it that way. 'Are you okay?'

The bridesmaid stared at her with glassy eyes.

'What's happening?' Sean barrelled out of the dining room into the hallway, his bride's arm entwined around his.

She peered at her friend on the floor. 'What's wrong?'

Cora took a step backwards. 'I should probably go.'

The hallway was starting to fill up with people, apparently thrown out of the function room so that the staff could reset for the evening party. Cora could see her parents, and Sean's family peering to see what the to-do was about.

The pale blue bridesmaid was still frozen to the floor.

Cora took another step away. 'I'll be getting off then.'

Sean narrowed his eyes. 'What did you do?'

Cora shook her fuzzy head. No. This wasn't right. She

wasn't going to get the blame for this. She wasn't going to run away. She crouched down next to the bridesmaid. 'I'm really sorry.'

The pale face turned towards her. It wasn't an angry face, or a sad face; there was simply no emotion there at all, as if the woman had retreated inside herself and shut down all external functions.

Cora swallowed. She leant closer and whispered. 'He told me he was single. I'm sorry.' She heard Sean groan. Obviously she hadn't whispered quietly enough. 'Honestly, I didn't know he was married.'

In the corner of her eye she saw Sean round the corner. Cora jumped to her feet to follow, in time to see Sean's fist land squarely on Patrick's nose. She heard the crack of knuckle against bone, and watched as her lover staggered backwards clutching his face, a trickle of dark red blood oozing between his fingers.

Mutters and whispers rippled back through the crowd of guests. Those at the back who couldn't see the bridesmaid on the floor, but could hear the crack of fist on bone, demanded hurried updates on the situation from their friends in front. Cora looked around. Her mother's face was fixed in an expression of gleeful intrigue. Other people's misfortune – her mother's favourite hobby. Cora didn't want to be there when she found out that her own daughter was at the centre of the current scandal. The bride was dragging Sean away from Patrick. Patrick's wife was still sitting on the floor. Patrick crawled over to her. 'Sweetheart, it's not what you think.'

Cora turned her heel and walked away. She didn't need to hear how he could explain, how it had all been her fault, how he'd been under a lot of pressure, how it hadn't meant anything. She'd been stupid about Patrick all summer. It was up to his wife to decide whether she wanted to be stupid now.

'You walked away?'

Rudy nodded.

'Wow.' Liam paused. She hadn't corrected him when he said 'you' rather than 'your friend.' Normally he'd make a joke of that but this time he didn't want to break the mood. 'And you hadn't seen him until yesterday?'

She nodded.

'You should have said. I could have punched him for you too.' And he knew he would have. He was furious with a total stranger over a woman he'd met less than four weeks earlier.

She managed a half-smile at him. 'That wouldn't be very Father Christmassy.'

'I guess not.' He remembered her reaction when Patrick had come into the grotto. At the time he'd harboured a quiet relief that Cora was clearly no longer with him, but now another, less welcome, thought pushed its way to the fore. 'So are you still hung up on him?'

She shook her head. 'It was an infatuation. I didn't really know anything about him, and I never told him anything about me.' She took a sip of tea. 'But I think he must have known. He was Sean's friend. He must have recognised my name. I guess he didn't think Sean would invite his ex-wife to the wedding.'

Liam didn't respond. He'd lied a lot this year, mainly by omission, but lying about loving someone, lying to your wife, that was unimaginable.

Rudy stood up and brushed the crumbs off her costume. 'So ...' She clapped her hands together in the universally understood gesture of changing the subject. 'So have you done all your Christmas shopping?'

Liam closed his eyes. 'I haven't started.'

'Why not?'

'It's the money. Everyone knows about it, so what do I get them? If I spend loads I'm being flash and that makes people uncomfortable. If I get a normal sort of thing then they know I can afford loads more and I look tight.'

Rudy leant on the wall and looked at him. 'Go for something personal. If it means something to them you can't go wrong.'

'So what about you?'

She shrugged. 'Nobody to buy for.'

'What about your mum and dad?'

Rudy stared at the floor. 'Well, I'm no longer invited home for Christmas.'

'How come?'

'Apparently I embarrassed them terribly.'

Liam shook his head. 'But you didn't do anything wrong.'

As she looked up their eyes met. 'You might be the only person who thinks that.'

That was so unfair. Family was supposed to stick together. That's what Mama Lou taught him. He'd always known that he could never do anything so bad that he couldn't go home to be met with unconditional love. She might be angry. She might be disappointed, but there was nothing that one of her kids could do that would stop her home from being theirs. That was what family meant to Liam. Everybody should have that certainty somewhere in their life. He struggled for the right words to make Rudy feel better. 'I know the whole story though, don't I?'

She nodded.

'Then my opinion counts. You didn't do anything wrong.'

# Chapter Fourteen

## October, earlier in the year

'Just sell it as quickly as you can.'

The estate agent making notes on his iPad on Cora's kitchen worktop couldn't have been more than twenty-two. At the start of his career, still all hopeful, no idea that everything could crash and burn in an instant.

'You're sure? That might not get you the best price.'

Cora nodded. 'So long as it clears the mortgage.' She didn't add that she had no other choice. She didn't add that the mortgage company had only put a hold on the repossession proceedings because she'd told them the house was already on the market. That had been a week ago. Now she had to make it true.

The baby estate agent busied himself taking measurements and photographs.

'How quickly do you think it'll sell?'

He shrugged. 'We've got buyers looking for this sort of thing. If you're really happy to be flexible on price, we should have some viewings by the weekend.'

Cora nodded. She knew what 'flexible on price' meant. It meant she should get enough to clear the worst of her debts, but that was all. Even when she had an offer, there'd be chains and solicitors and surveys to worry about, but that was okay. An offer would be enough to keep the mortgage company out of court and the bailiffs from the door. For now at least.

She waited until the agent had finished his inspection and headed back to the office before she switched on her laptop. It was three weeks since the wedding. Since then she'd ignored eight calls and two emails from her mother, three texts from Sean, and one single solitary voicemail from

Patrick sent at about 3 a.m. the morning after the wedding. At least she hadn't replied to any of them. The voicemail she replayed to herself three or four times a day, trying to find some nuance or hint of explanation amongst the self-justification and bile. Out of habit, she hit one on her phone to speed dial her voicemail and chose the option for saved messages.

'Cora, it's Patrick. I can't believe you turned up like that at the wedding. That was well out of order. Jess is really upset because of you. She won't let me in the hotel room. Sean threw me out of the reception. I can't believe you did that to me. I thought we had something special. I'm not surprised Sean divorced you. You're total poison.'

Maybe Patrick was right. Maybe it was somehow her fault. Breaking things and hurting people was what she did. She'd hurt her parents by running away with Sean, and then she'd hurt Sean by running away to London. She closed her eyes and sucked breath into her lungs. One thing at a time. One thing at a time was all she could do. She was selling the flat. That meant she needed a place to live. Focus on the practical. Don't think about the emotional. Keep breathing in and out. It was all she could do.

Cora pulled her laptop onto her knee and browsed through a few London lettings sites. The problem was obvious. They needed a deposit and first month's rent. Until she sold the flat she had neither. Okay. That was another practical problem. She needed money. She didn't have a job. She'd hit rock bottom the night before and phoned her parents to ask for help. Her father's response had been simple – they would help her generously if she moved home, and in his words 'made things right with the village.' Unless she agreed to that, she wasn't welcome and would have to get by on her own. Cora tried to picture herself back in her teenage bedroom, her mother constantly popping in to 'tidy round' and have a jolly good snoop through Cora's things, her father's silent disappointment at the breakfast table. No, she wasn't going back.

What else then? She could rob a bank. Technically she'd already been under suspicion of that once this year but, from her limited viewing of heist movies, robbing a bank involved a whole heap of accomplices. You needed a driver, and a safe cracker, and an inside man. Cora just didn't have the contacts.

She could sell something. Cora paused. Maybe, yes. She could sell some stuff. She glanced around her apartment. If she was going to move into rented accommodation, what would she need? A bed, some kitchen things. What else? She wasn't working. She could definitely live without at least some of her work dresses and suits. She had shoes the cost of which had made her wince when she'd bought them, and the pain of which made her wince when she wore them. They could all go.

Cora stood up, and walked into her bedroom to survey the options. She would sell some things. It was a plan. This was how she was treating life now. Breaking it up into single tasks. Lots of doing. Not too much thinking. She opened her wardrobe. She would keep one suit for job interviews, if she ever got any. Apart from that she lived in pyjamas and yoga pants. Everything else could go. She pulled clothes out of the closet and laid them on the bed. Suits. Designer dresses. Four different pairs of nude heels. Then she stopped. In her hand was a long, silver evening gown, strapless, fitted to the waist and then flowing out and down to the floor. That dress was the first designer piece she'd ever bought. She'd worn it for her first work party as a team leader. She ran her fingers over the fabric. It was as exquisite as she remembered. Without thinking she pulled her top over her head, kicked off the jogging bottoms she was wearing, and stepped into the dress. Cora inspected herself in the mirror. The woman in the dress was the woman she'd set out to be.

The walls inside Cora's head, the walls that kept her day to day activities separate from Patrick and losing her job and her home, cracked a little. The woman in the dress stared back at her from the mirror. Cora stared at the stranger, a memory from long ago, far removed from the person who'd taken over her body. This new Cora lived day to day. Dreams and hopes had been put firmly on hold. Cora stared at the stranger in the mirror and realised that both of them were crying.

Bang, bang at the door.

Cora wiped her eyes on the back of her hand. That didn't make sense. The building had a secure entry system, so only people who lived here could get in, and Cora didn't have the kind of neighbours who just popped round.

She padded through the lounge, still in her evening gown, and put the chain on the front door before she opened it a crack.

A woman leant on the wall outside Cora's front door. Her hair was scraped back and unwashed. She was wearing skinny jeans under a shapeless hoodie. Cora stared into the eyes of her boyfriend's wife.

'Can I come in please?'

## December

Rudy sighed. 'Well maybe we should get back to work.'

Liam slammed his mug down on the table. 'No way. You can't leave me on a cliffhanger like that.' He pointed at the clock. 'We've got loads of time.'

As soon as he said it, he realised it wasn't true. They had two more days. Two more chances to say something about what he was feeling, about how desperate he was to keep seeing her, about how much he loved the time they'd spent together. Two more days and then all of this – the hiding, the grotto, the stories, the two of them – was over.

Rudy grinned at him from the doorway. 'No. Your turn next. I'll tell you the rest after you've done a bit.'

## October, earlier in the year

'You're firing me?'

Across the desk from Liam the producer of *Lamplugh and Sons* shook his head. 'We're not firing you. We just think it would be best for everyone, including you, if you took a bit of time off.'

Liam shook his head. 'You said you wanted more publicity.'

The producer sighed. 'Apparently this is the wrong sort of publicity.'

There was nothing he could do, but Liam didn't like to go down without a fight. 'It's not fair. You know those stories aren't true. And our ratings are up.'

The producer nodded. Liam had always got on well with his boss. They tended to keep the dramatics for the show. Behind the scenes *Lamplugh and Sons* had always been a rather sleepy, and fundamentally good-natured, workplace. Liam couldn't deny that the last few weeks had been different. In the wake of the initial story in the paper, journalists had been doorstepping people across the country who'd grown up in the care of Mama Lou. None of them had had a bad word to say about Lou or their sort-of foster brother, but that hadn't stopped the papers painting a lurid picture of an out-of-control hippy commune funded by the hard-working British taxpayer. There'd been three different stories about his sexual prowess from women who claimed to have bedded the caricature of Liam who was now a tabloid sensation. After scrutinising the pictures of all three women wearing little more than a smile, which the papers so thoughtfully included with their articles, Liam was convinced he'd only met two of them, and one of those he'd not even so much as snogged at an office party.

On the one occasion Liam had allowed Raj to drag him on a night out since the story broke, he'd been photographed buying his round, holding a pint in each hand, and two different papers had written concerned columns about his alcohol-hell. All of which was topped off by a set of CCTV photos from his night at the casino, and a rather lurid quote about him throwing money around like it was confetti. So far as Liam could make out, that was the only story about himself with any sort of grain of truth to it, but the bottom line remained this: all those things that people said about news stories being here today and gone by the end of the week – all those platitudes about it being tomorrow's fish and chip paper – all of that was lies. Liam wasn't a person any more. He wasn't a moderately successful actor. He was a character in a story who had a life entirely independent of his own.

Liam tried to work out what he could say to change the producer's mind. 'I thought all publicity was good.'

'I'm sorry. It seems the view from above has changed. They think you're ...' He looked away. 'They think you're bringing us into disrepute.'

There was nothing else Liam could offer. He squeezed his eyes shut and decided that he definitely wasn't going to cry. He'd cried once in his adult life, that he remembered, sitting at Mama Lou's bedside while she drifted between life and death. This was just a job. He wasn't even losing a job. He was taking a break. Most people would be over the moon to get an unexpected holiday from work. Most people would be over the moon to get an unexpected twelve million in their bank account. Maybe Liam wasn't like most people. He lifted his head. 'I'm sorry about all this. I thought it would have blown over by now.'

The producer nodded. 'So did I. Look, you've got a lot to think about too. Take a bit of time. Things will calm down, and if it's still what you want, you can come back to work in January. For now we're going to send Lamplugh junior to Cuba.'

Liam nodded. It made sense. 'To look for Matilda's evil twin sister?'

'Exactly.' The producer paused. He was a decent sort, who Liam had known since he joined the series eight years ago. Liam watched as the older man walked around the desk, checked that his office door was fully closed and came back to face him again. 'Look I'm not trying to get rid of you. You're great, but that's sort of the point. You're really great Liam. Great actors don't stay in this sort of job for decades. They move on. They do theatre, TV, movies. In one way, I hope this all calms down and you're back in the New Year, but seriously, take some time. Think about what you could be doing.'

That again. His agent had said the same. The money in the bank could buy him freedom. So far all it had bought him was infamy, a broken friendship and a gaggle of photographers following him every time he went to the shop.

Across the city, Cora opened the door. Her boyfriend's wife popping round was a social situation Cora wasn't sure she had the skills for. Should she offer her a cup of tea? Something stronger perhaps? Cora glanced down at her dress. 'I don't normally wear this. I was just trying it on.'

The other woman nodded. 'Are you going to a party?'

Cora shook her head.

'Right.'

They stood opposite one another in Cora's open plan lounge-kitchen-diner. Her guest walked over to the window. 'You have nice views.'

Cora followed her gaze across the view she'd soon be leaving behind. 'Would you like a cup of tea?'

The other woman shook her head.

'Okay.' Cora sat down on the leather sofa and waited. The silence extended and prodded at her until she gave in. 'I'm Cora.'

'I know.' Her guest perched on the furthest end of the sofa. 'Jess. You're probably wondering why I'm here.'

'Not really.' Cora knew exactly why she was here. She'd come to look and see what she was up against. She'd come to assess the enemy in its lair. It's what Cora would have done.

'Patrick won't tell me anything. I said we could try to move past it and now he won't tell me anything. He says I have to stop dwelling on it.'

Cora's insides burnt hot and red. She ought to be angry with Patrick. She ought to be angry with Angus for framing her for fraud. She ought to be angry with London Fairweather for treating her and all her colleagues like worker ants who could be crushed under the heel of a bigger richer man. She ought to be angry with her parents. But none of them were here. Jess was here. Something inside Cora burst. She yelled. 'You said what?'

'What?' The other woman looked startled.

'You forgave him?' Cora could hear her own voice getting louder and louder. It was as though some forgotten part of herself was fighting its way to the surface. 'He cheated on you for six months. Pretty much every day for six months. You've not even been married a year. He lied about losing his job. He lied about where he was going, who he was seeing. He lied about everything. To both of us. For months.'

Jess closed her eyes, not quickly enough to hide the tears that were desperately trying to fall. 'You don't understand.'

Cora could see the hurt on the other woman's face. She softened her tone. 'What don't I understand? What have I got wrong?'

Jess's voice was tiny now. 'Nothing, but we're married. You were a fling. He's my husband.'

'He doesn't deserve forgiveness.' Cora was sure about that, and it was exhilarating to be sure. She didn't think she'd been sure about anything since the day in February when London Fairweather had crashed and taken her whole life with it.

Jess wiped her thumbs under her eyes. 'Well he's getting it. I just wanted to know what I was forgiving.' She stood up. 'And now I know.'

'He'll do it again.'

Jess shook her head. 'It was a blip. The first year of marriage is a transition, especially for men.'

Cora actually laughed that time. 'Really? Did you read that in some 1950s guide to being a good wife?' She forced herself to breathe and keep her voice calm. 'He cheated and he lied to both of us for months. The only reason he's not still doing it is that he got found out. It will happen again and again and again until you either walk away or get so beaten down that you start to find ways to lie to yourself about what he's doing and who he's with.'

Jess smoothed down the shapeless hoodie. 'Well I'm glad I'm not that cynical.' She walked back over to the door and stopped. 'Do you know when he lost his job?'

Cora nodded. 'April. That was the day we got together. We went to Clacton on the train and ate candyfloss.'

Jess put one hand on the wall. Cora saw her body sway slightly. 'Are you okay?'

She nodded. 'I like Clacton. He used to take me there.' She steadied herself. 'Thank you. I needed to know. I won't bother you again.' She stopped in the doorway, as if unsure what the polite way to end the exchange would be. 'I like your dress.'

# Chapter Fifteen

## December

Chris shook his head. 'So she came to your apartment?'

Cora nodded. 'And she forgave him.'

He was staring down at the floor. 'I don't feel like I should judge. I spent most of my year lying to people.'

Cora shook her head. 'That wasn't the same.' In fact it was entirely different. He hadn't lied to hurt anyone. 'We've stopped saying "my friend".'

He nodded. 'I noticed.'

How did she feel about that? It meant he knew, really knew, that she'd lost her job and her home, and had an affair with a married man. It meant that she knew that he wasn't just a struggling actor. He was a tabloid celebrity with twelve million quid in the bank, which still didn't quite tally with the laid-back guy she'd been getting to know. 'I can't imagine you being super rich.'

He lifted his head to meet her gaze. 'Neither can I.'

Something else didn't make sense. 'You got suspended from work, but you're still rich. You don't need to be doing this.'

He shrugged. 'I kind of do.'

'How do you mean?'

He shook his head. 'We're not at the end of the story yet.'

She was glad about that. They were getting close to catching up with themselves, but she didn't want it to end. The knot that was building in her stomach came down to one thing. It was almost Christmas. Almost time for the magic grotto to close, and then it would be goodbye Chris, and hello to a whole new year. That reminded her. 'I had a job interview last week.'

'That's great. What for?'

'Payroll admin. Here. They offered me it.'

'You should have said. We could have had ...' He looked around the kitchenette. 'We could have had slightly nicer sandwiches or something. You don't look that pleased.'

Cora paused. It was hardly high finance. She wouldn't be buying another South Bank apartment, but it was a job. 'Is it too much of a step down?'

Chris shook his head. 'From being a reindeer?'

Cora opened her mouth and closed it again.

'Stop worrying about not having the life you planned for Rudy. Why not make the most of the life you've got?'

Cora paused. She should call him out on not taking his own advice, but she didn't. The tension she was carrying in her gut eased a little. Chris did that for her. 'Thanks.'

## November, earlier in the year

Liam sat on the sofa. *Homes under the Hammer* had finished hours ago. He'd sat through the actual news at one o'clock because the remote control was at the other side of the room and moving was beyond his mental effort. The idea that he would have some time off, and reassess his situation while the whole tabloid storm blew over had been fine in principle, but having nothing to do, and the financial means to do absolutely anything, was paralysing. His time was his own. Money was no object, and Liam couldn't work out where to start.

Being alone so much wasn't helping either. He was a social animal, definitely better in groups, instinctively drawn to social situations. Damon had moved out, at Raj's insistence, and Raj had gone and got himself a job in the food court at Golding's of Knightsbridge, a department store so posh it boasted a dress code. So Liam sat on the sofa and waited for inspiration about the future to strike.

Raj's key in the lock disturbed his fruitless contemplation.

His housemate stood in the door to the lounge and crossed his arms. 'Right. We're doing an intervention.'

'On who?'

'On you. You're being a miserable git. And I'm sick of it. We need to get you off the couch.'

Liam rolled his eyes. 'Everyone recognises me. It's horrible. They all think I'm a millionaire rent boy alcoholic.'

Raj glanced at the growing pile of empty cans around Liam's spot on the settee. 'Well you're not a rent boy. And not everyone's thinking that. Most people don't read that stuff anyway, and if they do they don't pay any attention to it.'

That was easy for Raj to say. His face hadn't spent the best part of the last two months as the traditional accompaniment to the nation's commute.

'Anyway, it doesn't matter. In the plan I've come up with you get out of the house, you get to meet lots of people and not one of them is going to recognise your face.'

'And that's the bathroom, and that's it really.' Cora peered past the woman with the dreadlocks pulled back into a pony tail and tried to make an appreciative noise in response to the avocado-green bathroom suite. Her guide, and prospective housemate, pulled a face. 'It's horrible, but we can't afford a new one, and everything works. Charlie says I should describe it as wild sage, rather than green, but it's not like that's gonna stop people noticing, is it?'

Cora found herself smiling. After a week traipsing around 'stylish one-bedroomed apartments' that Cora would have struggled to consider a stylish cupboard, the honesty was refreshing. She hadn't really wanted to have housemates, but the reality was that she couldn't afford not to, and these people weren't bothered about her paying a deposit, on account of how somebody called Tonka had done a flit without getting her share back anyway. So far as she could make out the household now consisted of the dreadlocked woman, apparently called Trish, her girlfriend Charlie and somebody referred to as Fake Alan whose room had been omitted from the tour on account of him still being asleep in there. When Cora had queried why he was called 'Fake Alan', Trisha had looked blank. 'Because Alan isn't his real name.'

It was, in many ways, Cora's worst nightmare. She hadn't shared a house since university, and then she had gravitated towards the neatest, quietest, most organised looking girls and done everything possible to keep herself to herself. Nonetheless, needs must.

'I'll take it, please.' Cora expected her tour guide to need to run it by her housemates or the landlord or something but apparently not.

'Cool. When do you want to move in?'

The official completion date on Cora's apartment was Friday. It was Thursday afternoon. Another very good reason that she needed to learn to love this house pretty damn fast. She tried to smile. 'Tonight?'

Four hours later, Cora's stuff was all moved in. Her vague plan to ferry it across London on the tube in multiple trips had been pooh-poohed. Fake Alan had been dragged from his slumber and made to drive Cora and her increasingly meagre set of belongings to her new home. Requests en route for details behind the moniker 'Fake Alan' had, again, been met with a laugh and a simple explanation. 'Because I'm not really called Alan.'

Four and a half hours later, she was sitting on the rather beaten up couch, with cheap wine in her hand and a bowl of chilli on her lap, being interrogated by Trish and Charlie, while Alan drifted back to sleep at the other side of the room.

Charlie tilted her shaven head in his direction. 'He's always asleep. None of us have ever seen him going to work or out with friends or on dates or anything, but somehow he pays rent every month, and he's the lowest maintenance housemate you could hope to have so we're not gonna complain.'

Cora nodded. 'So what do you do?'

Charlie grinned. 'I do art therapy. I was an occupational therapist for years in the NHS. Now I do art, mainly in old people's homes.' She nodded towards her girlfriend. 'And she's a rock star.'

Trish laughed. 'I'm not a rock star. I'm a session singer, which pays like nothing, so at the moment I mainly update websites for businesses and stuff. It's so boring.'

Cora closed her eyes. 'At least you've got a job.'

Trish furrowed her brow. 'So what did you do? Fake Alan said your old flat was well nice.'

Cora gave the summary version of her financial breakdown. The version that involved her old company closing, but omitted to mention that they'd been all over the news for stock market fraud. The version that mentioned the futility of her endless rounds of recruitment agencies but left out one particular recruitment agent. 'Anyway, at the moment I'd take any job.'

'Really any job?'

Cora nodded. 'Short of getting my tits out.'

Trish smiled. 'I might know of something, if you're really not fussy.'

# Chapter Sixteen

### Christmas Eve

Today was her last day as Rudolph. As Cora pulled her brown nylon tights on, she felt sick. It was the end of a short, but strangely significant, era. In January she would start her new job. It wasn't the dream she'd harboured when she'd moved to the big city all those years ago, but she'd lived the dream and ended up here. Now it was time to give real life a try.

She went to the mirror and started putting her make-up on. She was kidding herself. The anxious knot in her belly had nothing to do with her new job, or even her old job. It had everything to do with Chris. Her last day as Rudolph was their last day together. It was the end of the story, and also time to tell him what she'd found out about Robert Grey. She smiled at the thought. At least she could give him something as a thank you for all the hours he'd spent listening to her sad story.

She glanced at the clock. It was time. She followed a gaggle of elves down to the toy floor, and waited for the morning inspection. Seconds later Chris appeared, blue eyes twinkling above his beard. Mrs Atkins followed him, surveying the line. She ticked off an elf for wearing mascara. Cora grinned. It wouldn't have been right for them to pass inspection on the last day. They never had before. She followed Father Christmas into the grotto and started checking through the sack of presents in the corner.

'Rudy?'

'Yeah?'

'What are you doing when we finish today?'

The grotto closed at four p.m. on Christmas Eve. Was he

asking her out? Something fluttered in Cora's stomach. 'I think some of the elves are going for a quick drink.'

'And after that?'

He *was* asking her out. Cora concentrated on the present sack, trying to ignore the quickening beat of her heart. 'Nothing.'

'So you're not dashing off anywhere for Christmas?'

'No.' So that was it? Just curiosity about her plans for the festive season. Why would it have been anything else? He was a multi-millionaire actor. She was basically a down and out adulteress who, so far as he was concerned, lived in brown nylon. There was no reason to think he'd look twice at her.

'Cool.' She heard him take a deep breath. 'It's just ... I wondered if you might want to do something later.'

'Together?'

He laughed. 'Yeah. Together.'

'Okay.' Cora's answer came out in a squeak. She needed to get a grip. He was a mate. He was probably just suggesting a Christmas drink. And she'd never seen him out of his costume. Sure. He had a nice face, but she didn't know how much of that belly was padding and how much was him. It was perfectly possible that she wouldn't even be attracted to him in the cold light of day. She tried to remember the pictures she'd seen in the papers. She knew he was blond and blue-eyed. She liked her men tall, dark and handsome. He wasn't even her type. Cora clung onto that thought, but it was no use. He could turn out to have two heads and she didn't think it would deter the butterflies currently flying loop-the-loops around her tummy.

The day went quickly. Most of the parents who'd booked a ticket for Christmas Eve were the ones who'd planned well in advance. Lots of gold ticket holders, which meant not too many anguished faces when children requested top-end, top-priced presents in their stockings. That made Cora's life a lot easier. The general sense of frantic activity, that built through the day, also meant that most of the parents were keen to be straight in and out on their little darling's visit to the big guy, so they were generally co-operative with Cora's attempts to keep the whole thing running to time. By ten to four they'd managed to clock up only two criers, one refusal to sit on Father Christmas's lap and no impromptu wee-wees at all. It was, in Cora's all new understanding of success, an entirely successful day.

The last child of the season was led into the grotto by the Chief Elf, bounding ahead of her mother, eager for her audience with Father Christmas. Her mum looked tired, lank hair pulled back into a pony tail, long cardigan hanging over leggings with a hole at the knee. In contrast, the little girl looked pristine. Possibly her clothes had the slightly ill-fitting air of hand-me-downs about them, but she was clean and smiley and as bright as the proverbial button. There was no hiding where the love and attention in this family was spent.

Cora watched her lean in towards Chris's ear. 'I'd really really like a doll's house,' she whispered. Across the room her mother looked stricken.

Chris bounced the little girl on his knee. 'Okay. Well Father Christmas will see what he can do, but I'm sure there's lots of things you'd like and even if you don't get them all, I'm sure you'll still have a great Christmas.'

Cora saw the girl's mother blinking hard.

'And,' Chris continued. 'I've got presents for you to take away today.'

Cora pulled an age-appropriate parcel from her sack.

Chris shook his head. 'Not just one present Rudolph.' He turned back to the child on his knee. 'Ho! Ho! Ho! Silly Rudolph. She can have the whole sack.'

Cora paused.

'Come on Rudy!'

Well she was supposed to be his faithful helper. She hauled the sack over to the child's mother who gasped. 'She can't have all these.'

'Is there anyone you can share them with?'

The woman nodded. 'We go to a day centre.'

Chris lifted the child down. 'Excellent. Merry Christmas to everyone at the day centre then. Ho! Ho! Ho!'

The mother and child dragged their mass of presents out of the grotto.

'Are you even allowed to do that?'

Chris pulled his beard away from his face. 'I'm Father Christmas. It's in keeping with my character.'

'What if Mrs Atkins finds out? I'm supposed to be carrying on working here in January.'

He paused. 'Then I guess I'll pay for them.'

Cora stopped. That seemed fair. 'It was a lovely gesture.'

'Thanks.'

She pointed back at his face. 'You need that back on. We've got to parade out, waving goodbye to the children.'

A groan.

'Come on. Where's your Christmas spirit?'

'A month of being Santa broke it.'

'Father Christmas.' She corrected the S-word without thinking.

'Sorry. Actually I've had an incredible month. I was thinking of asking if we could keep doing it in January.'

Cora moved towards him, still sitting in his festive throne. She lifted the beard off his lap, and hooked it back over his ears. Their eyes locked for a second, as she smoothed the beard against his face. Under her painted red cheeks, her real cheeks flushed pink. 'Come on. One last bit of festive mood and then you can be as grumpy as you want.'

The Chief Elf popped her head into the grotto. 'What did you say to that last one? They practically danced out.'

Cora flicked her eyes towards Chris who shrugged, full of innocence. 'Nothing.'

'Okay, well that's us done. Time for you to head back to the North Pole.'

'I thought I was from Lapland.'

The Elf shook her head. 'No.'

Cora followed him out of the grotto, watching him shaking hands and smiling for photos with families and children. There was definitely something about him, but she'd told him everything about her year. She was kidding herself if she thought there was even a passing chance he'd be interested in her.

Finally free from the grotto Liam stripped his costume off for the last time. His status as Father Christmas somehow earned him privileged access to the directors' bathroom. He had yet to establish who the directors were, or why they needed a private bathroom. He suspected that Mrs Atkins had some rather Victorian ideas about the appropriateness of Father Christmas sharing a changing room with young impressionable elves. Nonetheless, he wasn't complaining as he washed away the layer of sweat that built up under the thick foam belly for the final time.

He'd managed to bite at least one bullet today. He'd asked the lovely Rudy out. Admittedly, he'd rather panicked and asked her out for tonight, which wasn't ideal given where he absolutely had to be tonight. He checked the time. There were still a few hours before he had to get to the train. A drink with the elves. A drink with Rudy, and he'd still be on time. That was the plan. He'd take her for a drink, and then he'd go.

He dried himself quickly with the thick, white company director-quality towel. Maybe that was something he could do with his money. He could get nicer towels. He pulled on his jeans and shirt and boots, and slung his battered leather jacket over the top. His hair was still damp, but it would do. He made his way down the staff staircase and out of the door at the back of the shop. A gaggle of elves were waiting in the loading bay, almost unrecognisable out of costume and in their Christmas Eve mini-dresses and heels. He scanned the group for Rudy. Behind him, he heard the door swing open and bang shut. He turned. Everything stopped.

The woman standing in the doorway was beautiful. Properly beautiful. He'd met pretty girls before, all cute dimples and unnecessary sundresses. He'd met attractive women, even sexy women. What he was looking at now was something else. Something less familiar, that couldn't be broken down into its individual parts. Long, brown, glossy hair – perfectly nice. Big, oval, hazel-brown eyes – absolutely lovely. Thick, pink lips – very good. But this wasn't a result of good features, or nice clothes, or pretty hair. The woman was beautiful. 'Rudy?'

'Chris?'

He nodded.

She smiled.

He reminded himself to start breathing again.

Drinks with the elves was good fun. If they knew who he was they were either too polite, or too concerned with their own Christmas plans, to say anything about it. The pub was busy, but spirits were high and Liam would normally have been in his element. Today he wanted nothing more than for every other person in the room to simply disappear. They refused to co-operate. Every time he saw drinks around the table starting to drain away, someone would jump up and announce a new round. Time ticked down. Sooner or later he was going to have to make a decision. He needed to be with Rudy, just her and him. He needed to take his shot. He looked at his watch, and then checked it again. It was too late. He leant across the table to where she was sitting. 'I have to go.'

Something flashed across her face. Disappointment perhaps, or maybe Liam was seeing what he wanted to see. 'Okay.'

He took a breath. 'I wondered if I could get your number before I went?'

She nodded. He pulled his phone out of his pocket and let her type the digits in. There was more he should say, more he should do. *Fairytale of New York* came on the jukebox. All around him voices raised and sang along. It was no good. This wasn't the place. He shrugged in a way that he hoped communicated how desperately he wanted to stay, and stuffed his phone back in his pocket. 'I'll call you.'

He barged his way through the crowd and into the cold street, past the gaggle of smokers loitering around the door. *I'll call you?* Even to Liam that sounded lame, but it was what guys said, wasn't it? I'll call you, and then they never did. Everyone knew that. No guy ever calls. He pulled his phone out of his pocket. Why not? Why not be the exception to the rule? He hit call before he could change his mind and waited. When she answered he could barely make out her voice above the noise of the bar. He yelled into the phone. 'Come with me!'

'What?'

'I'm outside. Come with me.'

He heard her mutter something, and then muffled noises down the line.

'I can't hear you. What did you say?'

'I said I can't hear you. I'm coming outside.' Liam spun towards the voice, suddenly clear in the chilly air. He held out his phone and pulled a face, before clicking to end the call. He watched her do the same.

She stuffed her hands into the pockets of her long wool coat. 'So you rang?'

'Yeah.' With her in front of him he was suddenly nervous again. 'I wanted to ask you to come with me.'

'Where?'

He squirmed slightly. 'It's this Christmas Eve thing. A sort of family tradition.'

She shifted her weight from foot to foot. 'I don't know. A family thing?'

He held his hand out towards her. 'We're not really that sort of family. It'll be good. I promise. You did say you didn't really have any Christmas plans?'

He watched her scan his face and then drop her eyes to the hand. 'The last time I went somewhere on impulse with a man I ended up in Clacton with an adulterer.'

Liam grinned. 'You mean your friend did.'

He saw her cheeks flush pink as she smiled at the shared joke. 'Yeah. My friend.'

'This won't be like that.'

'I should hope not.' She took a tiny step forward and rested her fingertips on his palm. Liam didn't move. After a second she slid her hand across his. He closed his fingers around hers.

'Actually.'

'What?'

'We are sort of going to Clacton.'

He felt her stiffen. 'Just because that's where my family is. I don't think you should hold Clacton responsible for …' He paused. 'For what happened to your friend.' She was hesitating. Liam could understand that. It was hard to forget what it was like to be hurt in the past. He rubbed his fingers across the back of her hand. 'Come on Rudy. Trust me.'

He felt her hesitate for a second before she nodded, and joined him pelting down the pavement towards the tube. It wasn't until they were inside the carriage that she spoke. 'So we're going to Clacton?'

Liam nodded.

'Why?'

The why was more difficult. It was what he'd done on Christmas Eve every year for the last six, every year since Mama Lou died. He glanced at her face. 'It's tradition.'

She furrowed her brow. 'So you *are* taking me to some big family Christmas tradition thing?'

Put like that it did sound a little odd. Liam shook his head. 'It's not really a Christmas thing. It's ...' *What was it?* 'You'll see.'

She was staring straight ahead. 'I'm not really great with big traditional family things.'

'Why not Rudy?' He grinned. 'Did the other reindeer used to laugh and call you names?'

She giggled. 'No. They can just be a bit oppressive.' He saw her glance at his face. 'My friend Cora ...'

'Yeah ...'

'Her parents were always very big on tradition. Things had to be done a certain way, in a certain order, wearing the right clothes, the right wine with the right course. Everything just right.'

Liam shook his head. 'That's not tradition. Tradition is when something goes stupidly wrong, but everyone laughs so much that you decide to do it wrong every year, and then the next year it's a bit different again and it sort of evolves.'

He saw her scrunch her eyebrows together. 'I don't think my parents would approve of that.'

'Your parents?'

She smiled. 'I meant my friend's parents.'

'Of course.'

At Liverpool Street they got on the train to Clacton. Cora found herself squashed into the window seat, Chris's long limbs taking up most of the space, even with one leg stretched out into the aisle. She took the chance to take a proper look. He was tall, which she already knew, but it turned out the padded belly had been hiding a lean, muscular body. She'd never really fancied muscly guys, and she didn't go for blonds. In his Santa outfit with his big jelly belly and white wig, she'd been able to pretend that all that was true. She'd kidded herself that she could tell him all her stories because he was an anonymous friend who, after Christmas, she would never see again. Now the idea that she would never see him again was making her insides ache. So what if he wasn't her type? You didn't fall in love with a type. You fell in love with a man. Cora stared at the man sat next to her. She wanted to touch him, feel his skin against hers, drink him in and never stop.

Her previous December had been spent mainly in New York, courting clients, shopping on Fifth Avenue, living the high life, and she'd thought she was living her dream. Dreams changed. This new Cora, jammed into a train seat with too little leg room, would swap a year in New York for one more day in an itchy polyester reindeer suit sharing stories with the man sitting next to her. But now it was Christmas Eve and their little bubble of time ... Wait a second. It was Christmas Eve. This was the last train. 'How are we getting home?'

Her companion paused a second. 'I had not thought about that.'

'Really?'

He turned his electric blue eyes in her direction. 'Ah. I was intending on going on my own. Sorry.'

'Okay, so how were you planning on getting home?'

He shrugged. 'Usually someone gives me a lift back, or a couple of times I've crashed at Auntie Val's. She doesn't mind.'

Cora gestured at her body. 'I can't stay in Clacton. I don't have clean clothes, or a toothbrush, or anything.'

He frowned. 'No. Right. It'll be fine. Someone'll bring us back. I'm sure.'

'How sure?'

'Almost totally sure.' He flashed a smile.

'You didn't really think this through.'

He shook his head. 'I'm sorry.' She watched his chest rise and fall as he inhaled. 'It's quite hard to think around you.'

She pursed her lips, which did nothing to hide the smile in her eyes. 'What do you mean?'

Another deep breath. 'I mean that all I really thought was that I didn't like the idea that we'd both leave work today and I'd never see you again, Rudy. And I know that I got your number and I could have called you after Christmas and that would have been sensible and everything, but ...' He paused. 'I wanted to be with you now. Right now. I didn't want to wait.'

'Oh.'

'I'm sorry. That was too much, wasn't it? You're probably terrified now aren't you?'

Cora shook her head, but didn't speak. He wanted to be with her. He wanted to be with her right now. He found it hard to think straight around her. She opened her mouth and closed it again.

'Say something, Rudy.' She glanced up. His eyes were fixed on her face. 'I'm kinda out on a limb here.'

What could she say? It had to be right. It had to tell him that she was here too, one hundred per cent here with him right now. It had to tell him that she didn't regret getting on the train, that she wasn't freaked out, or at least, that the being freaked out wasn't making her want to run away, because running away would mean not being with him. She bit her lip. Eventually, she held out her hand towards him. 'Hi.'

He looked confused. 'Hi.'

She took a breath. 'I'm Cora. It's nice to meet you.'

The grin spread across his face as he understood what she was doing. Not hiding. Not lying. Choosing to be real. He took her hand in his. 'I'm Liam. It's nice to meet you too.'

She giggled, nervousness mixing with relief. So what now? 'So tell me about yourself Liam.'

And so he did. New stories. Tales from childhood rather than the last year. Anecdotes from drama school and recordings of *Lamplugh and Sons*. Horror stories from horrendous auditions. And she reciprocated with stories of her own. The pony her parents had bought her that had absolutely refused to be ridden by Cora while acting like a pussy cat around everyone else. The daily two-hour bus ride as a day girl at the private school on the far side of Edinburgh, because the village primary was not good enough for Princess Cora. The country rolled past in the darkness outside the window and then they arrived. Liam pulled himself out of his seat and held his hand out to Cora. 'Come on.'

She wrapped her hand around his and let him lead the way out of the carriage, across the station and into the street. 'Where are we going?'

'You'll see. It's not far.'

They made their way, hand in hand, through the town and up a hill away from the seafront until they reached a large cast iron gate. Beyond the gate was darkness. Cora scanned around for a notice or sign offering some clue as to where they might be, but she couldn't find a clue. Liam pushed the gate open and paused. 'Why do I never bring a torch?' He squeezed Cora's hand. 'You're not scared of the dark, are you?'

'No.'

'Excellent. I hate it.'

They made their way along the path beyond the gate. Slowly Cora's eyes adapted to the lack of streetlights and she started to make out shapes amongst the trees that lined the path. Short stubby shapes close to the earth, and then, to the other side, taller squarer shapes with a hint of a gleam to them. 'It's a graveyard.'

Liam nodded, and then stopped, spinning around to face her. 'Too creepy?'

Cora had been telling the truth. She wasn't scared of the dark, but graveyard on a first date – if that was even what this was – was a tiny bit on the twilight spectrum. 'It's a bit weird.'

'Sorry. We're nearly there. It won't be weird when we get there. I promise.'

Liam followed a smaller path that forked off to the right and came to a stop in front of one of the newer grave markers. The grave was well tended, fresh flowers sitting at its head, and a stone clean of moss and dirt. Cora couldn't make out the inscription in the darkness.

'Hold on.' Liam fumbled in his pockets and pulled out a small white candle and a lighter. He lit the candle and handed it to Cora.

She leant towards the headstone and read.

**Mama Lou**
**Here lies Louise Brown.**
**Daughter of Gladys and Fred.**
**Sister of Valerie.**
**Mother to all.**

'Mother to all?'

Liam nodded. 'To anyone who needed her.' He glanced at his watch. 'We're a bit early.'

Cora frowned. 'I'm sure she doesn't mind.'

Liam smiled.

'And you come here every Christmas?'

'Every Christmas Eve.' Another smile. 'Only it's not just me.'

Cora heard the sounds of footsteps coming along the path from the way she'd just walked, and then voices from the other direction, and then the faint hint of candlelight in the darkness behind the grave. As she watched candle flames flickered into life all around her. At first one or two more to join her own, and then tens, and it didn't stop. She leant towards Liam. 'How many people are there?'

'I'm never exactly sure. A hundred maybe. Or more.'

'It's beautiful.'

Liam wrapped one arm around her shoulder and flicked his lighter into life with the other. 'Wait.'

Cora waited, watching the candles flicker in the darkness, and then it started. One voice at first singing soft but clear across the dark cemetery. *Silent Night*. And then another voice joined in, and then another and another, until a whole choir of men and women joined together in the cold, black night.

She felt Liam's arm squeeze tighter around her and she rested her head onto his shoulder, listening to him sing. It was like no Christmas Cora had ever known, and none she could ever have dreamed about. Love swept through the air, carried on the voices of the strangers gathered in the darkness to pay their abiding respects to the woman who'd given them a home and a chance when they needed it most. *Sleep in heavenly peace. Sleep in heavenly peace.*

The group fell silent, for a second or two, and each person offered up their own quiet memories. Something caught in Cora's throat. Each of the people here had lived through their own year. Some filled with joy, some heartbreak, and most, she imagined, somewhere in between, but they all had somewhere they could bring those joys and disappointments and offer them up. And Liam had brought her here too.

The quiet broke as spontaneously as it had settled. Voices erupted all around her. Hugs and greetings were being exchanged. A short, ruddy-faced man appeared out of the gloom, and whacked Liam on the back. 'Liam! I wasn't sure you'd come.'

Liam dropped his eyes to the ground. 'Couldn't not.'

'Quite right too. You can't let the bastards grind you down.' The man's eyes drifted to Cora. 'You're new!'

She extricated the hand that was behind Liam's back and offered it for shaking. 'I'm Cora. I'm Liam's friend.'

The man laughed. 'Liam's friend? Course you are.'

Cora could feel her cheeks flushing and hoped it wasn't noticeable in the darkness.

She felt Liam's body shift against her but his arm didn't move from her shoulder. 'Are you heading back to London tonight?'

The man shook his head. 'Sorry mate. I've got Archie with me. First Christmas Nat's let me have him. We're staying at Val's.'

An older woman with a small child balanced on her hip bustled over. 'Terry, Archie needs taking back and putting to bed.' Terry wrestled the toddler from the woman's grip, leaving her attention free to turn to Cora and Liam. She kissed Liam enthusiastically on the cheek. 'Did you grow?'

Liam shook his head. 'I'm thirty, and you saw me in April, so no.' He finally uncurled his arm from Cora. 'Val, I'd like you to meet Cora. Cora this is Auntie Val.'

Cora's brain flickered into action. 'Val! With the letter in the box!'

Liam nodded.

Cora found herself enveloped in a hug heavily scented with lily of the valley and fruit cake. The woman stepped back and took both of them in for a moment. 'So you'll both be staying for Christmas then.'

'Er.'

Cora heard the pause in Liam's voice. *Enjoy the life you have.* That's what he'd told her. She slid her hand into his and squeezed. 'That would be lovely.' She glanced up at Liam. 'If that's okay with you?'

'That's perfect with me.'

\* \* \*

Liam followed Val and Terry along the path, pausing to accept hugs from other foster siblings and their families along the way. Every time he moved back towards her, he felt for Cora's hand, and every time it was there. Eventually they were clear of the crowds of extended family, walking a few metres behind Val and Terry.

'So they're all people who Mama Lou fostered?'

Liam nodded. 'Pretty much. And their families as well now. And Val.' He gestured ahead of them. 'Terry's about ten years older than me. Nice guy, but not the sharpest. Romantic though.'

'How?'

'Archie's mum. Natalia. From Belarus. Everybody said she was only interested in a visa, but Terry thought it was true love. They got married and now there's Archie.'

'That is romantic.'

'Not really. She divorced him as soon as she got permanent permission to stay here.' He glanced down at their clasped hands. 'Is this okay?'

'Is what okay?'

'All of it. Bringing you here. Staying over. Is it too fast?'

She stared away from him down the road. 'It should be, shouldn't it?'

*Should? Should wasn't really an answer, was it?* 'But?'

'But, I don't know. I don't have anywhere I'd prefer to be.'

That would have to be good enough for the moment. They wandered up the path to Auntie Val's bungalow. Val was already inside bustling around the kitchen. She smiled as they came in. 'Terry's taken the little one straight to bed.' She glanced up at the kitchen clock. It was close to midnight. 'I'm guessing you'll want to do the same.'

Liam nodded.

'I'll show you where you're sleeping then.' Val led the way upstairs, stopping on the landing to point at the various doors. 'Terry and Archie are in my room. I'll go in the box room. Cora – bathroom's through there.'

She pushed the final door open. 'There you go. The back bedroom's all made up.'

Liam opened his mouth to explain that he and Cora weren't really at the sharing a bed stage, but Val was already out of the door and across the hall.

'I'm going to turn in then. See you both in the morning.' He could have sworn there was a twinkle in her eye.

He let Cora's hand drop. 'I'll go on the sofa downstairs. I'm sorry.'

There were clean towels on top of the chest next to the bed. Liam glanced around the room. 'Have you got everything you need?'

She nodded.

And yet he still hadn't left the room.

'I ...'

'Actually ...'

They both spoke at once. Liam smiled. 'You go.'

Cora stared down at the floor. 'Actually, I'm not that tired.'

'Me neither.' He stretched out his arms and shoulders. 'And I am hungry.'

Cora nodded. 'I had wine and diet coke for tea.'

'Food then.' He swung the bedroom door open. 'Come on.'

In the kitchen he found bread, and rifled through the fridge. 'I'm a bit scared to use anything. When we were kids I remember not being allowed near the fridge on Christmas Eve in case we ate something that was meant for the big day.'

Cora laughed. 'It was like that when I was really little.'

'What about later?'

Cora rolled her eyes. 'We moved to the bigger house when I was about nine. After that my mother would hire a caterer.'

'You had a caterer do Christmas dinner?'

Cora nodded.

'How many people for?'

'Just me and my mum and dad. Sometimes my grandma.'

'Wow.' Liam stared at his guest for a second. 'How rich are your family?'

He saw her pout before a twinkle flashed across her eyes. 'Not as rich as you.'

'Touché.' He pulled a half used chunk of cheddar from the fridge. 'I reckon this is fair game. So an exciting choice. Would madam prefer a cheese sandwich or cheese on toast?'

Cora smiled. 'On toast.'

They carried their plates into the living room and sat together on the small sofa. Liam watched her eat. 'You're remarkably relaxed. Given that I'm guessing this isn't where you thought you were going to finish up tonight.'

Cora peered around the room. Liam tried to imagine it from her point of view. The flock wallpaper and velour-covered three piece suite were hardly the height of London chic. She shrugged. 'I like it here. It feels homely.'

'That wasn't what I meant.'

'I know.'

'I meant that you're the woman with a plan. This is quite a long way off piste.'

'Well this is my new attitude to life.'

'Really?'

'Really. I had this friend, you see.'

Liam laughed. 'A friend.'

'Yeah. My friend Rudy, and Rudy met this guy and he told her that you can't always plan for the future. Sometimes you have to enjoy the moment.'

'He sounds very wise.'

Cora pulled her feet up onto the settee and twisted her body to face Liam. A new, determined expression settled on her face. 'He was. Only he didn't always take his own advice.'

Liam suspected he knew where she was going, but didn't raise his eyes from his plate.

'Because this guy, Chris ...'

'Chris?'

'That's right. Chris inherited some money. A lot of money, and it just sat in the bank gaining interest.'

'That does sound stupid.' She had a point. It was what Val had told him, and Raj, and even the solicitor, but now Liam, finally, thought he might have an idea of what he wanted to do with the money. He turned to face her. 'Actually, I think I've decided what I'm going to do.'

'Yeah?'

'I've sort of been thinking about it all month, and then tonight the whole idea sort of came together.'

'So tell me.'

And he did. The realisation that Mama Lou's legacy wasn't the sense of responsibility she instilled, it was her love. The love she had given freely to any child who needed it. The love that had never been rationed, and was set alongside her heartfelt belief that every child deserved chances. He was going to found a charity, a charity to give chances to children who might never have a Mama Lou of their own.

Cora frowned. 'Twelve million isn't that much for a trust. You'd have to invest.' She sucked the air through her teeth. 'But you don't want to risk too much of your capital, and anything with a guaranteed yield is going to limit how much you have to distribute.' She reached for pen and pad from the coffee table in front of her and started making notes. Investment ideas. Different ways of setting up a trust. Areas they'd have to look into – charity commission rules, tax implications.

Liam reached across and took the pen and paper out of her hand. 'Cora, it's Christmas Eve.'

She glanced at the clock. 'No. It isn't.'

She was right. It was Christmas Day already. Liam smiled. 'Merry Christmas Rudy.'

She met his gaze. 'Merry Christmas.'

The silence hung between them for a moment, neither of them daring to break it, neither of them daring to make the first move. Liam waited. Somehow, he sensed, it was important to let her come to him. Christmas was an emotional time, and she'd already wasted most of her year on a man who'd taken advantage of Cora at her most emotional, her most vulnerable. Liam didn't want to be anything like that guy. He waited. Eventually she tilted her head, just slightly. That was all he needed. He leant in, wrapping his arms tight around her body, pulling her into him, pressing his lips urgently against hers. He felt her fingers slide to his waist and bury into the soft wool of his top. He slid one hand to the back of her head and stroked her hair. Her lips parted and he felt her shift her body against him. She swung one leg over his thighs and straddled him. Without thinking, he slid both hands under her shirt. Cora lifted her arms to let him pull it away over her head. He wrapped his arms tight around her again, kissing her deeply on the mouth before peppering kisses down her neck and towards her breasts.

Suddenly, she jumped, pushing herself away from him. She stood for a second in the middle of the room, before scooping her shirt from the floor and holding it in front of her chest.

'What's wrong?'

Cora stared around the room.

'They won't be able to hear us from upstairs.'

Cora shook her head. 'Do you mind if we don't do this?'

'Of course not.' He leaned towards her. 'Are you okay?'

She nodded. She pulled her top back over her head and

sat down next to him on the sofa. 'I really, really want to do this.'

'Okay ...'

'But it's what I always do. I jump in and then when it gets heavy I run away.'

'You didn't run away from Patrick.'

Cora nodded. 'But I sort of knew that had a time limit. I didn't know he was married, but we were in a bubble. We were ignoring all our problems. He was a way of running away from all the heavy stuff that was going on.' She swallowed hard. Sean popped into her head. She'd done this before. She'd taken a good man, a kind man and she'd broken his heart. Only that time she was a kid. Now she was an adult. She looked into Liam's perfect blue eyes. 'I don't want to run away from you, but I want to give you the chance to run from me.'

He shook his head. 'Never.'

'You don't know that.' She dragged her eyes away from his face. 'What if I'm just too poisonous? Look at what I did to Sean. I hurt him so badly. And Patrick's wife.' Cora stared at the space behind Liam's head, the image of Patrick's wife crumpled and devastated on the floor in a hotel lobby playing in front of her eyes.

Liam reached a hand to hers. 'You are not poison. Patrick might be poison. He's the one that lied. Not you. And Sean's fine by the sound of it.'

She let him wrap his fingers around her own.

'You're great Cora. You don't need to be so hard on yourself.'

The tiny spark of hope that Cora was harbouring deep inside flickered a little brighter. 'Is it okay if we take things slow though? I think I need to try not to repeat all my old mistakes again.'

'So what? No sex before marriage and babies?' Liam flashed a grin.

Cora laughed. 'No. Just no sex before ...' Her voice tailed off. Before what? '... before I'm sure I'm not using it to distract me from my other problems.'

Liam raised an eyebrow. 'Seriously, what other problems?'

'Well ... being broke. The fact that I'm barely speaking to my parents. Not having anywhere to live.'

'You have somewhere to live. It sounds completely mad, but it has a roof and housemates who don't keep their drug stashes in the oven. You've got a new job lined up. And being broke and in angst about your parents is the natural order of things for anyone under about sixty living in London.' Liam pulled her back into his arms. 'We can wait as long as you want, but you've got to stop telling yourself that your life's a mess. You're doing fine Cora. You're doing absolutely fine.'

# Chapter Seventeen

### Christmas Day

Liam opened his eyes to the sight of his foster nephew toddling into the living room and plonking himself down in front of the tree. He took a second to acclimatise himself to the scene. Cora was still fast asleep, stretched out along the sofa, head pressed into the nook of his shoulder. At some point during the night, the pair of them had both been covered with a soft blanket. Auntie Val, he assumed. He sneaked a peek under the blanket. They were both still wearing enough of yesterday's clothes to be respectable. He was only half relieved.

'Uncle Liam!'

Liam held his finger up to his lips in a shushing gesture, but it was too late. He felt Cora move against him.

'Good morning.' He leant straight down and pressed a kiss onto her lips. 'Happy Christmas.'

'Happy Christmas.' He watched a string of emotions dance across her face. Confusion, sleepiness, happiness, anxiety. 'Oh God! I can't stay here. I bet your aunt doesn't have enough food.'

'She'll have enough for half the town. And it's Christmas Day. You can't get anywhere now.' He leant towards her and whispered. 'And I don't want you to go anywhere. No running away. Remember?'

She gazed into his eyes and nodded, before sitting up on the sofa.

'Uncle Liam's friend!' The toddler in front of the tree addressed the guest directly.

'Yes?'

'Can I open my presents yet?'

Cora glanced uncertainly at Liam. 'I think maybe you should wait for Daddy.'

The boy stared at the pile of gifts and then back at Cora and then at Liam. 'She's right,' said Liam. 'Go and see what's taking your dad so long.'

Archie marched out of the room, leaving Cora and Liam to disentangle themselves from the blanket and make the best they could of their lack of change of clothes or toiletries. Despite that, the morning was great fun. Archie opened his presents with glee, and then moved onto 'helping' his dad and Auntie Val open theirs with equal vigour. Once all the gifts under the tree had been opened, Liam pulled Cora by the hand into the hallway, and pulled a tiny, wrapped parcel from the recesses of his leather jacket. He held it out to her. 'Happy Christmas.'

Cora stared at the gift. 'I didn't get you anything.'

Liam shrugged. 'That's okay. There's next year.'

Cora nodded. Next year sounded good. She lifted the present from his hand and pulled off the paper.

'It's not much. I just … I saw it and I thought of you.'

Inside the wrapping was a small, square jewellery box. Cora opened it cautiously. She wasn't expecting a ring, but the thought of him spending huge amounts of money on her at this very early stage made her anxious. As the box flipped open, she broke into a smile. Inside was a silver necklace chain. Hanging from the chain was a tiny pendant in the shape of a reindeer dashing and dancing through the sky. She laughed. It was just right. Simple, but personal. 'It's lovely.'

She clutched the box in one hand, and reached the other up to Liam's face, stretching up to kiss him softly on the lips. She felt his arms wrap, strong and tight, around her waist, and his lips responded to her kiss. So this was what it felt like when you fell in love with the person before you fell in lust. Cora pulled her head back from his embrace, and screwed up her courage. 'Liam … I…' She couldn't quite say it. She'd promised him she wouldn't run away, and she'd promised herself she'd be honest this time. She'd let him in. 'I think … I think I … I'm falling …' She stuttered.

Liam kissed the top of her head so gently she might almost have dreamt it. 'I love you Cora.'

Cora gasped.

'Was that the sort of thing you were trying to say?'

She looked up into his eyes, and nodded. Him going first made it so much easier. 'I love you too.'

She tilted her chin as he bent his head towards her, and then jumped back. There was something, something she should have shown him days ago. 'Actually I did sort of get you something.' She ran into the living room and pulled a handful of paper from her bag. 'I was going to give you this last week, but there wasn't really a good moment.' That wasn't true. There'd been plenty of moments. 'And I chickened out.'

She watched him unfold the paper and read. She knew what it said. She'd practically learnt it by heart. It was an email from Nathan Glover, Tennessee-based private detective, explaining that he did indeed remember Robert Grey and that, although normally client details were confidential, as Mr Grey was now deceased, with no known family, he felt he could give her some information.

She heard Liam gasp. 'He left twelve million pounds to hundreds of people.'

Cora nodded. 'Apparently he never found his son or daughter, but during the investigation they found all these different children with different stories and different problems. When he made his will I guess he sort of decided that they were all his children, even though really none of them were.'

She watched him reread the message, brows knotted together.

Doubt rushed in. Was it too much? Was she interfering where she had no business? 'I thought it would help you to know.' She paused. 'Sorry. Am I interfering?'

'How did you even find him?'

Cora shuffled. 'It wasn't a big deal. I just sent a few emails.' Actually over three hundred emails. It turned out there were a lot of private investigators in Tennessee.

Liam shook his head. 'Thank you.'

'You're not mad?'

'Not at all. This is ...' He swallowed. 'This is exactly what I needed.'

'Good.'

'It means I'm doing the right thing, doesn't it? With the charity. It seems like the sort of thing he'd have approved of.'

Cora nodded. It absolutely did.

Liam folded the email and stuffed it into his back pocket, before reaching his hand to her waist. 'Thank you.'

'It's okay.'

'It's more than okay.' He bent his head towards her once again, and she raised her lips to meet his.

A crash from the kitchen stopped them in their tracks. 'What the ...?'

Terry ran past them from the living room, and Liam followed. By the time Cora made it to the kitchen door she was peering between the shoulders of the two men, but she could see enough to make out the turkey on the floor, and Auntie Val's cockerpoo already taking a big chunk out of the breast. Liam shooed the dog away as Terry lifted the roasting tin, and the remains of the bird, back onto the table. Auntie Val surveyed the destruction. 'Well, that's buggered,' she announced.

The four adults stood around the kitchen table for a second considering the remains of their dinner.

'Whooooosh!' Archie ran from the living room around their legs waving his lightsaber happily.

Terry crouched down to talk to his son. 'Archie, mate. I'm not sure we're going to be able to have turkey for dinner.'

Archie whooshed his lightsaber one more time. 'Can we have ice cream instead?'

At the other side of the room Val let out a big throaty chuckle. 'I don't see why not.'

An idea was starting to form in Cora's head. She glanced at the clock. Only just after ten. 'Terry, do you have a car here?'

He nodded.

'Hold on.' Cora pulled her mobile from her pocket and stepped into the hall.

Three hours later Cora's new family sat down for Christmas dinner. Trish, with a party hat balanced on top of her dreadlocks. Fake Alan, wide awake and carving the turkey like an expert. Charlie cheerfully forcing portions of nut roast on to everyone's plate. Terry balanced on a plastic garden chair with a book under one leg to make it stand up, full of pride as his son ate all his carrots. Auntie Val, three sherries down and regaling anyone who'd listen with stories of how she was once runner-up in a beauty pageant, and would have won if it hadn't been for what the eventual Miss England was prepared to get up to under the judges' table. Raj, who was tucking in to a full Christmas dinner, despite having 'just popped by' and being committed to eating it all again that evening at his parents' house. And Liam. Liam who kept catching her eye across the table, and her foot underneath it. Liam who was prepared to wait as long as she needed, and from whom, Cora promised herself, she would never run away.

*What does perfection look like? Cora Strachan knows. Perfection looks like an inexpensive reindeer on a fine silver chain. Perfection looks like a room full of people prepared to see the best and the brightest in everyone they meet. Perfection looks like nothing you could ever have planned for at all.*

# Jessica's Christmas Kiss

# *Prologue*

## Christmas Eve, 2000

The perfect boy had dyed black hair that flopped in front of his face, not quite obscuring a pair of bright green eyes. He wore a single silver earring and black trousers and a faded T-shirt. He reminded her of the goths and indie kids at school. Jess sometimes wished she had the confidence to dress like them; standing out in a cool and uniform way was totally the best sort of fitting in.

He was leaning on the kitchen worktop next to the bottles of soft drink and pile of plastic cups. Jess poured her own drink. She could go back into the living room with the grown-ups and that Slade song playing on a constant loop. There was no reason to stay in the kitchen with a stranger. She made a deal in her head. If he spoke in the next five seconds then she'd stay. One... two... three... four... fi—

'So you know this Janine then?' He had the slightest hint of a local accent, hidden under something else. American maybe. It sounded amazing.

'She used to work with my dad. What about you?'

He shook his head. 'I came with a friend.'

'Right.' They fell into silence. Jess could run back to the party but somehow she didn't want to. She wanted to find out more about the boy in the kitchen. 'So what school do you go to?'

'Er ... I went to Colesworth.'

'That's primary. What about now?'

He shook his head. 'I don't go to school any more.'

Jess's stomach flipped. He must be older than her then. An older boy. She sighed. 'Sixth form? University?'

'No. I'm working.'

He was so grown-up. Jess beamed. 'What do you do?'

He shrugged. 'Nothing exciting. What about you?'

Jess dropped her gaze to the floor. 'I'm still at school. Septon Grove.' He was going to think she was a stupid kid, wasn't he? 'I'm in my last year though.'

He sipped his coke. 'So what's school like?'

She shrugged. 'It's school. S'boring.' She glanced around the pine and laminate kitchen. 'My whole life's boring. It's just normal, you know.'

A smile spread across his face. 'It sounds great.'

'S'not.'

'I don't believe that. Tell me about your life.'

Jess scanned his face for the inevitable twitch of a laugh at the side of his lips, or the look in his eye that would give away the fact that he was mocking her. It wasn't there. He looked interested. People generally weren't very interested in Jess. She was dull. She knew that. She wasn't a high academic achiever like her oldest brother, or a great creative talent like the youngest. She was just Jess.

'Seriously. I'm interested.'

She squirmed. 'What in?'

'Christmas. Tell me about what you're doing for Christmas.'

So she did. She talked about her mum and dad and the well-rehearsed routines of Christmas Day. She talked about the sorts of presents she hoped for and the sorts of presents she might actually get. She told him about her trio of perfect brothers, and she admitted that sometimes being the baby and the only girl made her feel out of place and unsure of her role.

He nodded at that.

'You know what I mean?'

'Sometimes when there's a lot of people who want you to be a certain thing, it's hard to try to be anything else.'

'Exactly.' Jess paused. She'd never tried to put this into words before. 'It's not even that they want you to be that thing. It's just that that's what they think you are.'

'Yeah. And then you end up becoming the thing they think you are. Even if you're not, but then you sort of are and ...' The beautiful black-haired boy's voice tailed away. 'I'm not really making sense any more, am I?'

'You are to me.'

'Cool.'

They were both still leaning on the worktop, but Jess realised that he was moving ever so slightly closer to her. She twisted to face him. His body was inches away from hers. He bent his head ever so slightly towards her. 'Is this okay?'

It took a second to realise what *this* was. This was it, wasn't it? It was actually happening. She'd come to a party and she'd met a boy. This was the beginning. Jess nodded. It was more than okay. She tilted her head and let him press his lips against hers. They were warm and firm, and they tasted of coca cola and salt and vinegar crisps, and it turned out that they were the absolute most perfect things for lips to taste of.

Jess leant further into the kiss, parting her lips ever so slightly, like she'd practised, so he could kiss her more deeply. She felt his hand move to her cheek and then to the back of her head. And then he pulled away.

'Sorry.' He was staring suddenly at the floor.

'No. Don't be. It was ...' Jess didn't have the words. 'Did I do it wrong?'

She saw the horror on his face. 'No. You were great. You are great. I ...' He glanced around the kitchen. 'Your parents are through there.'

'Right. Yeah.' He was right, of course. If Jess's mum or dad walked in on her kissing a boy she'd never met before at a party they'd probably keel over right there and then. 'Okay.'

He looked up and their eyes met for a second. He smiled. Jess's nerves calmed. 'I guess we should probably go back through then.'

He nodded. 'Sorry. You didn't say your name.'

She felt herself blushing. 'I'm Jess.'

He grinned. 'Hi Jess.'

'And yours?'

His brow furrowed instantly. 'What?'

'Your name?'

'Erm …'

'You've forgotten it.' She prodded him playfully on the arm and then pulled her hand away; the boy grabbed it, wrapping his fingers around her own.

'No. I know. It's … er …' He hesitated again. 'Alan. I'm Alan.'

He kept hold of her hand as long as he could, until finally the distance was too great and he had no choice but to release her. She flashed a smile back over her shoulder. She thought he was going to be there in a second. She thought that before they went home they'd probably exchange numbers, and that after Christmas he'd ring and they'd go and hang out at McDonalds or the shopping centre or whatever it was that normal teenagers did. Was it kinder to let her think that? Lucas wasn't sure.

He was sure that he couldn't follow her back into the living room. If he did then every second in that room was a second more risk of somebody recognising him, or of the mate he'd got dragged along with getting careless and calling him Lucas, and when people knew who he was everything changed. Everything always changed. Lucas knew what he had to do. He had to walk out of the back door, call a cab and get himself back to the hotel, and then he had to forget about the blonde girl with the perfect coca-cola lips.

Lucas paused at the back door, his unfamiliar reflection with its newly dyed hair staring back at him. It was one kiss. It didn't mean anything. As soon as the thought came he wished it away. He shouldn't be this cynical this young, but he'd been kissed a lot. Not by girls his own age, not with warmth or affection or desire. He'd been kissed by producers, and agents, and money-men, and co-stars, and by endless people who were always around and who apparently had some reason for being where Lucas was and for bending and planting air kisses in the vicinity of his cheeks. Kissing him like a gambler might kiss the dice for luck, hoping to absorb a little bit of whatever it was that had made Lucas, fleetingly, the most famous kid on the planet. Cheek-kiss after cheek-kiss from a parade of strangers who told him they were friends.

Lucas opened the back door. It might be cynical. He might not like it, but he knew it was right. Kisses didn't mean anything.

Lucas made his way around the side of the house and into the street. It was cold, and ice was forming on the puddles in the gutter. He glanced at his watch. 11.45 p.m. Nearly Christmas Day. He wondered what the normal people were doing. Probably spending their evening at parties, rather than running away from one. His mobile phone buzzed in his pocket. What now? Probably his mate trying to find out where he'd disappeared to. He answered the call without looking properly at the screen. 'I'm sorry. I needed ...'

A stranger's voice interrupted him. 'Is this Lucas Woods?'

'Er ... yeah.'

The voice at the other end of the line giggled for a second. 'Sorry. Mr Woods, I'm calling from the Monarch car service.'

Lucas frowned. He'd got in the habit of using the car service when he came back to the UK, back when the studio were picking up the bill. He hadn't used them for months though. 'Right?'

'I'm afraid there's been an incident with a vehicle on your account.'

Lucas shook his head. 'No. I haven't booked a car.'

The woman was insistent. 'One of our drivers was booked to collect you from ... hold on one sec ... from the Central Leeds Plaza at 8 p.m.?'

That didn't make any sense. 'No. I've been out with a friend all evening.'

'I'm sorry sir. The booking was on your account.'

Lucas realised what that meant. His account wasn't him, was it? He closed his eyes for a second before answering. 'You said there was an incident.'

'Yes.' The woman hesitated. 'I'm afraid the vehicle appears to have been stolen.'

Lucas was confused again. You booked a car from Monarch with a driver. The car belonged to them. Why was it his problem if one got stolen? 'What do you mean?'

'I mean that the gentleman who booked the vehicle appears to have taken it.'

All Lucas wanted was to head back into the party and be a normal sixteen year old. He wanted to be back in that kitchen listening to a beautiful girl moaning about how lame her parents were. He wanted to be eating crisps and trying to flick peanuts straight into his mouth. He wanted to be anxious about exams and whether to go to university. He wanted to be that boy in the kitchen that nobody knew. He wanted to be Alan. He didn't want to be Lucas Woods.

The woman on the other end of the line was still talking. 'I have to ask Mr Woods. Do you know who the gentleman might be?'

Lucas tried to swallow down the anxiety that was rising from his belly. 'It might be my dad,' he said.

# 2014
## *Chapter One*

### 23rd December, 2014

*Lucas*

'How is he today?'

The nurse shrugged. 'He's fine. A bit cranky still, since we put the decorations up. He still won't have any in his room.'

Lucas nodded. It was the same every year. The Christmas trees and tinsel sparked half-formed memories of better days and worse. You never quite knew how he was going to react.

The nurse smiled encouragingly. 'He's in his room.'

Right. There wasn't really any reason to hesitate. Lucas had been visiting this place every day since he'd moved himself and his dad to London five years earlier. Leeds had been fine, but he'd been too conspicuous. It was too easy to be recognised. The capital was better, and he'd been twenty-five by the time he'd moved down here. Nearly a decade had passed since his last film. Fifteen years since the one that had made him a temporary star. His face had filled out and he'd taken to maintaining a shadow of stubble across his jaw. He answered to his adopted name as naturally as to his real one. He barely even recognised Lucas Woods when he looked in the mirror any more.

Lucas knocked lightly on the door of room twelve before pushing it open. 'Hello?'

His dad was sitting in the good chair at the far side of the lounge area. The nurses and careworkers called them 'rooms', but really the residents here had suites comparable with most good hotels. There was a bedroom, a sitting room and a bathroom. Some of the apartments even had a kitchen. This one didn't. After the fire at the last place Lucas had decided that wasn't a good idea. His dad looked up as he came in. 'I thought you'd forgotten about me.'

Lucas forced himself to smile. So guilt was going to be the mood for the visit. 'Of course not. I was here yesterday. Remember?'

His father didn't respond. Lucas sat opposite him. 'So did you have a good night?'

A shrug.

'Okay. I was working on the helpline yesterday.' Lucas listened to himself trying to make some sort of conversation. 'It was pretty quiet. I'm at the advice centre this afternoon.'

'Bloody do-gooder.'

'I like to keep busy.'

Lucas watched his dad stare out of the window. He wasn't an old man at all. Forty-five. Only fifteen years older than the son he was so keen to ignore. Lucas realised that he, himself, was nearly the same age now as his dad was when he'd had the crash. He was embarking on the life that his father had missed out on. 'I got a Christmas card from the twins.'

His father didn't reply. Lucas couldn't even be sure that he remembered who his son was talking about. Some days the memories seemed as fresh and raw to his dad as they remained to Lucas. Some days he either didn't know, or didn't care. 'Ruth's getting married again, apparently. You remember her? The mum.'

Again he got no response. Lucas could still picture Ruth's face, wracked with grief even as her voice was telling him it wasn't his fault. She'd been kind, but she'd been wrong. All of this was Lucas's fault. He'd done everything he could to make it right, but there were some debts that even the kid whose wildest dreams came true couldn't repay.

'They won't let me go out.'

Lucas closed his eyes. 'You can go out if you want. I'll come and take you out.'

His dad shook his head. 'I don't need you to take me.'

'Well Carys then.' Carys was his dad's favourite carer. 'I can pay her extra to take you out on her day off. We've done that before.'

'She's gone.'

Lucas frowned. He was sure he'd seen Carys in the hallway on his way to his dad's room. 'I don't think she has.'

His father had gone back to staring sullenly out of the window. 'Well she won't come and talk to me. I get this big bloke now.'

'Well I'm sure there's a good reason.' Worryingly, Lucas really was sure there was a good reason. He spent a few more fruitless minutes trying to talk to his father, before heading out. Carys was leaning on the desk in the main lobby shuffling through some papers. Lucas hesitated. He didn't know her that well. She was very young, but seemed to cope better with the work than a lot of the young girls who arrived and disappeared again after two weeks when they discovered the realities of the job. 'Excuse me.'

She turned. 'Oh. Hi.'

'I wanted to check something. My dad says you're not caring for him anymore.'

Her gaze fixed itself somewhere to the left of Lucas's shoulder. 'No. I thought Julia was going to talk to you about that.'

Julia was the manager. Lucas shook his head.

'Right. She's off today. Maybe you should talk to her after Christmas.'

Lucas's stomach tightened. His father had been moved from home to home over the last fifteen years. He was too disruptive, or his condition was too complex, or his behaviour was too much for the staff. Lucas wasn't sure his dad would cope with another move. 'Just tell me what the problem is?'

He caught the hint of frustration in his voice, and forced

himself to take a deep breath. 'I mean, I'm sure whatever it was wasn't your fault.'

The girl's cheeks flushed pink. 'No. It wasn't.'

'Right. But what happened?'

'Mr Woods ... well, you know he got hold of some whisky last month.'

Lucas nodded. It wasn't the staff's fault. His dad was an addict. He was an addict with the brain of a child trapped inside an adult's body. If he could find drink, he would. 'Well, it wasn't so much the drinking that was the problem. He tried to ...'

Lucas desperately wanted to block his ears. He couldn't.

'... he tried to touch me on the ...' Her voice tailed off. 'You know. He was quite ...' She hesitated again. 'I was scared.'

'I'm really sorry.'

She nodded. 'It's not your fault. Anyway it's fine. I shoved him away, and pressed the buzzer. Julia and one of the blokes from estates were there before anything really happened.'

'Good. Right. I'm sorry though.'

The girl shrugged. 'Julia was supposed to talk to you. Explain why we'd changed around.'

'That's fine. I know now. I'm so sorry.'

'No need.' She picked up her bundle of papers. 'I'd better get on.'

'Right. Of course.'

'Merry Christmas.'

He nodded. 'Same to you.'

He walked out into the chilly air feeling grim. Maybe, whatever he told himself, this wasn't for the best. Maybe it was time to admit that and find a house where he could care for his dad himself. He thought back to when he'd tried before, rubbing his fingers over the bridge of his nose where he could still feel the bump from the years old broken bone. He was older now though, if not wiser. Maybe things would be different.

Christmas drinks before Michelle and Sean headed up to Scotland. Jess took a deep breath. It was nice, just her and her best friend, her best friend's husband, and the youngest of Jess's three big brothers, Simon. These were probably the three people she was closest to in the world. Apart from her husband, of course.

Simon picked up a card from the pile on the table between them. 'Okay. The question is ... your first kiss? Truth or dare?'

Jess shook her head and sipped her wine. 'I don't think so.'

Her best friend, Michelle, and Michelle's husband, Sean, stared at her expectantly. 'Why not?'

'Because you're sober, so I'm at a disadvantage. And you already know anyway.'

Michelle patted her growing belly. 'Well I'm only sober because of this little one. And Sean doesn't know.'

Simon laughed. 'And I'm not sober, so it all works out.'

Jess shook her head. 'I thought it was Sean's turn anyway.'

There was a second of silence, before Jess realised why Sean wasn't talking. Sean's first kiss would have been with his childhood sweetheart, wouldn't it? An image popped, uninvited, into Jess's head. *Cora.* She tightened her grip on her wine glass. 'What about you Simon?'

'It's not my turn.'

Jess pursed her lips. 'Well I'll tell mine, if you tell yours.'

Her brother shook his head. 'Well there were a couple of girls during school, but my first proper kiss was a boy called Craig on the school residential trip to Norfolk.' He grinned. 'I saw him again a couple of years after when I was with Anthony, who was insanely jealous of course.'

The group fell quiet for a second. Anthony had been Simon's first, and only, serious boyfriend. He'd died, after a long illness, when Jess was in her teens, but she could still picture her brother's devastation.

Simon broke the silence. 'Right. Your turn.'

Jess took a drink. 'Fine. ' She closed her eyes for a second and thought back. 'It was 2000 I think. It was Christmas Eve, so I was fifteen.'

'Quite old.'

'Fifteen's not that old.'

'It is,' Sean insisted.

'Well maybe if you grow up with nothing but trees for miles around and there's nothing else to do.'

He opened his mouth to protest before Michelle whacked him over the head with a cushion. 'Let her tell her story.'

'Thank you. Anyway I was fifteen. It was Christmas Eve. I was at some horrible party at this friend of my mum's house.' She turned towards her brother. 'Aunty Janine, you know?'

Simon shook his head. 'Not a clue. Definitely not a proper aunty.'

Jess pursed her lips. The twelve year age gap between her and her youngest brother meant that more often than not their childhood memories failed to overlap. 'Well anyway, it was all vol-au-vents and mini sausage rolls ...'

'I like a mini sausage roll.'

Jess shrugged. 'Well everyone likes a mini sausage roll. That's not the point. Anyway it was a horrible party, and I was in a massive sulk because I hadn't been allowed to go to Keeley Andrew's party at her house which everyone in our year went to.'

Michelle pursed her lips. 'I didn't.'

Jess grinned. 'That's because you refused to engage in any form of Christmas celebration. All the normal people in our year went.'

'Get to the point.'

'Sorry. So anyway, it was in the kitchen. He had dyed hair and an earring, so I basically thought he was the most worldly and glamorous being I'd ever met.'

'So you snogged him?'

Jess didn't meet Sean's eye. 'I did. And so that's that. My first kiss story.'

But of course that wasn't quite that, was it? Jess let her mind take her back to that kitchen, and that boy with the shock of black hair hanging in front of his bright green eyes. She remembered the touch of his fingers against her cheek, and the taste of his lips – cheap cola and a hint of salt. She remembered the cheesy Christmas music coming through the wall. She remembered the cupboard door handle that had been digging into her side, and she remembered not caring at all. She remembered friends at school describing their first kisses as gross or sloppy or icky, but hers had been nothing like that. It had been warm and soft and she'd felt somehow like she'd arrived home. She wondered if she'd ever been kissed like that since.

'What was his name?' Sean interrupted her thoughts.

Jess heard Michelle and Simon snigger. 'She doesn't know.'

'What?' Sean frowned.

'I do know. He was called Alan.'

Michelle shook her head. 'Only you checked and there was nobody called Alan at that party.'

Sean grinned. 'You got fake named.'

'I did not.'

Michelle was staring down at her glass, but Jess could see the smirk pulling at her best friend's lips.

'Well I never met him again anyway. He was there at that party and then he was gone.'

'Oh I get it.' Sean was grinning. 'He's the one that got away.'

Simon nodded vigorously. 'That's what I said.'

'Wise man. One perfect kiss and then he vanishes. Definitely the one that got away.'

Michelle sighed. 'You are such a girl when it comes to romance.'

'And you have no soul.'

Jess let them replay their regular argument. Of course the boy at the party wasn't her "one that got away". Okay, so she might have thought that once, but she wasn't a teenager any more. She was an adult and that meant not getting swept away by silly romantic ideas. There was no perfect guy out there pining for her. There was her husband, Patrick, and she was going to find ways to compromise, and they were going to make things work. That was realistic, not some hopeless teenage fantasy. Another memory forced itself to the front of Jess's mind. Cora. Was she Patrick's "one that got away"?

Jess had actually been to confront the other woman, and had instantly regretted it. Cora's apartment was a penthouse on the South Bank, and the woman herself was a picture of old school glamour. Perfect chestnut-brown hair, creamy skin, and the sort of figure that would have made Cindy Crawford look a bit frumpy. Jess was a scruffy, dowdy mess by comparison. And rather than Cora apologising to Jess for trying to steal her husband, Jess had found herself apologising for taking him back. Nothing about the visit had worked out like she'd imagined it.

Michelle glanced at the clock. 'I guess we'd better get going.'

A knot formed in Jess's stomach. Her friends wanted to leave before Patrick got back. He'd gone for a drink with some friends from where he used to work, at least that's what he'd told her. Jess took a deep breath. That's what he'd told her, and she believed him, like she believed him every time he popped out to see a recruitment agent, or go for a run, or to the gym. On the settee, Sean glanced at his watch and raised an eyebrow to his wife. Even he didn't want to stay, and he was Patrick's best mate. At least he had been. Was it always going to be like this? Jess frowned. 'You could stay to say hello.'

The look they exchanged was fleeting but Jess saw it. Michelle shook her head. 'It's not that. We've got a long drive tomorrow. Back to Scotland for Christmas.'

A noise in the hallway interrupted Jess's reply. 'That must be him now.'

She pulled herself to her feet and dashed the four paces to the door. Patrick was peeling off layers of coat, scarf and gloves. He was handsome. Properly handsome. Underwear model handsome. She watched him run his fingers through his hair and waited for the pang of desire she was used to feeling to hit her. It didn't quite come. Jess pushed the corners of her mouth wide. 'Michelle and Sean are still here. And Simon.'

Patrick nodded and flashed his perfectly even smile. 'Great.'

Jess followed her husband into the lounge. He asked after Sean's business and Michelle's health. Both replied grudgingly. Jess could feel her muscles tightening. Patrick was trying to put everything with ... her brain pushed the details of the thought away ... Patrick was trying to put everything that had happened behind them. She could see that he was trying. Why wouldn't her friends see that too?

She took a deep breath. The fairy lights were twinkling on the Christmas tree in the corner. Her present for Patrick was wrapped and waiting. In a couple of days it would be Christmas and then New Year. Once January came they really would be able to make a fresh start. All she had to do was hold on until then.

# Chapter Two

## Christmas Eve, 2014

*Lucas*

'Alan!' Lucas didn't hesitate before responding to the name. 'What's up?'

His supervisor, Viv, held a green form out towards him. 'You couldn't see one more, could you?'

Lucas sighed. It was nearly lunchtime. The morning hadn't been busy. Christmas Eve morning never was, but the people who did come in were in genuine crisis. 'I'm supposed to be going to see my dad.'

Viv pulled a face. 'I know. But there's only you and Gwen still here, and she's got two cases to write up.' Lucas looked across the office at his colleague. Gwen was lovely, fantastic with the clients – she'd taught Lucas a lot when he first started, but she was notoriously slow on the computer. She'd probably still be writing up her notes on Christmas morning. Viv held out the form. 'And I'd really really like to get home at some point this afternoon.'

Lucas nodded.

'Thanks.' Viv grinned. 'I can always rely on you.'

He picked up the form and scanned the details. A new client. Housing issue. No other details. Great. He headed into the waiting room. There was only one person waiting. Lucas had long ago stopped trying to guess clients' ages. Life put lines on people's faces that time couldn't justify. Lucas led the man into an interview room and gestured for him to take a seat. As he waited a stench of sweat and stale alcohol settled around the room. Lucas swallowed. 'So you've got a housing problem you're wanting some help with?'

The man nodded. 'Not got anywhere to stay.'

'You're homeless?'

'That's what I said.'

Lucas ran through his questions, to increasingly brief and irritated answers, and established that the man had been released from prison, and had been promised that his probation officer would find him temporary accommodation. He established that the man had a brother who lived locally, but couldn't stay there because the terms of his probation forbade him from contacting family members. Lucas didn't question why and he kept his expression as neutral as possible. He was here to help, not to judge. 'Okay. If you can hold on there for a few minutes, I'll see what options we can find you.'

Lucas left the man in the interview room and went back into the office. It was after lunchtime on Christmas Eve. His chances of getting anything from the council were slim to non-existent. A call to the probation service confirmed that the client's probation officer was off work and there was no temporary accommodation available that anyone else could arrange. It was going to be a question of night shelters and rough sleepers' charities. Lucas made a few more calls, grabbed a map and then went back to his client. 'There's spaces at the night shelter here.' He marked the location on the map. 'And they're doing Christmas dinner tomorrow in the community centre next door. Do you think that would be all right?'

The man shrugged.

'And can you get there okay?'

'Dunno. How far is it?'

Lucas drew another circle on the map to show where they were now. 'It's not that far. Are you all right walking?'

'Walking's all I can do.' The man peered at the map. 'Got chucked out of my last hostel for the booze.'

Lucas nodded. 'Do you want any help with that?'

'Had help before. It doesn't last.'

Lucas watched the man shuffle out into the cold. He hadn't done much. Every day he hoped that today might be the day he made everything better for someone, and every day he made a suggestion here and a compromise there. It was always one night out of the cold and a hot meal tomorrow, but never anything more.

The man stopped outside and turned back. 'Well Happy Christmas mate.'

'Happy Christmas.' Lucas closed the centre door behind the client, dropped the latch and pushed the two bolts across. So the guy had had help for his drinking before. What had he said? *It doesn't last.*

That wasn't true. Lucas had seen people who'd got off drink, or drugs, and stayed sober for decades. There were volunteers he'd worked with who were alcoholics themselves but were managing to leave their addiction behind. It had to be achievable. He just needed to find the right support, the right programme, the right help. He glanced at the clock. If he wrote his notes up quickly he still had time to see his dad. Maybe he'd be in a better mood today.

## Christmas Eve, 2014

### *Jessica*

Jess was ready too early. Of course she was ready too early. She'd been up at six o'clock, at the supermarket by six-thirty, and back home, cleaning the oven, soon after seven. She'd noted the hint of laughter in Patrick's expression when she'd made him lift his feet up so she could vacuum in front of the settee, and she'd ignored it. It wasn't *his* mother who was about to descend on the flat. Jess reconsidered the thought. *At least* it wasn't his mother who was about to descend on the flat.

And Patrick had helped. He'd put the beers and wine she'd bought in the fridge. Okay, so he'd helped himself to one while he was there, but it was, as he'd pointed out, Christmas Eve. You were allowed a sneaky beer on Christmas Eve. And now he'd gone to get some flowers to, in his words, brighten the place up. To be fair, Patrick had always been generous. Their relationship had been on and off for years before they'd finally got engaged, and every time they got together again he would woo her with gifts and flowers. Jess was aware that plenty of her friends – wise only after the event – were now convinced that Patrick's lack of early commitment was a warning sign. She was equally aware that they were wrong. It hadn't been Patrick dragging his feet for all those years.

Jess surveyed the tiny living room, trying to picture it from her mother's point of view. It was a disappointment. She knew that, but a single wage didn't get you very far in London. The fact that they had a second bedroom that they'd somehow managed to crowbar a double bed into was a hangover from the days when Patrick was working full time as well. When they'd looked at the flat Jess had thought it would make a nice nursery. A lot had happened since then.

She busied herself plumping up cushions and straightening the Christmas cards blu-tacked to the back of the door. As she lifted the cushion at the far end of the sofa, something caught her eye. Half-wedged down the side of the seat was a sleek black rectangle. She picked it up and placed it carefully on the arm of the settee. Patrick's phone.

Jess sat down in the armchair at the other side of the room and tried not to stare at the handset. It reminded her of the diet she'd been on before the wedding. She was fine, so long as there were no cakes or biscuits in the house, but as soon as there were, they would call to her. The idea that she could have half a piece would burrow into her head and refuse to go away, and then half a piece would become a whole piece, and, more often than not, two or three pieces. The phone was like that. It was goading her to take a look. It was tempting her to quickly check his texts. It would be so easy. She could sneak a peek at his call list and his contacts. Just to put her mind at rest. She jumped out of her chair and grabbed the phone. They didn't have secrets any more, did they? That's what he'd promised. So it wasn't snooping if he didn't have anything to hide. Her finger hovered over the unlock key. Only, if there weren't any secrets, what was she expecting to find?

The sound of Patrick's key in the lock made her jump. She dropped the phone onto the sofa and pulled the cushion over it. 'I'm back. And look who I found outside.'

Her parents followed Patrick into the living room, an already weary-looking Simon trailing behind. Patrick smiled broadly, full of festive spirit. 'I'll get some drinks.'

Jess's mum cast an obviously appraising gaze around the room. 'Very nice dear. You've decorated since we were last here.'

It was true. She'd painted most of the flat by herself one weekend in October. She'd wanted to make everything clean and fresh and new. She nodded brightly and told herself it was working.

Patrick re-appeared from the kitchen. She'd thought he was making tea, but the tray in front of him had a bottle of bubbly and five champagne flutes. He popped the cork to appreciative murmurs. 'I know it's a couple of days since our anniversary, but I thought a little pre-Christmas, post-wedding anniversary celebration was in order.'

Jess let him pour her a glass. They'd got married on the 22nd December. A year and two days ago. That was all. They were still newlyweds really. He'd bought her a necklace for their anniversary. She fingered the pendant at her neck. Jewellery, champagne and Patrick was all smiles.

Maybe she'd been right when she'd told ... her mind pushed the name away ... when she'd told that woman that it was a blip. Maybe Patrick had just been struggling to adapt to married life. She'd decided to make this work. Now she needed to work on believing that he was doing the same.

She let the pendant drop against her collar bone. He'd told her the necklace was silver, but the label he'd left in the bag said platinum, and they were drinking proper champagne not Prosecco or Asti. She didn't know where the money had come from. She had to stop thinking like that. She never used to be a suspicious person. She'd simply loved Patrick and she'd known that he loved her. He'd probably have married her while they were still at university, but Jess had said they were too young. You had to be sensible about love when you were starting out. Jess had seen friends make all the mistakes in the book. She'd seen people rush in to relationships; she'd seen people diving into something on the rebound; she'd even seen people tear themselves apart trying to make long-distance work. Jess hadn't done any of those things. She'd waited until they both had jobs in London. She'd waited until they could afford to buy a flat, and when she'd accepted his proposal she'd thought that that was that. She didn't think she needed to worry that he wasn't where he said he was, or wonder whether the little gifts he brought her were inspired by guilt rather than affection. Now she wondered about everything.

Her husband moved to stand beside her and clinked his glass against hers. 'Happy Christmas.'

She smiled, and opened her mouth to return the good wishes. Patrick frowned, and patted his jeans' pocket. 'Have you seen my phone?'

Jess took a sip of champagne and shook her head.

# Chapter Three

## Christmas Eve, 2014

### *Lucas*

'We've been waiting for you.' Two of Lucas's three flatmates were already huddled up on the settee when he got in.

He glanced at the clock. 'Sorry. I was ...' He didn't tend to tell his flatmates that much about his life. They were good friends but there was stuff he preferred not to share. His background. His work history. His real name. They knew, he presumed, that he had a dad, and they knew he did voluntary work, and they speculated wildly about how he managed to make the rent without any obvious source of income, but they were generally refreshingly happy to let him be. 'I had a couple of things to sort out.'

Trish, the de facto mum of the household, shook her dreadlock covered head. 'You're disrespecting Christmas film night.'

Lucas grinned. 'It's about the eighth Christmas film night we've had this month.'

Trish's girlfriend, Charlie, rolled her eyes. 'And your point is?'

In truth, he had no point to make. He'd learned from experience that only a fool got between Charlie and a festive movie. He grabbed a beer from the fridge and settled on the sofa. He spent a good amount of his childhood in trailers and hotel rooms, never quite knowing where his roots were. Their shared house was on the shabby side, but it was closer to being home than anywhere else he'd lived in the last two decades. He took a swig of beer. A quiet Christmas with undemanding people who wouldn't ask too many questions ...

'Anyway, before the film, Charlie has a new theory!' Trish prodded him in the ribs.

'Really?'

Charlie grinned. 'I think you escaped from Alcatraz.'

'What?'

'There were these three guys who escaped from Alcatraz in the sixties, and were like never seen again.'

'The sixties?'

She nodded.

'So you think I escaped from a high security prison on an island off San Francisco fifty years ago.'

'It's the only logical explanation, Fake Alan.'

The 'Fake' had been added to his name a few days after he'd moved in. Charlie had been standing in the hallway yelling his name repeatedly, before she marched into his room and demanded to know why he wasn't replying. He'd hesitated, only for a second, but it was long enough. Her eyes had narrowed. 'It's not your real name, is it?'

'What?' Lucas had been astonished. Nobody had ever called him out on the lie before. 'Course it is.'

Charlie had laughed. 'Bollocks.'

And so, somehow, he'd become Fake Alan, first at home and then at the pub on the corner, and the shop opposite, and then with Mrs Kingsley next door. And yet the story of who he really was, and why he called himself Alan had never been told. Sometimes, when all the beers had been drunk and they were toying with opening one of the random liqueurs from the back of the cupboard, Trish or Charlie would offer a theory. He was in witness protection. He was undercover. He was an alien sent to investigate earth culture. And Lucas would laugh and the conversation would move on. The Alcatraz theory was a new variation of the oft-repeated idea that he was, for some reason, on the run. 'You know that I'd have to be about eighty for that to make sense.'

Charlie tapped her nose. 'Plastic surgery. After your escape.'

Lucas shook his head. 'Just start the movie.'

'Cora's not here yet.'

Cora was the newest addition to the household. He'd helped her move her stuff in from some swanky place on the South Bank. Charlie had been very excited that they might have a wealthy flatmate, until Trish had pointed out that if Cora was rolling in money she wouldn't be renting a room off them. Lucas had kept his mouth shut.

Trish took a swig from her beer. 'She'll be mooning over Santa Claus.'

Cora had got herself a seasonal job at the department store Trish worked for, playing the part of Rudolph and was, quite clearly, smitten with the guy playing Father Christmas. Lucas nodded. 'She's right. We can't wait all night.'

'Fine.' Charlie stood up and pulled two DVDs from behind the telly. 'So we have Christmas classic, *Die Hard*, or we have *The Santa Clause 2*.'

Lucas shook his head. '*Die Hard* is not a Christmas film. It's a film that happens at Christmas. Not the same.'

Trish grabbed the other DVD. 'Well I haven't seen *The Santa Clause 1*. I might not understand the second one.'

Charlie flicked the TV on, and scrolled through the programme guide. 'What about this? *Miracle at the North Pole* is on at half past.'

'That's a classic.' Trish nodded her approval. 'A proper Christmas movie.'

Her girlfriend shrugged. 'But everyone must have seen it like a million times.'

Lucas never had.

'I wonder what happened to the kid.'

'The actor?' Trish screwed up her nose. 'Didn't he have some kind of meltdown?'

Lucas let the conversation wash over him. *Miracle at the*

*North Pole*? He'd managed to get to thirty without seeing it. It was one of those films that was on somewhere every Christmas. An instant classic apparently, but Lucas didn't believe in Christmas miracles. He grabbed a DVD box from Charlie's lap. 'You're right. Everyone's seen that. Let's do *Die Hard.*'

'You said *Die Hard* wasn't a Christmas film.'

He flipped open the case and slid the disc into the player. 'Then this is your chance to prove me wrong.'

## Christmas Day, 2014

### *Jessica*

Jess stirred her gravy. Last year it had been just her and Patrick and she'd given up part way through the process, and used granules out of a jar. This year her parents were here, and everything had to be right. On cue her mother appeared in the kitchen doorway. 'Are you sure you don't need any help dear?'

Jess shook her head. 'I'm fine.'

'Only we normally eat around one. Otherwise you're not done in time for the Queen.'

Jess glanced at the clock. 1.45 p.m. She could say that it didn't matter. She could point out that Christmas was about spending time together and it was fine to be relaxed about what time they ate. She made her lips into a smile. 'Nearly ready. Just letting the turkey rest.'

Jess wasn't a big cook, but she knew the turkey had to rest. When she'd first read that she'd thought it was a typo. The turkey was dead, but no, it turned out resting meat was a thing. It stopped it being tough and dry apparently, like cooking vegetables for less than three hours meant they tasted of something. Moving out of her mother's home had been a culinary revelation.

Simon appeared in the doorway. 'Come on. Let Jess get on with things.'

She mouthed a silent 'thank you' to her brother as he led their mum back into the living room, and turned her attention back to the gravy. It was nearly there. She pulled her list from where it was jammed under the corner of a dirty pan and smoothed it flat on the workshop. Starters were ready. Red wine was open on the table. White wine was in the fridge. The roasted veg needed another ten minutes. The turkey was done. Jess took a breath, untied her apron and picked up the tray of starter plates. 'Lunch is served.'

Her mum, dad and brother hauled themselves off the sofa and gathered around the dining table squashed into one corner of the lounge. Jess frowned. 'Where's Patrick?'

Simon shrugged. 'His phone rang. Think he went to answer it.'

The knot in Jess's stomach, that tightened every time her husband's phone rang unexpectedly, constricted even further. She handed the tray to her brother and plastered a smile on her lips. 'I'll go find him.'

In a flat the size of theirs finding Patrick wasn't difficult. Jess could hear his voice from the hallway, and followed the sound into the bedroom. He was on the balcony – well they called it the balcony; it was supposed to be a fire escape but the ladder was broken. She opened her mouth to call to him, and then closed it again. The knot hadn't loosened. Somebody had phoned her husband on Christmas Day. The only people who phoned on Christmas Day were parents and lovers, and he wouldn't be freezing himself half to death on the balcony to exchange seasonal good wishes with his mum.

Jess sat on the corner of the bed, feet away from the half-open door, and listened, waiting to be proven wrong. Patrick had promised after all. They'd made a fresh start, but the image she always carried with her swam in front of her eyes. Cora, Patrick's other woman. She corrected herself instantly. His former other woman. It was over. They were trying again. As always, the Cora in Jess's mind's eye was almost impossibly beautiful – Jess's polar opposite. Jess was short and, at best, curvy, or at worst, slightly plump. Her hair spun out in erratic blonde curls. Cora was tall with sleek brunette waves. Jess glanced down at her own body. She had a gravy stain on her nice top that she'd worn especially for Christmas lunch. How could she compete?

Through the door she could hear her husband mming and aahing. Clearly the other person was dominating the conversation. A shoot of hope jumped into her heart – maybe it was his mother after all. There were other things she could do. She could go back into the hallway and call to him that lunch was ready and then take her seat at the table with the others. She could choose not to know. That was what she'd promised. He'd promised that it was a one-off, and she'd promised to trust that. She'd promised not to snoop and pry. She'd even agreed that was for her benefit. Patrick had nothing to hide, so she'd only be torturing herself. All she needed to do was stand up and walk away.

Jess stayed sitting on the bed. She'd heard of the thing that happened in America. They called it suicide by cop. It was when someone was desperate to end it all, but couldn't quite bring themselves to pull the trigger, so they simply stepped outside, waved the gun in the direction of the police and waited for the inevitable. That was sort of what Jess was doing now. Checking his phone, following him, going through his credit card statement – those would have been like she was pulling the trigger herself. Sitting here, quietly listening, that was just accepting her inevitable fate.

'You know I can't.'

Jess's whole body stiffened at the sound of her husband's voice.

'You know why not ... Because it's Christmas ... Of course I'd rather be with you.'

A wave of nausea swept through Jess's body. This was it. All she had to do was let the truth wash over her.

'Seriously, her whole family are here. They're even more boring than her.'

Another wave of nausea. The moment to walk away had passed. Jess closed her eyes.

'Anyway, I'm gonna tell her. You know that. After Christmas it'll be you and me. A fresh start.'

A fresh start? Jess's mind seemed to float somewhere outside of her body, wafting around the bedroom on its own little cloud of serenity. Patrick had promised her a fresh start. Now he was promising it to someone else. It showed a sort of consistency, if you thought about it.

'Look, I gotta go. I love you babe.'

Jess opened her eyes as Patrick came back into the room. He stopped in the doorway, and she watched the split second it took his face to arrange itself into an utterly relaxed smile. 'What are you doing in here? I thought you'd be through there.' He flicked his eyes towards the kitchen. 'Dealing with lunch.'

Jess shook her head. 'Lunch is all ready.'

'Right then.' He walked past her towards the hallway. 'Are you coming then?'

'I'll be there in a minute.'

Patrick frowned. 'You weren't listening to me on the phone were you? We agreed. We have to trust each other.'

Jess thought for a second. 'I wasn't listening.' That was true. She hadn't set out to come in here and listen to him. She just happened to have heard. That was quite different.

'Good. It was my mum. She says Happy Christmas.'

'Okay.' Jess pointed at the stain on her top. 'I'm going to change this, and then I'll be through. You go and make a start.'

He nodded and she listened to his footsteps followed by the sounds of voices rising in the lounge. The lunch was done, and Simon was an excellent cook. She was sure he'd be able to find the brandy butter for the pudding and dish up the vegetables. Really everything was in hand. There was no reason for her to be here at all. Jess pulled a fleecy jumper off the back of the chair at her side of the bed and put it on. The little mini-satchel handbag she always carried outside of term-time was dumped on the same chair. She slung it across her body and stood up. There was really no need to make a fuss. There was definitely no need to spoil everyone else's Christmas. It was probably for the best for everyone if she slipped away.

She lifted the latch on the front door as quietly she could and then changed her mind. She quickly tiptoed back to the kitchen and pulled a bottle of Baileys from the cupboard. Then she stepped out into the stair well. She'd always found Christmas dinner a bit much if she was honest. She didn't like the bloated feeling afterwards. A nice long walk would be far better for her, and the Baileys was very Christmassy so nobody could accuse her of not getting into the festive spirit. She unscrewed the cap and took a good long swig.

# Chapter Four

## Christmas Day, 2014

### *Lucas*

Lucas watched his dad pull the wrapping off his final present. It was a comic book. It was always a comic book. Years ago, before everything had changed, comic books had been one of their great shared loves. They could spend hours looking at comics and movie memorabilia. Lucas remembered being allowed to choose one comic book, with a strict price limit, and he remembered how his dad would pause over the special editions and rare copies that could run to hundreds of pounds. Maybe in another life his dad would have been a proper collector, but in this life he'd had a son, and until everything in both their lives had changed forever, every penny his dad had struggled to earn had been spent on Lucas.

Some years the comics were greeted with childlike glee and Lucas would get to share a few happy minutes poring over the artwork and the story. This year his dad threw the gift directly at Lucas, missing his ear by an inch at most. Lucas sighed. 'Well I'll put this on the table then. Maybe you'll want to look at it later.'

'Why do you come?'

'To see you Dad.'

'I don't want you here.' He glared at Lucas and then twisted his head away. 'All of this is your fault.'

Lucas swallowed. 'I know. I'm sorry.'

His dad turned back towards his son and spat a long stream of saliva in his direction. His face was turning pink with rage. 'I said I didn't want you here.'

'Right.' Lucas made his way to the door. 'I'll get off then. I'll come back tomorrow.'

'Don't bother.'

'Well I will. Happy Christmas Dad.'

Lucas leaned on the door outside his dad's rooms for a second. Carys, the young carer, was coming out of the room opposite. 'Are you okay?'

Lucas shrugged. 'He's not in a good mood today.'

The young girl smiled. 'Well a lot of people find Christmas difficult.'

'Yeah.'

'Maybe he'll be brighter tomorrow.'

Lucas stood up straight. 'Right. Well, I'd better get going. Are you working all day?'

She shook her head. ''Til four. We're going to have our dinner at tea time after I get off. My boyfriend's cooking it.' She pulled a face. 'It think it'll be okay.'

Lucas smiled properly. 'It sounds great.'

She nodded, and then paused. 'Look. It's not my place but ...'

'But what?'

'Well, a lot of the people who live here, they're difficult. Brain injuries, mental health problems, addiction. It's no-one's fault but it's tough. Lots of the families don't visit that much. And that's okay. I mean maybe not okay, but nobody'd judge them.'

'You mean nobody would judge me?'

She nodded.

She was trying to be kind, but she was wrong. Someone would always judge Lucas. Lucas would always judge Lucas. He wished Carys a Merry Christmas and wandered back to his car. Carys was wrong about the rest of it too. Not about it being hard. Not about the fact that lots of families didn't visit that much. But about the fact that it was nobody's fault. He'd known, all those years ago, that his dad was drinking too much. He'd known that he was vulnerable, and he'd chosen to take a day off from the life he'd felt trapped in to piss about with a mate and go to a party and kiss a girl. The girl crystallised in his imagination. He could still see her perfectly in his head. Round face, button nose, bright blue eyes, blonde curls pulled back into a pony tail. He could remember her telling him about her parents and her school and her mates. He could remember her looking embarrassed at how lame it sounded, and he could remember being entranced by the sheer normality of her life and the sheer remarkableness of her. And that's what he'd been doing while his dad was drinking a whole bottle of whisky on top of a stomach full of pints and then taking a rental car for a spin across the north of England. It had been Lucas's unique situation that had given his dad the means to take that drive, and Lucas's lack of care that had given him the opportunity. Lucas wasn't like those other families who could decide to walk away, because what had happened to his dad really was his fault.

He drove back across the capital on auto-pilot, mentally taking Lucas off and putting Alan back on as he went. The lack of Christmas day traffic meant that the parking space outside the house was still empty. He pulled in and made his way inside. Trish and Charlie were in the kitchen, cheerfully bickering over a nut roast. Trish grinned as he came in. 'Charlie says her nut roast won't fit in the oven with your turkey.'

'Course it will.' Lucas got down on his hands and knees and opened the oven, pulling the turkey out and moving the shelves around until everything, just about, squeezed in. 'There you go.'

Charlie feigned a swoon. 'Oh Fake Alan. You're our hero.'

'Where's Cora?'

Trish frowned. 'Dunno. Still in bed?'

Lucas pulled potatoes and carrots out of the cupboard. 'I didn't hear her come in last night.'

Charlie grinned. 'I bet she's banging Santa.'

Lucas laughed. He hoped Charlie was right. He didn't know the details but he was pretty sure Cora was due some good luck in life. The house phone next to the front door rang. All three of them frowned. Who even knew their landline number? Lucas followed Charlie into the hallway and watched her tentatively lift the handset. She grinned and nodded. 'Okay ... All right ... Okay. See you then.' She hung up. 'That was Cora. Santa and Santa's whole family are coming for dinner.'

Lucas paused. They'd been planning a quiet dinner, just the four of them. That had seemed okay. He was going to be quietly at home. If he wasn't having too much fun, then it didn't need to make him feel any guiltier.

'What's up?' Trish leaned on the wall next to him.

He shook his head. He could hardly turn Santa away on Christmas Day. All he could do was make the best of things. 'Nothing. I guess I better do some more potatoes.'

## Christmas Day, 2014

### *Jessica*

Jess had walked a really long way. She wasn't sure how far, but the streets had started looking unfamiliar about an hour ago and she'd kept walking. Her phone had rung a lot, but she'd switched it to silent so it wasn't really bothering her anymore. The Baileys was three-quarters gone, but her head felt surprisingly clear, as if all the alcohol had done was take the edge off the anguish enough to bring her back into equilibrium. Everything was calm. All there was to think about was the walking.

Patrick's affair hadn't ended.

He'd promised her that it was over, but then she'd heard him promising that other woman, the perfect woman with the perfect hair, that he was going to end it with Jess and be with her. Both promises couldn't be true, could they? And there was no reason to expect him to break his promises to his perfect lover.

Jess kept walking.

She knew that she was probably supposed to be more upset than this. She remembered when she'd first found out about the affair back in September. It had all come out at Michelle and Sean's wedding. The shock had ripped through her whole body. She'd cried. She thought she might have shouted. There was none of that now. Maybe it was the drink, or maybe the horror was already out of her system. This was much better. This time she was going to deal with the whole thing maturely and calmly. She wasn't going to show herself up or make a scene.

Jess stopped walking and looked around. The Thames flowed alongside her and this part of the South Bank was lined with apartment buildings. So here she was. Of course. Where else could she possibly have been heading? She stepped up to the column of doorbells and pressed the button. A few seconds later the intercom crackled. A man's voice. That was odd. 'Who is it?'

Had she pressed the wrong buzzer? She checked again. The sub-penthouse bell was all lit up. 'Er ... I'm here to see Cora.'

'What? Oh Miss Strachan? She moved out.'

'What? Where did she go?'

'Dunno. Sorry.' The intercom fizzled for a second and went quiet.

It shouldn't matter. Jess wasn't even sure why she'd come here. She didn't need to see Cora. She'd heard quite enough already from Patrick, but suddenly seeing Cora was the only thing that mattered. She had to confirm that it was true, and Patrick would lie. The realisation made her pause. It wasn't something she'd discovered today. She'd always known.

She'd just never called it what it was before. He made big gestures and sweeping declarations. He bought her presents and whisked her away on exciting trips. She'd told herself that Patrick was romantic. Patrick was impulsive. Patrick didn't always remember details, but really Patrick lied.

It was part of who he was, but Cora might tell her the truth. Jess stared up at the apartment building as if the bricks and mortar might give a clue as to where she'd gone. And then she realised. Sean would know where Cora was. Or if he didn't know, he'd be able to find out. They'd been childhood sweethearts and next door neighbours. If he didn't know, then someone in his family would.

She pulled her phone from her pocket, ignored the flashing message notifications and phoned Michelle. Her friend was initially reluctant. Why did Jess need Cora's address? It was Christmas day. Was something wrong? Jess didn't intend to lie, but she wasn't ready to tell the truth. Michelle would worry, and that would spoil her Christmas, and that wouldn't be fair. So Jess told her friend that Christmas was a time for forgiveness, and she wanted to write a letter to Cora to get closure on the whole thing. And no, she didn't have to do it today, but if she didn't she might lose her nerve, so could Michelle please ask Sean or his mum if they had Cora's new address? Michelle agreed and a few minutes later a text arrived with the address.

Jess took a final big gulp from her bottle, tapped the postcode into her navigation app and set off walking again.

## Christmas Day, 2014

### *Lucas*

Lucas was enjoying himself. Despite his best efforts and his promise to himself that he would have a quiet Christmas, he was actually having fun. Cora had appeared with her department store Santa, whose real name turned out to be Liam, the Santa's brother and nephew and aunt. As they were piling the mountains of food on the table, Liam's flatmate turned up as well. They had a proper houseful, and Lucas had never experienced a Christmas Day like it. When he was little, Christmases had been low key affairs – usually just him and his dad. They might go and visit his grandparents, or even his mum, on Boxing Day but the family weren't particularly close. After everything changed there'd been Christmases in swanky hotels, and at least one year on the beach in LA. There'd never been a big traditional Christmas dinner with family and friends. Lucas leant back and watched the room full of people talk and eat and joke. There was a pull of something in his chest. The feeling that this was the right place for him to be. The feeling that this was somewhere he belonged.

It wasn't a new feeling, but it was one he'd forgotten. It was the feeling he'd had as a kid on Saturday afternoons poring over comic books in the shop with his dad. It was the feeling he'd had at drama club, where his dad had sent him for two hours every Saturday morning. It was the feeling he thought he'd had for a moment in a kitchen at a Christmas party many years ago. And that was the last time. That was the last time that Lucas had even believed that it was possible to simply be himself.

After what seemed like several hours, people pushed chairs away from the table, and rubbed overfull bellies. Lucas started to clear the dishes as everyone agreed that they couldn't possibly eat another thing. A second later they were agreeing, just as loudly, that he could leave the cheese out. And the mints. But that would definitely be plenty.

Cora and Liam followed him into the kitchen. 'We'll wash up mate. We kinda overran your Christmas.'

Lucas shrugged. 'That's okay.' He started clearing up as

Liam filled the sink and Cora hunted for a dry tea towel. 'So what do you do?'

Liam frowned. 'You don't recognise me?'

Lucas shook his head.

Cora laughed. 'Fake Alan doesn't read the tabloids.'

'Why do they call you Fake Alan?'

Lucas kept his mouth shut, and let Cora provide the answer. 'Because Alan's not his real name.'

Then it was time for Lucas to jump in and head off further questions. 'What have the tabloids got to do with anything?'

Cora held up a tea towel of indeterminate cleanliness. 'Liam's an actor. He's been a bit torn apart by the papers lately.'

Lucas nodded. 'Right. That must be tough.' He couldn't say anything else. He felt as if his skin was burning red already. He couldn't say he knew how it felt.

At the sink Liam nodded. 'I'm getting through it.'

*How? How do you get through it? How do you keep hold of who you are in the midst of notoriety?* That was what Lucas wanted to ask. He didn't. The doorbell rang. Lucas grabbed the excuse to escape.

Somehow the conversation had got to him. He was remembering that Christmas Eve night fourteen years ago. The party. The crash. The girl. And then the papers afterwards. They'd vilified him. It sort of made sense. No-one could account for Lucas's whereabouts that day. Nobody had ever reported outright that he was driving, but the story of a mixed-up kid who'd gone off the rails was a familiar narrative and the papers had latched onto it. All because of that one night. The party. The crash.

He opened the door.

The girl.

# Chapter Five

## Christmas Day, 2014

### *Jessica*

Great, thought Jess. Another wrong address. The man on the doorstep was staring at her. He was good-looking with light brown stubble around his jaw, and bright green eyes that made Jess feel like she'd seen them somewhere before, and he was definitely staring at her. Jess had turned up on his doorstep on Christmas Day though – that was probably to be expected. Bodies appeared in the hallway behind him. None of them were Her. 'Does Cora live here?'

The man's jaw dropped open, but he didn't reply.

'Cora Strachan – is she here?'

Eventually the man nodded. 'Cora!'

She appeared from the end of the hallway, tea towel in hand, cheeks pink from the heat inside the flat, dark brown hair pulled up into a pony tail. She looked disappointingly normal. 'What?' She stopped as she saw Jess. 'Oh.'

This was the moment. This was what she'd walked across London for. This was her moment to find out the truth. Jess opened her mouth and wailed. She listened to her own wail. It wasn't what she'd expected. She didn't know how to make it stop. It was rising up from somewhere inside her chest and pushing its way out of her. She tried to swallow it down, but it bubbled up again, accompanied by a big gulping sob.

'Right.' The doorstep man put a hand under her elbow. 'Maybe you should sit down.'

She let him usher her, past Cora, and past a whole lot of other faces too, into a living room. She sat on the sofa and accepted glasses of water and offers of tissues. This wasn't right. Wasn't she supposed to be angry? She thought she probably was. She was a woman scorned. She'd intended to be calm, while channelling her fury in a controlled sort of a way. She wasn't supposed to be sitting on a sagging settee in the middle of somebody else's Christmas party blubbing uncontrollably.

She forced herself to look around. She'd been aware that it was Christmas Day, but somehow she'd still imagined Cora on her own in that perfect apartment. That was what other women did, wasn't it? They spent Christmas alone. They didn't have lives. They had affairs. In reality, her rival had a houseful of people. She had friends, and a tea towel. That seemed wrong. Mistresses weren't supposed to do the washing up. Jess looked around the room. Two women stood close together, holding hands and staring at her. Then there was doorstep man, and another guy the same age, and an older woman, and a man with a little boy. People were bustling around putting coats on and making excuses. 'You don't have to go on my account.'

The older woman nodded. 'You're all right pet. We've got to get back.' She looked around uncertainly. 'Well we'll leave you to it.'

That left the two women, the doorstep man, Cora and a blond guy who seemed to be hanging back. Cora sat down next to her. 'Why are you here Jessica?'

That was the question, wasn't it? Why was she here? She remembered. 'I know it's still going on.'

Cora frowned. 'What?'

'I know. You're still seeing my husband, aren't you?'

This time Cora exchanged a look with the blond man. 'I'm not. I promise you I'm not.' She was looking at the blond man, rather than at Jess now. 'I haven't seen him since the wedding.'

Jess shook her head. That wasn't right. She'd heard him

on the phone this morning to the woman he wanted to be with instead of Jess. 'I heard you. This morning.'

The blond man stepped forward. 'This morning?'

'Well lunchtime. I heard her on the phone to him.'

Cora was still shaking her head. The blond man put his hand on her shoulder. 'Cora's been with me all morning. Up until now.' He gestured around the room. 'At lunchtime we were all here together. I promise you. Whoever you heard on the phone, it wasn't her.'

That didn't make sense. Patrick had to have been talking to Cora. A glimmer of hope flickered to life on the horizon. If he really hadn't been talking to his lover then maybe Jess had misunderstood. Her husband's words from earlier in the day replayed in her head. *I'd rather be with you ... After Christmas it'll be you and me. A fresh start ... I love you babe.*

She closed her eyes and slumped back in the chair.

'Cora, can we have a word in the kitchen?' That must have been one of the women, and the question was followed by the sound of footsteps trooping away.

'I'll stay, and make sure she's okay.' Jess opened one eye. Doorstep man had sat himself down in the armchair next to the TV.

Jess opened the other eye and looked around the room. There were still cheese and biscuits on the dining table. Her stomach turned over unpleasantly. She'd walked out on her own dinner. Simon and her parents would be worried. She needed to look at her phone. Her phone was in her pocket. The effort of moving her arm, reaching into her pocket, switching on the screen was too much. She looked at the doorstep man again. His gaze was still fixed on her. 'Why are you staring at me?'

He opened his mouth.

Jess didn't need an answer. 'I've barged into your Christmas haven't I?' Somehow that hadn't seemed a bad idea at all while she was marching across the deserted streets of the capital, but this stranger was clearly horrified by her. 'I'm sorry. It's been a weird day.'

'I got that.'

'And I drank a whole bottle of Baileys.'

'Like a mini-bar bottle?'

Jess shook her head.

'Right. Okay. Well let me know if you're going to puke.'

'I'm not.' She closed her eyes again. 'I don't feel drunk. Just a bit numb.'

'That'll be shock. I'd offer you a whisky for it, but maybe not.'

Jess shrugged. 'I don't know how I got here.'

'No. I mean there's no tube today.'

'No! I know how I got *here*. I don't know how I got here in life. It was all going all right, you know. I've got a job. We managed to get a mortgage, just. And we had a lovely wedding.' She took a deep breath. 'It was last Christmas. And then she happened.'

Another surge of sadness hit Jess when she mentioned Cora. It felt good in a way. If she was feeling something, it meant she was still alive, somewhere inside the shell of Jess that was walking around and talking to people.

Doorstep man moved to sit next to her. 'Look. I've not known Cora that long, but I don't think she's been seeing anyone, and she was here at lunchtime with all of us.'

Jess looked properly at the stranger. Her gaze met his. Those bright green eyes. 'Do I know you?'

## Christmas Day, 2014

### *Lucas*

Lucas hesitated. He'd known the girl from the kitchen the second he'd opened the door. She looked, to his eyes at least, exactly the same. The same open face. The same bright blue eyes, but fourteen years, washing the dye out of his hair and growing a beard had clearly made him less recognisable. And what if that wasn't even what she was thinking of? What if she recognised him from somewhere else? He ignored the racing of his heart and shook his head. 'I don't think so.'

She frowned but didn't argue. She obviously had other things on her mind.

'I might go and see what the others are doing. Do you want anything? Water? Tea?'

The woman shook her head.

Lucas made his way into the kitchen. Cora was leaning on the worktop with a very large glass of wine in her hand, and Liam's arm around her shoulders. Trish and Charlie were casting anxious glances towards the lounge.

'Is she okay?'

Lucas nodded. 'I think so. Will someone tell me what's going on?'

Cora sighed.

'The short version.'

The short version was surprisingly short. Cora had had an affair with the woman's husband. Cora definitely had not known he was married, and had definitely ended things as soon as she'd found out. The woman seemed to be under the impression that her husband was still seeing someone, but that someone was not Cora.

Poor girl from the kitchen.

Trish cleared her throat. 'So what are we going to do with her?'

Cora took a glug of wine. 'Well I don't see why she's our responsibility.'

Lucas thought back over his meal. One glass of wine. Nothing before that because he'd driven to and from his dad's. Then he thought about the woman. He should let her walk away. He didn't need ghosts from the past. 'I could give her a lift home?'

Trish shrugged. 'Is she going to want to go home?'

A cough from the doorway interrupted the conversation. 'A lift would be very kind. Thank you. I walked here, and I'm not entirely clear on the way home.'

Charlie boggled. 'You walked here? Where do you live?'

She gave them an address a long way south of the river.

'But that's like what? Two hours? I don't even know.'

The woman nodded. 'Sorry to have interrupted your day.'

Lucas led the way to his car, and waited for her to get in.

'It's nice of you to take me home.'

'It's fine.'

'Why are you being so nice to me? I ruined your day.'

'It's just a lift.' That wasn't a reason. The reason was that he didn't want to let her go yet. She was the girl from the kitchen. She was from the time before everything in the world had gone wrong. Kissing her was probably the last good thing he'd done. However much his head told him to steer clear, something else was making him want to eke out every available second in her company. That wasn't the only thing though. 'It looked like you were having a crap time. I know what that's like, when everything falls apart.' He paused. He wasn't sure what to say that would help her. 'Look. If you don't mind me saying, you seem very calm.'

'What do you mean?'

'Well if my husband …' That didn't sound right. '… or wife, or whatever was having an affair I'd be furious. Why aren't you throwing his stuff out of an upstairs window? Or cutting his suits up? Or whatever it is that wronged women do?'

'I don't know.' Lucas let her think about it for a moment. 'I'm numb. I was devastated the first time, when I found out about Cora. This time, it's more like I've been waiting for the axe to fall and now it has. And there's no point getting angry.'

It seemed to Lucas that there was every point, but it wasn't his place to say. 'So what are you going to do?'

'I have no idea.' She fell silent for a second. Lucas tried to concentrate on driving rather than the thoughts that were crashing around his head. The girl from the kitchen had walked back into his life, onto his doorstep. The younger Lucas would have thought that was fate, but he wasn't that boy anymore. And, he reminded himself, she wasn't that girl. She was married. Whatever was going on there, that fact remained, she was married. Her voice interrupted his train of thought. 'Talk to me about something.'

'About what?'

'Anything. Distract me.' She sighed. 'What's your favourite bit of Christmas?'

Lucas didn't know how to answer that. 'Christmas was never really a big deal when I was a kid. It was just me and my dad, so it was kinda low key.'

She frowned. 'Was your dad there today?'

Lucas shook his head. 'He's not very well. He lives in a care home.'

'Sorry.'

'It's okay.'

'I used to love the romance of Christmas.'

'The romance?'

'The magic of it, you know. I actually had my first kiss on Christmas Eve.'

Lucas glanced across at his passenger. She was turned away from him, staring out of the window. Did she know? 'Really?'

'Yeah. Long time ago though. Never saw him again.' She laughed a brittle little laugh. 'And I got married at Christmas, so maybe I'm better off not believing in romantic Christmas miracles, because they really don't last.'

'I'm sure he had a reason.'

'He'll have a hundred reasons. He always does.'

Lucas stopped. She meant her husband. Of course she did. She wasn't thinking about some kid she'd snogged half a lifetime ago. 'I meant the first kiss boy.'

'Reasons for what?'

'Not getting in touch.'

'You don't have to be nice. He didn't call because he didn't fancy me. Like my first boyfriend at university forgot to tell me he was gay because he didn't really care about me. Like Patrick cheats because he doesn't really love me. It's not them, is it? It can't be all the men. It must be me.'

Lucas didn't know what to say. If he told her would it lay one tiny ghost to rest or would it make her hate him forever?

'It's left here.'

'What?'

'Left at these lights.'

Lucas followed her directions for the rest of the journey and pulled up outside an uninspiring modern block of flats.

'They used to be council, but it was what we could afford.'

'I'm sure they're great inside.'

She shook her head. 'Not really.' She twisted in her seat to look at him properly. 'I don't want to go in.'

'Do you want me to come with you?'

'I can't ask you to do that.'

'I don't mind.'

'No. I have to deal with it, don't I?' She was still staring at his face. 'Are you sure we don't know each other?'

This was the moment. She'd asked twice now, and she'd explicitly mentioned the kiss. Before he could have pretended not to recognise her. Now he really had to say something. His phone played the theme from *Star Wars* in his pocket. 'Sorry.' The screen showed *Morning Rise Care*. 'It's my dad's home. I'm sorry.'

She nodded. 'It's fine.'

He watched her getting out of the car. She walked up the path and then paused. The phone was still ringing. He hit answer and spoke into the phone. 'Hold on a second.'

Lucas jumped out of the car, rummaging through his pockets for a bit of paper. He found an old receipt. Wait. No pen. Back in the car and he pulled stuff out of the glove box. A tiny length of pencil. It would do. He scrawled his number on the receipt and handed it solemnly to the girl from the kitchen. 'Let me know you're okay. Or not. If you need anything, you can give me a call.'

She nodded. 'You're really very kind.'

Lucas shrugged. 'Not really.' He glanced down at the phone in his hand. To call on Christmas Day afternoon it must be some sort of crisis. 'I really have to go.'

He strode back to the car, jumped into the driver's seat and lifted the phone back to his ear. 'Sorry. What's the problem?'

# *Chapter Six*

## Christmas Day, 2014

### *Jessica*

She watched the guy from the doorstep drive away, and realised that she hadn't even asked his name. Another man choosing to walk – or in this case drive – away from her. She looked at the scrap of paper he'd given her. She wasn't going to call him. He was just being kind. She'd probably throw it away. She folded the tiny piece of paper carefully and pushed it deep into her pocket.

So there was nothing else for it. It was time to go inside and face the rest of her life. She headed up the stairs to the flat, and opened the door tentatively. 'Hello?'

'In here.' The voice came from the living room. It wasn't Patrick.

'Simon?' Her brother was sitting on his own flicking through a magazine. 'Where is everyone?'

'I gave mum and dad the keys to my place. They're going to stay there.'

Jess nodded. She couldn't pretend she wasn't relieved. 'Are they cross with me?'

Simon hesitated. 'They didn't really say anything.'

That figured. Jess's parents weren't people who liked to cause a stir.

'And Patrick?'

'I asked Patrick to leave.'

'Why?'

'Why do you think?'

'He told you?'

Simon raised an eyebrow. 'I didn't give him much choice.'

'You didn't hit him, did you?'

Her brother shook his head. 'I didn't hit him. I should have hit him.'

Jess sat down. 'What did he tell you?'

'Not much. Stuff you already know, I guess.'

Jess hesitated. She didn't actually know very much. 'Tell me anyway.'

'Well, when you disappeared I looked all around the flat for you, and then outside and then I checked with your neighbours, and nobody had seen anything. And then Patrick said, "She must have heard me ..." I don't think he realised anyone was listening, but I was, so I made him tell me what you heard.'

'Him on the phone?'

Simon nodded. 'To this new girlfriend of his.'

New girlfriend? So Cora had been telling the truth. Jess closed her eyes. 'It's definitely somebody new?'

'He said he'd met her in November. He said that he couldn't help who he fell in love with.'

Love? Patrick had mentioned love on the phone, but it hadn't really sunk in. Her husband loved somebody else. Well that was probably final then wasn't it? 'Did he say anything about her?'

Simon shook his head. 'She's called Vicky.'

'Right.' Jess wasn't sure what she'd been expecting when she got home. Probably some sort of emotional scene. Even in her head that idea looked more like a soap opera than real life. She could picture the soap opera Jess shouting and throwing crockery across the room. She couldn't quite imagine doing it herself.

'Where have you been all day?'

'I went to see Cora.'

Simon raised a questioning eyebrow.

'The last one. I thought it was her again.'

'He says it's not.'

'No.' Jess looked around the room. 'You've cleared up.'

'Yeah.'

'Thank you.' She paused. 'And thank you for sorting mum and dad, and dealing with Patrick. So he's gone to hers? To this Vicky person's house.'

Simon nodded. 'I guess so. He said to ask you to call him. I promised I would.'

'Do you think I should?'

Simon didn't answer straight away. 'I told him I'd pass on the message. Jessie, it can't be up to me what you do now.'

Jess nodded. He was right. It wasn't up to Simon what happened next. It wasn't really up to Jess. All the decisions were Patrick's now, and he seemed to have decided to love someone else. Jess just had to go along with things. 'I'm tired. I'm really really tired.'

'I'm not surprised. Do you want me to stay tonight?'

He could. The spare room was already made up. Jess shook her head. 'I'm okay on my own.'

'Are you?'

She nodded. 'I'm going to have to be.'

She walked into the hallway with her brother, and let him hug her on the doorstep. 'Jessie ...'

'What?'

Her brother shook his head. 'It's not my place ... No. Sorry. I shouldn't tell you what to do.'

'What?'

Her brother stared down at the floor and answered in a whisper. 'Just don't take him back this time.'

Jess swallowed. Of course she wasn't going to take him back. It didn't sound like she was going to get the chance.

## Boxing Day, 2014

*Lucas*

For a brief moment it had been the best of Christmases, but

then it had been the worst. Well not the worst. That title had been wrapped up fourteen years ago, but it had been pretty awful. Lucas leant back against the wall in the hospital and rubbed his back. Hospital waiting rooms hadn't got any more comfortable in the last decade and a half.

A nurse cleared her throat somewhere near his right elbow. 'Er ... Mr Woods? Your father is awake. He seems quite well, if you want to see him.'

Lucas nodded. 'Will you be discharging him?'

The nurse paused. 'We're waiting for the consultant. We need to evaluate your father's mental state.'

Lucas shook his head. 'Well he has a brain injury. The carer said she'd explained all that last night.'

'Maybe you should speak to the consultant.'

'I'm speaking to you.' The edge of frustration that Lucas tried so hard to avoid was there in his voice.

'Right. Well, we need to establish whether your father's overdose was accidental.'

Well no. Obviously. You couldn't secretly keep half of your pills for six months under the noses of a building full of trained carers by accident. But somehow Lucas had mentally filed it as another crazy thing his dad had done. 'You mean you think he was trying to kill himself?'

'It's difficult with your father's other conditions. It might not even be something he'd thought out to that extent.' She paused. 'That's what the consultant will be trying to establish.'

Lucas slumped back into the chair. His poor dad. Lucas had been too busy feeling sorry for himself, hadn't he? He hadn't thought about what his dad was going through all this time. He swallowed down the guilt as best he could. He could make this better. Things could change. He could change them. He'd find his own place, somewhere where his dad could live with him this time. He had to take responsibility properly. He'd been pretending, trying to live half a life out there in the world, rather than really dealing with what he'd done to his dad.

He took a deep breath and took the short walk into the ward. There were six beds, separated by curtains. Two were empty – Lucas guessed that all the non-urgent patients got sent home before Christmas. The others were occupied by thin white-haired men, dozing, heads lolling on their pillows. His dad's bed was at the farthest end of the room, next to the window. His father was sitting up in bed looking around eagerly. 'Lukey! Is it Christmas Day yet?'

Lucas shook his head. 'It was Christmas Day yesterday, Dad. It's Boxing Day now.'

His father frowned. 'Did I get my presents already?'

Lucas nodded. 'You did. You had a selection box, and some socks and a comic book.'

The older man's eyes lit up. 'Avengers?'

'Avengers.'

'Who's your favourite Avenger Lukey?'

'Iron Man.' It had always been Iron Man. Thor was a god. Captain America sort of had stuff done to him. The Hulk was out of control. Tony Stark had decided what he wanted to be. He'd planned and worked and designed. His superpowers weren't the result of a freak accident. Iron Man made it seem like it might be possible to be in control of your own life. It was a fantasy, obviously, but it was a good one.

'I like Thor.'

'Thor's cool too … Dad, do you remember yesterday you took some pills?'

His dad pulled a face. 'I take pills every day.'

'But yesterday you took more.'

'Will you bring my comic books in Lukey?'

Lucas nodded. 'Sure.'

The nurse appeared at the end of the bed. 'Sorry

Mr Woods. It's not officially visiting time at the moment. It'll be breakfast soon and then the consultant should be round.'

'Okay.' He peered at his dad. 'I've got to go for a bit. This lady is going to look after you. They're going to bring you breakfast.'

'Cornflakes?'

Lucas glanced at the nurse. 'Of course.'

His dad seemed quite happy. That was definitely getting rarer, but at least it meant that Lucas could leave him for a couple of hours without worrying about coming back to stories of him trying to punch a nurse or get out of bed and make a run for the nearest off licence.

He rubbed his eyes as he waited for the lift. He'd barely slept in the plastic waiting room chair, and every time he'd started to drop off he'd been woken up by a nurse telling him he didn't need to stay overnight. He needed caffeine, and then he needed to go to the care home and pick up some stuff, and then ... and then what? It was Boxing Day. Could he really get things moving on Boxing Day?

He ordered a double espresso and found a seat in the corner of the hospital coffee shop. He didn't want to put things off any longer. If he waited, he'd persuade himself that how things were at the moment was good enough. And besides, he'd called this long-time solicitor on Christmas morning back when his dad had had the actual accident. Boxing Day was quite civilised by comparison. He scrolled through his phone until he found the number of Mr Daley of Daley, Callendar & Associates, and let his finger hover for a second over the 'Call' button. And then his phone rang. The incongruity made him pause. *Unknown Number.* Normally he didn't even answer those, but it wouldn't be a sales call on Boxing Day, would it?

# Boxing Day, 2014

## *Jessica*

This was a mistake. She should be ringing Simon or Michelle. They always knew what to do. They always knew when she was taking a wrong turn. She made a deal with herself. If he didn't pick up in five rings, then she'd hang up. One ring.

He'd probably be freaked out to hear from her anyway. He'd clearly only given her his number out of pity.

Two rings.

Michelle would tell her that the last thing she needed was some random bloke hanging around.

Three rings.

Simon would add that she needed to resolve things with Patrick. Maybe she should be calling him.

Four rings.

Jess's mother would mutter something about Jess needing to pull her socks up a bit around the house.

Five rings.

She moved her finger to the 'End call' icon.

'Hello.'

'Hi. Is that ...' She stopped. She didn't even know his name. 'I mean, this is Jessica.'

'Jessica?'

And he wouldn't remember hers, would he? 'Jess. From yesterday. The crazy woman.'

She could hear the smile in his voice. 'What's up Jess?'

Such a simple question. 'Well my husband's having an affair. His second affair in about six months. In fact I think he's left me for her. I guess it's not actually an affair if he really does leave his wife is it? It's like she's his girlfriend now. That must make me the other woman.' Her words came out in a torrent, and she was giggling as she spoke, which was strange because nothing she was saying was funny, but now she'd started the laughter didn't seem to want to subside.

'I'm sorry.'

'It's fine.'

'No. It's not. It's shit.'

She stopped laughing. He was right. That was exactly what it was.

'What can I do?'

She took a deep breath. 'I need someone to help me find him.'

'Are you sure?'

'Absolutely.'

'Okay, well I understand if you want to have it out with him.' He paused. 'Am I the best person though? I mean, don't you have friends you can ask?'

Of course he didn't want to help. Why would he? She was a stranger. 'Right. Yeah. Sorry. I don't know what I was thinking.' Jess pulled her phone away from her ear and hit 'End Call.' A second later it rang again.

'Hello?'

'I didn't mean I wouldn't help. Of course I'll help.'

Jess didn't know what to say.

'Right. I've got to do one thing, and then I'll come over there?'

'Thank you.'

'Give me an hour.'

That gave Jess an hour to work out where on earth Patrick actually was. She couldn't very well ask … she swore under her breath – she still didn't know his name … but she still couldn't very well ask him to drive around London looking for a house that looked like a whore might live there. But how did you go about finding a missing husband?

She could phone him and ask, but that would mean talking to him now, and if she talked to him now she might lose her nerve for the talking to him face-to-face she needed to do later. She'd had all night to think about everything. All night lying in bed staring at the wall, waiting for morning, to decide that she needed to talk to Patrick face-to-face. She needed to know for herself what was going on. If it was over, if he was never coming back, she needed to hear that from him.

So she wouldn't phone him. What then? She tried Facebook, but it was too much to hope that he'd tagged his location in the last twenty hours. She paused. That wasn't the only thing that Facebook could tell her though, was it? She swiped and clicked her way to his friend list and scrolled down. Vicky? Simon had said her name was Vicky. Amongst Patrick's two hundred friends there were two Victorias. One Jess recognised. She'd been at the wedding, and was, apparently, happily married and living in Alicante. She seemed unlikely. The other Victoria was unfamiliar. Jess clicked on the name. She was beautiful. Smooth dark brown skin, and super-short buzz cut hair. You had to have an amazing face to wear your hair that short, and this woman did. She looked like Grace Jones and Beyonce had got together and made an even more luminous daughter.

The voice in Jess's head told her that she ought to stop looking. Victoria (Vix) Morris's timeline was a cascade of beautiful people having tremendous times. From November, there were photos of champagne on a roof garden with views across the city. Two glasses of champagne, Jess noted. From December there was a selfie of Victoria in a bodycon tube dress and heels captioned 'On the way to meet my boy #datenight.' From Christmas Eve a single status update 'Totally can't believe some women. Would never get all clingy and nagging around my man. Have some self-respect sisters.'

*My man.* But he wasn't Victoria's man. At least he wasn't supposed to be. He was supposed to be Jess's man. That's what he'd promised. He'd hired a suit and bought her a ring and stood up in front of all those people and promised that he loved her. He'd promised, explicitly, that he wasn't going to do this. Jess had meant it when she'd promised. She'd thought that she was sorted now. No more horrible dates. No more first kisses or first times going back to his place. No more dissatisfying first shags. She was done. She was his and he was hers. Only now he was Victoria's.

Jess sat down on the floor, in the middle of the hallway of the flat she'd bought with the husband she loved, and waited. Every inch of her body was on the brink of breaking down. She could feel the tears building behind her eyes, pressing for release, but refusing to fall. She was stuck somewhere in between, not quite together but not even managing to properly fall apart.

# Chapter Seven

## Boxing Day, 2014

### Lucas

Jessica. Lucas remembered the name from that night in the kitchen, but somehow it had never stuck in his imagination. She's always been the girl from the kitchen to him, but as he hadn't explained that to her, it was probably easier to try to get used to using her name. And he'd promised to help her this morning, and he'd promised his dad he'd be back in a couple of hours. The voice in Lucas's head pointed out that he couldn't fix everything, or everyone. Lucas ignored the voice. His dad was quite safe in hospital for now, and they knew not to discharge him unless it was to Lucas or the home's care, so he had plenty of time to help Jessica. He was being a Good Samaritan. That was all.

Everything in his dad's rooms was stored in drawers and cupboards marked with stickers saying what was inside, so it hadn't taken long to gather together a couple of comic books, some toiletries, pyjamas and a change of clothes. Half an hour later he was pulling up outside Jess's front door. He slipped in as a neighbour was coming out, took the stairs two at a time, and then stopped. He didn't know which flat she was in, did he? Shaking his head, Lucas pulled his phone from his pocket and rang the last number again. 'Hi. I'm in your building, but I don't know which flat it is.'

'Oh God! Sorry. I should have said.' He could hear her moving around through the phone, and a second later a door on the landing next to him opened. 'I'm coming to the door. I— '

She stopped as she saw him. Lucas waved awkwardly. 'Hi.'

'Hi.' The jolt of emotion he'd felt when he'd opened the door on Christmas Day punched him in the gut once again. Good Samaritan, he reminded himself. She needed support, not complications. 'How are you getting on?'

She shrugged. 'Thanks for coming. I don't know why I called you really. It's just …'

'Just what?'

She shrugged. 'I don't know. Sometimes things are easier with strangers.'

Lucas followed Jess into the flat. That was it. He was a stranger. He could understand that. Once people knew too many facts about you they started thinking they knew who you were. Anonymity was easier. It meant you could just be. 'So what's the plan?'

'Well I think I know who the other woman is, but I don't know where she lives, so we need to find that out.'

'Okay. And then what?'

'Then we're going to go around there.'

Lucas raised an eyebrow.

'I need to see him. Even if it's horrible news, I need to hear it from him.'

Even if it's horrible news? Lucas wondered for a second what sort of non-horrible news she was hoping for. He stopped himself. He knew what a seductive drug hope could be. 'So why do you need me?'

She sighed. 'I was hoping you could drive me. Patrick took our car. My car. Patrick took my car.'

So he was the chauffeur for a woman who clearly wanted her cheating husband back. The feeling in his gut fizzled away. 'Right then. You don't know where she lives?'

Jess shook her head. 'Just a name. It's hopeless isn't it?'

Lucas frowned. The internet had really wreaked havoc with people's ability to think. 'Have you looked her up in the phone book?'

She hadn't looked her up in the phone book. She didn't even know the phone book was still a thing. 'I don't know if we've got one.'

'Everyone's got one. It'll be on a shelf or in a drawer under your landline phone.'

Jess shook her head. The landline was on top of the little table in the hallway. She turned to check. There was nothing underneath except a pile of takeaway menus and junk mail that neither of them had got around to throwing away, and ... and a phone book. 'Wow. You're a phone book savant.'

He moved past her and picked the book up from the floor. 'So what's her surname?'

'Morris.'

'M – O – R – R – I – S?'

Jess nodded, and watched him flick through the pages.

'There's two V Morrises.' He showed her the page.

'So how do we tell which it is?'

He shrugged. 'What else do you know about her?'

'Not much. Does it say that either of them's a husband stealing whore?'

'Strangely no.'

'Okay.' Jess flicked back to Victoria's Facebook profile. 'She checked in at South Kensington Tube on 22nd December, and twice at places on Gloucester Road the week before.'

'Hold on. I think one of these is near South Ken.' She watched while he got his own phone out and tapped an address in. 'Yep. Well it's not much, but I guess she's our best bet.'

Jess nodded. This was it then. They had a name. They

had a probable address. She had a willing chauffeur. There was no reason not to go around there and have it out. 'Do you think I should take some of Patrick's things?'

He shrugged. 'Well if it's definitely over it would save you having to see him here again, I guess.'

Jess looked around the flat. Beyond clothes she wasn't sure what was really his and what was hers. There was the mirror in the hallway that his dad had made for them, which should make it Patrick's, but he'd made it to Jess's specification, so she didn't really know. There were the four good dining chairs which they'd bought together, but which had replaced four chairs Patrick had had in his old flat. So did they get two each? Then there were the wedding presents. They had a fondue set that had never been taken out of the box. Was it too late to send it back? Or would everyone want their pressies back? How long did you have to stay married to be allowed to keep the gifts?

She shook her head. 'I'll worry about his stuff later.'

In the car she wondered again if she should have more of a plan. 'What am I going to say to him?'

'What do you want to say?'

'I want to ask him what's going on.'

'Will he tell you?'

Jess didn't answer. Patrick was good with words. He'd been good with words in September when she'd found out about his thing with Cora. Was there a part of her that wanted him to be good with words now? Was there a part of her that wanted him to find the thing to say that would make everything all right? Maybe if she was willing to take him back, if she opened up her heart a fraction, then he'd be able to find the perfect thing to say to make her believe that he could be happy with her. That wasn't what she was supposed to be hoping for. She was supposed to be angry. She was supposed to be full of fury and rage. She was supposed to know that she was the wronged woman, and that he had no right to expect her to take him back. That was what Simon would tell her. That was definitely what Michelle would tell her. She hadn't phoned either of them.

'So this is it.' He found a parking space and the two of them wandered along the street. 'It's 17a, so I guess it's above one of these shops.' They came to a stop in front of a florist. He nodded. 'Here. Are you ready?'

Jess shook her head. It felt very final. Before, when she'd tracked Cora down, she was relying on someone outside of her and Patrick to do something or to tell her something. This time it was just her and him. If they couldn't work it out, that would be it. She forced air into her lungs. 'All right then.'

The buzzer light flickered and a crackling female voice came through. 'It's open. Come up.'

'Guess they're expecting someone?' suggested Jess.

'Maybe. Remember this might not be the right V Morris. Do you want me to wait down here?'

Jess didn't. She wanted him to come with her and stand close enough to catch her if she fell down into a faint. 'Okay.'

The stairwell was dark and smelt of mould. At the top of the stairs a door was being flung open. 'Mum!' He stopped, stared at Jess, and folded his arms. Patrick. 'How did you find me Jessie?'

Jess didn't answer straight away. He'd said 'mum.' That must mean that her in-laws knew about this woman. Was she simply a laughing stock for his whole family? 'Hello Patrick.'

'Seriously, how did you find me?'

Jess shrugged. 'Facebook and the phone book.'

'Right. Cool.' He shuffled his feet. 'You probably shouldn't be here.'

She wasn't sure what she'd been expecting. Even in her fantasies he hadn't quite run into her arms declaring that he'd made a terrible mistake and begging her to take him back. At best he'd sort of assumed she would take him back, and Jess hadn't argued. It didn't seem like things were going that way.

'I wanted to see you.'

He rolled his eyes. 'Why?'

'To see what's going on. Simon said you admitted you were having an affair.'

Patrick shook his head. 'Come on Jessie.' He raised his fingers to make air quotes. 'An affair? We both know that us isn't working.'

'We've only been married a year.'

'Yeah. Since you finally decided I was worthy.'

That wasn't right. 'What do you mean?'

'Oh come on. How many times did I suggest moving in together or getting married?'

Jess shook her head, indignation rising from her gut. So what if the timing hadn't been right before? She swallowed back the impending tears. 'But we're married now.'

'Look, I am sorry.' He tilted his head and his eyes glinted in the light. 'Part of me will always love you, you know.'

'So we can ...'

A voice called out from inside the flat. 'Is that your mum and dad, hon?'

Patrick looked over his shoulder. 'No. It's Jessica.'

'Really?' Now the voice sounded excited. Footsteps made a rapid stomping noise and then a second face appeared in the doorway gawping down at her. 'Wow. That's the sweetest thing. Has she come to win you back?'

None of this was going the way that Jess had thought, but somehow it was all entirely right. She hadn't deserved him. She had been slow to commit, and now she was the naïve little girl who didn't understand. Patrick and Victoria were the grown-ups who thought everything she did was the sweetest thing. Sweet. Dull. Not sexy. Not smart. Not intoxicating like the woman who was currently snaking a perfectly toned arm around Jess's husband's torso. 'Right then. Well I'll go then.'

Patrick nodded. 'I think you should.'

The buzz of the intercom sounded. The other woman – this Victoria – ducked back into the flat. A second later she reappeared. 'Your parents are on their way up.'

Patrick looked down at Jess. 'You should go. You don't want to embarrass yourself.'

No. Of course she didn't, but it was too late now, wasn't it? They were already laughing at her, and she could hear footsteps at the bottom of the stairs. She was trapped. A second later Patrick's mother turned the corner, closely followed by his dad. Jess had always felt out of her depth with Patrick's parents. They were rich, which was one thing, but they weren't like Jess imagined rich people being. They exuded an air of worldliness. Patrick's mother threw her arms around Jess. 'Jessica, I didn't know you were going to be here.'

'I'm going.'

Patrick's mother shook her head. 'Oh, I do hope you weren't making a fool of yourself darling.'

All at once Jess found that her whole body felt out of shape. This always happened around Patrick's mother. It was as if the older woman's ease overwhelmed her and made everything about Jess feel awkward by comparison.

'I mean, things clearly weren't working out with you two, were they? And young people don't really accept the paradigm of traditional marriage anymore, do they?'

'I have to go.' It was all she could do. She couldn't stand here and make chit-chat about the outmoded construct of marriage. She couldn't persuade Patrick to change his mind. She needed to be somewhere else.

Patrick's voice carried down the stairs behind her. 'Are you going to bring my stuff over?'

Jess kept walking. Footsteps followed her down the stairs. 'Jessica!'

She stopped. It was Patrick's dad. He was a quiet man, usually found standing a few paces behind his wife. 'Look. I know you probably don't want to talk to me at the moment, but are you all right?'

She shrugged.

'Right. Well you will get through this. Just don't ...' he hesitated.

'What?'

'I know he's my son and everything, but promise me you won't take him back.'

'I know. You don't think I'm right for him.'

The older man shook his head. 'No. I meant for your sake.'

## Boxing Day, 2014

### Lucas

Lucas leant on the car and waited. What did a person say to their husband and his new lover, he wondered. And how long did it take? Was she going to be invited in for coffee and mince pies? It didn't take long to get an answer. Apparently not. Jess shot out of the door to the flats and straight back into the car.

'How did it go?'

'I don't want to talk about it.'

'Okay.' Whatever had happened clearly hadn't been what she was hoping for. 'What do you want to do?'

She sat very still for a moment. 'I'm not sure.'

'If you wanna talk about it ...'

She stared away from him out of the window. 'There's nothing to tell.'

'You didn't punch him or anything? Or punch her?'

She shook her head. 'No. Do you think I should have?'

'I think he probably deserved it.' She didn't reply. 'You're very calm again.'

She turned back towards him. 'Well what would getting upset solve?'

Lucas didn't reply. Getting upset didn't solve anything, but it was what people did. They cried and shouted and complained, and Lucas listened and advised and made things right again. 'Is there anything I can do?'

'I think I probably need to get my car back.'

It wasn't the answer he was expecting, but it was something they could actually do. 'Okay.'

'Unless you don't think that's fair? I mean I think I'm getting to keep the flat. Should I let him have the car?'

Lucas stared at her in disbelief. 'You found out he was shagging around on Christmas Day. I don't think you have to let him keep his bollocks if you don't want to.'

'Right.' She peered up the street in front of them. 'I can't see it.'

'What sort of car is it?'

'Silver 206.'

Lucas drove slowly around the streets near the flat, scanning the rows of parked cars as he went.

'Wait! There.' Jess was pointing across the road.

He pulled in and followed her across the street to her own car. She giggled awkwardly. 'Well then …'

She had her car back. That meant she didn't need him to drive her around. It meant he had no reason not to get back to the hospital. 'I guess I'll let you get on.'

'Right. You too.' She paused. 'Thank you. For today. And last night.'

'It's fine.' He wasn't sure what else to say. He couldn't tell her that he thought, no he knew, that he'd kissed her once years and years ago. He couldn't tell her that she was beautiful and whatever this Patrick guy thought was better in some dingy flat above a florist couldn't possibly be even a fraction as incredible as Jess herself. Saying any of that would lead to questions that Lucas wasn't ready to answer. 'I probably should go. My dad's in hospital, so ...'

Her hand flew up to her mouth. 'Oh my god. Why didn't you say? You shouldn't have been running around after me all morning.'

'It's fine. I wanted to help.'

'Well, thank you.' She turned away and opened the car door. 'Wait. I never asked your name.'

'No. Right.' Lucas paused. Suddenly he didn't want to lie. 'People call me Alan.'

She frowned and stared into his face just for a second.

He dropped his gaze to the floor.

'People call you Alan? So that's your name?'

'Not exactly.' This was another moment. He could do it right now. He could say, 'My name is Lucas and we've actually met before,' but if he did that then it was only a matter of time before she knew everything. 'It's kind of a long story.'

She shook her head. 'Well bye then, People-call-you-Alan.'

'Bye Jess.' He stood back on the pavement and watched her drive away. So that was that. It was for the best. They both had far too many other things on their minds to rake over a moment from years ago.

He made his way back to the hospital. The ward was busier now. It was regular visiting hours and the other occupied beds in the bay had people sitting around them chatting to the patients. Lucas was surprised to find his own dad asleep. He sat down in the chair next to the bed and waited. After a few minutes a tall, young man appeared at the foot of the bed. 'I'm Mr Herrera. Are you Mr Woods?'

Lucas nodded. 'You're the consultant.'

'That's right. I wondered if I could have a quick word.'

Lucas followed the man past the nurses' station and into a consulting room.

'Unfortunately we did have to sedate your father after you went. He was distressed and aggressive.'

Lucas dropped his gaze to the floor. 'I'm sorry. It's since the brain injury. He doesn't ...'

The consultant held up a hand. 'I understand your father's condition. Problems with impulse control, short and medium term memory loss, increased aggression?'

Lucas nodded.

'And I also understand that he is an alcoholic?'

Lucas nodded again.

'And that pre-dates the brain injury?'

Another nod.

'Okay.' It was that annoying doctor's 'okay', the one that implied that things weren't okay at all. 'And your father lives at Morning Rise?'

'Yeah.'

Lucas saw the slight flick of the eyebrow. Morning Rise was expensive. Lucas was aware that he didn't look like a man who'd be able to afford it. 'But I'm going to move him in with me. He'll be a lot better if he's with me.'

The consultant frowned. 'Well that is your decision.'

'Yes. It is.'

The man half-smiled. 'Of course. I do have to say though that it would seem to me that your father needs long-term professional care. His problems aren't simply physical.'

'I know that.' Lucas could hear the defensiveness in his own voice. Of course he knew what his dad's problems were. He'd been living with them for half his life. 'But I'm responsible for him, aren't I?'

The consultant frowned. 'You were sixteen when he had the accident?'

Lucas nodded.

'Look. I don't know you, and I don't know your situation,

but let me tell you what I do know about young carers, not all of them, just some of those I've seen. When you're only a kid yourself and you find yourself caring for a parent, it's very easy to take on too much responsibility. You assume that everything is down to you somehow. It isn't. And for your dad, Morning Rise is probably one of the best places he could possibly be.'

'But ...'

The man held up his hand. 'As I say, it's your decision, but your father's underlying condition isn't likely to improve significantly. It might be managed more or less effectively, but you understand that he isn't going to recover?'

Lucas didn't reply.

'Look, what I always say to families in this sort of situation is this. Make sure you're thinking about what's best for the patient, not what's going to make you feel better.'

Lucas stormed out of the consulting room. Presumptuous idiot. What did he know about Lucas's life? The thought stopped him short. What did anyone know about Lucas's life? His closest friends were his housemates, and all they knew was that he wasn't really called Alan. He'd never had a girlfriend who'd lasted more than a few weeks. It was hard to keep things going beyond the third or fourth date when all your anecdotes about your childhood stop aged ten, and you couldn't tell them who you really were. The only person who knew who he really was was his dad, and some days his dad barely recognised Lucas at all. He was a ghost, living half a life out here in the world, while the real Lucas drifted away into the ether. He sat down again next to his dad's bed, and watched the man sleep. He looked peaceful.

Lucas swallowed back the beginnings of a tear. He couldn't remember his dad ever looking peaceful. Before the accident he was always bouncing off the walls, buzzing over the next excitement. Even before everything changed he remembered his father as a restless soul. There'd been one day when Lucas had arrived home from school and found all the dining room furniture laid out on the lawn, and his dad with a paintbrush in hand, painting rainbow colours across the table top. Another time he'd set out to build a play house, but he'd run out of wood part way through. Lucas frowned as he remembered the other side of his dad's restlessness, the inability to stop after just one drink, the money lost in the pub or at the bookies, the tension he'd felt when he was the last child to be collected from the playground wondering if this was the day when his father wouldn't come.

Lucas shook his head. His dad had done the best he could, whereas Lucas had failed his father in so many ways. Right from being born when his dad was too young and changing the whole track of his life, through to Christmas Eve fourteen years ago when he should have stayed in, through to right now when he couldn't make it better – he'd failed every single time.

# Chapter Eight

## New Year's Eve, 2014

### *Jessica*

'I'm fine.'

At the other end of the phone Michelle didn't sound convinced. 'Are you sure? It's not too late to get a flight up here.'

Jess hesitated. The idea of seeing her best friend was tempting, but a last minute flight would be expensive, and Michelle was ensconced at Sean's farm in the depths of the Scottish wilds. She had her own new husband, and no doubt Sean's family would be there in force. Jess wasn't sure she could cope with quite that much domestic bliss at the moment. 'I'll be fine. I'll come up and see you at half-term.'

She could almost hear the frown over the phone. Jess knew Michelle liked things dealt with properly. It must be breaking her up not being able to march around to Patrick's new girlfriend's flat and give the pair of them a piece of her mind. 'But you're not going to be on your own tonight? New Year's Eve can be weird. I don't want you getting all weepy and taking him back.'

Jess was glad her friend couldn't see her face. Would she take Patrick back? It didn't matter. She wasn't going to get the chance. All that was left was to put her brave face on, and carry on as best she could. 'I won't. I might see what Simon's doing.'

That seemed to satisfy Michelle. They talked for a few minutes more about Michelle's bump and about which of the eccentricities of Sean's family might turn out to be genetic, before Michelle rang off.

That left Jess with six hours to fill until 2014 was officially over. Her first instinct was to get in bed with a book and ignore the whole thing, but she knew it wouldn't work. She couldn't concentrate enough to read, and sleep hadn't been coming easily of late. She could do what she'd told Michelle and call Simon. No. She could do better than that. She could go round there. She knew her brother. He'd have people around for New Year. His clubbing days might be behind him, but he was a consummate host, and always had a houseful at New Year and on birthdays and holidays. The only time he didn't volunteer to play the host with the most was when their family was involved. Jess might find her mother a little judgemental, but Simon increasingly considered her beyond the pale.

On New Year's Eve he was bound to have friends around, and he'd be more than happy to include his little sister in the group. Jess pulled on her coat and then stopped. The flash of reflection in the hall mirror was not heartening. She still hadn't cried beyond the odd stray tear, so she'd escaped the classic pink blotchy heartbreak face, but nothing could disguise her grey pallor. Her hair was scraped back into a greasy, unloved ponytail. She didn't exactly look party ready.

Jess dragged herself to the bathroom and let the shower water run over her body. She wasn't entirely sure when the last time she'd taken a shower was, but there were lines of black grime under her fingernails, and her armpits had turned into a hairy sweaty fug. She didn't just need a shower. She needed industrial levels of scraping, tweezing and moisturizing. It was still early in the evening. She had time. It might be therapeutic. She could wash away the trauma of the last week, and transform herself into a new woman for the New Year.

Jess started with the simple stuff. Legs were shaved. Hair was washed and conditioned. Out of the shower,

Jess trimmed and filed her nails before painting her toes and finger tips in deep purple. And then she stopped. The full length mirror showed her the reality. Tummy rounded with what, she believed, was known in her magazines as relationship weight. Dimples of cellulite on the backs of her thighs. Half a chin more than she was happy with. It was no use primping and preening. There was no way she could paint her tired married body, pushing thirty as it was, back to being twenty-one and ready for anything. She couldn't pluck out the memories of Patrick that were all around her, and inside her head. She couldn't wash the years of her life she'd wasted away. And they had been wasted. She'd been sensible. She'd taken things slow, and she'd ended up tossed aside anyway. Putting her face on and painting her nails wouldn't make her a new woman.

Instead of hunting for a party dress in the wardrobe, she pulled her balled up pyjamas from under the duvet and threw them on. It might be the start of a new year, but, whatever she did, she was still the same old Jess.

She dragged the duvet off the bed and carried it to the living room, before gathering her provisions together. Tissues. Leftover Christmas chocolate. Leftover Christmas alcohol. That was all she needed. There was no way she was venturing out there. 2014 had been horrible. There was no reason to start 2015 pretending it was going to be any different.

The door buzzer interrupted her wallowing. Jess glanced at the clock. Twenty to eight. She wasn't expecting anyone. A bubble of anticipation rose up from her belly. Patrick? It was New Year's Eve. It was the sort of night where people took stock and reflected on the mistakes of the past year. Maybe he was coming back to her. She jumped off the sofa and ran into the hallway, slamming her hand against the intercom button when she got there. 'Hello.'

'Hi.'

It wasn't Patrick. She squeezed her eyes tight shut against the tears that threatened to come but never quite fell. 'Who is it?'

The voice hesitated, and the intercom crackled with interference. '... from Christmas. And Boxing Day.'

'Right.' Embarrassment replaced despair. The poor bloke she'd harangued into taking her to find Patrick. What on earth must he think of her? 'Come in. I guess.'

Jess raced into the bedroom. She might have already established that she couldn't primp herself into anything nearing an attractive state, but she could, at least, have clothes on.

## New Year's Eve, 2014

### *Lucas*

He shouldn't have come here. He ought to be with his dad, but his father seemed to want Lucas around even less since his latest hospitalisation, and he'd had no luck finding a place for them both to live. He could have gone home, but Trish and Charlie had invited a houseful of guests around and Lucas wasn't sure he was feeling up to an evening of making polite chit-chat and side-stepping personal questions. He needed to hide away and somehow he'd wondered if Jess might be doing the same.

He knocked on the door to the flat. 'One minute!'

He recognised the slightly panicked voice of somebody who hadn't been expecting guests. Of course, it was New Year's Eve. He'd pictured her home alone, but that was the girl he'd been imagining. Real-life Jess might have plans of her own. She might have guests. She might have let her husband move back in. That thought didn't sit well. Lucas promised himself that he wasn't here to try to rekindle some romance that had never really happened from years ago, but he was absolutely sure that she deserved to be with someone better than a cheating loser.

The door swung open. Jess waved a hand downwards towards her body. 'Sorry. I'm a bit scruffy. I wasn't really expecting anyone.'

Lucas glanced down. She was wearing clothes. He didn't really know about women's clothes. He lived in jeans, T-shirt and a hoodie. She was wearing jeans and a top. She looked fine to him. Better than fine. Much much better. He smiled. 'You look great.'

She was still leaning on the door frame looking at him.

'Right. Yeah. I just ...' Lucas's voice tailed off. What had he 'just'? 'I just wanted to see if you were okay.'

Jess's face broke slightly from the mask of anxiety he realised she normally wore, and the edges of her lips turned ever so slightly up. 'Yeah. Well no.' She shrugged. 'I don't know.'

'Right. Well, I'm free if you want somebody to hang out with.' He glanced towards the stairway, trying to sound nonchalant. 'Or I can go if you want.'

She inched the door all the way open. 'Come in.'

Lucas followed her into the living room, and waited while she hurriedly gathered a duvet from the floor. 'I don't normally have this in here. I was ... sort of ...'

'You were having a duvet day.'

She nodded. 'Well duvet night. I hate New Year's Eve.'

Lucas took a seat on the sofa and surveyed the bottles in various states of emptiness on the coffee table. He picked up a full beer and flicked the top off with the opener on his key ring. 'So do I. Last year Trish and Charlie made me go out on New Year's Eve. It was awful. Overpriced. Full of people who only go out once a year falling over after three shots.'

Jess sat down next to him. 'Last year I was on my honeymoon.'

Lucas closed his eyes. 'Sorry.'

'Me too. We went skiing. Flew out the day after Boxing Day for a week. I hate skiing.'

'Then why do it for your honeymoon?'

She pursed her lips. 'Patrick loves it. He said he'd teach me.'

'Didn't he?'

Jess shook her head. 'No. He went off on the big slopes, and left me in the beginner's class.'

Lucas frowned. It didn't sound like much of a honeymoon. 'Bet you had some rows about that.'

Jess frowned even deeper. 'No. We never argued.'

'Why not?' Lucas had never really had a long relationship, and he'd never had a mum and dad who lived together, so most of his understanding of long-term relationships was based on his housemates, who were devoted to one another, and equally devoted to never losing a fight. 'Charlie and Trish row all the time.'

Jess took a deep slug of her drink. 'I don't like fighting. I hate it when people shout at me.'

Lucas grinned. 'I know what you mean. I had this ...' He paused. He'd almost said "director." 'There was a guy I worked for once who was always yelling at everyone. I used to feel sick every time he came anywhere near me. You never knew who was going to be the next person to get a rocket up their arse.'

'I know. And I didn't want Patrick to be upset. It was his honeymoon too.'

'So you never told him you were miserable?'

Jess pursed her lips. 'I wasn't miserable. I was happy that he was having a good time.' She paused a second. 'Anyway, what about you? Are you seeing anyone?'

Lucas shook his head. If he had been in a relationship he suspected that spending New Year's Eve alone with another woman would have been considered poor form. 'Free and single.'

'And how's your dad?'

'My dad?' Lucas didn't really talk about his dad. Even Trish and Charlie only knew that he had a dad who'd had some health problems. It wasn't something where he ever went into detail.

'He was in hospital?'

'He's home now.' That word – home. Was his dad home? Was Morning Rise really the best place for him? 'I told you he lives in a care home sort of place? Well, he had a car accident, years ago, and it affected his brain. He can't really live on his own any more.'

'Oh my god. That's awful.'

Lucas paused. Was it awful? 'It's normal for me.'

'Tell me about it.'

Lucas took another gulp of beer. She was a stranger. This was a bubble of time. This sofa on the last night of the year. It was another bubble like that Christmas Eve kitchen all those years ago. Maybe … and so he started talking.

And it was easier than he expected. The words tumbled over one another rushing to be free. He told her about that night. Christmas Eve, fourteen years ago. He told her that he'd been out with a mate and got a call to say his dad was missing. He told her about the police officer who'd come to his hotel room on Christmas morning and patted him on the head and pointed out that his father was a grown man who would probably roll home of his own accord when he slept off whatever he'd had to drink the night before. Then he told her about the call from the hospital, and the feeling that everything in his world had fallen apart and would never quite fit back together again. He remembered the family his dad had driven straight into. He told her that they'd been forgiving, but that they were wrong. And once he'd started talking he felt like he might never stop. He might tell his girl from the kitchen everything.

# New Year's Eve, 2014

## *Jessica*

And Jess listened. She listened to the story of the two young girls whose lives had been affected forever by the accident. She listened to the stories of the care facilities that hadn't been able to cope with his dad. She listened to the stories from longer ago – the comic books and the days out. She listened to the stories from more recently – the increasingly bitter man who sometimes knew his son and sometimes didn't and sometimes, it appeared, pretended not to know out of little more than spite. 'It puts the things I've been crying over into perspective.'

At the other end of the sofa her guest frowned. 'Not at all. Being let down by someone you love is horrible.'

'That sounds like the voice of experience.'

He shook his head. 'No, but I let my dad down. That's what I always remember when he's yelling or throwing things or refusing to let me in. I should have been there, the night it happened. I let him down.'

Jess reached along the sofa and took his hand. It was meant to be a gesture of comfort. There was nothing comfortable about it. The jolt of heat that ran through her body was pure sex. At least she imagined it was. She wasn't sure she'd ever felt anything like it before. She'd fancied Patrick. She'd known he was good-looking. She'd seen the way that other women looked at him. This was different. This wasn't about her finding someone attractive; it was about her suddenly feeling like a goddess when he touched her skin. She pulled her hand away. 'You were just a kid when he had the crash.'

He nodded.

'Then you weren't responsible. He was the adult. Not you.'

She watched her guest stare at his beer bottle for a moment.

'My childhood was kind of complicated. I ...' His voice cracked. She waited. 'I made quite a lot of money quite young. My dad wasn't used to being rich. It sort of went to his head a bit.' He shook his head. 'That's not fair. He was used to doing everything for me, and then when we had money maybe he felt like he wasn't needed? Or maybe he didn't know how to cope? He drank. A lot. Too much. He was drunk when he crashed the car. I knew what he was like.' She watched him screw his eyes tight shut. 'I knew what he was like and I went out anyway. I thought it was more important for me to go out with my mate and have a laugh than stay in with him.' He opened his eyes and looked straight at Jess. 'It was my fault.'

Jess recognised the child the man in front of her used to be. She'd had kids like that in her class. Kids from tough households. Kids who'd learnt to fend for themselves. Kids who'd grown up looking out for younger brothers and sisters, or for the parents who were supposed to look after them. Kids who wore a permanent mask of 'everything's all right.' Some of those kids got good at wearing that mask. Some never did. 'What were you doing?'

'What?'

'The night he had the accident, what were you doing?'

He stared at the floor for a second. 'Just went out with a mate. Stupid teenage boy stuff.'

'Right.' Jess could see that he didn't want to talk about it, and she didn't think she knew him well enough to force the issue. She needed a change of subject. 'So, what do you do now?'

'How do you mean?'

'Like for work and that.'

He shrugged. 'Bits and bobs.'

'Okay.' So he did something dodgy that he didn't want to

talk about. That didn't fit with the image in Jess's head. 'I'm a teacher.'

'What age?'

'Primary.' Jess sighed. She'd messed up, hadn't she? He'd been baring his soul, but somehow she'd said the wrong thing, and now he'd clammed up again. 'Another drink?'

She gestured towards the stack of booze, and watched as he flicked open another beer. His brow furrowed as he took an extended slug, before turning towards her. 'Look. I'm sorry. I've not been completely honest with you.'

Jess's stomach clenched. Of course he hadn't been honest. People weren't, were they? Patrick hadn't been. Why would this guy be any different?

'My name isn't Alan.'

Jess nodded. She sort of knew that already.

'It's Lucas.' He was staring at her full in the face. 'I'm Lucas.'

## New Years Eve, 2014

### *Lucas*

He looked into her face, waiting for a flicker of recognition. There was none. He took a deep breath. He wasn't entirely sure what he was doing, but he wasn't entirely sure why he'd come to this virtual stranger's home on New Years Eve, and he wasn't entirely sure why he'd been unable to stop thinking about her since she'd turned up at his house on Christmas Day, but he was here, and he was ever so slightly drunk, and so he'd decided that, for once, he would turn off his brain and let his mouth lead the way. 'My real name is Lucas Woods.'

This time there was a flicker. He took a deep breath. 'I don't really have a job at the moment, because of caring for my dad, and because I don't need the money, so I volunteer at an advice centre and on an addiction helpline.' He wasn't looking at her face now. If he saw her reaction that might be enough to make him stop. 'And I don't need the money because—'

'You're the *Miracle at the North Pole* kid!'

Lucas nodded.

Jess's jaw hung open. 'I thought you'd gone off the rails or something.'

It was what everyone thought. His dad's accident had made it into the papers, but with a couple of key details all the wrong way around. They'd picked up that the police were involved and that the car was hired on Lucas's account, and then Lucas had disappeared from public view, having been one of the best known actors on the planet for the previous five years. Once you added in the received wisdom that child stars always ended up losing the plot, it had been pretty easy for people to put two and two together and make something a long way north of four. 'I didn't go off the rails.'

'But your dad did?'

Lucas nodded. 'He was only in his twenties when I made my first movie, and he'd never had money before. Not like that anyway.'

'I can't believe you're a film star.'

'Was a film star. In the past.'

'Why did you stop?' She was frowning. 'Was it because of your dad?'

Lucas paused. Why had he stopped? He'd always told himself he stopped because of his dad. He'd been supposed to start filming on a weird cowboys and robots sci-fi western thing that January, a few weeks after the accident, but he'd pulled out. Why had he never gone back? Honesty, he'd decided was his watchword for the night. 'It was too much, everybody knowing who I was, everybody thinking they had a part of me.'

'So you liked the actual acting?'

He didn't know how to answer. In his head acting was all to do with the movie business, and that was all to do with fame and fakery, which he'd grown to detest. He thought back to drama club, before that first audition, back when he was playing second spear carrier in the background. 'It was okay.'

He paused. It wasn't the actual acting that he loved. 'I loved being part of a company. Even on the big movies. I liked working with all the other actors and the crew.' Lucas smiled. 'I wasn't that good though.'

Jess shrugged. 'You seemed to do okay.'

Lucas shook his head. 'I was lucky. For *Miracle* I just had to look innocent and make a few cute quips. And looking innocent was easy because I didn't have a clue what was going on. Nowt I did after that was any good though.'

He watched Jess's face change.

'What?'

She took a slug of her drink. 'Well I don't want to be rude, but most of what you did after that was awful.'

'Thanks.'

'No. I mean the films were awful. You were fine in them, but they were bad bad movies.'

'I didn't have you down as a film buff.'

Jess smiled. 'I'm younger than any of my brothers by like fifteen years which meant I had to entertain myself a lot, and so I persuaded my mum and dad to get me a TV and a VHS for my bedroom. If you could get it from the local library I've seen it.'

Lucas winced. 'Then I should probably be apologising to you.'

Jess shook her head. '*Miracle at the North Pole* is one of my favourite films. I cry at the end every time.'

Lucas hesitated. Honesty, he reminded himself. 'I've never seen it.'

'What?' Jess's eyes widened. 'Everyone's seen it.'

Lucas shook his head. 'I was too young to stay up for the premiere, so I walked down the red carpet and then got back in the car in an alley behind the cinema. So I didn't see it then, and paying to go see it at a regular screening seemed weird, so I never did.' He stopped. He thought he might be all talked out. He told her all the things he usually kept locked away, and now he was ... what? Lighter? Definitely. Happier? He wasn't sure. He was spent though. He knew that. He took a long gulp from his drink. 'I'm going on about me. How are you?'

Jess shrugged. 'Single. Apparently.'

'I'm sorry.'

She laughed. 'You're the only one that is. Everyone else either thinks I was a lousy wife because I couldn't even keep hold of him a year, or tells me I'm better off without him.'

'Well I agree with the better off without him people, obviously. But I'm sorry you're sad.'

## New Year's Eve, 2014

### *Jessica*

He was sorry she was sad, and she definitely was sad. She'd been sad all week. Really she'd been sad since September when she'd found out about Patrick's affair with Cora, and realised that her whole idea of what her own life was like was a fantasy. She blinked her eyes tight shut to block out the world for a second. Being sad wasn't getting her anywhere, and when she thought about it, Jess realised, the harsh ball of wretchedness in her guts wasn't quite there anymore. Not right at this moment at least. Right this second what she was feeling wasn't sadness. It was something else entirely.

Lucas was sitting next to her on the sofa, body twisted towards her, his face full of concern. She raised her head and looked back into his bright green eyes. She hadn't really looked at his face properly before. She'd been preoccupied with Patrick and the marriage-wrecking harlot. It was a good face, a really good face. Patrick was always perfectly put together, clean-shaven, groomed – Jess had a suspicion that he tweezed his eyebrows. Lucas was a man who didn't bother with any such vanities. His chin was lined with stubble, and his brown hair was functionally short – the sort of hair that could be washed and then safely ignored. Michelle had always called Patrick a 'pretty boy.' Lucas wasn't pretty, and he definitely wasn't a boy.

'Are you okay?'

'What?' Jess shifted back in her seat. She hadn't been leaning towards him, had she?

'You were looking at me funny.'

'Sorry.' Jess stopped. Was she sorry? She'd spent a lot of time recently being sorry. She'd said sorry to her parents for running out on Christmas dinner. She'd said sorry to Cora for crashing her Christmas Day. She'd said sorry to Lucas for using him as a chauffeur service. She even thought she might have said sorry to Patrick. She was sick of being sorry. She was sick of acting like everything she'd done was wrong. And she was sick of being sensible. She'd been sensible all her life, and where had it got her? She pulled her glass to her lips. It was empty. That didn't seem right. She'd planned to keep filling it up until the bottles of random alcohol were all gone. She didn't think it ought to be empty yet at all. She refocused on Lucas and fought her way back to her train of thought. That was it. Sorry. Being sorry. Not being sorry. Not apologising for every little thing. 'I'm not sorry.'

He frowned. 'Okay. What are you not sorry for?'

'For snogging you.'

The frown deepened, but a hint of a smile tugged at the edges of his lips. 'You haven't snogged me.'

Jess thought through the conversation. He was right. She hadn't snogged him. That was embarrassing. 'Sorry. I didn't mean ... I ...' Jess listened to her own voice, doing what it always did. Apologising. Avoiding awkwardness. Not saying what she wanted. It was the last night of the year. It was a man she could simply choose never to see again. Why not go for it for once? Why not see what it would be like to be Cora or Victoria or any one of those perfect, confident women who got the things they desired? She didn't let herself hesitate. Hesitation would leave time for reflection and reflection would lead the way to thinking about risks and consequences. She didn't want to do any of that. She leant towards him, bringing her hand to his cheek as she pressed her lips to his.

## New Years Eve, 2014

### *Lucas*

He hadn't expected her to kiss him. He'd hoped. He couldn't kid himself that he hadn't hoped. He'd told himself he was going to see her because he was avoiding the party at home, or because he was at a loose end, or because he was worried about her, but really he'd come to see her because he was hoping that whatever had been there in that kitchen fourteen years ago would still be there now. He'd hoped that whatever it was that had come over him when he'd seen her standing on the doorstep on Christmas Day might have come over her as well. He'd thought it was foolish to hope; he'd pretended that he wasn't hoping at all, but hope was never quite that easily put down.

She pulled away from his lips. 'Sorry.'

'What?'

'Sorry. That was ... you probably don't ...' She stared for a second at the bottle and glasses on the table. 'I should clear these ...' She stood and started gathering debris into her arms.

'Wait.' Lucas had messed this up, but for once in his life he knew exactly how he'd messed up. He'd forgotten that he was supposed to be being honest. He'd started thinking about the kiss, and wondering what it meant. He'd forgotten to stop worrying and kiss the damn girl back. 'Wait.'

He stood up and lifted the bottles out of her hand. She pursed her lips slightly. 'What are you doing?'

'What I should have done two hours ago.' Lucas placed one hand on her waist and the other to the side of her face, before lowering his lips to meet hers. She responded immediately, snaking her arms around his neck and pulling him towards her. This felt honest.

He let her lead, sliding her hands under his T-shirt and peeling the fabric away from his skin. He followed her to the bedroom, watching as she slipped her own top over her head, before finding his belt with her fingers and pulling and fumbling to release him. He grinned as she swore to herself under her breath as she tipped out the contents of her bedside drawer hunting for a condom, and then he took her beneath him and all around him and let her soothe him and stop him thinking about anything at all beyond the scent, and touch, and taste of the very second he was living in.

# Chapter Nine

## New Year's Day, 2015

### *Jessica*

'Happy New Year.'

Jess swallowed hard. Someone seemed to have stuffed her mouth with sand while she was asleep. She forced an eye open, and lifted her head from the pillow. The voice was lying next to her in bed. It smiled. 'Happy New Year.'

'What time is it?'

'Nearly ten.'

Jess shook her head. 'Don't believe you. Still the middle of the night.'

She closed her eyes for a second. She was in bed with Lucas. She hadn't woken up in her own bed with anyone who wasn't Patrick for years. There'd been men, during her and Patrick's 'off' periods, but none that had been serious enough to stay the night for a very long time. It ought to feel awkward. It didn't. Being here with him felt like the most natural thing she could imagine. She opened her eyes again. 'Happy New Year to you too.'

The daylight coming in through the curtains was too much for Jess's drink-addled retinas. She closed her eyes. Flashes of last night whipped through her mind. The scent of his skin as she buried her face in the crook of his neck. The roughness of his stubble against her cheek. The warmth of his body beside her as she drifted into sleep. And then other things. Snippets of conversation. Oh god. Jess pulled the duvet up to cover her reddening cheeks.

'What's up?' He gently tugged the covers away from her face.

'I'm sorry.'

'What for?'

'I said all your films were shite. I'm so sorry.' Jess was mortified. She could blame the alcohol. She could blame a stressful week, but it was no excuse. 'I'd never normally say that.'

She forced herself to look at his face. He was grinning. 'You were honest. No need to apologise for that.'

'But I'm so sorry.'

'You said. And it's fine.' Lucas turned over and shifted down the bed so he was lying on his side facing her. 'So do you have any plans today?'

Jess shook her head. New Year's Day had always seemed like a peculiarly pointless bank holiday. It was a day entirely set aside for sleeping off hangovers and throwing away Christmas food that was turning manky. 'What about you?'

'Well I need to go see my dad later, but I could go this evening, if you wanted to do ... something?'

She nodded.

'Like a date sort of something?' he added.

Jess nodded again. Why shouldn't she go on a date? Why shouldn't she have her fresh start?

'Okay. I don't know about you but I need something to eat.'

Jess realised that that could be a problem. 'I haven't been to the shop since ... well, you know. I'd basically got down to leftover booze and Quality Street.'

And she was pretty sure they'd cleared the leftover booze already.

Lucas grinned. 'All right then. I guess we'll start by finding somewhere for breakfast. What do you reckon? Coffee shop and croissants? Or full English?'

Jess's hangover answered before her budding resolution to lose weight had a chance to intervene. 'Bacon. Need bacon.'

So an hour later they were snuggled into a booth in a less

than stylish pub chomping their way through bacon, eggs, sausage, beans, mushrooms, tomatoes and toast. They'd established that brown sauce was very wrong, and agreed to disagree about ketchup at breakfast time. And Jess had discovered that she was hungry. Ravenous. It was her first proper meal in a week, since she abandoned Christmas dinner and set off to walk across the city. And now she was out with her new man. Everything had worked out. Really, when she thought about it, it was for the best that she'd found out about Patrick's affair, because that's what had brought her here.

'Jess!'

Lucas's voice brought her back to the table. 'Sorry. What?'

'Nothing. You were miles away.'

She smiled. 'Sorry. I was just thinking about Patrick.'

His eyes narrowed slightly.

'Not like that. Just that it's all worked out. I know my brother and Michelle, my friend, they were expecting me to fall apart but I didn't. I got through it and now we're here.'

Lucas didn't answer straight away. 'You don't have to be okay, you know.'

'But I'm fine.'

'Okay. But it was only a week ago. This ...' he waved his fork to gesture the space between the two of them. 'We can take this slow, if that's what you want.'

Jess shook her head. 'I told you. I'm fine.'

'All right. So what else do you want to do?'

She didn't know. She was used to Patrick having an idea or a plan. She was used to going skiing because he wanted to go skiing. She was used to entertaining herself on her own in her room, because her brothers were too big to be interested in her. She was used to Michelle organising her and giving advice. 'I don't know. What do you want to do?'

Lucas leant back. 'Let's be tourists.'

'What do you mean?'

'Let's go to one of the parks, or Harrods, or Madame Tussauds, or the zoo.'

'Harrods on a Bank Holiday during the sale?'

'No. Fair point. You know what I mean though. How long have you lived in London?'

'Er ... we ... I moved here after Uni, so nine years.'

'Okay. I've been here about five. And how often do either of us actually go out and do tourist stuff?'

She shook her head. 'Never?'

'Well then.'

So they walked the length of Regent's Park, bundled up in coats, scarves and gloves against the January chill. Jess felt like all the big, serious talk had been spent last night, so they talked about little things. It was silly inconsequential chatter, but when they reached the gates of London Zoo, Jess found she didn't want to go in. 'I'm happy just walking, if that's okay.'

Lucas nodded. 'That's fine.'

'I'd forgotten how much I like Christmas.'

'It's not really Christmas anymore.'

'Course it is. It's Christmas until I have to go back to school, thank you very much.'

'Tell me what you like about it.' She felt his fingers rub against hers as he spoke, and she wrapped her hand around his.

'Well, it's romantic.'

'You still think that?'

She nodded. 'I got married at Christmas for a reason.' Another memory stirred. 'I had my first kiss at Christmas as well.' Had she told him that already? 'It was at this stupid party of some friend of my mum's.'

Her arm pulled backwards, and she realised Lucas had stopped walking. She turned around. 'What's up?'

'There's something else I should have told you last night.'

The knot in her stomach reappeared. Maybe it had never really gone away. 'What?'

'It's not a bad thing. I don't think. It's romantic.'

'Just tell me.'

He was gazing down at the floor. 'We've actually met before.'

'On Christmas Day?'

'No. *Before* before. Years ago.' He lifted her face and stared straight at her. Those bright green eyes.

'No.'

'Jess!'

'No.' It didn't make sense. He couldn't be. Of course he could be. She hadn't connected the Alans because she'd known, this time around at least, that that wasn't his real name. 'I asked you. I asked you if we knew each other.'

'I know.' He was still gripping her hand. 'I just ... I don't really talk about my past, and you were upset, and there was never a good moment.'

'Last night? The whole of last night there was no good moment?'

She pulled her hand away from his. There was too much going on inside her head to process. She couldn't make sense of it all. Patrick lied. She'd accepted that, and she'd decided that she was moving on, and Lucas was different. That's what she'd thought. Lucas was going to be different. Lucas wasn't going to make her feel out of control, and like she was constantly swallowing back this wave of darkness that threatened to overwhelm her. One thought crystallised in front of her. 'You lied.'

'I'm sorry. I didn't mean to.'

It didn't matter. 'You lied. You lied to me last night. And you lied to me back then.'

'No!'

'You did. You told me your name was Alan. That was pretty much all you told me about yourself and it was a lie.'

And that was it, wasn't it? Men lied to her. 'That was where it all started …'

'What?'

She was right. She could see it all now. 'That was where it all started. You were the first. I liked you. I thought you liked me. But you lied and then you just … you went away.'

'I'm sorry.'

Jess shook her head. They were always sorry. And then Jess was sorry. Everyone was sorry. Patrick had been sorry, at least the first time. Sorry didn't mean anything. 'I want you to go.'

'What? No. We can sort this out.'

'No. I want you to go.' She risked a glance at his face. He looked defeated. She repeated her point. 'I want you to go.'

He stood a few feet away for a few seconds before he nodded.

'And I never want to see you again.'

Jess waited until his back was receding into the distance before she walked the few yards to the nearest bench and sat down. At least she'd done better this time. With Patrick she'd listened to his explanations and apologies and she'd taken him back. At least she'd learnt. This time she'd been sensible. Lucas was a worse sort of liar. He was the sort who made you believe he was telling the truth. And then, finally, she started to cry.

# 2015
# *Chapter Ten*

### 23rd December, 2015

*Jessica*

'I can't believe you're moving two days before Christmas.' Michelle was sitting on the floor in Jess's now bare living room, bouncing Jess's nine-month old goddaughter, Izzy, in her arms.

Jess looked around the bare room. The sale wasn't scheduled to complete until January 2nd, but she hadn't wanted to wait any longer. An extra fortnight's rent in her new apartment was more than she could afford but worth it in the circumstances. 'I don't want another Christmas in this flat.'

Michelle cuddled her baby girl. 'So what next?'

'Well new flat obviously. Once this is sold Patrick will get his half of the equity.'

'I can't believe you're giving him half.'

Jess shot her best friend a look. 'His parents helped with the deposit.'

'And then he promptly lost his job and spent the rest of your marriage shagging around.'

It was true, but there was no point getting wound up about it now. 'It was the easiest way to get it over with. This way the divorce will be done by the end of next month.'

'I know.' Michelle pulled a face at her little girl. 'But that wasn't what I meant.'

'What then?'

'What's next romantically?'

Jess shook her head. 'You've changed.'

'What do you mean?'

'What happened to the woman who said romance was just a posh word for deceit?'

Michelle's husband appeared in the doorway. 'She's a convert.'

Michelle shook her head. 'I am not, but I think it would do Jess good to get out there again.'

Sean pulled a face. 'She doesn't need to put herself out there. She's got the reappearing Christmas Kiss guy.'

Jess knew Sean was unlikely to let this one drop, but there was really nothing to talk about. 'I think that was over before it began.'

Sean frowned. 'No chance. Two meetings. Years apart. Both at Christmas. That sounds meant to be to me.'

Michelle set Izzy down on the floor and struggled to her feet. The little girl set off, shuffling on her bottom towards Daddy. 'Don't be ridiculous. I'm not saying she should fall in love straight away, just that it might be good for her to get out and meet new people. The Christmas guy was a rebound thing. That never works.'

Jess nodded.

Sean crouched down to pick up his little girl. 'But that's my point. You can't choose when you fall in love. Love is just love. There's no right time or right way of finding it.'

'But he lied about who he was.'

'I know.' Sean shuffled to let Izzy get settled against his chest. 'But everybody lies, sometimes. It depends why he lied.'

'No!'

Jess listened to their argument. Michelle was right. She'd thrown caution to the wind with Lucas a year ago and, of course, it had been a mistake. The bickering rumbled on around her. She coughed loudly. 'I'm still in the room.'

Her friends exchanged a glance. 'Sorry.'

Sean nodded. 'Ignore us. I'm a hopeless romantic and she's got no soul.'

'Oh, I know.'

'But, have you thought about getting in touch with him?'

Jess didn't answer. Of course she'd thought about it. She'd almost done it a hundred times, but the realistic conclusion was that she'd missed her chance. Maybe she could have called him that very first day and said she'd overreacted. Maybe she could have explained that she was still upset about Patrick, and she hadn't meant to take it out on him. She could have called him and said sorry, but what was the point? There was no point trying, no point pretending that it had been anything more than a fling. And so that first day had turned into a second day, and then a week, and a month and she'd had to accept that he wasn't going to call her, and she'd missed the moment to call him. It was probably for the best, when she'd had so much else to think about – filling divorce forms in, selling her flat, dividing up her and Patrick's things. 'Maybe we could concentrate on the moving?'

Sean sighed. 'Okay. All the boxes are in the van. Apart from …'

'From what?'

He gestured towards the bedroom door. 'There's one marked *Patrick*. I wasn't sure what you wanted to do with it.'

Jess hesitated. It wasn't anything important. Patrick had sent his father to collect his clothes and computer in January, and she'd made Simon drop off the few bits of furniture she couldn't bear to keep using. What was left was tat really, stuff that she'd found over the year and couldn't quite bring herself to throw away. 'I guess I'll take it to him.'

Michelle frowned but didn't object. Jess didn't need her to. She was well aware that her best friend would have cheerfully dowsed Patrick's stuff in petrol and chucked in a flame. There'd been moments over the last twelve months when Jess would have lent her the lighter.

Sean cleared his throat. 'We could take it, if you want.'

Jess shook her head. 'You've done loads to help already. I'll take the box to Patrick's and meet you at the new place.'

Sean strapped Izzy into the car seat in the van, and Jess watched as her possessions drove away. She stuffed the box of Patrick's things into the boot of her own car and set off across London. She found a parking space around the corner from the florist shop she'd visited a year before and pulled in. The street was busy with last minute Christmas shoppers, and she struggled through the crowd with the taped up box. She rang the buzzer for 17a and waited.

## 23rd December, 2015

### *Lucas*

Lucas pulled into the car park at Morning Rise. He'd promised himself he wouldn't still be coming here. He'd promised himself that this was going to be the year when he took responsibility properly, and he'd tried. He'd really tried. He'd found a ground floor flat with a secure garden. He'd talked to social workers and advisers from the local carers' helpline and to consultants and addiction specialists. He'd done it. He'd moved his dad out of the home and in with him. And he'd lasted seven weeks.

Seven weeks.

Seven weeks before he found himself fighting with his dad in the hallway, because he'd picked up Lucas's car keys and made a dash for freedom. Seven weeks from absolutely believing that what he was doing was for the best, to physically restraining the man who raised him, while his dad struggled and kicked and spat. Seven weeks to realise that wanting to care for his dad wasn't the same as being able to.

So now his dad was back here, and Lucas was back to driving across the capital every day to visit. Only now he was doing it from an empty flat. He got to the room, knocked, and pushed the door open. There were Christmas decorations up inside his father's room, which was a first. Normally he had a fit of temper when decorations were mentioned, but this year he'd been part of the occupational therapy group making streamers and had consented to a string across the ceiling. 'How are you today?'

The older man looked up from his chair by the window. 'Lukey!'

Lucas smiled. 'Hi Dad.'

'I was watching a squirrel.' He gestured out towards the garden. 'It's gone now. Do you remember the squirrels in Roundhay Park, Lukey?'

Lucas nodded. He realised now that his dad took him to the park so often because he could get a bus straight there and it was free once they arrived, but at the time the wide green space had been his personal playground. 'Are you looking forward to Christmas?'

'Yeah.' His dad went back to staring out of the window. 'It were in Roundhay Park that your mum told me she was pregnant.'

Lucas didn't reply. His dad never talked about his mother. It wasn't a secret exactly. Lucas had met his mum; he knew who she was. She'd been fourteen when she had Lucas, and she was just too young to cope. His dad had never taught him to be angry or bitter about that, and he knew that his mum was married now with kids still in primary school. She sent him cards at Christmas and birthdays, but she was never talked about.

'She were so scared, but I wasn't. Everyone said it wasn't fair on you, trying to bring you up when I was just a kid, but you were my son. I was going to make sure you had the most incredible life. I wanted you to have everything. I wanted you to be able to do anything you wanted.' His dad didn't look at him. 'Did I do all right?'

Lucas swallowed hard. 'You did brilliantly.'

'Good. That's all you want when you're a dad. You want your kids to be happy.' His dad turned back towards him and scanned across the room. 'There was a thing about your film in the paper. Mrs Julia showed me it.'

The manager, Julia, was one of the few people who knew Lucas's full story. 'It's twenty years since it came out. They're re-releasing it.'

'Can we go Lukey?'

Lucas had actually been invited to a 'premiere' for the re-release in Leicester Square, but he'd politely declined, and it would be too much for his dad anyway. 'Maybe next week. Or we could get the DVD?'

His dad fell silent and then looked up, as if he'd forgotten Lucas was there for a moment. 'Have you brought my lunch?'

'You've had lunch. It's nearly dinner time.'

His dad nodded but didn't respond.

# Chapter Eleven

## 23rd December, 2015

### *Jessica*

Jess had never thought she'd be back here again. She pressed the buzzer and waited. A woman's voice crackled over the intercom. 'Yes?'

'I've got a delivery.' Jess wasn't sure if that was the best thing to say, but she was aware that if she explained who she was the beautiful Victoria might not deign to open the door. As it was, she was buzzed in without another word.

Jess dragged the box up the stairs, and rapped on the door to 17a. She could hear slow footsteps from inside.

'Just a minute!'

Eventually the door swung open. Jess took a moment to process the evidence of her eyes. Victoria was still beautiful. She still had the same buzzcut hair on top of huge dark brown eyes and perfect cheekbones. She was radiant. You might say glowing, because she was also pregnant. It was hard to tell exactly under the voluminous maternity top she was wearing, but from what Jess could see, Victoria was very very pregnant indeed.

'So he's sent you?

'What?'

'He's sent you to get his things. Typical.'

Jess opened her mouth and closed it again. She wasn't getting his things. She was bringing his things. 'No. I don't understand.'

'Jessie!'

The voice behind her made her spin around. Patrick. Standing on the stairs holding his key.

Victoria snorted. 'So you both came. Awesome.'

'What are you doing here Jessie?' She decided to focus on Patrick's question, because at least it was one she could answer.

'I'm moving house. I found some of your things. I thought you might need them.'

'What things?'

In the doorway, Victoria opened her mouth and closed it again before she spoke. 'Is this some kind of joke?'

Jess shook her head.

'But Patrick doesn't live here. He left. He went back to …' Victoria held a finger out pointing, accusingly, straight at Jess.

'What?' Jess turned to her ex.

He shrugged. 'Well it wasn't working out and …'

His words washed over her as the shock sunk in. Patrick wasn't with Victoria any more. That shouldn't be surprising. Long-term didn't seem to be one of his favoured things, but all year Jess had been picturing the two of them together, snuggled up in cosmopolitan domestic bliss, drinking overpriced wine and laughing at stories of Patrick's provincial-minded ex-wife. Of course that wasn't what he was doing. Patrick was built to want things, she realised. Once he had them, he inevitably wanted something else.

Victoria leaned against the door frame. 'So he didn't come back to you?'

Jess shook her head. She wasn't sure what the other woman was going to do. What if the shock sent her into labour right here? Jess really wasn't certain what the socially acceptable thing to do would be in those sort of circumstances.

Victoria's face froze for a second, and then cracked, not into the tears Jess might have expected, but into a huge, uncontrollable laugh. When she did her whole face crumpled into something far less perfect. Less beautiful, much prettier.

'Are you okay?'

'I'm fine.' Victoria nodded, and something inside Jess broke a little. That wasn't right. She shouldn't be fine. She was pregnant. She should have a partner she could rely on.

Patrick cleared his throat. 'So if I could just get my things?'

The feeling in Jess's gut exploded out of control. It wasn't a nice feeling. It wasn't a quiet feeling. It was the sort of feeling that might make somebody cause a scene. 'How could you?'

She screamed the words at Patrick, still skulking two steps below her.

'How could you? Who have you run off with this time? You absolute sleaze.'

Patrick held up his hands. 'Come on, Jess. What makes you think there's someone else? Maybe I did leave her for you.'

Had he? She paused but only for a second. 'Don't be ridiculous. You don't care about me, or her, or Cora or whoever you've shacked up with this time. You're just a …'

She ran out of steam. There weren't any words for what he was.

Victoria leaned forward. 'You said sleaze before.'

'Yes!' Jess could hear that she was yelling. She wasn't a person who yelled. She wasn't a person who acted on impulse. She wasn't a person who threw things either. She bent down and opened the box of his things. 'I brought your stuff back.'

One by one she hurled the contents of the box down the steps to where her ex-husband was cowering. A possibly broken charger for his electric razor whipped past his ear. A set of Russian dolls with faces like American presidents clapped him square in the chest. A box of cuff-links bounced off his shoe.

'Can I chuck something?'

Jess turned towards her former rival. 'Help yourself.'

'This is ridiculous. If you two can't act like adults, I don't have to stand here and take it.'

And the anger subsided as quickly as it had arrived, and Jess found herself laughing. Patrick's prettiness looked like vanity. His assertiveness was just high-handedness. All those years when she'd thought she was dragging her feet, and he was ready to commit, were an illusion. He'd wanted her precisely because she was just out of reach. Once they were married it was only a matter of time before things fell apart. Whatever it was that he'd held over her, even during a year of absence, was gone. The two women watched him stalk away down the stairs.

'Wow.'

'What?'

'Patrick told me you were a quiet little thing.'

Jess smiled. 'Well isn't it always the quiet ones you have to watch?'

'I am sorry.'

'Did you know he was married?'

Victoria shook her head. 'Not at first. And then he told me ...' Her voice tailed off. 'He told me you didn't understand him.' She closed her eyes as she uttered the cliché.

'And you believed him?'

'I guess I wanted to. I am sorry though.'

Jess waited for a new wave of anger, but it didn't come.

Victoria looked her up and down. 'You look different from a year ago.'

'How?'

'I don't know. Brighter somehow.'

'Thanks.' She jumped down a couple of steps and picked up the cufflinks and the Russian dolls, and chucked them back in the box. 'I guess he didn't want these.'

Victoria shook her head. 'I can get one of the neighbours to put it out by the bins if you want.'

It was a curiously unceremonious ending for a marriage, but somehow it felt right. 'Will you be okay?'

'I'll be fine. If you'd said a year ago that I'd be about to become a single mum, I'd have run a mile, but actually it's all good.' She rested a hand on top of her expansive belly. 'Really good. What about you?'

Jess paused. What about her? It had been a horrible year. She'd reached a point of acceptance. She wasn't intoxicating like Cora or Victoria. She wasn't the girl destined to get the guy, but when she'd seen Victoria's belly, and thought of her ex starting a whole new family, the pang hadn't hurt like she'd expected it to. 'I'm okay.'

She turned away to start down the stairs.

'Jessica!'

She stopped.

'I really am sorry, about ...'

Jess shook her head. 'It's fine. It's over.'

The other woman smiled. 'So no regrets?'

Jess nodded in agreement. No regrets. 'Actually one thing. Not a regret. A parting gift, if you like.'

'What?'

'I've sold our flat. Patrick's getting half the money. Just so you know.'

Victoria frowned.

'For when he tells you he can't afford to pay child support.'

The other woman nodded. 'Thank you.'

She walked down the stairs, and along the crowded street. She'd parked, she realised now, in the same place that Lucas had stopped a year ago, when they'd driven around the back streets looking for her car. No regrets, she'd said, but that wasn't quite true. No regrets over Patrick maybe, but Patrick wasn't the person on her mind. Christmas ought to remind her of her December wedding, but it didn't. The fairy lights, the Christmas tunes, the mince pies all sent her back to that kitchen fifteen years ago. They sent her back to that sofa on New Year's Eve twelve months ago. Being cautious about love was the sensible choice. There was no reason to think that Lucas had even given her a second thought. Jess told herself to stop, but every time she thought about Lucas a tiny nugget of hope crept into her heart. She had to stop. Hope wasn't her friend. Hope was just the thing that came before disappointment.

## Christmas Eve, 2015

### *Lucas*

What his dad wanted him to do was be happy. That was all. He wanted Lucas to have an incredible life. Lucas wasn't sure that hiding away in his flat, rarely even telling anyone his real name, could be considered an incredible life. He wasn't sure that what he was about to do was the best first step to remedying that, but at least he was trying. He gripped the box tightly in one hand and rang the doorbell.

'Fake Alan!' Charlie flung herself through the door and hugged him vigorously. 'We thought you'd done a runner. Or the mafia finally caught up with you or something. That's it, isn't it? You're hiding from the mafia.'

He shook his head. 'Can I come in?'

'Course you can come in. Don't you still have a key?'

He followed his former housemate into the lounge.

'Look who I found.'

He was greeted with similar enthusiasm by Trish.

'Cora not around?'

Trish grinned. 'Cora has moved in with lovely Liam.'

That was a shame. Well, obviously it was good, for Cora, but Lucas had planned to do this once for the whole group. Never mind. In for a penny and all that.

The two women squashed onto the sofa on either side of their guest. 'So what brings you here?'

He took a deep breath. 'I hoped you might fancy a Christmas movie night?'

Charlie nodded. 'Always.' She grabbed the box from his hand. 'So what's the movie?'

He watched her scan the DVD case. '*Miracle at the North Pole*. Good choice.'

'Didn't we have that last year?'

'No.' Charlie narrowed her eyes. 'Fake Alan didn't want to watch it last year.' Her face suddenly broke into a smile. 'Pay up.'

'What?' Trish was looking blank.

'I think you owe me twenty quid.'

'What are you two talking about?'

Charlie turned the DVD box around and tapped her fingertip against the picture of Lucas's ten year-old face on the cover. 'Anything you want to tell us?'

Lucas leaned back. 'You already know?'

She raised an eyebrow. 'Know what?'

He took a deep breath. He'd come here to tell his closest friends the truth. And being a real friend, Charlie was going to make him go through with it. 'You already know that I'm Lucas Woods. I'm the kid in that film.'

Trish leapt off the sofa. 'No!' She jabbed him in the chest. 'You take that back. I'm not having her win a bet that's stood for the last six years. You tell her you're an undercover detective and you do it right now.'

Lucas laughed. 'Sorry. I can't believe you already knew.'

Charlie leaned her head against his shoulder. 'I didn't *know* know. I suspected.'

'But you never guessed that? And you guessed everything.'

She swallowed and glanced at her girlfriend. 'I didn't guess that because I thought it might be true. I figured it was up to you to tell us.' She grinned. 'And now you did, and she owes me twenty quid.'

Trish sat back down. 'Okay. Okay. She wasn't as restrained as she's making out though. Last Christmas she wanted to do an intervention on you.'

'Why?'

'She saw a documentary about them.'

Charlie nodded enthusiastically. 'They do them for alcoholics and that to help them get over denial. They look awesome.'

Lucas shook his head and tried to take it all in. 'When did you work it out?'

'About twenty minutes after you came to look at the room. I love Christmas movies. You know I love Christmas movies. I pretty much recognised you before you'd had chance to get your coat off.'

'So does everyone know who I am?'

His friends shook their heads.

'Don't think so,' Trish reassured him. 'I mean some of them might have thought that you look like that guy from that film, but you say you're called Alan and people go along with it. It's a bit different if you're living with someone.'

'So what else haven't you told us?'

'What do you mean?'

Charlie held up the DVD box. 'Well this was twenty years ago. I know you made a couple more films after this, and then you turned up here. Fill in the gaps a bit?'

'I wouldn't know where to start.'

Trish folded her arms. 'The beginning.'

And so Lucas talked. He told them the story of his dad's accident. And then he told them about the visit to his dad's previous care home in Leeds when his father had persuaded an agency gardener to bring him in a bottle of whisky. Lucas relived the terror of going into his father's room and finding him unconscious on the floor. He described the wait for the ambulance while the nurses had pumped at his dad's chest, and the wait at the hospital until the consultant came out and told him his dad was awake and Lucas could see him. He couldn't quite bring himself to describe the tiny part of him that had wished his father hadn't made it through. He described the time he'd been to Morning Rise in August when his father had been sober but still threw his dinner plate across the room at his son's head. 'I moved out of here to have him with me, but I couldn't do it.'

Charlie shook her head. 'It sounds like he needs professional care.'

Lucas nodded. 'I know.'

Trish frowned. 'So you're living on your own?'

'Yeah.'

'And do you like it?'

Lucas shook his head. In truth he hated it.

'So move back in here.'

'Really?'

'Please. We've had four housemates since you moved out and they were all nutters.'

Charlie nodded. 'One of them used to take a spatula in with them when they went to the toilet.'

'What? What for?'

'We don't know.'

Trish dropped her gaze to the floor. 'We don't want to know.'

'Okay.'

And then he was being hugged from both sides.

'You're not pissed off with me?'

'What for?'

'Well, lying, moving out. All of that.'

Both women laughed. 'Don't be ridiculous. You're part of the family Fake Alan. You don't get rid of us that easily.'

# *Chapter Twelve*

### Christmas Eve, 2015

*Jessica*

Simon pulled an armful of DVDs from one of the boxes. 'Oh my god. You own some cheesy films.'

In reality Simon, and his lovely new boyfriend, Zac, weren't really helping. They were mainly mocking Jess's possessions. Zac pulled a couple of DVDs out of Simon's hands. 'You've got Christmas movies. We should watch one.'

Jess pursed her lips. 'We're supposed to be unpacking.'

Simon wrinkled his nose and looked around at the mass of boxes and piled up possessions that currently formed Jess's new lounge. 'Are you sure you don't want to keep it like this?'

Jess nodded.

The couple exchanged a look. Zac grinned. 'But we're all going to his tomorrow, so we could totally leave this 'til after Christmas.'

Jess folded her arms. Her 'assistants' had already set up the TV and DVD player and filled her fridge with 'new home' gifts of champagne and chocolates. Her bed was set up and made. She'd found the kettle and unpacked most of her clothes and toiletries. 'It's half past ten in the morning.'

Simon leaned towards her. 'On Christmas Eve. Normal rules don't apply.'

He was right. It was Christmas Eve. And it was gearing up to be a refreshingly relaxed and chilled out Christmas. Just her and Simon and Zac. Her mum and dad were in Leeds with her eldest brother's family. She didn't have Patrick to keep happy. The thought made her pause. That's what she'd done, wasn't it? She'd spent her marriage making Patrick happy and trying to keep him that way. This Christmas was going to be about her, and she was spending it with people who seemed to genuinely like her. 'All right. I'll get something to drink. You shove the worst of the mess out of the way and pick a film.'

Zac clapped his hands. 'Open the New House champagne.'

Jess stared at him. 'Still half past ten in the morning.'

He stared back. 'Still Christmas Eve.'

Jess knew when she was beaten. 'All right then.'

Simon followed her into her new kitchen. 'Thanks Jess.'

'What for?'

He shrugged. 'Being so nice to Zac. Mum was a bit ...' His voice tailed off. Jess didn't need him to explain how Mum had been. Their parents had never expressed any problem with Simon being gay, but had quickly developed the same aspirations for his perfect partner as they had for Jess's. They were waiting for a responsible, hard-working, and preferably, high-flying man to come along for Jess's brother. Zac was more of a free spirit. 'He's a lot younger than me.'

Jess handed the champagne bottle to her brother to open, while she pulled glasses out of the cupboard they'd only been unpacked into an hour earlier. Maybe a year ago stuff like Zac's age would have bothered her. She'd had a lot of time to think about what made relationships work since then. 'But he patently adores you.' She grinned. 'And quite right too.'

Simon leaned back against the worktop. 'I didn't expect ...'

'What?'

'Another chance. After Anthony.'

'I'm happy for you. You deserve to be happy.'

She let Simon lead the way back into the living room, where Zac had spread what looked like her full stock of Christmas movies out on the floor. 'So what do you fancy?

I'm thinking either *Miracle at the North Pole* or *Miracle on 34th Street*. You can't beat a small child experiencing a Santa-related life-changing moment at Christmas.'

Jess picked up the two copies of *Miracle on 34th Street*. 'Original or remake?'

Zac sucked the air through his teeth. 'Tricky. Normally I'd say original is always best, but Dickie Attenborough as Santa? What's not to like?'

Simon leaned through the gap between them and picked the *Miracle at the North Pole* DVD up from the floor. He shot Jess a look. 'I think we should watch this one.'

Simon was the only person Jess had told the whole Lucas story to. Even with Michelle she'd omitted the small detail of him being an international child movie star. It was Lucas's secret to tell, not hers. Jess pursed her lips. She couldn't really object without explaining her reasons and Zac, though lovely, probably wasn't the most discreet person in the world. She took a gulp of her champagne and let the bubbles fizz and tickle on her tongue. 'Fine.'

They shoved the remaining boxes to one side of the room and squashed together on the sofa. The film hit all the right emotional Christmas marks. It was sweet but not sickly, and tugged at the heartstrings in the best possible way. The final scene saw Lucas's character back home in his suburban cul-de-sac after his adventure at the North Pole. Santa's sleigh stood in the road alongside him, and the big guy in the red suit crouched down to the young Lucas's height. 'So what would you like for Christmas now son?' he asked.

On screen Lucas furrowed his brow. 'Something for my mum. Something she lost when Dad went.'

Father Christmas frowned. 'You know I can't bring him back.'

Lucas nodded. 'I know but she lost something else. She lost hope. I'd like her to get that back.'

And, with a nod, Santa smiled the twinkliest of smiles,

ruffled Lucas's hair, let out a hearty 'Ho! Ho! Ho!' and steered his sleigh out into the night.

It was ridiculously sentimental, but that didn't stop the tears streaming down Jess's face. Hope. The fifteen year old girl who'd met Lucas in that kitchen had been full of it. Where had she disappeared to, Jess wondered. That girl had been happy to dive in with both feet. She hadn't been sensible when that perfect boy had tried to kiss her. She hadn't come up with problems or objections. She'd been brave enough to enjoy the moment. She'd been brave enough to hope.

Simon squeezed her arm. 'Love that film. Have you got the sequel?'

Jess shook her head. Even for her, that would have been a step too far. 'The sequel's awful.'

Zac jumped in. 'It's not really. It's exactly the same again.'

Jess nodded. 'Which makes no sense, because it's the same again, but this time Santa lives in Lapland instead of at the North Pole. You can't just move Santa.'

Simon laughed. 'So we'll agree that the sequel is an anathema but that this one is a classic.'

'Total classic.'

'It's twenty years old you know.' Zac turned the DVD box over in his hand. 'They're doing a re-release with a big premiere thing tonight in Leicester Square.'

Jess nodded. She'd read about it on the entertainment pages, telling herself she was interested in the nostalgic movie from when she was a kid, and that she wasn't desperate for news of Lucas. Of course there wasn't any. All any of the articles said was that Lucas Woods had disappeared from the public eye.

Simon glanced at the clock. 'We should get going. I've got seven types of veg to prep this afternoon.'

Zac rolled his eyes. 'There's only three of us. It's basically just Sunday dinner.'

Simon gave him a look. 'It is not Sunday dinner. It's a

Christmas feast. And you're not doing anything until all my potatoes are peeled.'

Zac mouthed a weary 'So not going to happen' at Jess.

'Are you sure you don't want to stay over at mine tonight?'

She refused her brother's invitation. 'No. I'm going to unpack a few more things, and I think I've got something else I need to do.'

'On Christmas Eve?' Simon frowned.

'Yes.' She led the way into the hall and picked up her handbag and winter coat. It was a silly idea, a silly romantic idea, but watching the movie had made her think. And if she wasn't going to do it now, then when?

## Christmas Eve, 2015

### *Lucas*

Lucas lay on the bed in what was, apparently, his room again. He'd drunk too much to drive home the day before, and given that he was planning to move back in anyway, staying had seemed like a sensible option.

'Fake Alan!' The voice was accompanied by a knock on the door and, a second later, Cora shuffling into his room.

'I'm assuming they've told you that's not my name.'

She frowned and sat down on the bed. 'Well, we always knew that wasn't really your name, but yes. I wasn't even all the way through the door before Charlie cracked. I can't start calling you something different now though. It's too weird.'

'Fair enough. What are you doing here?'

'Just dropping off some food for tomorrow. I'm still coming for Christmas lunch.'

'Quite right too.'

She nodded. 'So what are you going to do now?'

And that was the question Lucas couldn't answer. He wondered if he'd been hiding because he didn't want to face up to his past, but caring for his dad, keeping in touch with the two girls who'd been hurt in the accident, living with the constant guilt, all made it feel like dealing with the past was all he ever did. It wasn't the past that Lucas had trouble facing up to.

Cora cleared her throat. 'Or think about it another way. What do you really want?'

'In what way?'

'Any way you like. Work or life or relationships or family. What's the one thing? The thing that you want more than anything?'

'I guess I want to be happy.'

She shook her head. 'Well everyone wants that. Be specific. What do you hope for?'

Lucas had the beginning of the tiniest edge of the hint of a thought, but he couldn't put the words together.

'What's made you happy in the past?'

His face broke into a smile. The idea wasn't a beginning anymore. It was fully formed and screaming at him. He knew exactly what he wanted. He'd known all year. Lucas was a fool. He hadn't just known all year. He'd known since he was sixteen years old.

'I have to go.'

'What?' Cora jumped slightly as he leapt up from the bed.

'I have to go.' Lucas was suddenly buzzing. Time, so much of which had passed him by unnoticed, was suddenly precious. If something was to be done, then it was going to be done right now. 'She was right.'

'Who was right? Right about what?'

'About everything. Christmas is romantic.' He checked his watch. 'I have to go.'

# Chapter Thirteen

## Christmas Eve, 2015

It was three hundred and sixty four days since the last time she'd knocked on this door. What an incredible difference a year made. Last time she'd been numb; this time she was fizzing inside. She'd lost her temper with Patrick and it had felt liberating, and now she couldn't let go of the idea that it might not be too late. Years of disappointment had taken away her hope, and replaced it with a constant nagging fear. That wasn't okay. It was time to start hoping again. The door opened. Cora. Jess had to admit that she hadn't quite considered that. Cora folded her arms. 'Are you going to be doing this every year?'

Jess shook her head. 'I was looking for Lucas.'

One exquisitely sculpted eyebrow rose on the face in front of her. 'Lucas?'

'Alan. Lucas. Alan.' Jess shook her head. 'You know who I mean.'

The perfect face cracked into a smile. 'You've just missed him.'

'Right.' Setbacks hadn't really fit into Jess's thinking. Her plan, roughly speaking, had gone: One: Seize the moment. Two: Well, one was really the end of the plan. She'd seized but the moment had slipped out of her grasp. 'Do you know where he's gone?'

Cora shook her head. There was a silence. Cora unfolded her arms. 'You can come in and wait if you want.'

Jess didn't particularly want, but her only other idea was to pace up and down the street until he came back, and it was freezing outside. She followed Cora into the living room, which was full. Jess wasn't sure if that was better or worse.

Cora paused. 'So you remember Liam? And this is Charlie and Trish.'

Jess nodded at the assembled household, but then something else caught her attention. The DVD. 'You know about this?'

'Yeah.' Cora sounded wary. 'Officially only since last night though.'

Jess stared at the poster. 'And you talked to him about it?'

Cora nodded.

Jess smiled, and let the feeling of hope rise through her belly again. 'I have to go. I think I know where he is.'

Across town Lucas pressed his finger to the buzzer and waited. No answer. That wasn't the plan. He wasn't fully sure what the plan was, but it definitely involved her being home. In frustration he pressed the buzzer and then the one above and below it. The intercom came to life. 'Jess?'

'Who is this?'

'I'm looking for Jess. Jessica. Flat four.'

The voice crackled. 'Not here any more. She moved out.'

'Do you know where she went?'

'Sorry mate.'

The intercom hummed for a second and then fell silent. So that was that. She wasn't here any more. He'd taken half a lifetime to work out what he wanted and now it was gone. He stuffed his hands in his pockets and turned to walk away. Inside his pocket his fingers wrapped instinctively around his phone. Lucas really was an idiot sometimes. He might not know where she was but, of course, he knew how to find out.

Jess stood on the edge of the crowd and tried to get her bearings. The cinema was at the far side of Leicester Square, and there was a fenced off area for the red carpet. The barrier was already lined with film fans, many of whom were dressed as elves or in the distinctive NHS glasses Lucas's character had worn at the start of the movie. Jess had to get to the front. That was the only way he'd see her. She wasn't normally the sort to push to the front. She was the sort to hang back and wait and see what everyone else wanted to do. And this is where it had got her. Alone on Christmas Eve getting bustled out of the way by people who thought their lives were more important than hers. Well no more. For once Jess was going to be the star. She stuck her elbows out to the sides and started to work her way through the mass of bodies. As she got to the front and rested her hand on the railing her phone vibrated against her leg. She squirmed to pull it out of her pocket and realised that she'd already hit answer as she was trying to get the handset clear of her jeans.

'Hello? Hello? Jess?'

'Hello.'

'Where are you?'

'Who is this?' She could hear herself shouting over the noise of the people talking on either side of her.

'I tried to find you.'

She pulled the phone away from her ear for a second and glanced at the screen. *Lucas*. Jess gasped. 'I'm here. I'm waiting for you.'

'Where?'

'Leicester Square.'

'What are you doing there?'

'The movie thing. I'm waiting for you to come down the red carpet.'

There was a long pause on the other end of the phone. 'Leicester Square?'

'Yeah.'

'Wait there. I'll find you.'

Lucas hung up the phone and started running. The tube would be heaving but it was still the quickest way. He wound his way through the packed bodies and squashed into a corner. It was going to take a while. What if she didn't wait? What if she had second thoughts? What if the whole idea of the girl in the kitchen was a mirage, a fantasy he'd made up at the worst time of his life? He remembered last Christmas; the taste, the feel, the realness of her. That hadn't been a fantasy. That had been something genuine and he'd stuffed it up. He checked his watch and willed the stops to fly by faster.

Jess watched the stars of the movie make their way down the red carpet, interspersed with a whole load of pop singers and TV personalities, many accompanied by perfectly dressed children who'd clearly been prised away from the nanny for half an hour to make a pretty picture for the paparazzi who had assembled opposite. An announcer was keeping the crowd entertained, drawing their attention to whoever was stopping to sign autographs, and grabbing people for thirty second interviews as they passed.

Jess let the hubbub wash over her. Lucas wasn't among the stars on the red carpet, but on the phone he'd said he was coming. Her head span slightly. He'd said he was coming, but the last few celebrities were making their way past and he wasn't here. She'd thought hope would be better than fear. Maybe she'd been wrong. If you dared to hope, you were daring to lose that hope all over again. She turned away from the barrier. Lucas had lied. He wasn't coming. She pushed her way forward.

The crowd parted before her.

Lucas.

She walked towards him, letting the bodies close back together behind her until they were inches apart.

He bent his head to her ear, and half-shouted over the crowd. 'What are you doing here?'

'I was looking for you.'

'Why did you think I'd be here?'

'Cora said you'd gone out, and I saw the DVD and they said you'd told them everything and I thought ...'

He pulled his face back slightly and she could see the confusion on his face.

'I thought you'd sort of come to terms with your past or something.' It sounded lame as soon as she said it, but Lucas was nodding.

'I did. I think I have, but all this ...' He waved an arm at the crowd and the cinema and the red carpet. 'This *is* the past.' He was having to yell so she could hear, but the noise around them made it a completely private conversation. 'I went to find you.'

Jess shook her head. 'No! I came to find you, but you were out ...'

'Looking for you.'

'Looking for me.' Everything was falling into place. He'd been looking for her. She'd been looking for him. Jess reached forward and wrapped her fingers around his. He bent his head towards her. Jess stepped back. Concern filled his eyes. Kissing him would be easy. Kissing him would be so right, but there were things she needed to say first, because she knew that once the kissing started there wasn't going to be much talking at all. 'I need to say sorry.'

'What for?'

'Last year. I overreacted.'

Lucas shook his head. 'I should have told you who I was.'

Jess swallowed. 'I should have given you a chance to explain ...' She paused. There was something else. 'It wouldn't have made a difference.'

He nodded. 'It's okay. I can understand you not wanting to rush into anything after ...'

'It wasn't that.' She felt him inch away from her. She squeezed his hand a fraction tighter. It was so hard to explain. She'd been cautious about romance her whole adult life. She'd believed the rules she'd heard. She'd believed that rebound things were a bad idea, and that you should take your time. She thought she'd learnt how relationships worked, but she'd learnt nothing that prepared her for how Lucas made her feel. 'It wasn't you though. I think I told myself it wasn't the right time. You gave me an excuse not to get close and I grabbed it.'

She could see the beginning of a smile in his eyes. 'Like maybe fifteen years ago wasn't the right time for me?'

'Your dad?'

He nodded.

'And now?'

He was quiet for a long long time. Jess waited.

Lucas thought about everything that had happened. He'd been a kid. He'd been a normal kid who'd made a completely exceptional film. It had changed his life, and the lives of the people closest to him. And then his dad had got off his face and driven a car into a group of pedestrians and everything had changed again. And somewhere amongst all that he'd met a girl, and even though he'd only known her for one evening, everything about her had been right. And then he'd met her again. And she was still right. And he'd thought that he was ready, but the past was always there, and now she had a past as well, playing on her mind and changing how she reacted to the here and now. The past wasn't going away, but maybe they didn't have to live there all the time. Eventually he spoke. 'Now is good.'

She smiled.

'What about for you?'

'I think I've learnt that now is all we have.'

She was right. Lucas was used to dealing with his past and worrying about the future, but right now was what mattered. He bent his head towards her again and this time she let his lips brush hers. Then she pulled away.

'What's wrong?'

'Nothing. But they keep announcing how child star Lucas Woods vanished from public view, and going on about how it's a great mystery, and you're standing right here.'

Lucas looked around at the crowd, all turned towards the bright lights and the shiny, famous people who'd been laid on for their entertainment. 'So?'

'So I don't mind if you want to go and ...' She waved a hand towards the red carpet. 'Be Lucas Woods for a bit.'

Lucas couldn't stop himself laughing. That seemed to be what everyone expected him to want. 'No. I didn't quit acting because of my dad's accident. I think I only kept going for as long as I did because he wanted me to. I grabbed an excuse as well.'

'One more question.' He knew what she had to ask. 'Why did you lie to me back when we first met?'

'I didn't.'

She narrowed her eyes.

'Well I did. I lied about my name, but that was all. I didn't want to be Lucas Woods any more. I wanted to be normal. I wanted to have mates, and meet a girl I liked and for it just to be simple. I wanted to do a job where I got to help people and nobody gawped at me. Alan wasn't a lie. Alan is more me than Lucas Woods, the movie star, ever was.'

She smiled. 'That's a good answer.'

He shook his head. 'It's a stupid answer, but I promise you, it's the truth.'

She glanced back towards the red carpet. 'So you're walking away from all this? No regrets?'

He shook his head. 'I'm not walking away from that. I'm walking towards the thing I really want.'

'Which is?'

'You.'


Jess let the thought sink in. She'd worked so hard to make Patrick happy, but in the end what he wanted wasn't her.

She'd given up on romance and miracles. She stopped believing that she could have perfection, but, in the end, there was no point giving up on miracles, because the miracles didn't care if you believed or not. They didn't reward effort, or beauty. Miracles were miracles. Love was love and all you could do was hope, and when your miracle came to find you, you could grab on and never ever let go.

She smiled and raised her lips towards his to claim her perfect moment, with her perfectly imperfect man.

# About the Author

Alison May was born and raised in North Yorkshire, but now lives in Worcester with one husband, no kids and no pets. There were goldfish once. That ended badly.

Alison has studied History and Creative Writing, and has worked as a waitress, a shop assistant, a learning adviser, an advice centre manager, and a freelance trainer, before settling on 'making up stories' as an entirely acceptable grown-up career plan.

Alison is a member of the Romantic Novelists' Association. She writes contemporary romantic comedies. In 2016 Alison's novella *Cora's Christmas Kiss* was a finalist for the Romantic Novel of the Year ROSE award.

You can find Alison on: Twitter: @MsAlisonMay and on Facebook. You can also visit her website and blog: www.alison-may.co.uk

# More Choc Lit

*From Alison May*

## Sweet Nothing

Book 1 in the 21st Century Bard series

**Is something always better than nothing?**

Ben Messina is a certified maths genius and romance sceptic. He and Trix met at university and have been quarrelling and quibbling ever since, not least because of Ben's decision to abandon their relationship in favour of ... more maths! Can Trix forget past hurt and help Ben see a life beyond numbers, or is their long history in danger of ending in nothing?

Charming and sensitive, Claudio Messina is as different from his brother as it is possible to be and Trix's best friend, Henrietta, cannot believe her luck when the Italian model of her dreams chooses her. But will Claudio and Henrietta's pursuit for perfection end in a disaster that will see both of them starting from zero once again?

*This is a fresh and funny retelling of Shakespeare's Much Ado About Nothing, set in the present day.*

Visit www.choc-lit.com for more details, or simply scan barcode using your mobile phone QR reader.

# Midsummer Dreams

Book 2 in the 21st Century Bard series

**Four people. Four messy lives. One night that changes everything …**

Emily is obsessed with ending her father's new relationship – but is blind to the fact that her own is far from perfect.

Dominic has spent so long making other people happy that he's hardly noticed he's not happy himself.

Helen has loved the same man, unrequitedly, for ten years. Now she may have to face up to the fact that he will never be hers.

Alex has always played the field. But when he finally meets a girl he wants to commit to, she is just out of his reach.

At a midsummer wedding party, the bonds that tie the four friends together begin to unravel and show them that, sometimes, the sensible choice is not always the right one.

*A modern retelling of Shakespeare's Midsummer Night's Dream.*

Visit www.choc-lit.com for more details, or simply scan barcode using your mobile phone QR reader.

# Introducing Choc Lit